Sarah wasn't sure she'd heard Aiden's words correctly. They were surprising. They were scary—driving her to a place where she surrendered to her deep longing for him.

He granted the smallest fragment of a smile, looking at her with his heartbreaking blue eyes. He tenderly tucked her hair behind her ear, drawing his finger along her jaw to her chin. "I don't know what force in the universe brought you to me, Sarah. I only know that right now I need you. I want you. And I'd like to think that you want me, too."

The air stood still, but Sarah swayed, light-headed from Aiden's words. Their one night together had been electric, filling her head with memories she'd never surrender, but judging by the deep timbre of Aiden's voice, they might shatter what happened in Miami. "I don't want to ruin our friendship. And no strings attached only breaks my heart."

"Is that why you shut things down after Miami?"

"Yes." It wasn't the whole truth, but it was enough. As much as sleeping with Aiden might be a mistake, she didn't want to deprive herself of him. Would one more time really hurt? And I've spent the last two nights regretting it."

"Then I say we have no more regrets."

Before she knew what was happening, he scooped her up into his arms.

* * *

Ten-Day Baby Takeover
is part of Mills & Boon Desire's
No. 1 Bestselling series
Billionaires and babies: Powerful men...
wrapped around their tiny, little fingers.

THE TEN-DAY
BABY TAKEOVER

BY
KAREN BOOTH

First Published in Great Britain 2017
By Mills & Boon, an imprint of HarperCollins*Publishers*
1 London Bridge Street, London, SE1 9GF

© 2017 Karen Booth

ISBN: 978-0-263-92814-3

51-0417

Our policy is to use papers that are natural, renewable and recyclable products and made from wood grown in sustainable forests. The logging and manufacturing processes conform to the legal environmental regulations of the country of origin.

Printed and bound in Spain
by CPI, Barcelona

Karen Booth is a Midwestern girl transplanted in the South, raised on eighties music, Judy Blume and the films of John Hughes. She writes sexy big-city love stories. When she takes a break from the art of romance, she's teaching her kids about good music, honing her Southern cooking skills or sweet-talking her husband into whipping up a batch of cocktails. Find out more about Karen at www.karenbooth.net.

For my dear friend in the writing world
and the real world, Margaret Ethridge.
I will always want to stay up way past
my bedtime, talking and giggling
in the dark with you.

One

The lobby of LangTel's Manhattan headquarters was practically a shrine to order and quiet restraint. It was not the place to bring a fussy baby. Sarah Daltrey had done precisely that. Marble floors, towering ceilings and huge expanses of windows facing the street made any sound, especially baby Oliver's errant cries, echo and reverberate like crazy.

Sarah kissed his forehead, bouncing him on her hip as she paced in the postage stamp waiting area. For such a massive building, taking up nearly an entire city block, LangTel had been distinctly stingy with the amenities for the uninvited. Two chairs and a ten-by-ten rug sat opposite a closely guarded bank of elevators. It was clear that no one occupying this space should stay for long.

Oliver whimpered and buried his head in her neck. Poor little guy—none of this was his fault. Oliver hadn't asked to take a four-hour train ride that morning. He certainly hadn't asked to come to an ice-cold office building in the middle of his nap time. More than anything, Oliver hadn't asked to lose his mother three weeks ago, nor had he asked to have a father who refused to acknowledge his existence.

Sarah took her cell phone and dialed the number she'd memorized but wasn't about to add to her contacts. As soon as she got Oliver's dad to accept his paternal responsibility, she'd force herself to forget the string of digits that led to an office somewhere in this building, most likely the top floor. There would be no maintaining ties with Aiden Langford. Their connection was temporary, albeit of paramount importance. She had his son and he was going to take custody, even if it killed her.

"Yes. Hello. It's Sarah Daltrey. I'm calling for Aiden Langford. Again."

One of the two security guards manning the lobby gave her the side-eye. Meanwhile, the woman on the other end of the phone line expressed equal disdain with her snippy tone. "Mr. Langford has told me a dozen times. He does not know you. Please stop calling."

"I can't stop calling until he finally talks to me."

"Perhaps I can help you."

"No. You can't. This is a personal matter and Mr. Langford should appreciate that I'm not sharing the details of this situation with his assistant. I outlined it all in the email I sent to him." *More like seven emails, but who's counting?* "If I can just have five minutes of his time, I can explain everything." Five minutes was a lie. She'd need at least an hour to walk Mr. Langford through Oliver's schedule, his likes and dislikes, and to make sure he was off to as good a start as possible.

"Mr. Langford is very busy. I can't put through the call of every person who claims to need his time."

"Look. I just spent four hours on a train from Boston to New York and I'm downstairs in the lobby, caring for a ten-month-old sorely in need of a nap. I'm not leaving until I speak to him. I'll sleep here if I have to."

"I can have security escort you from the building, Ms. Daltrey. Surely you don't want that."

"Does LangTel want the embarrassment of their security removing a kicking and screaming woman with a baby from their lobby?"

Mr. Langford's assistant said everything with her momentary silence. "Can you hold, please? I'll see if there's anything I can do."

Sarah had very little hope for this, but what other options did she have? "Sure. I'll hold."

Just then, a statuesque woman with glossy brown hair dressed in a tailored gray dress and black pumps came through the revolving door. Sarah might not have noticed her, but she had a baby bump that was impossible to miss. The security guard beelined to her, taking the stack of papers in her arms. "Good afternoon, Ms. Langford. I'll get the elevator."

Anna Langford. Sarah recognized her now, from the research she'd done on the Langford family while trying to find a way to get to Aiden. Anna was one of two LangTel CEOs, along with her brother Adam. She was also Aiden Langford's younger sister.

Oliver dropped his favorite toy, a stuffed turtle, and unleashed a piercing wail. Sarah cringed, crouching down, scooting across the carpet in her wedge sandals, scrambling for Oliver's toy while cradling the phone between her ear and shoulder. Anna came to a dead stop and turned her head, zeroing in on Sarah and Oliver.

Great. Now we really are going to get kicked out of the lobby.

Anna frowned and strode closer, but when she removed her sunglasses, there was only empathy in her eyes. "Oh no. Somebody's unhappy."

Certain that she'd been banished to the land of horrible hold music, Sarah ended her call and tucked her phone into the diaper bag. "Sorry about that. It's nap time. He's tired." When she straightened to face Anna, she felt as if she needed a step stool. Anna was tall *and* in heels, while Sarah was height challenged even in her strappy sandals.

Anna shook her head. "Please don't apologize. This is the highlight of my day. He's adorable." She reached for Oliver's pudgy hand and smiled. He responded by gripping her finger, his head resting on Sarah's shoulder. "I'm Anna Langford, by the way."

"I'm Sarah. Daltrey. This is Oliver." Sarah watched as Oliver smiled shyly at Anna. He was such a sweet and trusting boy. Saying goodbye to him was going to be heartbreaking, especially after three weeks of caring for him all on her own, but that was her charge and there was nothing to be done about that. She was done with being a nanny, and caring for a child that wasn't her own, regardless of the circumstances, felt far too much like her old life.

Anna's eyes didn't stray from Oliver. "Nice to meet you both. I'm due to have my own little one in about six weeks. Middle of June. I have baby fever right now, big time." She studied the baby's face. "Your son's eyes are incredible. Such a brilliant shade of blue."

And exactly like your brother's.

Sarah cleared her throat. "He's not mine, technically. I'm his legal guardian. I'm in the process of connecting him with his father. That's why I'm here."

Confusion crossed Anna's face. "At LangTel. The father works here?"

Sarah had committed herself to discretion for the sake of everyone, especially Oliver, but this might be her one real chance to get to Aiden. She was getting nowhere with his assistant. "I came to see Aiden Langford. He's your brother, right? I need to speak to him about Oliver, but he won't take my phone calls."

"Oh." A flicker of surprise crossed Anna's face as her eyes darted between Oliver and Sarah. "Oh. Wow." She kneaded her temple with the tips of her fingers. "The lobby doesn't seem like a good place to talk about this. Maybe you should come upstairs with me."

Aiden's assistant buzzed his extension. "Mr. Langford? Your sister is here to see you. She's brought a visitor."

Visitor? "Sure. Send them in." Aiden set aside the LangTel global marketing report he'd been skimming, easily the driest thing he'd ever read, which was saying a lot. With more than a dozen years in business under his belt, he'd digested his fair share of dull financial projections and legal briefs. He preferred to rely on his gut when making decisions. Billions later, the strategy had served him well.

In walked Anna with a blonde woman he didn't know. To say the stranger was eye catching would've been dismissive. With full pink lips and big blue eyes, wearing a black sundress, she was natural femininity embodied. Their gazes connected and he noticed the faintest of freckles dotting her cheeks. His tastes in women were wide and varied, but this woman ticked off more of his "yes" boxes than he cared to admit. Unfortunately, one thing about her made her absolutely not his type—the baby asleep in her arms. As a skilled avoider of emotional entanglements, moms were not on his list of women suitable for dating.

"Aiden, I want you to meet Sarah Daltrey," Anna said softly.

That name ended all thought of sexy sundresses and freckles. "You're the woman who keeps calling. You just called from the lobby. How in the world did you get to my sister?"

Anna shushed him. "The baby. He's sleeping."

The baby. His brain whirred into overdrive. He'd read Sarah's email. Well, one of them at least. That was enough to help him decide he shouldn't speak to her. He'd had false paternity accusations thrown at him before. When you have a vast fortune and come from a family well-known for success, you might as well have a target on your back. "This isn't right." His gut told him this was all wrong. "I don't know what Ms. Daltrey is after, but I'm calling security." He reached for the phone, but Anna clapped her hand over his.

"Aiden. Don't. Just listen. Please. It's important."

"I don't know what she's told you, but it's all lies." His pulse throbbed in his ears.

"Five minutes is all I ask, Mr. Langford." Sarah's voice suggested nothing less than calm professionalism. Not exactly the approach of someone unbalanced. But a baby? Oh, no. "If you don't believe me and what I came to tell you, you won't need to call security. I'll leave on my own."

Anna eyed her brother, asking his opinion with an arch of her eyebrows.

With pleas from two women who were obviously not going to give up, what choice did he have? "If it will put an end to this, then fine. Five minutes."

"I'll leave you two to it." Anna stopped at the door, turning to Sarah. "Stop by my office when you're done. I'd love to get the title of that book you mentioned about getting a baby to sleep through the night."

Sarah nodded and smiled as if she and Anna were best friends. What was he in for? "Yes, of course. Thanks so much for your help." The door clicked shut when Anna left, leaving behind a suffocating silence. Sarah cleared her throat and stepped closer, the baby's head still resting on her shoulder. "It would be great if I could sit. He's really heavy."

"Oh, sorry. Of course." Aiden offered a seat opposite his desk. He didn't know what he was supposed to do with himself—stand, sit, cross his arms. Nothing felt right, so he settled on his chair.

"I know this is strange," she started. "So I'll just get right to it. Oliver's mom was my best friend from high school. Her name was Gail Thompson. Does that ring a bell? She told me she met you at the Crowne Lotus Hotel in Bangkok."

Aiden's shoulders tightened. These tidbits of information hadn't been in Sarah's email. She'd only mentioned that she was guardian of his baby. To his knowledge, nobody knew about his brief affair with Gail. They'd met in the hotel bar and spent three days together before she went back to the US. That was the last he'd ever heard from her. "I do remember the name. Yes. But that doesn't mean anything." He shifted in his seat. He knew exactly where this was going. And that made his stomach lurch.

"Nine months after you and Gail had your little tryst in Thailand—" she fluttered her hand at him "—Oliver came along. Eight months after that, Gail called me and told me she had late stage cancer. I was the only person she could sign over guardianship to. She had no siblings— her parents died in a car accident when she was in college. She knew that I used to be a nanny and it just made sense. She said she tried to call you, but had even less luck than I did. It's hard to be persistent when you're dying."

Aiden swallowed hard. Sarah's email had mentioned that the baby's mom had fallen ill. He'd assumed that she was still alive and that this was a scam for money to pay medical bills. "She passed away?" An inexplicable tug came from the center of his chest as his vision drifted to the child. All alone in the world. He'd known that feeling well when he was young, and he despised the idea of any child growing up that way.

"Yes." Sarah pressed her lips together and nodded. She cupped the back of Oliver's head and kissed him softly on the cheek. "That left Oliver with no mom. I was left in charge of finding you so I can sign over guardianship. I think it'd be best for everyone if we kept this as simple as possible and try to wrap it up today."

Today? Did she say what I think she said? No. That was *not* happening. "You expect to waltz into my office, hand me a baby I've never seen in my life, and then what? You go back to wherever you came from and I'm expected to raise this child? I don't think so, Ms. Daltrey. You aren't going anywhere until I know for certain that the baby is mine. We need lawyers. Paternity tests. I'm not convinced this isn't a big fat hoax."

Her lips pressed into a thin line, but she otherwise seemed unfazed by his reaction. "First off, it's Sarah and his name is Oliver. And I understand you're shocked, but that's not my fault. If you'd taken my phone call, you could've been prepared for this."

"I seriously doubt I would've felt prepared. It's the middle of the workday. I'm a single man and an incredibly busy one at that. I am not prepared to care for a baby I didn't know about five minutes ago." Anger bubbled up inside him, but it was more than this inconceivable situation. He disliked his own dismissive tone. Considering the way his father had treated him, he didn't want to reject the little boy. No child deserved that. Especially one who didn't know who his father was.

"I understand you'll want a paternity test, but I think that the minute you see him awake, you'll realize he's yours. He looks just like you. Especially his eyes. Plus, he has the same birthmark you have on your upper thigh." A flush of pink colored her cheeks. She cast her eyes at her lap, seeming embarrassed. Despite the nature of their conversation, Aiden found it extremely charming. Sarah seemed to be the sort of person who wore her heart on her sleeve, a quality that made her incredibly sexy, too. "I mean, Gail told me you have one. And that's where Oliver gets it."

Sarah carefully hitched up the baby's pant leg. The child must've been incredibly tired—he hardly stirred when she revealed the mark. Aiden's breath caught in his throat. He rounded the desk, dropping down on one knee before them. He had to see it up close. He had to know this was real. The shape and size of the birthmark were indeed the same as his—an oval about the height of a dime, tilting to one side. The dark brown color was a match. *Is this possible?*

He reached out to touch the mark, but stopped himself. "I'm sorry. I'm a little taken aback."

"It's okay. He's your son." Sarah's voice was sweet and even. Given the impression he had of her from that first email, she was not at all the woman he'd envisioned.

The boy's skin was powdery soft and warm. Aiden gently tugged his pant leg back down, then studied his face. His eyelids were closed in complete relaxation, lined with dark lashes. His light brown hair had streaks of blond, admittedly much like Aiden's, although Oliver had baby-fine curls and Aiden's hair was straight and thick. Still, he knew from his own baby pictures that his hair had once been like Oliver's. Was this possible? Was this really happening? And what was he supposed to do about it? He had no idea how to care for a baby. This would change his entire life. Just when he was getting settled back in New York and trying to find a place for himself in his own family.

Oliver shifted in Sarah's arms, and for an instant, he opened his eyes and looked right at Aiden. The familiar flash of blue was a shot straight to Aiden's heart. It was like staring into a mirror. *Oh my God. He's mine.*

Two

Things weren't going terribly. Awkward, yes. Terrible, no.

It was really only awkward on Sarah's side of things. Aiden was still on bended knee watching Oliver sleep, and it was impossible not to stare at him. She tried to look elsewhere, to feign interest in the framed black-and-white photographs of exotic locales on his walls, or the view out his office window overlooking the Manhattan skyline, but she could only sustain it for a few moments. His blue eyes would draw her back in, so vivid and piercing she was sure he could hypnotize her if their gazes connected for more than a few heartbeats. They were topped by dark brows that suited his hard-nosed demeanor, accentuated by just a few tiny crinkles at the corners. The scruff on his face was a warm cinnamon brown, neatly tended, but gave him an edge that made her wonder what he was like when he wasn't so guarded. And there was something about the way he carried himself—more than self-assured, he came across as superhuman. Bulletproof. Sarah was certain Aiden Langford did precisely what he wanted to do, when and how he wanted to do it. He was not the sort of man who cared to be told what to do.

Too bad she had to do exactly that. The thought made her pulse race like an overcaffeinated jackrabbit. There was no telling how he would react, but judging by the look on his face, there was a chance it might go okay. However much of a handsome jerk he'd been when she walked in the door, his demeanor had softened in the last few minutes, ever since he'd taken a good look at Oliver. Surely she realized now, that even in the absence of hard evidence like the results of a paternity test, the baby was his.

"So," Sarah started, recalling the speech she'd practiced many times, words she dreaded saying because they would signal the end of her time with Oliver. "I was thinking that I'll leave Oliver with you now and I'll check into a hotel while we get this straightened out. A paternity test is a quick thing. We'll get your name on Oliver's birth certificate. I'll sign over the power of attorney and guardianship. All we need is a lawyer and a few days and then I can be out of your hair."

A crease formed in the center of Aiden's forehead as he stared at her. "Out of my hair?" It was just as tough to look into his eyes as she'd guessed it would be—they really were the spitting image of Oliver's. She'd fallen in love with that shade of blue over the last three weeks. "I already told you that you are not handing me a baby and walking away." He stood and straightened his charcoal suit jacket, which showed off his wide shoulders and broad frame. The way he loomed over her only accentuated his stature. There must've been something in the water in the Langford household—the two she'd met were ridiculously tall. "It seems to me that the more sensible course is for you to keep Oliver until this gets straight-

ened out. You said it yourself—you used to be a nanny.
You're used to caring for a child. I have zero experience
in this area."

Of course, most single men, especially those who notoriously played the field, weren't in a position to drop everything and care for a baby. But Aiden Langford wasn't
most men. Didn't he have a pile of money to throw at
the problem? "I used to be a nanny. Past tense. That's
no longer my vocation." She stopped short of admitting
that she didn't have the stomach for it anymore. "You'll
need to hire someone. I wrote down the number for the
top nanny agency in the city for you. One phone call and
they'll send someone over to help you."

"So I'm not only supposed to work with a complete
stranger to take care of a baby, but the baby is supposed
to accept that, too?"

He'd gone for the jugular with that one, although he
seemed to be doing nothing more than making his case.
The thought of anyone aside from his own father caring for Oliver made Sarah's chest, especially everything
in the vicinity of her heart, seize up. "I'm a business-
woman, Mr. Langford. I need to return to Boston and
my work."

"Business? What sort of business?" Although he was
following the logical course of their conversation, Sarah
couldn't help but bristle at his dismissive tone.

"I run a women's apparel company. It's really taking
off. We can't even keep up with demand."

"Good problem to have. Until your vendors get tired
of waiting and move on to something else."

Wasn't that the truth. Half of her day was spent reassuring boutique owners that their orders would be there
soon. "That's exactly why I need to be back in Boston.
And don't forget that I have been caring for *your* child
full-time for nearly a month. It's time I go back to my life

and let Oliver start his new one. With you." That last part
had been particularly difficult to say, but the fact that her
voice hadn't cracked only bolstered her confidence. She
hadn't even shed a tear. It was a miracle.

Aiden sat on the edge of his desk and crossed his arms.
His suit jacket sleeves drew taut across his muscles. How
was she supposed to hold her own in an argument when
he was distracting her with his physique? "So, I'll pay
you for your time."

Ah, so he *did* know how to throw money at a problem.
He was just lobbing it in the wrong direction. A breathy
punch of a laugh left her lips. "I'm not for hire."

"I'll pay you double whatever your going rate used
to be."

She huffed.

"Fine. Triple."

"You're a terrible negotiator."

He shrugged. "I do what's necessary to get what I
want."

"That would make me the most expensive nanny in
the history of child care. I was paid very well for my services. I was very good at my job."

"You're only making my argument for me. Money is
no object, Ms. Daltrey. If Oliver really is my son, he de-
serves the best. Sounds to me like that's you."

She shook her head. "No way. Absolutely not." This
was not the way this was supposed to go. She needed to
put an end to Aiden Langford and his money-throwing,
muscle-bulging ways.

Oliver fussed and rubbed his eyes, moving his head
fitfully as he woke.

Sarah had spoken too loudly. Nap time was apparently
now over. She stood and attempted to hand the baby to
Aiden. "Here. Take your son. At least for a minute."

Oliver refused, clinging to Sarah.

"See? He clearly wants to be with you. I'm a stranger to him. Would you really leave a baby with a stranger?"

She pursed her lips, calculating her best response. Of course she wouldn't do that. But after the extensive research she'd done on Aiden, he didn't really seem like a stranger. That, however, was not information she cared to share. Which meant she was back at nothing.

"Even worse," he continued. "A stranger who doesn't know how to change a diaper, or what to feed him, or what to do if he starts to cry."

"No idea? I know you have two younger siblings. You never babysat?"

Aiden threaded his fingers through his hair, tousling it in the process. "No."

Well, shoot. She couldn't hand over Oliver to a man he didn't know, especially not one who might not be able to care for him, even if that had been her plan. Her horribly simple plan. "I don't think it's a good idea for me to take Oliver to a hotel, either. He needs to get used to being with you. And you're apparently going to need to learn how to take care of him."

"Excuse me if I haven't thought it out quite that far yet. This is still a new concept for me." He blew out a breath, seeming deep in thought. "I guess the thing that makes the most sense is for you both to stay with me. Until we get things straightened out. And I can hire a nanny. I guess I have to buy a crib, too? I mean, really, this is a lot to pile on a person in one day."

He wasn't wrong. Maybe it would be in Oliver's best interest if she stayed for a couple of days, even if it would make it exponentially more difficult to say goodbye to him. As for the to-do list to get Aiden up and running with the baby, it was a long one if she was going to be thorough. They would need time. With the bad hand Oliver had been dealt in life, she owed it to him to spend a few days in New York so he could be off to the best possible start with Aiden. That was exactly what she'd promised Gail. "Okay. We'll stay at your place."

"You'll have to tell me what you want to be paid. I have no earthly idea how much money a nanny makes. Or even what a nanny does, other than everything a parent would do if they were around."

She'd first said no to Aiden's money on principle, but if she was going to help him with Oliver, she could get something from him that was far more valuable than a paycheck. She knew from her online snooping that he was a whiz when it came to growing companies. It was in his blood—the Langfords were one of the most successful entrepreneurial families in US history. Maybe he could help her solve the countless problems she was facing with trying to take her business to the next level.

"I don't want your money. I want your expertise."

"I'm listening." He cocked an eyebrow at her, threatening to make her throat close up.

"Business expertise. I want you to help me with my company. Help me find investors. Help me figure out my manufacturing issues and widen my distribution."

He nodded, clearly calculating. "That's a tall order. Between that and me going through baby school, this is going to take more than a few days. We'll need at least a week. At least."

How long could she do this? Every minute with Oliver only made her love him more. She clutched him, kissed his head, taking in his sweet baby smell. *We don't have to say goodbye today, buddy. I guess that much is good.* "Today is Friday. I'll give you ten days. I teach you how to care for Oliver. You help me with my company."

"I think I'd be a fool to say no. You have me in a corner here."

"I mean it, though. Ten days and I'm out of here."

"Like I said. In a corner."

"Okay, then. I want to have a say in the nanny you hire, too. And I want to help outfit the nursery."

Aiden then did the last thing she ever expected. He smiled. Not a lot, just enough to create the tiniest crack in his facade. Sarah felt as if she'd had the wind knocked out of her. His face lit up, especially his eyes. "Anything else?"

"That's all for now."

"Just so you know, fashion is outside my realm of expertise. Women's clothing isn't really my world."

Ah, but he hadn't let her finish. Given Aiden Langford's reputation for being a ladies' man, she had no doubt that he was well-versed in her specialty. "Actually, it's women's sleepwear and lingerie. Something tells me you know at least a little something about that."

Three

Oliver in her arms, Sarah climbed out of Aiden's black SUV, squinting behind sunglasses at the apartment building before them. About a dozen stories high, it had an antique brick facade blanketed in tidy sections of ivy and dotted with tall leaded glass windows. This was not what she'd envisioned for Aiden Langford's abode. She'd assumed a high-rise overlooking Central Park. Wasn't that his birthright? Ritzy address and an equally swanky apartment? Instead, he resided on Fifth Avenue at Twenty-sixth Street, in the Flatiron District with a view of Madison Square Park. She had a sneaking suspicion that Aiden was full of surprises. And that this was the first of many.

"Is that one yours?" She pointed at the highest floor. "The one on top with the biggest terrace?"

Aiden wheeled Sarah's suitcase from the car, lugging the teddy bear that was easily twice Oliver's size, while Aiden's driver John unloaded the remaining bags of toys and baby clothes. "The top four floors are my apartment."

Sarah gulped, surveying the manicured spaces—a formal balcony with stone columns and wrought iron on the lowest level all the way up to one that looked like a park in its own right, each spanning the building. He'd still gone for swanky, merely in a different corner of the city. "That's a lot of room for a single guy."

"My third floor is empty. And the fourth floor is all outdoors. I need my space."

"I'm surprised you don't live up by Anna and her husband. She was telling me she lives only a few minutes from your mom."

Aiden cast his sights down at her, his sunglasses revealing nothing but her own reflection. The crinkles in his forehead and the way his brows drew together were enough indication that he didn't like the question. The driver slammed the car tailgate. Sarah jumped.

"Like I said, I need my space." Aiden's voice was stern, like a father telling his wayward teenage daughter that she'd better be home before eleven.

Okay, then. Dropping the subject.

Together, they entered the beautifully appointed lobby. Black-and-white-checkerboard marble floors and a chandelier dripping with crystals hinted at both wealth and good taste. Sarah pushed Oliver in the stroller while she tried to remember to take deep breaths. Everything about this made her heart beat an uneven rhythm—entering into an agreement with a man she hardly knew, staying in his home, handing over the little boy she'd already grown to love more than she'd thought possible. She did everything she could to ignore the feeling in the pit of her stomach, the one saying that each passing minute was another step away from what she was supposed to be doing—leaving nannying behind, once and for all.

Stop being negative. This is good for Oliver. She had to believe that. Really, it was the best scenario for him—a transition period where his new dad could become acquainted with parenting. They'd find a nanny, set up the nursery. In ten days, this sweet little boy would be given the best possible start at a new life. And she'd get back to hers in Boston, a simple and solitary existence with its own rewards, the most notable of which was the chance to pursue a career that didn't leave her so open to heartbreak.

They stepped onto the elevator and Sarah closed her eyes to ward off her claustrophobia. Plus, every time she looked at Aiden, he got to her with his all-knowing gaze. No wonder the man had such a reputation with the ladies. Most women were probably too mesmerized by his penetrating stare to entertain a single lucid thought beyond, *Of course, Aiden. Whatever you want, Aiden.*

The elevator dinged, and John, loaded down with the bulk of the baby supplies, held the door for Sarah as she wheeled Oliver off the elevator. They entered a stunning foyer with glossy wood floors, an exotic carved console table and several colorful abstract paintings. Aiden followed with his laptop bag, Sarah's suitcase and the teddy bear, which was a nice counterpoint to his tailored gray suit and midnight-blue tie.

"Where would you like these, Mr. Langford?" John asked.

"Just leave them here. I'm not entirely sure where everything is going yet."

John did as instructed, neatly placing the bags on the table.

"Thank you so much for the help. I really appreciate it," Sarah said to John.

He turned and looked at her as if she had a unicorn horn sprouting from her forehead. "It's my job, ma'am."

"Well, we came with a lot of stuff. I'm sure Mr. Langford doesn't normally make you lug stuffed animals and diaper bags."

"I'm happy to do it. But thank you. For saying thank you." He smiled warmly.

Aiden watched the back and forth. "That's it for now, John. I'll let you know if I need anything else."

"I'll be downstairs, Mr. Langford." John stepped onto the elevator and the doors slid closed.

"He's really nice," Sarah said. "We talked quite a bit while we were figuring how to get the car seat into the SUV. He told me all about his wife and kids. Good guy."

"Of course. A very good guy." Everything in Aiden's voice said that he didn't know the first thing about his driver, and that it quite possibly had never occurred to him to ask.

"Now what?" Sarah wanted Aiden to take the lead. His house. His baby.

"Tell me why a baby needs a stuffed animal this large."

Sarah shrugged, unsubtly peeking ahead at what she could see of the apartment, which seemed to stretch on for days. "Kids love to have things to snuggle with. And eventually, Oliver will be bigger than the bear."

"Ah. I see."

"You'll learn."

"I have a feeling I won't have a choice." Aiden leaned her small suitcase against the wall and propped the bear up on top of it. "And how did you get all of this onto a train, then off a train and into the city, all by yourself?"

"Let's just say that I relied on the kindness of strangers. And I'm a very good tipper. I managed."

"You're resourceful. I'll give you that much."

Sarah went to get Oliver out of his stroller, but decided it was time to start the learning process. "Aiden. Here. You unbuckle him and get him out."

"You sure? I don't have the first clue what I'm doing."

"You have to start somewhere."

Aiden crouched down and Oliver messed with his hair while Aiden tried to decipher the maze of straps and buckles. Sarah watched, not wanting to interfere. Oliver was doing enough on his own, tugging on Aiden's jacket and kicking him in the chest.

Aiden sat back on his haunches, raking his hair from his face. "Is he always like this? So full of energy and into everything?"

"Unless he's asleep, yes. Now pick him up."

Aiden threaded his massive hands under the baby's tiny arms, lifting him as if he might break him if he went too fast, then holding Oliver awkwardly against his torso.

"Bend your arm and let him sit in the crook of your elbow." Sarah shifted Oliver into position. She straightened Aiden's suit coat while she was at it. She stood back and admired the change. The strong, strapping man holding her favorite baby on the planet was awfully sexy. "See? That wasn't so bad."

Oliver leaned toward Sarah, holding out his arms for her.

"I think he wants to be with you."

Sarah had to be firm. "He'll be fine. He needs to be with you. Let's start the tour so we can start planning the nursery. He'll stay in your arms if we're busy and there are things to look at."

Aiden blew out a breath and they strolled into the modern, open apartment. The space had very high ceilings and was decorated almost exclusively in white, black and gray. Everything was meticulous and neat, just like Aiden's office at LangTel. He was in for a big wake-up call when Oliver took over and there were toys everywhere. Best not to mention that, though. He'd learn.

To her right was a massive gourmet kitchen with an eight-burner stove and seating for six at the center island. Beyond the kitchen, she could see a hint of a dining room tucked away, then a staircase, and beyond that a room with a sofa and the beautiful windows she'd noticed on the front of the building. As a nanny, Sarah had seen grand displays of money, but nothing that hinted at this level of affluence. Although she was no real estate agent, the house had to be at least five thousand square feet if the other floors were the same size. By comparison, her Boston apartment probably could've fit inside the kitchen. When Aiden had said he needed his space, he wasn't kidding.

"The living room is at the front of the building, overlooking the park."

"Beautiful. Absolutely stunning." Sarah followed as Aiden led them in the opposite direction.

"This is the library." He nodded to his right, where black, open-back bookcases delineated the room. The shelves were packed with books. "The room with the French doors at the back of the building is my home office."

Aiden did a one-eighty and Sarah trailed behind him, past the dining room and stairs, to the living room. It was a grand and comfortable space with charcoal-gray sectional couches, a flat-screen TV above a stacked stone fireplace and a massive glass coffee table. "Another beautiful room."

"Thank you." He shifted Oliver in his arms, seeming ever-so-slightly more comfortable with holding him.

"Unfortunately, we're going to need to babyproof in here like nobody's business."

"Why? What's wrong with it?"

Sarah didn't know where to start. "There are outlets everywhere. The coffee table is a disaster waiting to happen. I can just see Oliver bonking his head. You'll probably have to put up a gate to keep him away from the fireplace.

As for the rest of the house, that's going to need an overhaul, too. Those stairs will need a gate, too."

"Isn't that how children learn? By making mistakes?" There was no misconstruing the annoyance in his voice.

"Not on my watch, they don't. At least not the kind of mistakes that put a child in the emergency room."

A low grumble left his throat. "Talk about turning my entire life upside down." He shook his head and took what seemed like his hundredth deep breath. "I'll need you to make a list. We'll tackle it that way."

"Not a normal nanny responsibility, but okay."

"I thought you weren't a nanny anymore."

"I'm not."

"Well then. This is part of our business arrangement. You need my expertise. I need yours."

"Fine." Sarah walked over to a long, dark wood console table against the wall, plopping her handbag down to dig out a piece of paper. A handful of framed photographs were directly above—one taken from the viewpoint of someone skydiving, one looking straight down the side of a cliff with a waterfall and jungle in the periphery, and another of a group of men and donkeys on a narrow path carved into a mountainside. Each looked like something out of a movie. "Nice pictures. Are these from *National Geographic*?"

"Remembrances of my adventures."

"Wait. What? These are yours?"

Aiden nodded, fighting a smile. He joined her, Oliver in tow. Aiden was doing well with the baby, and she was happy to see him master his first few moments of dad duty. "I enjoy pushing the limits," he said.

Goose bumps cropped up on Sarah's arms. A man with a dangerous side held mysterious appeal, probably because it was the opposite of her personality. She'd fallen for a few guys who liked to live on the edge over the years.

None of them was good at flexing their bravado in the realm of relationships.

"You're going to have to set aside your daredevil escapades for a little while. Skydiving is not an approved activity for a toddler."

He scowled. "I'm not enjoying this part, in case you're wondering. The part where you tell me how I have to construct my life around someone else's needs."

She patted him on the shoulder. "Welcome to parenthood. It's good for you. It'll remind you that the world doesn't revolve around you."

"Jumping out of an airplane reminds me that I'm still alive," Aiden countered. "And that I'd better find a way to enjoy my time on this planet."

There was a somber hint to that last string of words, but she was still piecing together who and what Aiden Langford truly was. It struck her as sad that he lived all alone in this big house, however much it was a showplace. Despite his protestations, Sarah couldn't imagine Oliver as anything less than a blessing in Aiden's life, quite possibly his salvation.

Oliver reached for the pictures, pointing to the skydiving snapshot. Aiden stepped close enough for him to touch it.

"Pretty cool, huh? I took that picture. I jumped out of an airplane. Maybe you and I can do that someday. Someday when Sarah isn't around to tell us what to do."

Oliver turned to Aiden, concentrating hard on his face. He flattened his palm against Aiden's cheek. Aiden reached up and covered Oliver's hand with his, a fascinated smile crossing his face. A sweet and tender moment, it left Sarah on the verge of tears. For the first time since she'd gotten off the train that afternoon, she was less worried about Aiden accepting fatherhood. They weren't out of the woods, but he was already showing signs of folding Oliver into his life. Which meant one step closer to Sarah being out of it.

Oliver needs his father. His new family. "For now, I still get to tell you what to do, at least when it comes to Oliver. I say it's time to find him a bedroom in this massive house of yours."

Aiden walked Sarah and Oliver up to the second floor, holding the little boy. He was slowly growing comfortable with this tiny human clutching the lapel of his suit coat, keeping him warm and reacting to the world Aiden walked through every day without giving it a second thought. It all was new to Oliver—sights and sounds, people and places. He didn't play the role of stranger though; he played explorer, full of curiosity. Aiden had to admire that disposition. He was cut from the same cloth.

They reached the top of the stairs and the hall where all four bedrooms were. At the far end was his master suite. There was only one other room furnished, for guests. The other two remained unused and unoccupied. With most of his family in the city, visitors weren't common, nor would they likely ever be. His friends, small in number and much like him in that they preferred to roam the globe, were not prone to planning a visit. No, the apartment with arguably too much space for a confirmed bachelor had been purchased with one thing in mind—breathing room.

He fought the sense that Sarah and Oliver were encroaching on his refuge. He made accommodations for no one and doing so put him on edge, but it was about more than covering electrical outlets and putting up gates. He hadn't come close to wrapping his head around his newfound fatherhood, even if he did accept that with the arrival of Sarah Daltrey, everything had changed.

He was counting on the results of the paternity test to help it all sink in. He'd already made the call to his lawyer. It would mean a lot to know that Oliver was truly his. Aiden had lived much of his own life convinced that Roger and Evelyn Langford—the people he called his parents—had lied to him about who Aiden's father was. Roger Langford's death nearly a year ago had made the uncertainty even more painful and the truth that much more elusive. He wasn't about to badger his mother, a grieving widow, over his suspicions. But he would confront her, eventually. He couldn't mend fences with his family until that much was known, and there was a lot of mending to be done. Aiden had made his own mistakes, too. Big, vengeful mistakes.

"I was thinking we could put Oliver in here." Aiden showed one of the spare rooms to Sarah. "It's the biggest. I mean, he is going to get bigger, isn't he?" Talk about things he hadn't considered…life beyond today, when Oliver would be older…preschool, grade school and beyond. No matter what, Aiden didn't need to think about where Oliver would go to school. He would be wherever Aiden was. There would be no shipping him off as his parents had done to him.

"Is it the closest room to yours?" Sarah asked.

"No. The smallest is the closest."

"That's probably a better choice for now." Without invitation, she ventured farther down the hall. "In here?" Sarah strolled in and turned in the small, but bright space—not much more than four walls and a closet. "This is better. It'll make it easier on you. He still gets up in the middle of the night."

"And I'll need to get up with him." He stated it rather than framing it as a question. He was prepared to do anything to feel less out of his element, as if any of this were logical to him, which it wasn't.

Oliver fussed and kicked, wanting to get down.

"Let's let him crawl around," Sarah said.

Aiden gently placed the little boy on the floor. He took off like a bolt of lightning, scrambling all over the room on his hands and knees.

Sarah pulled a few toys out of her bag and offered them to Oliver. "Yes. You'll need to get up with him and comfort him, especially when he's teething like he is now."

Aiden leaned against the door frame, acting as a barrier in case Oliver decided to escape. "Is that why he drools so much?"

Sarah smiled and sat on the floor with Oliver, tucking her legs beneath her, her dress flounced around her. "My mother used to say that's not drool. It's the sugar melting."

Aiden wasn't prone to smiling, let alone laughing, at things that were quaint and homey. But he couldn't have stopped if he'd wanted to. He drank in the vision of Sarah. She was so different from every woman he'd ever known. She was beautiful, but not made up. Eloquent, but not pretentious. There was no hidden agenda, nor did she seem concerned with impressing him. She just came right out with it, but didn't mow people over with her ideas. She simply stated what she found to be best, in a manner that made it seem as if it were the only logical choice.

Sarah again looked around the room. "We should probably order a crib online and see how quickly we can have it delivered, along with some other necessities. He'll need a dresser, a changing table. You should probably invest in a rocking chair for this room." She began counting on her fingers. "Then there's clothes, diapers, formula, bottles, toys, bath supplies, baby laundry detergent."

"Special laundry detergent?"

Pressing her lips together, she nodded. "When he's crying in the middle of the night, you don't want to be wondering if it's because his skin is irritated. One less thing to worry about."

Just when he thought he was getting a handle on things,

a new spate of information came down the pike. "Like I said before, it'd be great if you could make some lists. You can use the computer in my home office and get a lot of that ordered."

"We need to call the nanny agency, too. They probably don't take calls after five on a Friday. Sounds like we have a busy night ahead of us. Oliver's going to need a bath, too." Oliver crawled over to Sarah with a stuffed toy in his hand and showed it to her.

Aiden's cell phone rang with a call from his sister Anna. "Excuse me for a minute. I need to make sure this isn't anything important."

"Sure thing. I'll call the nanny agency and Oliver can play. Avoiding outlets, of course."

"Right. The outlets." *Gotta deal with that, ASAP.* He accepted the call and stepped out into the hall. "Anna, hi. Everything okay?"

"I was calling to ask you the same thing. Is everything going well with Sarah and Oliver? I can't believe it, Aiden. A baby. It's so amazing. Are you just bursting at the seams?"

Aiden wandered into his room and sat on the leather bench at the foot of the bed. "More like my brain is about to implode. I don't know what I'm supposed to feel. At least you've had time to get used to the idea of becoming a parent. It's only been a few hours for me."

"I'm sure it will take some time, but I'm so excited for you. You know, the minute I looked into Oliver's eyes, I knew he was yours. He looks just like you. It's going to blow Mom's mind when she sees him."

Oh no. The one thing he hadn't yet taken into account. "Please tell me you haven't said anything to Mom. Or Adam for that matter, but especially not Mom. I need to figure out how best to deal with this."

"I haven't said a peep."

He exhaled a little too loudly, if only to make the weight of dealing with his mother subside. "Good." His mind often raced at the mere mention of his mom, thoughts quickly mired in bad memories and sad stories. He couldn't fathom the moment when she'd meet the son he hadn't known he had. Would he feel better about his suspicions, a misgiving he'd shared with no one other than Anna? Or would he feel worse? Either way, his mother's reaction to Oliver would be telling. If she accepted him unconditionally, he'd always wonder why she hadn't treated him the same way. If she rejected him, he'd have a hard time not blowing up at her.

"When are you going to tell her?" Anna asked.

"Tomorrow. Or maybe Sunday. I need time to get us settled." He rested his elbows on his knees. "Sarah's calling the nanny agency, we have an entire nursery of furniture to order and I'm apparently in Daddy School after that. I have to learn how to change a diaper and give him a bath."

Anna tittered.

"What's so funny?"

"I like the image of you bathing a baby. It's sweet. And unlike anything I ever imagined you doing."

"You and me both. I never thought I'd have kids." *Not after everything with Dad.*

"Sometimes life gives us unexpected gifts. I felt like that when I got pregnant."

Anna was carrying a miracle baby. Her doctor had told her it would be nearly impossible to conceive and even more difficult to carry a pregnancy to term, but she was doing great. "I hear you. I'm still getting used to it."

"Well, promise me you won't keep Oliver to yourself. I want to see him, too. I could even come over and take care of him if you need help. I could bring Jacob. It would be great practice for us."

Anna always managed to take the edge off his greatest concerns. Even if he'd come back to New York and everything had been a total disaster with the rest of his family, he still would've forged a better relationship with Anna. "Thanks. I'll definitely need your help after Sarah leaves."

"She's staying for ten whole days? How'd you convince her to do that? She seemed hell-bent on only being in town through the weekend when we first talked."

"We made a deal. She gives me ten days and I help her with her business." Aiden then realized that his sister might be able to help. Before she'd taken a job at Lang-Tel, she'd been CFO for a company that manufactured women's workout clothes. "Did Sarah happen to tell you what she does?"

"She did. And the idea of you helping her with it is almost as amusing as the image of you giving Oliver a bath."

"I'm glad you find my life changes so entertaining right now. Do you think you could help me out with some contacts in the garment industry? I haven't talked to Sarah about it that much, but I know she needs manufacturing and warehousing and distribution. Maybe you know someone I could call."

"Oh, absolutely. Let me think about it and I'll email you a list."

"Perfect." One thing he could check off his to-do list. "God only knows how I'll get any work done on Monday when I'm back at the office. I doubt I'll get much rest this weekend."

"Don't worry about that. Work can wait. You're a dad now. That's the most important thing."

Four

Sitting on the floor in Oliver's room, Sarah ended her call with the nanny agency. She leaned down and kissed the baby's head. He'd been playing quietly in her lap for a few minutes. "Guess what? Your daddy's going to hire someone very nice to take care of you. Won't that be great?"

Oliver gnawed on a plastic teething ring, not interested in much else.

Sarah swept his soft curls to the side. "She'll play with you and take you for walks in the park and sing songs to you. Just like I do." Her voice wobbled as Oliver peeked up at her with wide eyes. She wrinkled her nose and forced herself to smile, if only to stop tears from gathering. The thought of leaving Oliver was as unhappy as it was inevitable. Getting attached to children who weren't her own was no longer part of her self-destructive pattern. Nor was getting wrapped up in the life of a single dad. The sooner she left Oliver with Aiden, the better.

"It really is too bad that you can't just stay and be his nanny," Aiden said.

Sarah nearly fainted. First out of surprise at his voice, then from the view as she slanted her sights to him. Leaning against the door frame, he stood there like he could hold up the whole world that way. He'd changed clothes. In a long-sleeved black T-shirt and a pair of jeans with a dark wash, he was now at a level of casual she hadn't pondered, although he had to take off the suit at some point. That thought sent her brain skipping ahead, especially now that she could better see the contours of his shoulders and how well-defined his chest was. No doubt about it— Aiden Langford logged his fair share of time in the gym.

Cut it out. The things cycling through her mind were not good—thoughts of peeling away his T-shirt and smoothing her hands over his chest, kissing him. Her curiosity was getting the best of her, and his presence was making it worse. Unfortunately, his expression was just as irresistible as the rest of the package—a look that said he didn't care what anyone else thought about, well, anything. Sarah could hardly keep her jaw in a place that suggested some measure of decorum. Forget ladylike—right now she was going for not ogling him like a sex-starved loon.

"I adore Oliver, but I told you I'm no longer a nanny."

Aiden stepped into the room and once again, something about the way he moved left her pulse unsettled. He held up his hands in surrender. "Got it. No more nannying for you. But did you call the service?"

"I did. They'll send candidates over on Monday morning. We can sit down before then and go over your priorities. And mine, of course."

"We? You know, I'm more than capable of conducting an interview. And you aren't going to have to put up with this person. I am."

She narrowed her focus on him. "You asked for my

help." She stood and gathered Oliver in her arms, settling him on her hip. "Some of these nannies will embellish on their experience just to get the primo jobs. I'll see past that."

"This is one of those primo jobs?"

"With this house? Yes. And you're going to need someone at your beck and call with your schedule. I told them you need live-in help." Sarah didn't like this idea, although she couldn't arrive at a sensible reason why. She only knew that the myth of the nanny falling for the father of her charge was very real. It happened all the time. It had happened to her. If Aiden were to be judged on his looks alone, she could see most women falling for him. Add in the money, power and semiarrogant veneer? Forget it. It was only a matter of time.

"Wait a minute. I'm not just getting one new member of the household, I'm getting two? Can't the nanny live at her house and come over when I go to work?"

"That might work if you had a backup, like a family member. Otherwise, I can't imagine you waiting for the nanny to show up so you can go to work. What about your mom?"

Lightning fast, Aiden plucked Oliver from her arms. "My mother will not be taking care of him."

Sarah grappled with his hyperprotective reaction. A few hours ago, he'd been ready to banish her and the baby from LangTel corporate headquarters forever. Now, there was something else to contend with, something that Sarah sensed went deep. "Why? Most people would do anything to have a grandparent around to care for their child."

"Not me."

"Technically, I'm Oliver's legal guardian. I have a right to know why." None of this added up. Aiden's sister Anna had spoken warmly of her mother. Sarah had read about Evelyn Langford when she was researching Aiden. She sat on countless charity boards and was known for her generosity with children's hospitals, cancer research and battered women's shelters. By all reports, her benevolence had grown in the wake of her husband's death.

"I'm not saying my mother would hurt him. Not that. It's…" He closed his eyes for a moment and Sarah's breath hitched in her throat. No air would go in, nor would it come out. She was too in awe of this glimpse of vulnerability. It was so incongruous with his personality. He was showing a different side of himself, a side Sarah wanted to know. A side Sarah wanted to comfort. "It's complicated. Let's just say that for now, it's best if you know that my mother can't be relied upon for anything."

There was a finality to his tone that said Sarah should leave it alone. "Okay."

"What's the schedule for the rest of the night? I have some work I need to tend to."

Sarah consulted her phone—nearly five o'clock. "Oliver eats at five thirty. Bath time at six o'clock, story time at six forty-five. Bedtime is at seven."

"Is that Oliver's schedule or yours?"

"It's everybody's schedule. That's how things work with a baby. It makes him feel secure. He knows what happens and when."

It was impossible to ignore Aiden's attitude. Once again, he seemed put out. "I see. I guess I still have a lot to learn. We can order some takeout to come for us around eight. I trust that will work?"

She nodded. "Yes. That will give us the perfect time to talk about my business." There had to be some payoff for allowing herself to get in deeper, when she'd told herself she'd never do that.

"I spoke to my sister Anna about it briefly. She may be able to help. I wasn't kidding when I told you that I don't have many connections in that business. I can't promise you the world."

But you can ask the world of me. She stopped before the words left her lips, but she was all too familiar with handsome, powerful men who expected everything for very little in return. "Well, if nothing else, I'm sure you can give me some good advice. That alone could end up being very helpful."

"Come on. Let's go down to my office and we'll get the nursery furniture ordered."

They headed downstairs and Aiden led them to the double French doors, into one of the coziest, most gorgeous rooms Sarah had ever seen. The office had a different feel to it than the rest of the house, warmer and more colorful. The walls were a deep navy, and an ornate Oriental carpet sat in the center of the room, topped with a pair of club chairs and a massive oak desk. Bookshelves lined two of the walls from floor to ceiling.

"More books? Even with the home library?"

Aiden shrugged and rounded to the chocolate-brown leather desk chair. "I like to read. It's a nice escape."

"Escape? From what?"

"Excuse me?"

"From where I sit, you have a pretty perfect life. You have this gorgeous home, a job that tons of people would kill for and you don't seem to be hurting from the financial end of things. More than anything, you don't seem to do anything you don't want to do. At all. Ever."

For a moment, he just glared, not saying a word. He wasn't angry, nor was he pleased. "You say whatever you want to say, don't you?"

"It's not that bizarre a question. I've seen the pictures. Skydiving. Hiking the Andes. I'm just wondering what you need to escape from."

"Stress," he answered flatly, methodically spinning a pen on a pad of paper. She hadn't noticed his hands much before now and she was kicking herself for not paying better attention. His fingers moved gracefully, demon-strating their ability to do things deftly, but they were manly, too—strong. Able.

"Stress." Her stupid brain leaped ahead to methods of reducing stress and none of it had to do with reading. Again she was knee-deep in thoughts of what he looked like under that T-shirt.

"Yes." He opened his laptop and placed his fingers on the keyboard, but stopped before typing. "I don't even know where to start. Do I just search for baby crib?"

"Here. Let me do it." She carried Oliver around behind Aiden's desk and handed him the baby. Oliver settled in on Aiden's lap, but reached for the pen.

"Can I let him have this?"

"No. He'll put it in his mouth. You can run upstairs and grab a toy out of his room."

Aiden raised an eyebrow as if she'd made the most lu-dicrous suggestion ever.

She shrugged and waved him off. "Gotta start being Daddy sometime. Now shoo. Let me see what I can find online."

Aiden trekked out of the office with Oliver. Sarah rested her chin on her hand, watching as they made their way down the straight shot of the house, past the library and the kitchen, until they disappeared up the stairs. Aiden was so big, Oliver so tiny in his arms. She hoped to hell they would be okay on Sunday, after she left. She couldn't bear the thought of anything else.

She pulled up a browser window and quickly found a furniture place offering next day delivery in Manhattan. That was the genius part of being in a big city. Virtually anything could be delivered at any time. Once she was done, a delivery truck would be set to arrive in front of Aiden's building tomorrow morning. And she'd be one step closer to removing herself from Aiden's and Oliver's life.

Five

Aiden had learned one thing already—fatherhood was no walk in the park. He'd struggled through his first attempt at feeding Oliver his dinner. With no high chair, they'd had to improvise by wheeling Oliver's stroller into the dining room. The baby rubbed his eyes and turned his head, refusing every spoonful Aiden offered. He had to hand it to Sarah, though—she only gave advice when asked. She'd otherwise sat by quietly and watched as a man capable of orchestrating billion-dollar deals and negotiating with cantankerous CEOs was unable to convince a fussy toddler to take a single bite of food. Frustrated, he'd finally asked her to do it. She took over, Oliver downing an entire jar of baby food with hardly a single complaint. Aiden walked away from the dinner table with a bruised ego. And baby food on his jeans.

He wasn't sure what to make of bath time, either. But this time, Sarah took charge.

"This is the only tub you have in the house?"

Aiden failed to understand the question. The tub was perfect, in that it fit two people. For him, seduction was the only reason to get in a bathtub. "Yes. What's wrong with it?"

"It's huge."

"Of course it is. It's a two-person soaking tub." He cleared his throat, waiting for her next comment.

"Well, you're going to have to get in there with him. I refuse to bathe a child in the kitchen sink. It's not sanitary."

He turned and dropped his head until his chin was nearly flat against his chest. He was at least a foot taller than her, maybe more, and they were nearly toe-to-toe. She was still wearing the sundress from earlier in the day. Had that really been today? So much had happened, it was hard to wrap his brain around it. "So you're going to see me naked before we've known each other for eight hours? You take things quickly."

"Very funny. No, Oliver gets to get naked. You're putting on swim trunks. If I had a bathing suit with me, I'd do it myself. But I don't, and you need to bond with him."

He raised an eyebrow. "This from the woman who swore I'd have no problem feeding him dinner."

She shrugged. "Babies are unpredictable. The sooner you learn that, the better. I promise you that physical contact will help you and Oliver to bond. It's a scientific fact. Now go change. I'll get the water running."

"I like it hot."

"You'll get lukewarm and like it."

He grumbled, but made his way into his walk-in closet, closing the door behind him. He took off his clothes and plucked a pair of board shorts from the bottom drawer of his bureau, slipping into them and tying the white string at the waist. He opened the door. "Ready."

Sarah turned, glancing at him over her shoulder. Every

muscle in his body tightened from that single flash of her eyes and the immediate connection he felt. Good God she was gorgeous, all deep blue eyes and skin flushed with rosy pink. She shied away. "So I see."

He liked getting that reaction. He liked it a lot. "What now?"

"Get in. I'll hand him to you." She tended to Oliver, who was pulling himself to standing at the edge of the bathtub. He bounced up and down on his toes while Sarah took off his pants and diaper.

"He seems excited."

"Just you wait. He loves bath time. It's a good thing you're in your trunks. I'm going to get soaked."

Aiden climbed into the tub, wrestling with the idea of Sarah, soaked, and the white-hot image it conjured. Sure, they only had ten days together, but that was plenty of time for him. In fact, it was his preference—a strict, short timetable. But was that a good idea? From a physical standpoint, sure. From every other standpoint, he didn't know. There were repercussions and awkward conversations to worry about. *Dammit.*

Sarah handed him the baby and he let Oliver sit on his lap while he wrapped his hands around his waist. The baby wasted no time slapping the surface of the water and sending it flying.

Sarah laughed and dropped a few plastic toys into the bath. "Told you."

Splash splash splash. Oliver looked at Sarah, who beamed at him as if she couldn't be any more in love with someone if she tried. She rested her elbows on the edge of the tub and leaned closer, flicking at the water with the tips of her fingers. Oliver giggled, then mimicked her in a far less delicate way. *Splash splash splash.* He laughed so hard his entire body shook. It was impossible not to find the fun in their game, even with water being flung at his face and shoulders, not to mention all over the bathroom.

"Is bath time always this chaotic?"

"Basically. Anything you can do to get him clean. And it helps relax him."

Splash splash splash. Another peal of Oliver's sweet giggles rang out.

"It relaxes him?"

"Believe it or not, yes. He has a lot of energy. This helps to get it out." Sarah pulled out a toiletry bag and poured a dollop of golden shampoo into her hand. "Get his hair wet. We don't have a cup, so just use your hands."

Aiden scooped water with one hand, curling his arm around wiggly Oliver. He started tentatively, unsure if the baby would like it, but quickly learned that he took no issue with water running down his face. Aiden had a little fish on his hands. How amazing it would be to teach him to swim, then snorkel and surf, another of Aiden's favorite pastimes. *Small waves at first. It's dangerous.* He was still getting used to these parental thoughts, but he was amazed how quickly they had kicked in. Especially when the topic of his mother had come up. He hadn't meant to impulsively take Oliver out of Sarah's arms. He only knew that was his gut talking—and reacting. Oliver would know nothing but unconditional love from his family. He wasn't certain his mother could offer it, and until she'd demonstrated as much, she would be kept on a very short leash.

Sarah leaned over and shampooed Oliver's head, his blond curls becoming matted and soapy. A soft fragrance filled the air.

"It smells nice," he said.

"It smells like baby, and that's the most wonderful smell in the world. Well, most of the time. There are times when it gets stinky, too."

"I bet." Like most things, there would be both good and bad to parenting. Aiden was optimistic about more good, mostly because he and Oliver had a clean slate. Aiden would not do to Oliver what his parents had done to him. Oliver would never wonder whether his father loved him. For that matter, he would never have to wonder *who* his father was. Once the paternity test was done, Aiden would have that sewn up for them both.

"Turn him around, facing you. So I can rinse out his hair."

He carefully turned Oliver in his hands, but it wasn't easy—it was like holding on to a greased-up watermelon with moving arms and legs. "I'm trying to figure out how I'm supposed to do this by myself."

"I ordered a seat that goes in the tub. That will help immensely. And it won't be long before he can sit up reliably in the bath on his own."

Now that he and Oliver were facing each other, Aiden had a chance to really study him. Oliver returned the gaze, chewing on a rubbery red fish. His eyes were so sweet and innocent, full of wonder. Aiden saw only hope, remarkable considering what the little guy had been through. As Sarah rinsed his hair, Aiden was overcome with the most unusual feeling. It was stronger than his inclination to protect Oliver from big waves. It was a need to keep him from everything bad. He never wanted Oliver's eyes to reflect anything but happiness. Had his own father ever looked at him like this? He didn't enjoy the role of pessimist, but the idea was implausible.

Sarah rolled a small bar of soap in her delicate hands and washed Oliver's back, shoulders and stomach, while Aiden held on tight. Every gentle caress showed someone who genuinely cared about her charge. He'd never really seen this side of any woman aside from on TV or in movies, and it was breathtaking to watch. If he were honest,

he'd never done so many things with a woman that gave
him a taste of what being a couple was like. Wining, dining and seduction were not the same. This was different.

Sarah swept her hair to one side, displaying the stretch
of her graceful neck, the contours of her collarbone. Her
skin was so touchable, and the urge to do exactly that
was strong with her mere inches away. His hands were
practically twitching at the idea. He had to set his mind
on another course.

"So. Tell me more about you," he said.

She smiled and sat back on her haunches. "Not much
to tell. Born and raised in Ohio, oldest of five. Moved
to Boston to study fashion design, stayed for the good
nanny jobs."

"Why not go right into design?"

She plucked a washcloth from the bathroom vanity
and wiped her hands. "Nannying was a detour. I grew
up helping out with my siblings, so it was a natural thing
to care for children. And Boston is not cheap. Nannying
pays well. It just worked."

"If you liked it that much and it paid well, how does
that stop working?"

She looked down at the floor, her golden hair falling
down around her face. "I burned out. Badly. Let's put it
that way."

That didn't make sense. She didn't seem at all burned
out on caring for Oliver. If anything, she had superhuman
stamina and patience when it came to it. "And the rest?
Surely there's a special guy in your life."

"There is." Her face lit up so brightly that it was as if
someone had sucker punched him. So much for seduction. There was another man.

"His name is Oliver," she continued. "He's so sweet.
He doesn't talk much. Drools a fair amount. Still learning how to walk. Exactly like I like my men."

He laughed and shook his head. She was ridiculously charming and clever, probably why he had such a strong reaction to the idea of her with a boyfriend.

She flipped her hair back and grinned at Oliver. "But seriously, the right guy hasn't walked into my life and I'm not about to wait. I'm too busy trying to build my business to think about stuff like that. Romance is not on my radar right now."

No wonder he'd been feeling as though he and Sarah might be kindred spirits, even though they came from different worlds. She wasn't looking for love. And neither was he. And with only ten days together, that might be perfect.

Sarah was ready to claim victory over bath time—Oliver was clean and she hadn't been caught staring at Aiden. It was a miracle since she'd been doing exactly that, sneaking peeks at his chest, broad and firm with the most perfect patch of dark hair in the center. Then there were his glorious shoulders and his sculpted biceps. She'd also spent a fair amount of time studying the tattoo on the inside of his forearm—a dark and intriguing pattern, impossible to decipher.

She bopped Oliver on the nose with the tip of her finger. "Hey, mister. It's time for somebody to get out of the bath and get into pj's."

Aiden furrowed his brow. "Sarah's no fun," he said to Oliver. "I don't know about you, but I'm good for at least another fifteen minutes."

She smiled. "The water will be freezing by then. And don't forget the schedule."

"Ah, yes. The schedule."

Aiden lifted Oliver out of the bath and handed him to Sarah, who had a towel at the ready. She wrapped up the baby, holding him close, gently drying his hair with an extra washcloth. Her vision drifted to Aiden as he climbed out and planted one foot on the edge of the tub and bent over to scrub his leg with the towel. She nearly bit right through her lip. His back was long and lean, his posture flaunting the definition—a railroad of muscle running north to that thick, touchable head of hair and south to a pleasingly tight rear view.

He dropped his foot and turned. Either she hadn't had *time* to turn away or she hadn't had the will. A devilish half smile crossed his face—a grin that said he knew she'd just committed his backside to memory. Sarah was petrified. If she shied away, she'd look even more guilty. It'd be tantamount to blurting, *I had to look. You're too hot not to look.* But if she kept staring, it would be hard to stop and that would further chip away at her resolve. No falling for the impossibly handsome single dad with the adorable baby.

"You're wet." Aiden nodded in her direction, wrapping the towel around his waist.

Sarah shifted Oliver to her hip. Her dress was streaked with dark patches and clung to her thighs. "Oh, shoot. Yeah. I should probably get out of this thing."

"Might as well get comfortable since we're in for the night."

"Comfortable?" *No, not comfortable. I need to get uncomfortable.*

"Unless an evening gown is more appropriate for story time. I'm still learning here." He took the baby from her. They were ridiculously cute together—Aiden bare chested and wearing a towel, Oliver bundled up in his arms. "If Oliver gets to wear pajamas, that's what I'm wearing, too. You might as well join us."

"I didn't pack for a pajama party. All I have is one of my nightgowns."

"I haven't seen your work yet. If I'm going to help you with your business, I need to know what you're selling."

"I'll show you pictures."

"Why? Too sexy?"

"No," she blurted, not taking the time to think.

"Then what's the problem?" He cast her a look of admonishment that left her quaking. "If this is what you do, you have to own it. You have to live it or it'll never work."

"I do live it. I do own it."

"Then show me. I promise I'll contain myself."

She stifled her exasperation. "Fine. Everything you need to get Oliver dressed is on your bed. I'll be right back."

"Don't take too long. I'm still figuring out this whole diaper thing."

Sarah hustled down the hall in her bare feet, muttering to herself. "Great job, Sarah. First you get caught staring and now he talked you into half-naked story time."

How had she ended up in this situation? *Aiden.* He was everything she hadn't expected. Once she'd gotten past the get-out-of-my-office exterior and been invited into his inner sanctum, he'd shown her a different side, one that was unfairly appealing. He was nicer, he was more amenable, he was generous. And then there were the things his physical presence did to her, making her tingle in places that hadn't tingled in more than a year. Not since she'd discovered that her employer Jason had been taking her to bed when he was in town and doing the same with countless other women when he traveled for work. She'd allowed herself to get caught up in their lives, and crossed the line no nanny should, and she'd paid the price. Her heart had been trampled by Jason, and even worse—she'd had to say goodbye to Chloe, his sweet, adorable daughter. That had hurt like nothing else. She couldn't repeat that mistake.

She ducked into her room and closed the door, sucking in a deep breath to reclaim some semblance of control. She would not be her own worst enemy. Time to get her act together.

Her eyes darted to her suitcase, perched on the bench at the foot of her bed. Unless some different pajamas had magically made their way inside, she had exactly one of her designs with her—a midthigh bias-cut nightgown with thin straps. The black raw silk held a subtle shimmer, embroidered with delicate silver threads at the hem and demure neckline. It didn't scream sexpot, but it wasn't anywhere close to frumpy either. Just risqué enough to give her an anxiety attack. Her shoulders dropped in defeat.

"He said I have to own it. I just have to do that." There was no more time for thinking. Aiden was indeed still figuring out the whole diaper thing, and Oliver would invariably pee all over him if she took too long. She wrestled her way out of her dress and threaded the chemise over her head. The silk skimmed her skin, reminding her precisely why her customers couldn't get enough of her nightgowns—they made a woman feel sexy.

But she could take the edge off. She grabbed her black cardigan and put it on, buttoning it up. She'd bought herself a small measure of modesty, but as she stole a passing glance in the mirror, she saw that she was not owning it—she was borrowing it. Frustration bubbled up inside her, but she couldn't simply traipse into Aiden's bedroom dressed for seduction. This would have to do. If she had to walk a narrow tightrope, she would. Even if she'd be donning a bizarre ensemble while doing it.

With no more time for second-guessing, she hurried back down the hall. Aiden's door was open. He was hunched over the side of the bed, attempting to dress Oliver.

Sarah joined them, perching gingerly on the edge of the mattress. The bedding was so soft and silky she had to stifle a moan of approval. In dark gray pajama pants and a black T-shirt that showed off the straight line of his shoulders, Aiden was dressed to kill. Why did everything about him have to be so enticing? "Looks like you did well with the diaper. What about the rest?"

"I'm worried I'm going to bend him in the wrong direction."

"Just think about how you would get ready for bed. Do that."

He arched an untamed eyebrow at her. "Then he's ready. Because I don't wear much to bed."

Of course he just *had* to plant that mental image in her head. He had to. "Then pretend you're putting on a shirt for work." She crossed her legs, noticing how parts of her were again tingling and zipping with electricity.

Aiden got Oliver into the sleeves and the legs, but then he hit another trouble spot with the snaps. "These things don't match up."

"Start at the top."

He did as she'd instructed and picked up Oliver when he was done. "Good?"

"Fantastic."

He sat next to her on the bed, Oliver in his lap. "You know, I can hardly see what you're wearing with that big old sweater over the top of it."

She wrapped her arms around her waist. "I was cold," she lied. Being this close to Aiden, she was about to go up in flames. "And we need to get going with bedtime."

"Right. The schedule."

Nightgown crisis averted, it was now acceptable to exhale.

"Since the crib doesn't come until tomorrow, Oliver can sleep with you tonight. It will be a nice way for you two to bond."

"But what if I roll onto him? What if he falls out of the bed?"

A breathy laugh escaped her lips.

"Something funny?" he asked.

"Careful. You sound like a dad."

"They're valid questions."

"And I'm glad you're concerned. We can put some dining chairs next to the side of the bed."

Aiden scratched his head, looking around the room. "Get up. Hold Oliver."

Sarah stood and took the baby, watching as Aiden pushed aside the bench at the foot of his bed and began tugging on his mattress. It only took a few pulls before it landed with a thump on the floor.

"There. Then if he rolls out of bed, he won't go far. It's only for one night."

Sarah could hardly believe her eyes. "Talk about problem solving."

"It's partly selfish. I won't get any sleep if I'm paranoid all night about what's going to happen to him."

She didn't bother containing her smile, even though she sensed that with every sweet thing Aiden did or said, she was being pulled more forcefully into his orbit. "You're turning into a dad right before my eyes."

Aiden retrieved the pillows from their resting place on the box spring—they hadn't made the trip. "I have a job to do, I don't shy away from it."

"I know, but you were bitching about baby gates a few hours ago. Now you're camping out in your own bedroom."

Aiden stepped over to her and took Oliver. "It was the bath. I guess it started to sink in that he needs me. It feels nice. Nobody's ever needed me like he does."

There was an edge of sadness to Aiden's voice that tugged at Sarah's heart. She needed to make a graceful exit, now. "You know, I think I'm going to get Oliver a bottle and walk you through the bedtime routine. Something tells me you'll do just fine."

"Oh, okay. Did you want to have dinner after he goes to sleep?"

I do. I really do. But I don't. "No, thank you. I've had a long day. I'll just turn in."

Aiden seemed puzzled, but didn't argue. "Okay."

Sarah retrieved Oliver's bottle and left Aiden to his own devices after a brief overview of what to do. Since Oliver's nap had been cut short that day, she was sure he'd fall asleep quickly. Apparently, exactly that had happened, since she didn't hear another peep for hours. She stayed in her room, tucked under the covers, trying to banish thoughts of Aiden from her head.

Deep in the middle of the night, Sarah woke to the sound of Oliver's cries. They caused her physical pain, made worse by the fact that she couldn't go to him. Aiden had to learn how to deal with it. The baby let out another screech and Sarah rolled onto her side, squinting at the alarm clock on the bedside table. Two forty-three.

This was normal. No big emergency. Oliver cried again and her instinct told her to go to him, and if she were honest, there was sympathy for Aiden, too. He'd been through a lot today and had risen to the occasion. She sat up, dangling her feet off the edge of the bed, listening. There was quiet. She was just about to lie back down when another cry came.

As did a knock on the door. "Sarah? Are you up?"

Hearing Aiden's voice in the middle of the night did something funny to her. "Yes. Need some help?"

Oliver wailed again.

"Yeah. If that's okay."

"Two secs." Sarah climbed out of bed and opened the door. There stood a nearly naked Aiden, wearing only a pair of gray boxer briefs, and a red-eyed Oliver. The baby lunged for her and Sarah took him, bouncing him in her arms to comfort him. "What's wrong, buddy? Why are we giving Daddy such a hard time on his first night?"

Aiden walked in and sat down on the edge of her bed, running his hands through his hair. "I thought I was in good shape. He started to get fussy and then he started to cry, so I got up and changed his diaper. He was pretty wet."

Sarah nodded, pacing back and forth, partly to comfort Oliver, and partly to distract herself from the vision of Aiden. "Good."

"He didn't want a bottle."

"Did you try his pacifier?"

"I couldn't find that thing. I think it's somewhere in the bed."

"That might help. Let's go look."

She followed Aiden down the hall into his bedroom, where he flipped on one of the bedside lamps. His daddy instincts were already becoming attuned. Most first-time parents would've flipped on the overhead light. She bounced Oliver up and down while Aiden kneeled down on the bed and began rummaging through the sheets.

"Ha. Found it." Aiden stood, victorious, and brought his finding to Oliver. The baby grabbed the pacifier with his hand and plugged it right into his mouth. "So that's what he wanted."

"Apparently."

Aiden blew out a breath. "I have a lot to learn. But thanks for your help." He reached for Oliver, but the baby was having none of that, clinging to Sarah and whimpering. "He wants you. Maybe you should take him for the rest of the night."

"Oh no. You have a way bigger bed than I do. And you two are supposed to be bonding, anyway."

"So sleep in my bed with us. I'm too tired to argue."

"That hardly seems appropriate."

"Why? We're going to have a baby between us. You'll have to trust me when I say that nothing will happen, however tempting you might be, Sarah Daltrey."

Tempting? Yeah, right.

"And there'll be plenty of room. You're practically a miniature human being."

"I'm not miniature."

"Like I said, too tired to argue. Just get in the bed. Please."

"Fine. But tonight only."

"I won't need to have you in my bed tomorrow night. There'll be a crib."

Well, that certainly solved that, didn't it? She walked around to the other side of the bed, and climbed in under the covers. Even with the mattress directly on the floor, she'd never been on a more comfortable bed in her entire life. Oliver must've been really unhappy to have had a hard time sleeping.

Aiden turned out the light and joined them, lying on his side, facing her and Oliver. The baby relaxed and let go of his iron grip on her shoulder, settling in on his back between them. The quiet was thick and nearly unbearable. She was too keenly aware that she was in bed with Aiden and that Aiden was aware of her and that Aiden was still awake. It was going to take forever to fall asleep.

"Sarah," Aiden whispered.

"What?"

"You let me see the nightgown."

Sleep deprivation makes me dumb. "I guess I did."

"It's gorgeous. I'm not surprised you're having a hard time keeping inventory."

She smiled to herself, there in the darkness.

"You were wrong when you said it wasn't sexy."

Sarah's heart galloped at an unhealthy speed. Now she'd really never get to sleep.

"It shows off your legs. You have nice legs," he continued. "And, well, it compliments other parts of you as well."

If it were possible to die from flattery, Sarah was DOA. What was she supposed to say to that? Was she supposed to reciprocate? *Those boxers you're wearing sure show off your three percent body fat and ridiculously alluring physique?*

"Sarah? Are you asleep?"

Dang. She should've pretended to be snoring. "Not quite," she whispered.

"Did I say something wrong?"

No. You said everything right. "I think we should get some sleep. And I don't want to wake the baby."

Six

Aiden was rarely overwhelmed. He didn't believe in it. Why panic when there's a lot to do? Tackle it, and move on. But bleary-eyed, navigating the maze of boxes in the hall outside Oliver's nursery and operating on very little sleep, he was officially off his game.

"How does a person who is so small need so much stuff?"

"You asked me the same thing yesterday. And I don't know why, they just do." Sarah balanced Oliver on her hip while she peeked into his room, where two delivery people were assembling furniture. "They should have the crib done soon. Somebody needs to sleep in his own bed tonight." She cleared her throat and looked square at Aiden. "That goes for me, too."

"Of course." Yeah, he'd gotten the hint last night when he'd tried to say a few nice things and she'd hardly re-acted at all. Although he'd caught her staring when he'd climbed out of the bath, and the look in her eyes said she approved, so which was it? It seemed like she was attracted to him, but maybe not.

It might have been a bad idea to invite Sarah into bed last night, but that was also his first dose of sleep deprivation at the hands of a crying baby. He could already see how a parent could end up giving in to any number of demands, just to have a respite.

Of course he hadn't slept soundly. He'd worried that he might crush little Oliver, so he'd made a point of not moving, which didn't lend itself to relaxation. He'd been intensely aware of every peep the baby made, hoping he'd sleep through the rest of the night. Sarah's presence hadn't helped. He'd ended up in bed with women in fewer than twenty-four hours before, but never like this, and never with a woman like her. As he'd studied her in the soft light that morning, he found himself not only admiring her uncommon beauty—the scattering of faint freckles across her cheeks, and lips that could make him lose all sense of direction if he thought about them too much—he had to extol the gumption contained in her small frame. She'd gotten through to him when that was the last thing he allowed.

"How are we supposed to get all of this put away with a toddler crawling all over the house?" he asked.

"Now you understand the challenge of caring for a child. It's a constant juggling act."

Oliver struggled and kicked to get down from Sarah's hip.

"So I'm learning." He yawned and took another sip of his coffee. This was going to be a long day. Not that he wasn't looking forward to it. As much as he'd never imagined spending his weekend this way, and as tired as he was, yesterday had been incredible.

"He'll go down for his morning nap soon and he'll have the longer one in the afternoon. That should give us some time. Of course, it'd be a lot easier if we brought in reinforcements. Maybe you could call your family?"

Not this again. "I already told you I'm not ready for Oliver to be around my mom at all, let alone have her come in and spend any time with him on her own."

"What about Anna? Didn't she offer to watch him? She could take him for a walk and some fresh air."

That could work. Anna was Aiden's strongest ally in his family. He and his brother Adam had their moments, but he also represented some of the most painful parts of Aiden's childhood—their father pitting the boys against each other, and deeming Adam heir apparent, even when logic said that Aiden, as the oldest child, should've eventually been handed the reins at LangTel.

Aiden's other family ally was Anna's husband, Jacob. He and Aiden were cut from a similar cloth—both dealing with the price a man must pay when he's had a strained relationship with his father.

"Anna would love it."

Sarah let Oliver down onto the floor. With the help of a cardboard box, he pulled himself to standing and began pounding on the top. "Yes. Please call your sister."

Anna and Jacob were over to the apartment in less than an hour. Oliver was still taking his nap when they arrived. Sarah and Anna had gone up to Aiden's room, so Anna could watch Oliver sleep. Talk about baby fever—Anna had it.

"Now that you've had twenty-four hours to come to terms with it, how's fatherhood?" Jacob asked, settling in on the living room couch.

"Surreal. That's the best way to describe it." He scratched his head and glanced out the window—the sky was crystal clear. Not a single cloud. "Honestly, it's the only way to describe it. It doesn't feel real."

"I take it you're going to have a paternity test?"

"We have to for my name to be added to Oliver's birth certificate. Then Sarah will sign over guardianship."

"Is there any chance he might not be yours?"

After his first look into Oliver's eyes yesterday, and especially after seeing his birthmark, Aiden had been viewing the paternity test as nothing more than a formality. There was no way that Sarah could've popped into his life with a baby that looked *just* like him. But the question brought up feelings he'd wrestled with for so long. Had his dad done a paternity test? Was that the moment when things went wrong? When Roger Langford decided he wanted nothing to do with him?

"I don't want to entertain the thought, to be honest. I look in his eyes and I know he's my son. It's the best feeling, even if it has been out of the blue."

Jacob smiled and stretched his arm across the back of the couch. "I can't believe Anna and I are so close. Only six weeks until her due date. Talk about surreal, try touching someone's stomach and feeling a kick and realizing there's a tiny person in there."

"Are your parents excited about becoming grandparents? That's a lot of pressure on you as an only child."

"My mom says she is, but we'll have to wait and see what happens. Your mom, on the other hand. All she talks about is the baby."

That gave Aiden a sliver of optimism.

"Look who's up from his nap." Anna waltzed into the room, talking in a happy singsong, holding Oliver and smiling warmly at him. It was funny the effect that Oliver had on people. Aiden felt as though he'd been given a ray of sunshine.

Jacob got up from the couch and went to Anna, wrapping his arm around her back. "Holding a baby suits you. You look perfect."

Anna's smile only grew. "Oliver is perfect. I have the perfect nephew. It's a fact."

Aiden soaked up the joy radiating from his sister. He needed to share Oliver with his family, which meant he needed to get his mother up to speed and invite her over to meet him. It was time to let her in. Aiden walked over to Anna as Oliver cuddled with her. He pressed a gentle kiss to his petal-soft cheek. *This child will always know love.* Oliver would never doubt that he was wanted and adored. Not for a minute.

"If you guys are going to take him on a walk, I'll show you how to use the stroller."

As she watched the elevator doors to Aiden's apartment draw closed, and Oliver, along with Anna and Jacob, disappeared from sight, Sarah was struck by one thought. *We're alone.*

She turned and walked square into Aiden's chest.

"Slow down, champ." He grasped her shoulders. "I know they won't be gone long, but we have time to get down to business."

Get down to business. Why did her brain have to translate everything he said into a rambling internal dialogue about *S-E-X*?

"No time like the present." She laughed nervously. He still hadn't let go, and his warmth poured into her like a waterfall into a thimble. She was sure he was trying to hypnotize her with his blue eyes.

A smile rolled across his lips and Sarah was now distracted by his mouth. It was so tempting, so kissable, and she was dying of curiosity. Which version of Aiden Langford would she get if she kissed him? The powerful, broad-shouldered businessman? Walking sex in a suit? He'd probably want to be in charge in the bedroom. Or would it be the effortlessly sexy tattooed guy in board shorts? The one who needed space and jumped out of planes? She could see that guy taking his time, tending to the small touches that send a woman over the edge. She shuddered at the realization—she wanted both.

"I just want to thank you." With no other sound in the apartment, the timbre of his husky voice echoed in her head.

"For what?"

"For bringing Oliver to me. I never imagined I would feel like this."

"That's a big turnaround from the guy who ignored my emails and phone calls for three weeks."

He nodded like a man accepting guilt, a storm of blues and grays swirling in his eyes. "I know. And I apologize. I didn't want to believe it was true. It's impossible to know how you'll feel about parenthood until you have a child. If you'd asked me two days ago if I wanted a baby, I would've said absolutely not. I don't feel like that anymore."

Sarah's ovaries were whispering to her, *God, he's good.* A ridiculously hot guy confessing his tender feelings for a baby? Forget about it. After the bath last night and later being in his bed, Sarah was tempting fate. She needed to keep things professional. "It's been nice to watch you and Oliver connect. That makes me happy. Now let's go upstairs and get his room squared away."

Aiden released her from his grasp, leaving shockwaves of heat. He drew in a deep breath through his nose, studying her face. "Okay. Whatever you say."

Sarah did an abrupt about-face to lead the way upstairs.

"Hold on a sec," Aiden said.

"What?"

"Since when do I have a cookie jar?"

"Since you left me alone with the internet and your

credit card. You have a little boy in the house. You need a cookie jar."

"I thought nannies didn't allow children to have things like cookies."

Sarah shrugged. "It's nice to show someone how much you love them by giving them something sweet." She resumed her trek to the stairs, holding her finger up in the air. "Just not every day."

Upstairs, the dark wood crib was waiting in the corner of Oliver's room. There was a combination dresser and changing table, and a beautiful rocking chair as well. All it needed were finishing touches—artwork, more books, his most precious toys—the special things that would make Oliver feel at home.

Sarah had already washed the crib bedding. "Let's make up his bed. I'll show you how to lower the side of the crib."

Aiden stood by her side, again making her nervous, as she showed him how to lift up on the side rail of the crib before lowering it. "Seems simple enough."

"Be sure that the side always goes up. You don't want him escaping."

"Or staging a coup."

"Very funny. Since Oliver's pulling up on furniture, the mattress is on the lowest setting. It goes at the top for a newborn. To save your back."

"Unless there's something I don't know, I wouldn't ever need to put it up higher, would I?"

Sarah started to put on the waterproof mattress pad and Aiden helped at the other end. "Maybe you'll get married and have another baby." Why she'd chosen to go on a fishing expedition was beyond her.

"I'd have to keep a woman around for more than a few days for that to happen."

Leave it to Aiden to casually own up to his playboy

ways. "I take it your very short relationship with Oliver's mom was the norm?" Gail had been spare with her account of Aiden, saying that he was charming and sexy and up-front about not wanting anything serious. Sarah couldn't blame her for a second for going for it. She would've done the same thing if she were brave enough to have a fling. She'd never had a talent for walking away from an amazing guy.

"Remember when I said that I need space? That includes my love life."

"Space. That's such a cop-out." Sarah might have subjected herself to horrible heartbreak, but at least she'd taken chances for love.

"Excuse me?"

"So, you'll jump out of an airplane, but getting serious with someone is off-limits? You meet a woman and you decide before the start that it's going nowhere."

"No, I decide precisely where it's going. I know how it ends. I know my limitations and I accept them."

Sarah draped two small blankets over the end of the crib. "If that's what makes you happy, that's great. I just don't think you're being honest with yourself. You said you need space, but it didn't take long for you to get comfortable with Oliver."

"That's not the same thing, at all. Oliver needs me. And what about you? You're the one who said you won't make time for a boyfriend."

"My situation is completely different."

"How?"

"Because I refuse to treat a man as temporary." *Exactly the way they tend to treat me.* "But you treat women that way. It's sad, really."

"I don't need you to feel sorry for me."

"Oh, I don't. So don't worry about it." She shook her head. She had to escape this line of conversation. She'd learned enough frustrating details for one day. Aiden was everything she'd first thought—the guy who does not commit. "Can we please talk about my business? I need you to hold up your end of the deal. I'm at the point where Kama could either take off or crash and burn."

"Kama? Is that what it's called?"

"Yes. It's the Hindu god of desire. Our fabrics all come from India, so I thought it was fitting."

He nodded and jutted out his lower lip. "I like it. Simple. Elegant. Plus, it makes me think of the *Kama Sutra* and you know what that makes me think of."

You walked right into that one. "Will you please take this seriously? The next six months are crucial and I don't know what I'm supposed to do. I'm terrified it will fail." That was an understatement. She couldn't imagine a future without Kama. She'd be left to start all over again, doing what, she had no idea.

"It really is important to you, isn't it? Your little business of making nightgowns."

"Don't be so dismissive. It's my livelihood. My career."

"And like I said last night, if it means that much to you you have to own it. You were hiding it from me last night. That's troublesome."

I was hiding me from you last night. Not the same thing.

"And whatever you say, you still have nannying," he continued. "There will always be children to care for and you're so good at it. Not everyone is an entrepreneur."

"I don't know how many times I need to tell you. I am *not* a nanny."

"Now who's living a contradictory life? I watch you with Oliver and you clearly adore him. So you love kids, but refuse to earn a living that way?"

"I want the challenge of making this work."

"That's it?"

"That's it." *That's all I'm going to tell you.*

"Okay, then. Walk me through the whole thing."

"Let me show you." She pulled up some photos on her phone. She'd taken them to show the bank when things started to take off and she'd tried to get a loan for expansion. "Flip through these. You'll see some of what I'm up against."

He swiped at the screen. "It's tiny. How can you get anything done in this space?"

"Honestly? I have no idea, other than I have some incredible employees who are willing to put up with a lot. I have six people doing assembly. If I were going to keep up with demand, I could easily have two dozen, but I'd have nowhere to put them. Moving means a huge lease, more equipment, health insurance and finding qualified people. It's a lot. I barely sleep as it is."

"So outsource. Let someone else do your manufacturing."

"I can't fire these people. They've been with me since the beginning, and they all do exceptional work. They have families to support."

"You're destroying your margins."

"Not if I'm in with the right retailers and can demand a better price point. Plus, our margins will improve once we've streamlined our manufacturing."

"Okay, then. Why don't I become an investor? I'll write a check and we can be done."

Here was Aiden's propensity for clean and simple, in sharp focus. It wasn't merely his attitude toward romance—he did this with everything that could get messy. No matter what, he was *not* going to become her investor. She needed to see out this ten days and get out of Dodge before his eyes made her do something she would regret.

"I need guidance. I need someone to give me advice and help make the right connections, not throw money at me and hope I'll go away. That's your role in our arrangement and now you're trying to get out of it." She didn't want to speak to him in this manner, but she hated being blown off. It felt too much like Jason discounting everything about her—her dreams, her desires, and most important, the feelings she'd thought were between them, the ones he'd said were a figment of her overactive imagination.

Aiden handed her back her phone, appraising her. It was as if she could see the gears turning in his head, and she was more than a little nervous to hear what he was going to say. "You're right. I said I'd help you and I will. Not having looked at your financials, I'm thinking we need to find you an exclusive partnership. Become a subsidiary of a larger fashion corporation to scale your production, help with facility and warehousing issues, and most importantly, take over distribution so you can focus on what you're good at."

Finally, he got what she wanted. And he wasn't trying to back out. "Yes. Great. I can spend my time designing." *And I can be back on track.*

Seven

Sunday had brought Aiden's less sunny side. He'd finally called his mother about Oliver that morning, which had not gone as he'd hoped. He'd assumed, and so had Sarah, that she would be eager to come over right away. Instead, she'd said she was busy and would stop by Monday. That response had prompted Aiden to hunker down in his home gym for hours, lifting weights and running on the tread-mill. As if the man needed to be in better shape.

Sarah had tried her best to go about her day, working on Oliver's room while he played, and during his nap, doing research on apparel companies she could partner with, per Aiden's suggestion. She'd also taken Oliver for a long walk, with a stop at a bookstore for some of her favorite children's reads. Considering how much Aiden loved books, she knew the gesture would be appreciated. Maybe someday those books would make him think of her—the woman who'd brought him Oliver out of the blue. And slipped away just as fast.

Now that it was late Monday morning, Sarah was still awaiting the return of pleasant Aiden. He'd been a real jerk during the nanny interviews, which was not the way it should've gone. The agency was the top in the city. Money was no object. All signs led to this being a short and simple process. But she hadn't counted on Aiden stonewalling.

"What is your problem?" Sarah asked as the elevator doors closed on the fourth and final candidate. "For now, the agency has no more nannies to send. The woman was practically Mary Poppins and you tell her that you don't think she's right for Oliver?"

Aiden shoved his hands into the pockets of his dark gray suit pants. He'd ditched the jacket and tie for the interview, but otherwise dressed handsomely, which was driving Sarah crazy. It took too much work to be mad at him when he looked so good.

"Did you see her face when she wasn't talking? It was so cold and stern. I want Oliver to be happy, not scared out of his mind."

"Are you saying she had resting bitch face? Is that really what this has come down to? Because you're being ridiculous."

"I didn't like her. End of story."

Sarah grumbled. Aiden might be right about the woman's austere facial expressions, but she was otherwise perfect. Plus, she was in her fifties and happily married and there was a very petty part of Sarah that wasn't about to leave Aiden with a perky twentysomething.

She flipped through the candidates' résumés. "What about Frances? She had a very sunny personality and came with impeccable references. She was a nanny for Senator Meyers, for God's sake. Do you think just anyone gets that job?"

"And why doesn't she have that job anymore? I'm not sure I buy her answer."

"She wanted to be in New York to help with her sick aunt. The Senator and his family are in Washington, DC. Seems reasonable to me."

"What if her aunt's illness takes over her life? I need someone who is solely focused on Oliver. That's what's best for him."

"You've spent all of three days with him. How can you say that you know what's best?"

Aiden shot her a look that said she'd taken it too far. He swallowed so hard that his Adam's apple bobbed. "I'm trusting my gut. That's the best thing I have to go on right now." He turned and walked out of the entryway and into the kitchen.

Sarah followed. They had to get the nanny situation resolved. "Don't forget that I'm the expert on this subject. I'm telling you right now that you're an idiot of the highest order for sending those four women away."

"We have to keep looking."

"I'm only here for a week, Aiden. It's Monday. Your ten days are up on Sunday and I'm gone. What are you going to do then?"

He grabbed an apple out of the bamboo bowl on the kitchen island. "Maybe I need you to stay longer."

So that's what he was doing—avoiding the potential mess of someone who might not be right by trying to keep the one thing he knew would work—her. "You're trying to force me to stay by sending away the other nannies?"

"Listen to what you just said. *Other* nannies."

"No way. I'm done with that."

"Honestly, I don't believe you're capable of walking away from Oliver on Sunday. You love him. I can see it."

Why did he have to make this so much worse? His words cut to her core. They were the truth and he knew it.

"Of course I love Oliver. How could I not? But he's not my child and just like every other child I've cared for, I eventually have to leave him." Just saying the words brought up an unholy mess of things she dreaded and terrible memories. If she was bad at anything, it was goodbye.

"So you've got leaving down to a science. You can do it. No problem." Everything in his tone was biting, dripping with sarcasm.

"I'm not heartless."

"Which is why I don't buy it."

"Look. You need to focus on holding up your end of our deal. Part of that is hiring a nanny. I'm calling the agency to see if they have anyone else for us to interview." She slapped the résumés down on the kitchen counter. "In the meantime, I'd appreciate it if you would please look these over again and see if you're willing to reconsider any of these applicants." She turned on her heel and took extralong strides to get to the stairs.

"Sarah. Hold on."

She turned back, just in time to see him push aside the résumés. "What?"

He blew out a breath. "I'm sorry. I'm sorry if it seems like I have ridiculous standards, but my gut is telling me that those women were not right. Remember, this is all new to me. Almost too new. I'm doing my best. I swear."

She crossed her arms, hoping it would make it easier to buffer her attraction to him. It was hopeless when he was being sweet about the baby and talking in that tone that made her want to flatten him against the wall and climb him like a tree. "I know you're trying. I'm just antsy about time. We don't have much and I have to get back to Boston and Kama."

"I know you do, which is the other thing I need to say to you. Anna and I are working on getting us into a charity fashion show, organized by *Fad Forward Magazine*. Apparently it's a big deal."

Holy crap. Sarah clamped her hand over her mouth to keep a string of elated profanity from leaving her lips. "The Forward Style show? Where is it this year?"

"Miami. I thought I'd just buy tickets, but you have to be invited, which seems ludicrous since it's a charity event…"

Sarah couldn't breathe. She'd seen the pictures in *Fad Forward Magazine* every year since she was a teenager. Their annual charity fashion show was a chance for designers to bring out their most adventuresome work, and was attended by fashion legends, rock stars, Hollywood bigwigs and sometimes even royalty.

"Everybody who's anybody will be there. But I'm not sure it will help me."

"Our target is Sylvia Hodge. She's the honorary host this year. Anna and I dug up some info that she's acquiring new brands, but she's about to spend six months in Europe and Asia, looking for designers. If we want to meet face-to-face with her, going to Miami is the only way. And we might have to just walk up to her and start talking. I can't get her to take my call."

"But you're Aiden Langford. Isn't your last name enough?"

"Sylvia Hodge's admin didn't seem to care who I was."

"If we go, what are our chances?"

He shrugged. "No idea. Right now I'm waiting to see if they'll let me buy tickets."

"But the tickets. I can't afford that. They're tens of thousands of dollars."

"It's my treat."

"But it goes so far beyond our agreement."

"You brought me Oliver. It's the least I can do."

* * *

After having been away from LangTel for much of Friday and all of Monday so far, Aiden had a mountain of work, but he couldn't focus, not even with the relative quiet of working from home. The clock on the wall was taunting him. Three forty-five. Fifteen minutes until his mother was set to arrive to meet Oliver.

Sarah poked her head into his office, Oliver on her hip. The baby smiled at him, sweetly tilting his head to the side. This child would be the death of him, in a good way.

"If you're still working, I can hang out with Oliver until your mom arrives," she said. "Then I'll clear out so you three can have some time alone."

Aiden was trying to be optimistic, clinging to the idea that Oliver would bridge the chasm between him and his mother, but he had too many reasons to believe that would not be the case. "Where are you headed?"

"Out for a run. With all of the excitement of waiting to hear about Miami, I'm way too tense. Plus, I haven't worked out in days. I feel like a slob."

His vision drifted over her. She was wearing black leggings that showed off her fit and healthy curves, with a formfitting top that left her bare shoulders on display. Her hair was back in a high ponytail. He stepped out from behind his desk and took Oliver, unable to keep from admiring her. He wrestled with a deep desire to thread his hands into the back of her golden blond hair and pull out the rubber band, tilt her head back and give her the sort of kiss that makes a woman linger for a moment afterward with her eyes half-open.

"You are not a slob. You look incredible."

"You're just saying that because you feel bad about the nanny interviews."

"I'm saying it because you're a beautiful woman and I'd be an idiot if I didn't at least say it out loud."

A wash of pink crossed her cheeks and she fought a smile. If only she knew that it made him that much more attracted to her. If only she knew that she was making every inch of his body draw tight and burn hot.

"Thank you. I appreciate the compliment." She pressed her lips together and gazed up at him. "If you're going to take Oliver, I'll just head out. I should be done in about an hour. I don't know how long your mom is planning on staying, but I can grab a cup of coffee if you want more time."

The gears in Aiden's head whirred. He'd first thought it would be better if he and his mom were alone with Oliver. Keep things simple. But the truth was that he couldn't imagine Sarah not being there. It didn't make any sense, although he wanted to know why. Then he realized that no matter the situation, Sarah calmed him. She took the edge off. She made him believe things would work out. Aside from his sister, he didn't have anyone in his life who did that, but this was different. Sarah wasn't obligated to make him feel good.

"What if I said I wanted you to stay?"

She scrunched up her adorable nose. "What? Really?"

"I could use the moral support. I could use someone on my side. Things with my mother are not easy. I think you've gathered that much by now."

"I have, although you haven't told me the reason why."

Because I don't want to talk about it. "It's complicated. If you're here, it'll keep the conversation light and fun. I could use that right now."

She looked down at herself. "Oh God. I look terrible. I should go change. I don't want her to see me like this."

Before he could think about what he was doing, his fingers cupped her chin. He shouldn't have crossed that line, but he couldn't help himself. "I think you look perfect. Don't change."

She didn't move. He didn't either. Neither of them said a thing, but their eyes connected, as if they were each digging deeper, wanting more.

Sarah broke the spell with a shake of her head. "You're sweet, but there's no way I'm wearing this to meet your mom. And I have no makeup on." She turned and headed out of his office. "Back in five minutes."

Aiden watched her jog away, her leggings accentuating every move. A ripple of steamy thoughts ran through his head—everything he wanted to do with her. It had been a long time since he'd wanted a woman as badly as he wanted Sarah. The question was whether the opportunity would present itself. So far, there was always something in the way.

Aiden wandered into the kitchen, where his housekeeper had put on a pot of coffee. She'd also stocked Sarah's cookie jar with an assortment of biscotti, some of it plain. Oliver regularly chowed down on teething biscuits, and Aiden decided that this was basically the same thing.

"Do you want a cookie?" He offered it to Oliver.

The baby snatched it from his hand and it went right into his mouth, like most things. His eyes grew wide once he'd gotten a taste. Aiden leaned against the counter, enjoying the moment. Sarah was going to leave behind a lot more than a cookie jar on Sunday.

"Good, huh? Just wait until you get older and I can take you out for hot fudge sundaes or we can get a hot dog at a baseball game." The thought brought with it a peculiar mix of hope and melancholy. Dads did those things with their children. Aiden very much looked forward to having those experiences with Oliver, but they were things he'd missed out on entirely.

Sarah hurried down the stairs. "This is as good as it's going to get. I really wish you would've given me some advance notice. I could've taken a shower and done something with my hair." Her face was flush with color, probably from rushing around. She wore a full black skirt that skimmed her knees and a white top that hinted at the curves he'd been admiring for days now. She'd put on the sandals she'd been wearing the day he met her, which gave her a few more inches of height. He still towered over her, but he loved the way they made her legs look.

"Once again, you look perfect."

The buzzer for the elevator rang.

"You're sweet. And you need to answer the door."

Aiden's heart went from racing over Sarah to plummeting to his stomach. His mother had arrived. He didn't bother with the intercom, hitting the button to grant her access to his floor. "Here goes nothing," he said to Sarah. He filed into the entryway, Oliver in tow and making excellent progress on his cookie.

When the doors slid open, Aiden managed a smile. It was only half-forced. He still loved his mother, despite his immense frustrations with her.

She actually gasped when she saw Oliver, breezing off the elevator in her usual garb of all black with a colorful scarf tied at her neck. She took a direct route to her grandson, her mouth softening to a tiny O. "Aiden, he looks just like you." She held on to his hand and shook her head in disbelief, but not enough to muss her short, dark hair. "What an angel." A tear rolled down her cheek, but then a steady stream started. Of the many reactions he'd anticipated from his mother, full-on crying was not one of them. She smiled through the tears, her eyes crinkling at the corners. "Can I hold him?"

Aiden was stricken with conflicting emotions, ones that didn't belong in one person's head at the same time. He wanted to protect Oliver. But at the same time, there was a yearning—so deep he could feel it—for his mother to accept and love Oliver. He had to take this leap, however much she could end up hurting either of them. "Yes. Of course."

He handed over Oliver, who seemed perplexed. She bounced him up and down as she plopped her handbag on the entry table.

"Come in, Mom. I want you to meet Sarah."

Sarah was pouring herself a glass of water. "Mrs. Langford. It's so nice to meet you. I've…" She paused and looked right at Aiden. "I've heard so much about you."

"Please, call me Evelyn. And I wish I could say the same about you. My son has been remarkably quiet about everything." She turned and shot Aiden a disappointed look, a wordless reprimand. Did she have any idea how hard he was working to keep up his hopes? Intentional or not, she expertly knocked them back down. "Not that I'm surprised. He keeps things to himself. Always."

Eight

Stress radiated off Aiden like August heat off a tin roof—jaw tense, shoulders rigid. Was he always this away around his mother? He must be, because she didn't seem to notice. She was too preoccupied with Oliver, sitting on the floor in the library, offering him toys from a bag Sarah had given her.

"He's smart. I can tell," she said to no one in particular.

Aiden stood sentry, arms crossed squarely at his chest. This was not a bonding moment for him. He was observing, like a hawk.

Sarah walked up behind him and placed her hand on his shoulder. He flinched, then relaxed under her touch. She might have underestimated this burden, and her heart ached because of it. Whatever there was between him and his mother, it was not good. Sarah desperately wanted to know more. Even if it was painful, she wanted to know.

"Is there anything I can get for you?" she whispered to Aiden.

He looked over his shoulder, lowering his face closer to hers. A waft of his heavenly scent hit her nose—warm and masculine, like the sheets on his bed, just like his entire bedroom. "Now who's the sweet one?" he muttered.

You are. When you want to be. "I'm sensing you could use a drink."

"It's only a little past four."

"It's five o'clock in Nova Scotia. I've heard it's lovely there this time of year. Bourbon?"

"On the rocks." He cracked a smile and his shoulders visibly relaxed. She fought the urge to dig her fingers into them, help him unwind while she committed the contours of his broad frame to memory.

"Cocktail, Evelyn?" Sarah asked.

She shook her head and started peekaboo with Oliver. "I'm too in love with my grandson for a drink. But I'll take a diet soda."

"Got it." Sarah went to work, getting Aiden his drink first. He was in greater need. "Here you go." Their fingers brushed when she gave him his glass, sending a tingly recognition through her.

"Thank you. For everything." His voice was low and soft, just as luxurious as the bourbon in the glass. Why did the man she was supposed to stay away from have to be so undeniably sexy?

The elevator rang again.

"That's odd," Aiden said. "I don't know who could be here."

"I'll get it." Sarah hurried to the entryway and buzzed the intercom. "Hello?"

"It's Liam Hanson for Mr. Langford. I'm one of the admins at Barkforth and Sloan."

The paternity test. "I thought you were coming tomorrow morning." Surely this was not the sort of commotion Aiden wanted while his mother was there.

"They asked me to come this afternoon since you need this done right away. They should've called you."

"Come on up."

Aiden joined her. "Great. With my mom here." He must have overheard. He raked his hand through his hair, again showing her the strain she hated seeing on any face, especially on one as handsome as his.

The elevator doors slid open. "Mr. Langford. I'm so sorry if there was a miscommunication. I promise this will be quick. Five minutes and I'm out of your hair."

Aiden nodded. "No, it's fine. We have to get it done. What do you need?"

"It's a cheek swab from you and one from the baby. That's it."

"He's in the other room."

Sarah followed Liam and Aiden into the library.

"Mom, I need Oliver for a minute. The lawyer's office needs to do the cheek swabs for the paternity test so we can take care of the legal end of things."

Evelyn picked up the baby, handing him to Aiden. "This seems silly. One look at him and it's obvious he's your son."

Aiden snatched Oliver away, much as he had the day Sarah had mentioned the idea of Evelyn caring for him. "It's important for Oliver and me, too. That we know he's my son, for sure."

She took a sip of her soda. "Of course."

Liam took out two plastic tubes and asked Aiden to open his mouth. He swabbed the inside of his cheek, then did the same to Oliver. "All done. We'll have this expedited. I understand the paperwork needs to be taken care of this week."

Aiden nodded. "Yes."

"If it takes until next week, I could always come back down from Boston, I suppose." Had she just said that?

She should *not* be straying from the timeline she'd established. With every passing day, they were more comfortable with each other, she more attracted to him, her resolve becoming flimsy. There were signs he might be feeling the same way—the moment when he'd slid his fingers under her chin? The comments about how good she looked?

"It's best if we wrap this up quickly," Aiden said. "Sarah needs to leave on Sunday and return to her business. Oliver and I need to start our life together, too."

Why was her body filled with such utter disappointment at his words? This was what she'd wanted, and it was no time to switch her priorities. *Stay with the plan, Sarah.* "Aiden's right. I really can't be running back to New York."

"Certainly." Liam packed up everything in a messenger bag, which he slung across his chest. "We'll take care of it, Mr. Langford. We should have the results by Friday."

Aiden walked Liam to the elevator and returned with Oliver. There was a shift in the mood, one impossible to ignore. Aiden had said he wanted to keep things short with his mother for this first visit. Evelyn showed no sign of leaving.

"Can I hold him again?" she asked, getting up from the sofa.

Aiden took in a deep breath. "For a few minutes, then Sarah and I have some things to do. Oliver needs a bath and quiet time before bed."

Even if it might have been an excuse, Aiden was clinging to the schedule, and it was adorable. He sat on the couch next to his mother and tried to hand over the baby, but Oliver wanted to stay with Daddy.

"Don't you want to spend time with Grandma?" Evelyn leaned into Aiden, trying to catch Oliver's attention.

"He's still getting used to you, Mom. It might take time."

"Maybe he's unhappy after having that strange man put a stick in his mouth. The whole thing really is silly. He looks just like you."

"We have to follow the proper channels. It's important." Aiden held Oliver close. "He lost his mother a month ago, and that will be something he'll always wonder about. A child needs to know where he came from. He needs to know where he belongs." Aiden's voice cracked, which Sarah had never heard before, not even in the tender moments with Oliver.

"I wasn't trying to upset you."

Aiden cleared his throat. "Mom. Listen to yourself. There's this dark cloud hanging over us and Oliver has given us the perfect chance to talk about it, but you won't let yourself go there, will you? You'd rather keep your secret."

"I have no earthly idea what you're talking about."

"Yes, you do. I've brought this up with you at least three times since I've been back in New York. It's the reason I've been unhappy for most of my life. It's the reason I tried to take over LangTel. And you're sitting here, talking about the paternity of my son like this hasn't been a question in your own life. It's so frustrating I want to scream." His voice didn't waver in the slightest now. It was sheer determination.

Oliver whimpered.

"You've upset the baby," she said.

Oh no.

Aiden pulled Oliver closer and rubbed his back, pecking him on the forehead. "I think you need to leave. I'm not going to pretend that my entire existence in this family hasn't been built on a lie and you won't own up to it. I know that your husband was not my father. I know it with every fiber of my being. And we all act as if that isn't the case."

Sarah gasped. She didn't mean to, but how could she *not*? Roger Langford wasn't Aiden's father? How could that be?

Evelyn reached out and set her hand on Aiden's forearm. "Aiden, darling. Haven't we all been through enough with losing your father? Don't tear us apart even more. I love you and you're my son. That's all that matters."

Sarah turned to sneak upstairs. She had no business being in the room for this.

"No, Sarah. Don't leave," Aiden said.

Did the man have eyes in the back of his head? Sarah looked down at her feet. Damn noisy shoes.

"So that's your response," he said to his mother. "And when you say we lost my father, do you mean my actual father, or Roger? Because I know they're not the same. There's no other explanation for you sending me off to boarding school. There's no other reason why Adam would be deemed heir apparent when I'm the oldest."

"Aiden, there's no good in dredging up the past. And I really don't think we should discuss this in front of a stranger."

"A stranger? You're calling Sarah a stranger? She's nothing of the sort." Aiden bolted from his seat. "It's time for you to go now. You can come back when you're ready to talk. Until then, I don't want to see you."

"You're going to keep me from my grandson?"

"That's all on you. I have nothing to do with it."

Evelyn blew out a breath, just as determined as Aiden. Family gatherings must be a real barrel of laughs with the Langfords. "You'll change your mind. A baby needs his grandmother." She leaned forward and kissed Oliver's forehead, but Aiden kept both arms firmly around him. "Bye-bye, sweet boy. Grandma will see you soon."

With that, Evelyn Langford traipsed out of the room. Aiden stood, facing the entryway, his back to Sarah. All Sarah could hear was her own pulse thumping in her ears. What she was supposed to say? What was she supposed to do? There was no mistaking the pain in his voice. True or not, he believed that he'd been lied to about his father.

"I'm sorry you had to see that," he said. "I'm sure that's the last thing you would've wanted to trade your run for."

She went to him, her heart heavy. "No, Aiden. I'm glad I was here. I mean, if that's what you wanted."

"It *is* what I wanted. Honestly, your presence probably prevented a bigger blowup. One that's been coming for thirty years."

She reached for his arm, wanting to comfort him even more than that. Here she was, stepping into emotional quicksand, the very last place she belonged if she was going to leave on Sunday with her heart in one piece. "I don't believe that you would've blown up in front of Oliver. I really don't."

Aiden managed a smile, but it was as if it had been broken and cobbled back together. There was some part of him inside that was fractured. She'd sensed that about him the day they met, but now she was beginning to understand what had caused it. Her own family was so important to her. They were always there for her. Always. She couldn't imagine growing up the way Aiden had. He might have had money and privilege, but that didn't replace love. That didn't replace knowing where you came from.

"Thank you for being here. That's really all I can say." He tugged her into an embrace with one arm while he held on to Oliver with the other.

She sank against his chest, so drawn to him, every inch of her wanting to make things better. Each second in his arms was another step into his world, but she would've needed a heart of stone to walk away. He needed her. And in that moment, him needing her was everything.

Oliver was sound asleep in his crib, but Aiden stayed, studying the steady rise and fall of his chest as he slept like a starfish—arms above his head, legs splayed, tiny rosebud mouth open. After the upset of his mother's visit, Oliver filled Aiden with contentment he'd never known. If he never had anything more in his life than Oliver, even if he never got the truth from his mother, he could be happy.

He flipped the baby monitor on, then crept out of the room, quietly closing the door. A few steps down the hall, a heavenly smell hit his nose. Sarah was cooking dinner and judging by that one whiff, it was going to be delicious. She was his savior today, but not because she was preparing a meal. She'd been there for him when his composure crumbled and anger threatened to consume him. She'd been his rock.

That left him in a peculiar spot. If he were smart, he needed to work very hard to keep Sarah as a friend, and as part of Oliver's life. He couldn't imagine her not being involved, even if it was only an occasional phone call or a visit on Oliver's birthday. Considering his zero percent success rate with keeping a woman around for more than a few days, logic said he shouldn't allow them to be anything more than friends. He shouldn't cross that line, however attracted he was to her, even when every inch of him wanted her. Between her beauty, her spark and the sweet things she did for him, he didn't see how he was supposed to stay away. He only knew he had to. Giving in to the temptation of Sarah—sweeping her up in his arms and finally tasting her lips, would likely end with her never speaking to him again. For the first time in his life, he didn't want that.

"Whatever you're cooking, sign me up." He strolled into the kitchen.

She had two glasses of red wine waiting. Was she the perfect woman? She was reading his mind. He wanted nothing more than to relax and put his afternoon behind him.

"Good. Because otherwise, it's toast or a protein bar." Her back was to him, and she was humming—something he'd noticed she did every time she was busy in the kitchen. He forced himself still, to keep from walking up behind her, wrapping his arms around her waist, leaning down and kissing the graceful slope of her neck. He wanted to bury his face in her hair, inhale her sweet scent, get lost in her.

But he had to be good. So he slugged back some wine. "What are we having?"

She turned and smiled sweetly. "Pasta. Almost ready."

"Perfect. Thanks for opening a bottle of wine. If you hadn't, I would have." What was he doing? He'd been reprimanding himself moments ago about how Sarah had to stay a friend, and yet he couldn't stop from talking as if he was in pursuit.

She dished the pasta into two bowls. "Sorry it's not fancy."

"If you want fancy, we could take this bottle of wine up to the rooftop when we're done eating. It's a beautiful night." Was this a good idea? No. Did it sound like fun? Yes. "We'll need to bring the baby monitor."

"Okay, Dad." She elbowed him in the ribs and flashed a flirtatious smile. That was it. She was going to kill him before the night was over.

They ate at the kitchen island, chatting about Oliver, squabbling about nanny candidates and whether or not there would be any more people to interview. It wasn't long before dinner was done, the dishes were in the dishwasher and Sarah suggested they open a second bottle of wine.

"The terrace?" *Stop encouraging this.*

"I should grab a cardigan first. In case I get cold."

I can keep you warm. He pressed his lips together to keep the words from escaping. "Okay."

He waited for Sarah outside her room, then led her to the second-floor stairs at the back of the house that took them up to the empty third floor and finally up to the terrace.

The darkening night sky was streaked with purple and midnight blue, the city lights casting a glow across Sarah's face. She rushed across the stone pavers, like a little kid who couldn't contain her excitement. "It's so beautiful up here. Like your own private park." Holding out her arms, she turned enough to make her dress swirl around her legs.

"It's nice, isn't it?" He smiled, admired her, wishing he could make everything in the world conform to his will— why couldn't he have a free pass for a night, kiss her and have everything return to normal tomorrow?

"After meeting your mom, I think I understand why you need space."

"Very perceptive. Although the physical space is nice for anyone, especially in the city."

He led her to an outdoor sectional couch and lit a kerosene heater. She plopped down, tucking her leg underneath herself. He set the wine bottle on a low table and joined her, keeping his distance, staying in check.

"Do you want to talk about today?" she asked. "Maybe you'll feel better about everything if you just get it out."

He wasn't much of a talker, especially when it came to things like this, but Sarah wasn't like anyone he'd ever considered confiding in. She had no agenda, nothing to gain. And she had to be wondering what was going on.

"I've suspected since I was eight that the man I called Dad wasn't my biological father."

Sarah pressed her lips into a thin line. "That's what I thought. I didn't want to eavesdrop on what you were saying to your mom, but it was hard not to hear."

"I'm glad you were there. It made it far less uncomfortable."

"It seemed pretty uncomfortable."

He had to laugh. She didn't shy away from the truth. "Honestly, that was nothing."

"How does an eight-year-old arrive at that conclusion?"

"I was home from boarding school for Christmas break and I overheard them arguing about it."

"Did you ever ask them about it?"

He took a sip of his wine, fighting back memories of standing in the hall of the Langford family penthouse apartment, late at night. He'd been unable to sleep and wanted to ask his mom for a warm glass of milk, but he'd instead heard her say something terrible. *If I could take it back, I would. But I can't change the fact that he's not your child.* "I never said anything to anyone until I was much older. You have to understand, Roger Langford was an imposing man. And he was never very warm to me. He was to Adam and Anna, but not to me. I didn't want to give him another reason to push me out of the family."

"Push you out?"

"They sent me to boarding school after Adam was born. I was seven. I didn't understand why, but they said it was for my own good. Now I suspect it was because he couldn't stand the sight of me."

Sarah's eyes became impossibly sad. He hated seeing that look on her face, even when it was *his* pain she was reflecting. She grasped his forearm, scooting closer on the couch. The distance he'd left was gone, and he was so glad. He craved having her close. He wanted nothing more than to erase the space between them.

"I can't even imagine what that must've been like. I'm sure you were just the sweetest boy. I'm so sorry."

Aiden wasn't much for pity, but it was healing to have Sarah see how wrong it all was. "It got worse over the years. I got in trouble at school a lot, mostly for fighting or practical jokes. I got kicked out of a few. That was never fun. It embarrassed my dad and confirmed to him that I didn't belong at home. I guess I was self-destructive, but I was confused. I certainly didn't feel loved."

Sarah was now rubbing his arm softly with her thumb. "Of course you didn't. No child should feel that way." She looked down at her lap and fiddled with the hem of her sweater. She was so gorgeous in the moonlight—it was like watching a museum masterpiece come to life. "I know that my arrival with Oliver was a shock, but you have such a big opportunity with him."

"Opportunity?"

She nodded and sucked in her lower lip. "You can give Oliver the childhood that you didn't have."

For a moment, it felt as though the earth didn't move. He'd thought that on some level, but hearing her say it made it clear how right it was. "I can break the cycle."

"Yes. Although I don't think you'll have real closure until your mom finally tells you the truth."

He downed the last of his wine. "I'm starting to wonder if that will happen."

"Have you told anyone else in your family?"

"I confided in Anna, but she thinks I'm crazy. She knows that something wasn't right in our household, but I don't think she wants to believe it. My father has only been gone about a year. Everyone is still grieving. No one wants to think ill of him."

"I don't think you're crazy, Aiden. It makes perfect sense to me."

Sarah's lips were right there, waiting for him, telling him everything he'd ever wanted to hear. The validation of his pain, his fears, the vulnerability that he wished didn't exist at all, was so powerful it made his entire body feel lighter. He wanted to kiss her so badly, to express his gratitude for her in a way that would leave no doubt in her mind that he appreciated her.

But he couldn't do that. Not when he needed her in Oliver's life. Not when he was sure it would ruin everything.

His phone buzzed with a text. Normally, he wouldn't stop to read it, especially when he was alone with a beautiful woman, but it was taking extreme effort to keep from kissing this one and it was his intention to do exactly that. "I'm sorry. I should check this." The message was from Anna—good news. "You and I are going to Miami. We have our tickets."

Sarah popped up out of her seat. "For Forward Style?"

He laughed, watching her bounce on her toes. "Yes. We go the day after tomorrow."

"Wednesday? Oh my God. We have to book flights. Who's going to take care of Oliver?" She looked him squarely in the face. "What am I going to wear?"

"We'll ask Anna and Jacob to stay with Oliver for the night. You know they'd love to do it."

Sarah's shoulders dropped with relief. "True. She and Jacob are so good with him. What about the rest?"

"We'll take the corporate jet. No need to worry about flights."

"Are you sure? That seems extravagant."

He grinned so wide it made his cheeks ache. The joy of seeing her happy and excited was his reward after a roller coaster of a day. "Yes. I'm sure. I told you I'd help you, and I'm a man of my word. As for what you should wear, we're in New York. Go shopping."

She shook her head. "There's no time. We have more nannies to interview tomorrow, and I know you need to get some work done. Plus, if I'm going to walk up to Sylvia Hodge and try to impress her, I need to be wearing one of my own designs."

"You're going to wear a nightgown?"

She slapped his arm and grimaced. "No, silly. I design other things. And I have the perfect gown at home. It's gorgeous. Emerald green, dangerously low-cut. Sylvia will love it." Her eyes flashed with mischief. "I just need to get Tessa in my office to overnight it to me."

Aiden felt like he couldn't breathe. In a little more than twenty-four hours, he'd be alone in Miami with Sarah and her dangerous dress. How he loved peril, especially at the hand of a beautiful woman. "Have her send you a swimsuit, too. We can't go to Florida without some fun in the sun."

Nine

Between leaving Oliver overnight, and knowing that in twelve hours she'd have to dazzle Sylvia Hodge at a fashion event most people would kill to attend, Sarah was so worked up she thought she might be sick. "I hope I haven't forgotten anything." Yesterday had been such a whirlwind, it'd be a modern miracle if she hadn't messed up something. Oliver'd had a fussy day, which probably meant he had another tooth coming in. Aiden had been shuttered in his home office for hours, coming out long enough to say no to three more nanny candidates.

Sarah had dealt with a million other details beyond that, including having Tessa, her assistant, overnight her gown and a few more clothes to the hotel in Miami. That meant she was in the same black sundress she'd had on the day she met Aiden. She didn't feel confident at all, but she'd only packed a weekend's worth of clothes when she'd come to New York. Two days had always been her plan.

"If we have any questions, we'll call you." Anna eased herself into a chair at the kitchen table. "I just want you to go to Miami and kick some serious butt."

"Any last-minute advice before we head to the airport? You worked in the garment industry for years. I really wish you could be there to make me look less incompetent."

Anna sat up straighter and reached across the table, placing her hand on Sarah's. "From the moment I met you, you struck me as nothing less than cool determination. You will have no problem with Sylvia Hodge. She's drawn to people who have a vision. Show her what you see for your future and everything else will fall into place. I promise."

Sarah blew out a breath. What a coup it was to have Anna's help, and Aiden's for that matter. He was bankrolling this venture, after all. But knowing he was putting so much money into it only made the pressure that much more intense.

"Ready?" Aiden strode into the room. In dark gray dress pants and a white dress shirt, he looked so good he could've sold her a magic bag of beans.

Jacob followed, holding Oliver. He'd just had his first diaper-changing lesson, courtesy of Aiden. The former daddy-in-training was teaching the daddy-to-be.

"You look extra handsome holding a baby," Anna said to Jacob, slowly pushing herself up out of the chair.

Jacob flashed his dazzling smile. "It's the ultimate fashion accessory. Women go crazy for it."

Anna rolled her eyes and sidled up next to them. "Don't push it."

Aiden watched Anna and Jacob with Oliver. He was anxious—Sarah could see it. That made a small part of her melt on the inside. There was nothing sexier than a man who was on edge about leaving his child.

For Aiden's sake, Sarah started the goodbyes. "Okay, sweet boy. Anna and Jacob are going to take very good care of you. We'll see you tomorrow when we get back." She kissed his forehead. Emotion washed over her. In a few short days she'd be doing this for real.

"Goodbye, buddy." Aiden's voice wobbled as he cupped the back of Oliver's head and kissed his cheek.

Aiden's driver John was waiting outside in the black SUV, idling at the curb. The ride to the private terminal in Teterboro, New Jersey, took nearly an hour with traffic. Aiden made work calls, leaving no time for them to talk. The way he laid down the law with people was inspiring and intimidating. Would she ever be that in control? Could she grow her company and give herself security, command respect and just tell people what she wanted? She had a hard time imagining she could muster that much mojo.

The car went through a security gate and drove up alongside the sleek white jet, tastefully marked with the royal blue LangTel logo. The plane's boarding stairs had been lowered to the tarmac. Aiden's driver opened the door for Sarah, and she dug her fingernails into the tender heels of her hands, reminding herself that this wasn't a movie. This was really happening. "Thank you so much, John. I don't know how you navigate traffic in this giant car, but I'm glad you can."

"Thank you, Ms. Daltrey."

She gently swiped at his arm. "Please, call me Sarah. It's only fair since I call you John."

An amused smile crossed his lips. "You're very gracious, Sarah. Excuse me while I retrieve the bags. I'll see you on board."

"Oh. You're joining us?"

"I always drive Mr. Langford. Everywhere."

Aiden climbed out of the car and placed his hand on

her lower back, only amping up her nervousness. That touch from any other man would've reminded her this was really happening. It would've taken her *out* of the dream. But Aiden? He put her that much further into it. He nodded toward the plane, his sunglasses glinting. "Shall we?"

They climbed the stairs and stepped into the luxurious cabin, piling one surreal moment on top of countless others. There were a dozen or so oversize cream-colored leather seats, mahogany and chrome accents. Everything gleamed—even the flight attendant's red lipstick and white smile as she said, "Welcome aboard."

"Anywhere special you want me?" Sarah asked Aiden.

He removed his sunglasses and cocked an eyebrow. "Wherever you'd like to be is fine with me."

Her face flushed with heat. Damn him and his comebacks. Damn her and her brain that just had to go there. She took the seat closest to her. Aiden took the one directly opposite, facing her.

"May I get you a drink before takeoff, Ms. Daltrey?"

Sarah hadn't had a chance to introduce herself. Nor did she have a chance to respond.

"We'll have the usual, Genevieve," Aiden answered.

"Yes, Mr. Langford."

"I trust that champagne is okay?" Aiden asked Sarah.

"It's nine in the morning."

Aiden ruffled the newspaper open. "You're on edge. I see it on your face."

My face is fine. John boarded, taking a seat in the front. Sarah glanced out the window as the plane began to taxi. She hated to fly and seeing outside after takeoff would only make it worse. She lowered the shade, doing her best to act as if this was exactly where she should be. If she seemed on edge, it was because she was as far out of her element as she could imagine, and this was only the start of her day on the brink. There was much more to deal with—Sylvia Hodge, the fashion show, the countless glamorous people who would be in attendance, who would undoubtedly be wondering how someone like Sarah got in. And then there was the not-small matter of spending twenty-four hours with Aiden, when she already didn't trust herself with him.

Own it, Sarah. Own it. "I'm not on edge. I'm just thinking over the things Anna and I talked about this morning. For the moment when I meet Sylvia Hodge." *God help me.* "She gave me some great pointers." Sarah sat up straight and crossed her legs. If only she was in her black pencil skirt, short peplum jacket and pumps, she'd be the epitome of put-together. Thankfully, Tessa had sent that power suit, along with the dress she'd designed and a bathing suit. The clothes would help her fake her way through today, and then she'd be golden.

In the interest of control and modesty, Sarah had been explicit with Tessa about the swimsuit, asking for the plain black one at the very bottom of her dresser. *Plain black. Got it?* Hopefully she could talk Aiden out of a trip to the pool and she wouldn't even need it. She'd seen him without his shirt and managed to keep her own clothes on. No point in pressing her luck.

The flight attendant brought two champagne flutes, filled with golden bubbles. Aiden folded his newspaper and reached out to clink his glass with hers. "To success."

She admired his optimism—success was not a familiar concept. "Yes. I'm hoping for success."

His vision narrowed on her, a crease forming between his eyes. "There is no hoping. You need to walk up to Sylvia Hodge tonight, tell her what you do and tell her what you want. That's how you make deals. By taking charge."

"And how, exactly, do I take charge with Sylvia Hodge? She's a legend. She's put more designers on the map than anyone, and she's probably destroyed more. Just saying her name scares me."

"I can tell. And it's not good. But don't worry. I have a solution."

A solution? "Please. Do tell. I'm all ears."

"How do you feel about heights?"

Uh-oh. Mr. Adventure-seeker was at play here. "Absolutely mortified. So whatever it is that you're planning, just forget it. I'm not climbing or jumping off anything."

"No climbing or jumping. Just fun. You don't have to do anything other than sit there."

"A roller coaster?"

"Parasailing."

"Over water? In the sky?" Sarah's brain sputtered. As if she wasn't already nervous enough. "No way. My hair looks amazing today. I'm not giving up a God-given good hair day."

He leaned closer and rested his elbows on his thighs. "Sarah. You made me step outside my comfort zone. It's time for me to do the same for you. Trust me. It'll be good."

"Maybe I forgot to ask my assistant to send a bathing suit. Oh well. Your plan won't work."

He shook his head. "I was in the room when you asked her. Unless she's terrible at her job, you should be all set. Stop making excuses."

Sarah blew out an exasperated breath, downed half of her champagne and slumped back in her seat. *Great. Now I get to risk life and limb right before I put my entire career on the line.*

Three hours later, they were on the ground in Miami. Sarah stepped off the plane, thick balmy air hitting her skin as she squinted into the bright Florida sun. At least summery weather made it feel like vacation. A black SUV like the one Aiden had in New York was waiting for them planeside. John had them off to the hotel in no time. As much as Sarah felt out of place, traveling with Aiden did have an upside. No waiting to check your bag or slogging your way through security. It was lovely.

She glanced over at him while the car sped along a causeway, palm trees fluttering in the breeze outside. He was so good-looking it sometimes hurt to set her sights on him for too long, as if her eyes grew weary of handsome. What would it be like to be Aiden Langford's female companion on a trip like this? Romantic female companion. She already knew the VIP treatment was wonderful, but sleeping in the same bed with six-plus feet of pure man? Kissing him, taking off his clothes… the thought of it made her squirm in her seat. She quickly turned away and stared out her own window. She had to stay focused on business, even if romantic fantasies about Aiden were a nice escape.

They arrived at The Miami Palm hotel, situated on a private key, a small island just off the coast of downtown, connected to land by a gated bridge. Inside, the hotel lobby had classic Miami opulence—art deco chandeliers, towering potted palms and a tropical color scheme of cream, coral and sea green. Aiden was apparently a frequent customer—every employee, especially every female employee, knew his name. They didn't even have to check in. The bellman brought them straight up to the top floor. And one room.

"One room?" Sarah said under her breath. "Isn't that a little presumptuous?" It was her duty to feign indignation, at least while her brain attempted to determine what exactly Aiden was up to.

The bellman opened the door and stepped aside. Sarah nearly gasped when she walked into the luxurious space. Heck, if this was where they were staying, Aiden could presume whatever he wanted to. A sprawling living area was before them, with two large sectional couches. A black baby grand piano was beyond that, flanked by linen-upholstered armchairs. A dining table for ten was on the other side of the living area, with a wet bar beyond that. Along the length of the room were a trio of sliding doors leading to the terrace, with palm trees, a cloudless sky and the ocean completing the view.

"The presidential suite, sir." The bellman wheeled their suitcases inside.

Aiden peered down at her. "See? Nothing presumptuous. Two bedrooms. Two master baths. Separated by this big room. And don't worry, your door has a lock."

Now Sarah felt stupid for saying anything. This was a business trip. She needed to start acting as such.

"It's wonderful. Thank you so much for arranging this. I really appreciate it."

"Holding up my end of the bargain."

And nothing more.

"Time to get settled," he added. "We leave in forty-five minutes."

Her shoulders dropped. "So you were serious about parasailing? Really?"

"Dead serious. I don't get to do this sort of thing nearly enough. I'm in Miami, I'm going parasailing. And you're coming with me."

"You know, I'm really more of a lounge-on-the-beach-with-a-mojito sort of girl."

"Although I'm enjoying the vision, that's not the plan today."

"But…"

He shook his head. "No buts. If you get scared, the boat can bring us in. But you won't get scared."

"Fine." Dejected, Sarah sucked in a deep breath and ambled to her room.

Once inside, Sarah's eyes were immediately drawn to

her gown, hanging neatly on a dressing rod next to the closet. Her suit coat and skirt were behind the dress. They must have been steamed by the hotel staff. They looked the picture of perfection. The emerald-green silk of the dress was just as exquisite as she'd remembered, the beading on the bodice and trailing down onto the skirt equally sublime. This was a good thing. She would be confident in this dress. It would be her superhero costume, the one in which she set aside her everyday persona and became an invincible woman.

Time to step outside her comfort zone.

She turned, her vision drifted to the bed and her inner peace sizzled away like a bead of water on a hot skillet. *Good God. No.* There sat her beach cover-up, along with her bathing suit. The aqua-blue caftan was great thinking on Tessa's part. Sarah hadn't thought to ask for it. Next to it was indeed her black bathing suit—a plain one at that, precisely what she'd asked Tessa to send. Only that it wasn't the one she wanted. *One-piece, dammit. One-piece. Not the teeny tiny bikini.*

Ten

If Sarah seemed apprehensive during the flight, now she was downright agitated—trudging out of her room dressed for the beach in a pretty blue cover-up paired with sandals and a scowl. The hair that had been perfectly in place on the airplane was in a ponytail. Her makeup had been removed. Sarah didn't wear a lot of it, but there was a difference and he liked the change. It harkened back to the only morning she'd been in his bed, and the way he'd pored over her as she slept, wondering if it was a good idea to pursue any of the ideas ruminating in his head—thoughts of kisses bestowed and returned, and every satisfying thing that it could lead to.

"Ready?" he asked.

"You're making me do something I am literally terrified to do. So no, I'm not ready." Clutching her handbag, she plodded toward him as if she'd been banished to the gallows.

He placed his arm around her shoulders and gave her

a gentle squeeze while unsubtly ushering her to the door. "You'll feel better after this. I promise."

"What do I get if I don't feel better? What if I feel worse? I'm already so worked up about tonight that I feel like I'm going to lose my lunch. We haven't even had lunch."

"You're just going to have to trust me."

She glared up at him when he opened the door. "You realize it's not my inclination to trust you, at all."

Her freckles again teased him, toyed with him. Now that they were completely alone, he wanted nothing more than to bend down and kiss her. Just get it over with so he could stop thinking so damn much and let his instincts take over. There was nothing stopping them—nothing stopping *him*, except the entirely foreign worry that sex might ruin what was already between them.

"You don't trust me even a little bit?"

"This is a trick question. If I say I trust you, it'll make your argument for letting a thin parachute carry me thousands of feet into the air over the Atlantic Ocean."

"Biscayne Bay. And it's five hundred feet, and that's only if they let us go all the way up. Not much more than a football field."

"Oh."

"I'll be right next to you. You can hold my hand."

"Oh. Okay." The faintest of smiles crossed her lips. "I guess that makes it a little better."

"Good. Let's go before you change your mind."

They headed down to the lobby. John was waiting outside and swiftly had them on their way to their beach adventure. This excursion was about more than distracting Sarah from her worries. He wanted her to see this side of him. She'd remarked about the photos in his apartment, comments that made him think she didn't understand why he did risky things. He hadn't always been the guy who jumped out of airplanes, but once you've done something that you could die doing, it takes away fear.

"I want to say one thing. Part of being successful in business is learning to fake fearlessness."

Sarah removed her sunglasses and shot him a very hot look of admonition. "Fake it? I assumed you were actually fearless. I've heard you on the phone. You're incredibly intimidating."

"I don't have to fake it now, but that doesn't mean there wasn't a time when I was scared to forge my own way."

"But you come from such an influential business family. Surely your dad helped you, even if you didn't have the best relationship."

It was Aiden's natural inclination to steer away from this topic, but Sarah knew his history. "That's one thing my dad offered, but I didn't want his help. By the time I graduated from college, I was too bitter to take anything from him anyway. I wanted to prove to my parents that I didn't need them. Now, granted, I had a trust fund that got me started, that was no small matter, but I did everything else on my own."

"Refusing your dad's help couldn't have made things better with your family."

"It didn't. But I also didn't feel that it was my responsibility to make things better." If ever there had been an understatement, that was it. "Regardless, I was terrified. I didn't know how to find the right companies to invest in or how to influence people. When a friend invited me to go skydiving in Peru, that changed my mindset. I realized that I could do anything because I had nothing to lose."

"Except maybe your life."

He laughed quietly. "Maybe. But when you give up a little control, you find out what you're made of. It's not my intention to scare you. I want to show you that you can do anything. You have no reason to be intimidated by Sylvia Hodge."

"I can think of fifty reasons, easy."

"No. Listen. You have a vibrant concept, you've demonstrated there's a demand for your product and most importantly, you have you. There's no substitute for a smart, creative mind. That brain of yours is pure gold."

Sarah's eyes swirled with wonder and emotion. Exquisite and teary, they took Aiden's breath away. He'd played a role in her reaction and that made his heart thump wildly.

"You make it sound like I can't fail."

"I don't think you can." Aiden blanketed Sarah's hand with his, unable to keep from touching her. He really did believe in her. After all, she'd found a way to reach him when he'd been determined to keep her away.

She turned her hand, allowing their palms to touch, wrapping her fingers around his. Her grip said that she didn't want to let go. Neither did he. Her skin was too soft, too warm. He'd waited too long for this. He had to know where this single touch led.

"Mr. Langford, the boat you hired is waiting. Anything I can carry out to the dock for you?"

John's voice yanked Aiden out from under the spell of Sarah. They were already in a parking lot adjacent to the beach.

"We'll be just fine, John." Even with the disruption, Sarah hadn't let go, and neither had he. Was his heart about to leave his body via his throat? Sarah was giving him a glimmer of hope he wasn't sure he should cling to. Why he was in any way unsure of himself with Sarah was a mystery. With any other woman, he knew precisely where hand-holding led…into his bed. With Sarah? They might never share more than what they just had.

They hiked across the hot white sand, sidestepping

people soaking up the midday rays. The crew was waiting for them on a shiny blue speedboat, bobbing in the water. The winch, which held the line for the sail, was all set up on the back. Aiden greeted the young man standing sentry on the dock, introduced Sarah and helped her aboard.

"Here are your life jackets." An older man handed a red one to Sarah and a larger blue one to Aiden.

Sarah placed her handbag on one of the benches lining the perimeter of the hull. Aiden removed his T-shirt and put on the life vest. His eyes connected with Sarah's— she'd been watching, again filling him with ill-advised hope. She turned her attention to getting her flowing cover-up sleeves through the armholes of the life jacket.

"You should get rid of the top layer," he said.

She blew out a breath. "Yeah. Okay."

She tossed the vest aside and turned her back to him, suggesting she wanted privacy. But this gave him the perfect chance to watch. The aqua fabric skimmed the backs of her toned legs, over her pleasantly round bottom, revealing the feminine curve of her waist, and the beautiful contours of her back and shoulders. With string ties at the back and at the hips, her bikini left little to the imagination, but his mind was racing to fill in the details. Blood rushed to the lower half of his body. Heat surged. Again.

She turned and sat on the bench as the boat puttered from the dock. Aiden wasn't sure he could sit alongside her and keep his hands to himself, so he kneeled on the bench, steadying himself with his hand. Ocean air rushed as the boat picked up speed, cooling his overheated skin.

The crew prepared the harnesses and called Aiden and Sarah over. Even with the boat jostling them as it bounced over the waves, it wasn't hard to see Sarah's nervousness. Her back and shoulders were stiff as a board as she stepped into the straps and they hooked her onto the winch. Aiden took his place next to her, the two of them sitting on the platform at the back of the boat. One of the men released the chute. The wind caught it, yanking on the line.

Sarah grabbed his thigh. "Oh, my God. I'm going to die."

No. But I might. He swallowed hard and took her hand. "We're in this together."

"What a comforting thought," she yelled, as the boat gained speed.

One of the crewmen leaned in closer, grasping the top bar carrying the harnesses. "We're sending you up now. Give us a signal if you decide to come back down. Have fun."

The boat engine revved. The winch creaked. The rope began to unwind and they were lifted to standing.

Sarah yelped and squeezed his hand even harder. "Don't let go," she screamed as their feet left the deck and they were carried up into the air.

The line unrolled, steadily carrying them up into the warm, cloudless sky above the crystalline sea. She'd never before wondered what it felt like to be on the end of a kite string, but this had to be what it was like, floating free while tethered to safety. As they reached a height that she'd been sure would terrify her, elation bubbled up from the depths of her stomach, giving way to breathy giggles.

Aiden laughed. "You okay?" he yelled, still holding her hand.

"Yeah," she shouted. She did have to work at focusing on the freeness of the moment, rather than the fact that she and her feet were dangling hundreds of feet above the bay. She'd never willfully experienced a height like this, outside of visiting the top of the Sears Tower in Chicago and pressing her forehead against the window for a second before she clamped her eyes shut. Somehow, the tautness of the rope and the tug of the chute made it feel as though they couldn't fall. Or perhaps it was Aiden. He did scary things all the time and he always lived to tell the tale.

Careful not to look straight down, she took in the view—high-rise hotels lining the beach, people dotting the sand and countless shades of beautiful blue composing the vista of sea. She sucked in salt air, relished the wind against her skin, and more than anything, the comfort of Aiden's hand.

If someone had asked her a month ago if she'd ever do this, she would have said no way. Now she had to wonder why she'd never allowed herself to try. Bungee jumping was definitely not on her list, nor was BASE jumping or skydiving—basically, jumping of any kind was out of the question. But this—flying in the air with a handsome, hunky guy holding on to her? *This* she could do.

Aiden was such a huge part of everything she was feeling right now. He'd been so sweet in the car, giving her the pep talk that helped her step back from the proverbial ledge. Even though they were only friends, they'd grown close, and she couldn't help but compare him to other men. Aiden, even when he made her question what she was doing, did not doubt her ability to rise to the occasion. So many men had dismissed her, especially Jason. Not Aiden. He thought of her as more. That made her see those things in herself.

She smiled. Bad memories would not dog her today. Today was full of possibility. Today was about taking risks. Aiden leaned into her, sending a zap of electricity through her. It made them pitch to one side, which made her heart race. Sarah angled toward Aiden and that became their game, back and forth, laughing, smiling at each other, shoulders touching, hand in hand. Her heart swelled with the way she felt right now—unhindered. She could do anything today.

It was hard to know how long they'd been up in the air, but all too soon the rope was pulling them back to earth. Without much trouble, their feet settled on the boat's landing pad, while the crew rushed to bring in the sail and help them out of their harnesses. Minutes later they were at the dock and trekking back across the sand to the spot where John was waiting.

Taking her seat in the car with sandy feet, windswept hair and the blood brought to the surface of her skin, Sarah's nervousness had been obliterated. Feeling invincible and exhilarated, she wanted to hold on to this moment forever.

Aiden handed her a cold bottle of water, which John had brought for them. "So?"

She smiled, turning away from him for a moment and watching South Beach whiz by as they headed back to the hotel. She knew the answer Aiden was waiting for. He wanted confirmation that he'd been right and she'd been wrong. Part of her didn't want to give it to the guy who always got whatever he wanted, but he'd earned it.

She turned back. "You were right. I loved it. It was scary at first, but I loved it."

"And how are you feeling about tonight?"

She took in a deep breath through her nose, waiting for the old nervousness to creep back in. She was on such a high that she couldn't fathom that old negativity. She could do what she set out to do. She was going to dazzle Sylvia Hodge tonight, impress her with her gown, the photos she had ready on her phone, and prove to her that her company was worth investing in. "Honestly? I feel great. Which is scary in its own way since it's not normally the way I feel, but definitely better than the other kind of scared."

"A little bit of scared keeps you on your toes, but you can get rid of the rest of it. It doesn't help you accomplish what you want." He took a swig of his water and screwed the cap back on. That little bit of time in the sun had darkened his skin, giving it a golden glow, making him that much more touchable.

"You tan quickly."

He removed his sunglasses and lifted his T-shirt sleeve, revealing the rounded curves of his muscular biceps. "I guess I did get some sun." He glanced over, setting his sights on her, making her feel exposed in a wonderful way. "You did, too. Your shoulder is pink."

Sarah turned her head. Her cover-up had slipped down and she did indeed look sunburned. "Oh, man. And I used SPF 700."

"They make such a thing?"

She shook her head. "I'm exaggerating." She examined her other shoulder, the one that had been closest to Aiden and shaded by the chute. "This side is fine."

"We'll take a look at it when we get back to the room."

We will?

"I don't want you uncomfortable tonight. I want you to walk into that room in that dress and slay everyone."

The thought of slaying a room full of people was laughable. "You do realize I'm short, right? Room slaying is more for a woman who's five foot ten."

"All that matters is that you have confidence. And I have complete confidence that you will look stunning."

Sarah swallowed, hard. The man was lethal. Her resolve was doing more than melting away—she was having a hard time remembering why she'd ever needed it in the first place. Would it hurt anyone if she and Aiden gave in to a night of passion? She'd promised herself she'd stay away from single dads if she were caring for their children, but maybe this was different. She and Aiden had already shared so much more than she ever had with Jason. And she wasn't really Oliver's caretaker. Not for long, at least.

They arrived at the hotel and rode to their floor, both

quiet. Considering all of the very sexual thoughts running through her head, Sarah was terrified to open her mouth.

"We have about an hour until we need to leave. I'm going to go ahead and hop in the shower." Aiden took his shirt off right there.

Sarah nearly choked. "Okay." She couldn't have moved if she wanted to. Not when the world's most gorgeous display was right before her. Considering that she'd never touched it, she had an irrational attachment to his chest, longed to spread her fingers across it, feel his skin against her palms and soak up the glory of Aiden Langford.

"Before you get in the shower, let me check your back for sunburn. I'm worried about that shoulder of yours."

"Oh, okay."

She stepped closer so carefully you'd think she was about to feed a lion from the palm of her hand.

"Turn around."

Goose bumps dotted her skin. He swept her ponytail to the side and teased her beach cover-up from her shoulder with his finger.

"Anything?" Her voice squeaked.

"I can't see very well. Take off this thing."

No no no. No taking off of things. Oh, but she wanted to. She really, really wanted to. He was so close, radiating heat right into her back. He towered behind her, making her wonderfully aware of his size. She crossed her arms, curled her fingers under the hem of the caftan and lifted it over her head.

"Much better."

She swore his voice was tailor-made for the bedroom. *Why is it hotter now that I'm wearing fewer clothes?*

He placed one hand on her left shoulder while brushing the right with the tips of his fingers, leaving behind a trail of white heat. His touch was heavenly and perfect.

She could have stood there forever and let him ever-so-slightly caress her shoulder. "You're a little pink, but I think you'll live."

That's rich since I feel like fainting. "Okay. Thanks."

Eleven

Sarah finished her makeup—a few dabs of powder and another swipe of deep red lipstick. "I can do this," she muttered. "I was born to do this." *I think*.

She took a final look-see in the full-length mirror. Was this dress the right call? It was certainly stunning. And if any garment, aside from a Kama nightgown, could tell the story of her design aesthetic, this was it. Still, with a neckline aimed straight for her navel, it was a bold statement. For Aiden, it was practically a lie detector test. If he showed no interest while she was wearing it? She'd know precisely how stupid her thoughts about him had been. Like most things she designed, the dress was meant to be left in a puddle on the floor at the end of the night. It was meant to leave a man with few defenses.

Not that she had a single guard against Aiden. If he made a move, it'd be painful to say no. It didn't help that her brain wouldn't stop obsessing on the blissful moment when he'd caressed her shoulder and only their bathing suits had kept them apart. What would he have done if she'd glanced over her shoulder and uttered the words she'd been dying to say? *Kiss me.*

Some part of her hoped that he wanted her the way she wanted him. Another part—the grumpy, sensible part— said that it didn't matter. Crossing that line would be foolish. It would never end well. He was worldlier and infinitely more powerful than any man she'd been with. How could she possibly make an impression on a man like Aiden? How could she not disappoint him with her relatively narrow frame of reference in the bedroom? And if it happened, and proved to be a misstep, there would be many awkward conversations to endure over the coming days. All while she was trying to save her business.

It was best not to push her luck. There were only so many things she could conquer in one day—Sylvia Hodge and building a fashion empire at the top of today's list. She needed to force herself to stop barking up the handsome billionaire.

Sarah grabbed her evening bag and marched into the living room. Aiden was standing near the door, talking on his cell. Even seeing him only in profile, he was too much to take in with a single look. So her vision landed on his black dress shoes, perfectly polished. Eyes traveling north, she savored every inch—his long legs in black tux pants, his heavenly torso in a crisp white shirt, topped off with an untied bow tie. However ludicrous the thought, she considered begging him to forget the Sylvia thing. Face time with a fashion icon? Who cared? She needed face time with him. Face-to-face. Lips to lips.

He turned, his vision unsubtly washing over her. "I need to go," he said to his phone, then tucked it into his pocket.

Sarah waited for his verdict, her pulse racing and her mouth dry.

"You look absolutely gorgeous," he said. "The dress is stunning."

The dress. The dress is stunning. She couldn't ignore his choice of words.

"You clean up pretty nice yourself." She stopped short of mentioning that his suit pants might look better draped over a chair, his shirt flung over a lamp.

He cocked an eyebrow and tied his tie without so much as looking in the mirror. Surely her heart was never meant to withstand these flirtatious blows. "Good?" he asked.

"Your tie?"

"Yes."

"It's a little crooked." He'd done a spot-on job, but this was too good an excuse to touch him. She set down her bag and straightened the tie, quickly learning that with her height disadvantage, she was giving him a bird's-eye view down the front of her dress. His warm smell teased her nose, making the proximity of his mouth impossible to ignore. Why was she torturing herself? She patted his shoulder and stepped back. "You're perfect." *Too perfect.*

"Good. Let's get out of here."

John quickly had them to the warehouse where Forward Style was being held. The show moved from city to city each year, and to make it that much more exclusive—and elusive—the exact location was never revealed to guests until hours before it started. Judging by the jam of limousines and expensive cars in front of the venue, along with the mass of people and photographers standing behind barricades, Sarah could only imagine the mayhem if the address were publicized ahead of time.

Sitting in the car, waiting for their turn at the red carpet, Sarah's earlier calm faded. The closer they crept, it got worse. Cameras flashed. Spotlights beamed into the night sky. Sarah's pulse acted like it was auditioning to join a Miami music rhythm section. This world they were about to step into was all kinds of intimidating, but she'd wanted this since she was a teenager. *You've waited long enough. This is your future.*

A valet opened the door and Aiden was out first. Sarah scooted across the seat, and just when she had another pang of doubt, he took her hand and gave it a squeeze. Regardless of what it meant, she was so glad to have her fingers safely tucked inside his grasp. He didn't have to give a speech to bolster her now. His touch was all she needed.

She'd worried that the photographers' camera flashes would stop when she stepped out of the car, but they kept coming. Of course, it was part of the excitement of the evening, or quite possibly the allure of Aiden, but she soaked up every second. She stood tall and smiled, hanging on to Aiden's hand just as she had in the air above Biscayne Bay.

Across the threshold, gorgeous women in supershort dresses offered glasses of sparkling wine. Aiden and Sarah filtered into the warehouse, which had been done up with glitzy lighting and cascades of white fabric hanging from the tall ceilings. A din of conversation and thumping dance music filled the room. Models, designers, rock stars and the Hollywood elite were decked out in a dizzying array of fashion choices—everything from priceless gowns to ripped jeans. They all seemed to know each other, embracing, laughing and chattering away.

A handsome young man in a tux offered to show them to their seats. As they walked up the aisle, Sarah couldn't believe it as they got closer and closer to the front. They stopped at the first row, taking their seats between one notorious magazine editor and renowned twin sister fashion mavens. "How'd you manage these?" she whispered in Aiden's ear.

He put his arm around her and nestled his nose in her hair. "I made an additional donation. I figured it would add to your mystery. Everyone will want to know who you are."

Sarah looked up at him, their lips only inches apart. With every crazy thing going on in this room, hundreds of endlessly wealthy and fabulous people milling about, she could only think about planting her mouth on his. Earlier, she'd wanted him just for being his sexy self. Now she wanted to kiss him for countless reasons. "I don't know what to say. Thank you."

He smiled. "Of course."

The music faded and there was a rush for people to take their seats. The song changed to a delicate instrumental and a hush fell over the crowd. Sarah's heart threatened to explode. This was really happening. Out strode a grinning Sylvia Hodge, lithe and graceful in a silvery-gray gown with a slit up one leg. Her black hair was pulled back in a high ponytail, her wrist weighed down with a stunning collection of diamond bangles. She carried herself as a woman who had the world at her feet. And she did, so it worked.

She raised a microphone to her ruby-red lips. "I want to thank everyone for joining us for this year's Forward Style. It's much more than a fashion event—it's a community coming together to support a worthy cause. This year, all proceeds benefit art programs in our public schools. That makes me incredibly proud. We must nurture creativity whenever possible. Speaking of which, I know you're all ready to see what our brilliant designers have in store for us this evening. Without further ado, on with the show." Sylvia worked it on her way backstage, hips swaying, hemline flapping around her ankles.

The music changed to another driving dance beat, and before Sarah could put a single thought into Sylvia, the show started. An endless line of models filed down the runway as the secret Forward Style collections were revealed. Sarah focused on design details, following along in the program until she noticed that none of the other VIPs were doing the same. She set aside her guide. An up-and-coming designer wouldn't be obsessing over who made what, she'd be enjoying the creativity of her peers. She sat straighter, watching the show, keenly aware of two people—Aiden right next to her and Sylvia, now seated in the front row on the opposite side of the catwalk. One person to be her rock, the other her greatest challenge.

After an unbelievable display of fashion, the show drew to a close with the designers' curtain call. The crowd gave a standing ovation, furiously clapping. Sarah kept her eyes trained on Sylvia. Once the final bows had been taken, it was time to act. *Goodbye comfort zone.*

"I'm going in," she blurted to Aiden.

Surprise crossed his face. "Yeah. Go."

Sarah pushed her way through the throng of people, easier said than done when you're height challenged, but she was not about to be thwarted. *Just fake it.* When she reached Sylvia, she didn't think. She acted. She touched her arm and started talking. "Ms. Hodge. I'm Sarah Daltrey and I need to tell you about my company, Kama. I know you're shopping for new brands and you need to see my designs. My company makes women's sleepwear and lingerie. There's a gap in your company's portfolio when it comes to that category."

Sylvia looked both astonished and amused. "Not many people have the nerve to be so direct with me. Can you show me your work?"

"I'm wearing one of my own designs tonight."

Sylvia quickly eyed the dress. "Okay. Show me more."

Not a ringing endorsement, but Sarah still couldn't get out her phone fast enough. She pulled up the gallery and handed it over to Sylvia, then began explaining each image. That was the easy part. And now that she'd gotten over her initial nervousness, every word out of her mouth became more natural.

Sylvia flicked back through the pictures a second time, nodding, as Sarah tried to interpret what each facial tic might mean. She returned Sarah's phone then gave her a business card. "Call my office tomorrow morning and ask for Katie. She'll walk you through what else we'll need from you before we can talk any further. I trust you have your financials in order? A website? Designs for next season?"

Sarah's mind whirred into gear. This was happening. "Yes. Of course. Katie. I'll call her."

"She gets in very early. I'd call before her day gets too busy. You have talent, but it won't do you any good if you don't find the right partner."

Sylvia Hodge, who Sarah now regarded as a powerful and intimidating fairy godmother, disappeared into the crowd.

"Well, that was intense," Aiden quipped. "You just did it. You didn't need my help at all."

Sarah grasped his elbow with one hand and his lapel with the other. She wasn't sure she should be so forward, but taking what she wanted and faking it when necessary had actually worked. "But I did need your help. Now let's get out of here. This music is making me crazy."

They made a quick escape into the Miami night, heading back to the hotel. Sarah settled into her seat—as much as a girl can when she's floating on air for the second time in one day.

Aiden turned to her. "If things don't work out with Sylvia, I want to invest."

"Fashion's not in your wheelhouse, remember?"

"Sarah, you could sell me the Brooklyn Bridge right now. That was a really tough thing you did. And you killed it."

Pride swelled inside her, as did her yearning for Aiden. However much she'd wished earlier that she could touch him, kiss him, run her fingertips over the intricate patterns of that tattoo on his arm, the desire was tenfold now. "You're so sweet."

"That's not what you'd say if you knew the thoughts going through my head when I look at you in that dress."

"Thoughts?"

Her face was on fire. Swallowing became an impossible task. *Kiss him. Just get it over with and if he turns you down, you can tell him it had been a momentary blip of insanity.* The car came to a stop. *Why are we not moving? We need to get to the hotel. Now.*

"We're here, Mr. Langford," John said.

"Good." Aiden gazed deeply into Sarah's eyes, taking away her ability to breathe, let alone think. "Time to retire for the evening."

Halfway through the lobby, Sarah was overcome with the feeling that everything was about to change. And not just with her career.

Aiden unknotted his tie on the elevator. He couldn't take it anymore. He'd started something in the car, something that was not smart, but he'd had enough. Being with Sarah all day had been too great a test. Every inch of her was temptation…he would've berated himself for suggesting parasailing and subjecting himself to hours with her in a bikini if he hadn't so greatly enjoyed it. He'd thought at least a dozen times about untying one of those bows on her bathing suit, caressing her soft skin, leaving her bare to him.

Next to her in the elevator, the view was incredible, but looking was no longer enough. He needed to touch her, without the dress, needed her in his bed, so he could finally get lost in her sweetness and beauty. He'd be kissing her right here and now if he thought for even a minute that he'd be able to stop.

Finally, mercifully, the elevator reached their floor.

Sarah stopped halfway down the hall, planted her hand against the wall and kicked off her shoes. "These things are killing me."

Aiden laughed quietly. Her career was built on aesthetics, but she wasn't afraid to be real with him. He opened their door, ready to sweep Sarah into his arms and finally just kiss her.

She had other plans. "Sorry, but I need to do one thing."

Before he could say a single word, she darted into her room and closed the door.

Well damn.

He stood there for a moment, unsure of what to do, which made no sense. He almost always knew what to do. *Come on, Sarah. Hurry up.* But she didn't appear. And there was no sign that she would return. What could she possibly be doing in there? *How long could it take?* So that was that. He'd crossed a line with that comment in the car, and it hadn't worked. Time to admit defeat.

He stalked to his room and closed his door, disappointment threatening to consume him. This was not the way things typically went for him. Hell, he couldn't think of any time this had happened. Then again, he'd never known a woman like Sarah. He stepped out of his pants, which oddly enough made his arousal a more pressing matter. It felt good to be less constrained, but now it was impossible to ignore how badly he wanted Sarah. *Should I go to her? Tell her how badly I want to make love to her? Or will I seem like a jerk?* They only had a few more days together.

A quiet knock came at his door.

Aiden looked around the room, unsure if it was a construct of his imagination. A second knock came. He lunged for the door and opened it, pure evidence of how little he was thinking. In his boxers, there was no hiding how thrilled he was to see her.

"There you are," she said, slightly breathless, in the tempting black-and-silver nightgown.

"Where else would I be?"

"I thought you would wait for me. I mean…after the car. It seemed like you wanted to, um, spend some time together." Her eyes flashed with something he'd never seen, which was saying a lot since she was such an animated woman.

"I do want to spend time together." Why couldn't he find something smooth to say? Oh right, everything below his waist was doing the thinking.

"What are you up to?" She looked everywhere—at the ceiling, the floor, the windows with the view of the water. Either she was trying to ignore the erection in the room, or she was waiting for him to make his move.

"I'm up to this." He leaned down and cupped the side of her cheek, placing a soft and tentative kiss on her lips. He choked back a sigh of relief. He'd wanted this more than he'd known.

She popped up on to her tiptoes and reached for his neck. Before he could think twice about what she was doing, she had him in the throes of the most enthusiastic kiss anyone had ever laid on him. He stooped to get closer, her lips wild and untamed, as if she'd been sent to consume him. For an instant he had to wonder if he'd fallen asleep and was stuck in a dream, but then she nipped his lower lip and the heavenly sting brought him to the present.

"Do you?" He wasn't sure what he was trying to prove by inquiring about her intentions. They were pretty clear.

She drew in a deep breath and nodded, never taking her eyes off him. "I do. I want you to take off my nightgown and kiss me again. I want you to touch me. I need to touch you. And I don't want to stop until we're both exhausted."

She gazed up at him, her eyes open and honest, while he teased one of the skinny straps from her shoulder. The corners of her sweet lips turned up when he reached for the hem of her gown and tugged it over her head, dropping it to the floor.

He couldn't have stifled the groan in his throat if he'd wanted to. Having her stand before him, completely naked, was overwhelming. He didn't know where to start—he wanted every part of her at once. Her breasts were even more beautiful than he'd imagined—full and luscious. The outline of her bikini showed from their time in the sun—stretches of creamy, touchable skin paired with the golden glow of her tan.

He snaked his arms around her waist, leaning down to kiss her, taking her velvety bottom into his hands. Was he the luckiest man ever right now? He'd been fantasizing about this five minutes ago and now it was actually happening.

He wanted to kiss her in a way that projected how badly he wanted her, but their height difference made it difficult. He turned and sat on the edge of the bed, pulling her along. She stepped between his knees, her body bracketed by his legs. In his eyes, she was the embodiment of luscious femininity. His arms reined her in, holding her close, as his lips traveled from her pouty mouth to her neck, down the center of her chest, and he took her pert nipple into his mouth as he plucked at the other with his fingers. He listened to the way her breath halted, took note of the subtle moves she made to get closer to him. He had so much to learn about what pleased her, and about what would make her unravel.

She dug her fingers into his hair, massaging his scalp,

soft and sexy moans coming from her gorgeous mouth. She dropped to her knees, seeking another kiss from him as she pulled at his boxer briefs and forced him to pop his hips up from the bed, so she could slide them down his legs. Kneeling before him, she took his length in hand, stroking firmly, making contact with her riveting gaze. It was everything he could do to hold his head up, let alone keep his eyes open. Her touch was bringing every nerve ending in his body alive, much as she was changing his entire life, bringing positive energy that hadn't been there before. She lowered her head and wrapped her lips around his tip, taking him into her warm and welcoming mouth. Aiden had to recline back onto his elbows—the way the blood was rushing through his body right now was enough to make him pass out.

She took her time with him, sweet and sensual with every pass, placing one hand flat on his stomach and caressing tenderly. The tension was coiling inside him like a rattlesnake about to strike. He couldn't hold on much longer.

"Sarah, come here."

She made a gentle popping sound when she released him from her mouth, but she kept her hand firmly wrapped around him. "I thought you were enjoying yourself."

The sight of her full mouth, her fingers on his body, her luscious curves, made it nearly impossible to form a coherent thought. "I was. You have no idea." He sat up and cupped the side of her face. "But I want to make love to you." His lips trailed from her mouth to her cheek and again down the graceful sweep of her neck. "If that's what you want."

"Aiden, I've wanted you from the moment I laid eyes on you. So, yes. That's what I want."

Did she really mean that? Aside from a few moments

of flirtation, and the time he'd caught her staring after the bath with Oliver, he'd assumed the attraction was somewhat one-sided. Most women were very up-front with him. Sarah had hidden it well. How she somehow managed to become even sexier to him was beyond him, he only knew that this particular revelation did exactly that. Not many people surprised him. Sarah did.

"I have a condom in my suitcase," he said.

She climbed up onto the bed and rolled to her side. "Hoping to get lucky in Miami?"

He smiled to himself and shook his head. "That wasn't what I was thinking. I just happen to have them with me when I travel."

"Best to be prepared."

"Yes." He presented her with the foil packet and cocked an eyebrow. "Care to do the honors?"

"I do." The flirtation in her voice was enough to send him sailing past his peak, until she touched him. Then it was as if he were clutching the crumbling edge of a cliff with his fingertips.

She lay back on the bed and he followed, settling between her legs, sinking into her. He bestowed kisses on her forehead, her cheek and then her lips as they rocked together. For someone so small, Sarah had a lot of power resonating from her hips. She was already gathering around him, which made thinking too great a demand, so he didn't bother. He brushed her hair back from her forehead, enjoyed the feeling of her heels on the backs of his thighs and her hands roving up and down the channel of his spine.

Their gazes connected in the soft moonlight filtering through the window as she reached her peak, her body tugging on him in pulses as she gasped for breath. He loved that blissful look on her face—so incomprehensibly beautiful. He gave in to the pleasure, steeped in the knowledge that he'd made her happy. He dropped to his side and she didn't hesitate to curl right into him. They fit so wonderfully together and he couldn't wait to have her again. He was damn lucky to be with her, even if they might never have more than one perfect night.

Twelve

Sarah wasn't sure she'd ever been so tired. Nor had she been so blissfully happy in her own skin. There in Aiden's bed, half-asleep in the early morning light, she replayed her favorite moments with him. The most captivating memory came when Sarah had gotten up in the middle of the night to use the bathroom, only to find him wide-awake when she returned. He hadn't let her get more than a few steps before she was in his arms, his hands roving everywhere as his mouth explored hers and he led her back into the bathroom.

The shower was magnificent—marble and glass, with enough room to play. Hot water covered them in a deluge but there were moments when she could've sworn the heat all came from Aiden's hands. He spread soapy suds across her breasts, and gave her kisses that hardly let her come up for air, all as steam swirled and for the third time in twenty-four hours, it felt as if she were floating.

The man was a magician, every move born of some innate ability she didn't understand. He was always a step ahead of her, anticipating. She never asked for a thing, but again and again he did exactly what she would've asked for if she'd had the guts to put it into words. He'd asked her to sit on the shower bench, then dropped to his knees before her. He hitched one of her legs over his shoulder, and brought her to heights she'd never seen. She was accustomed to being the giver, not the receiver. Sitting back and letting Aiden take control had been heavenly.

But of course she'd begged to return to the role she relished, the one in which she pleased, as it was his turn to sit on the bench and his fingers combed through her hair as she took his steely length into her mouth. Judging by the extended string of dirty talk, which ended only when his body froze and he reached his apex, she'd made him happy—very happy. That turned her on more than anything.

The mattress bounced when Aiden shifted his weight and rolled away from her. She fought disappointment that it hadn't been his body's inclination to seek hers while they were in bed, but perhaps that was for the best. Now that it was morning, and the high of yesterday had faded, reality was creeping back in. She was going home on Sunday. Aiden and Oliver would be starting their new lives then, too. That was as it should be, precisely what she'd come to New York for. She'd done her job; she and Aiden had had their fun. Aiden was not the settling down type. He needed his space—he'd said as much. Becoming a dad was already an awful lot of settling down for a man who needed his freedom. More than being used to those things, he needed them the way everyone else needed air and water.

She'd promised herself she wouldn't get attached or involved. That she wouldn't cross that line with Aiden, however badly she'd wanted him. So that was her one mistake. She'd given in to the way he drew her in. Now it was time to return to their old dynamic or tempt fate. One mistake was forgivable. Two would be idiotic.

She gently peeled back the sheet and sat up, glancing at the alarm clock. It was only a few minutes after five. Best to let Aiden sleep. She could shower and get dressed, pack her things and be ready to go whenever he was. Careful not to disturb the bed, she tiptoed to the other side to get her nightgown. But the sight of that black silk against the pristine white carpet was a snapshot from her painful past—nearly an exact replica. It sent an avalanche of hurtful memories crashing through her head—the morning after what became the final time with Jason, when she'd scrambled through the pile of clothes at the foot of the bed, desperate to find her nightgown and her dignity. That was the morning he'd scoffed at the notion that "sleeping with the nanny" meant anything. It was the morning he'd laughed when she'd said *I love you*.

She closed her eyes, willing the tears away. *You're stronger than this. It's not the same. You can stop before you get in too deep. Walk away.* That chapter was gone. She'd turned the page.

She picked up her nightgown and crept out of Aiden's room. What happened in Miami stayed in Miami. That was the only way this was going to work.

Aiden woke to an empty bed. He even rolled to his side to touch the spot where he was certain Sarah had been last night. The sheets were cold, as if she'd never been there. He propped himself up on one elbow and raked his fingers through his hair, scanning the room for evidence he wasn't dreaming. But last night had happened. He and Sarah had made love. More than once. It wasn't his mind weaving a fantasy. It had been real.

He sat up to see if his clothes were where he'd left

them. They weren't. They were draped over the arm of a chair. Most notably, her nightgown was missing from the floor. *Huh.* He'd made graceful exits from trysts. It'd never happened to him, but Sarah had a habit of keeping him on his toes. Luckily, there were only so many places she could be. He pulled on a clean pair of boxer briefs and began his search. He didn't need to go far.

"Morning." She spoke from behind the newspaper, seated at the dining table, a cup of coffee next to her. "I hope it's okay I ordered breakfast. I was starving and I figured we should get on with our day."

He rubbed his eyes and wandered over to her, struggling to make sense of this version of Sarah. This wasn't at all how he'd expected their morning would go. "You're already dressed and everything."

She didn't look up, eyes trained on the paper. "Packed and ready to go."

Sure enough, her suitcase was parked next to the front door. "You realize we can leave whenever we want, right? The jet will be waiting whenever we get to the airport. There was no need to rush." *I was hoping for some morning sex to start my day.*

"We have a lot to do today. I already spoke to Katie in Sylvia's office. We have a call this afternoon at four. I also called the nanny agency and told them we need more candidates to interview today. It's Thursday, Aiden. There's only so much time until I go home."

Well then. Aiden was used to being the distant one the morning after, the one who made it clear all roads ended here. He respected the tack Sarah took, even if it didn't add up. He'd been sure she was the girl who liked morning cuddles and romantic remembrances of the night before. Apparently not.

There was only one conclusion—her business was her top priority. He'd be a hypocrite to let that bother him.

She'd had her big break and it was of her making. She'd be a fool to lose focus, even if they'd shared what he believed to be a special night.

It still didn't sit well with him, although he couldn't discern why. What was this uneasy feeling in his stomach? The one that made him want to take her hand and say sweet things. What was the feeling that made him hope she'd say sexy things in return, flutter her lashes and deliver a proposition he couldn't refuse with her unforgettable lips? *Should we go back to bed?*

He pulled out a chair and took a seat at the table, pouring himself a cup of coffee. Caffeine might help him find clarity.

Sarah finally made eye contact. "No shirt at the breakfast table?"

Was he in some alternate universe? "You were fine with me not wearing a shirt last night."

She cleared her throat and folded up the newspaper, casting it aside. "That was last night. Today is today."

"Okay, well. I don't feel like getting up and getting a shirt. So you'll have to put up with my chest. Hopefully you can control yourself."

She rolled her eyes. "I'll manage."

This was so stupid. He didn't put up with crap like this. "Did I miss a memo or something? Did we not enjoy ourselves last night? Did I do or say something wrong?"

She downed the last of her orange juice and folded her napkin. "Of course we enjoyed ourselves. It was nice."

Nice?

"But it's time for me to get back to work." With that, she got up from the table.

Aiden grasped her arm. "Okay. I get it." Touching her was a bad idea. He was overcome with that unfamiliar feeling again. It made him want to say things he'd normally never say. *Can we talk? What are you think-*

ing? What was wrong with him? Too much sun? "You're right. We need to get back to New York to take care of the nanny situation."

"The clock is ticking."

"It is." He let go of her arm, now struck with the feeling that *not* touching her was the bad idea. He needed to get his head on straight. He was not himself this morning. "Give me a few minutes to scarf down some breakfast and read the sports page, then I'll hop in the shower and we can be out the door."

"Do you want me to call John and let him know we'll be ready in a half hour?"

Talk about being in a rush. "Tell him forty-five minutes." He watched her walk away. She wasn't wearing her usual sundress and sandals. Today, she was all business—a straight black skirt and tailored jacket with heels. She looked every bit the role of take-charge entrepreneur. And maybe that was all she wanted to be.

His interactions with Sarah didn't improve over the next several hours. Not in the car on the way to the airport, not on the plane, not in the car back to the apartment. Aiden wasn't sure what he wanted from her—something more than a minimal acknowledgment that they'd shared a fantastic night? He hated the thought of wanting that or needing it, but he did. He had this need for her approval that he'd never experienced before. He needed her to say that she'd enjoyed it—even though he was certain she had. More than a small part of him wished that she'd say that she wanted to do it again. He'd been right to worry that sex would ruin their friendship. And for now, he had to focus on salvaging it.

Of course, his deadline with Sarah loomed. Ten days had seemed like a long time the day she walked into his office, but it had gone so fast. There was so much left to do, especially after the paternity results were back tomorrow. First to tackle was the nanny situation, which Aiden wasn't looking forward to revisiting.

They arrived back at his building midafternoon.

"I just got a text from the nanny agency," Sarah said. "They're sending one more candidate over at three."

"One? That's it? You'd think that with the money I would be paying that there would be more options than one more."

"Between your standards and mine, the pool is limited. Plus, it takes time to find a good nanny. And we don't have any." Sarah put on her sunglasses and climbed out of the car.

Aiden grumbled and followed, not wanting to chase after her, but he had to—she was walking at a clip. "Do you mind telling me what's going on? You've been weird since last night and I don't like it. If we need to talk about something, then please let's do it so that the next few days can be tolerable."

"I don't want to talk about it on the sidewalk. Can we wait until we get upstairs?"

John was blazing his own trail up the walk with their suitcases.

"Yes. Of course." Aiden turned and stopped him. "You know, John. I've got this. Why don't you knock off for the rest of the day? I'm sure you'd like to spend some time with your family." Aiden took the luggage.

"Sir?"

"Is there a problem?"

"No, sir. None at all. I just…you've never sent me home early before."

"Some things are more important than sitting around waiting on me. I realize it's your job, but I also just took you away from your family for a night. If I need to go anywhere, I'll get a cab."

John shook Aiden's hand. "Thank you so much, sir.

I appreciate it. I'll be here bright and early tomorrow morning."

"Great. I might go into the office for a few hours." *It'll keep my mind off the paternity test.*

Aiden bid John his farewell and caught up to Sarah in the lobby. They rode in the elevator in silence. He didn't want to launch into everything right now anyway. He was looking forward to seeing Oliver too much and he didn't want to be in a bad mood when that happened.

His normally quiet apartment was noisy when he and Sarah stepped off the elevator. Music was playing and there was laughter, too—Oliver and Anna both, from the sound of it. Aiden left the suitcases in the entry, in search of the fun. He found them in the library. Jacob was lying on the floor, holding Oliver by the waist above him, letting him drop a few inches, and quickly catching him. Oliver unleashed peals of giggles, as did Anna, who was sitting next to Jacob on the floor. They were oblivious to Aiden and Sarah, too stuck in their happy world.

Aiden was overcome with a feeling impossible to label—longing, regret, sadness and joy. He loved seeing Anna and Jacob like this. He loved hearing Oliver's laugh. He loved seeing what a family looked like against the backdrop of his own home. It gave him an entirely different lens through which to see his future, a view that filled him with optimism and yet there was a nagging sense that not all was right. There were pieces missing. Aiden not only didn't know how to find the pieces, he didn't know what to look for.

Anna turned and her face lit up. "Look who's home, Oliver. It's Daddy."

Tears welled in his eyes. *Daddy. That's who I am now.*

Jacob got up and handed over Oliver, who snuggled right into Aiden's chest. "We had a great time, Aiden.

You have an awesome little boy here." He helped Anna get up from the floor.

"You had a good time?" Aiden asked Oliver, rubbing his back and breathing in that magical baby smell.

"He had the best time," Anna said. "He's such a good baby."

Oliver tugged the sunglasses threaded on Aiden's shirt, smearing them with his tiny fingers. Aiden didn't care that they were five-hundred-dollar shades. He merely took the chance to kiss Oliver's temple and hold him close.

Sarah peeked around Aiden's shoulder. "Hey, sweet pea," she said.

Oliver's face lit up, and an elated gurgle rose out of him when she went in for a kiss. They rubbed noses, mere inches from Aiden's face. Sarah's soft, musical laugh filled his ears. Something deep inside him wanted to hold on to that moment forever. Disappointment washed over him when it ended.

Sarah was a missing piece. And that piece was leaving on Sunday.

Thirteen

As every minute passed, it became more difficult to be with Aiden. Sarah had entered territory she'd vowed to avoid, and she'd been a fool to think she could step out of it by adopting a steely demeanor. She could convince her brain of a lot of things, but it didn't mean her body was going to be on board. Just sharing the same air made everything harder—it only made her want him more.

The apartment buzzer rang. "That must be the final nanny," Sarah said to Oliver, scooping him up.

Aiden emerged from his office, where he'd been working. "What's this one's name? Lucy?"

His voice dripped with doubt, saddling Sarah with the fear that he'd turn down their final option. If he did, *he* could deal with the repercussions. Oliver was his responsibility, not hers, and she wasn't going to stay because Aiden refused to make a decision.

"Her name is Lily. Her credentials are exceptional. I think she could be the one."

"I read her résumé, Sarah. You don't have to keep selling me on these people."

Sarah choked back a frustrated grumble. If he were going to sabotage this, he'd better be prepared for a lecture when Lily left.

The elevator doors slid open and Lily roved into the foyer. Her wavy auburn hair was past her shoulders, barely tamed. She wore a swishy orange skirt that grazed the floor and a white tank top—not the professional interview attire Sarah expected. Maybe Aiden wouldn't have to ruin this. Maybe Lily would. "Langford residence?"

"It is. I'm Aiden." He stepped forward to shake her hand. "This is Sarah. She's been filling in as nanny until we find a permanent replacement."

His choice of words stung, especially after what had happened last night. It was confirmation of the way he saw her—as a temporary fixture. "Hi," Sarah said. "This is Oliver."

Lily's eyes grew impossibly large and she tilted her head as she went to him, taking his tiny hand. "Hello, Oliver. Aren't you the cutest thing ever?" Her voice was pure fairy-tale princess—full of magic.

Oliver was immediately taken, going to her.

"If it's okay with you," Lily said, "I'd like to play with him while we chat. I'm not big on formality."

Sarah never would've deigned to dictate the course of an interview when she was nannying, but she couldn't argue with Oliver's reaction to Lily. He was infatuated, babbling away and tangling his fingers in her hair. Aiden gestured for them to go into the library, where many of Oliver's toys were spread out on the floor.

Lily plopped down on the rug and jumped in with playtime. "I assume you've seen my résumé."

Aiden sat while Sarah stood, observing. "It's impressive," he answered. "You've worked for some very high-profile families."

"I've been lucky to have had the chance. And every child I've ever cared for has been wonderful. It worked well with those families because they appreciated my approach to nannying."

"And how would you describe that?" Aiden asked.

"Well, of course I'm firm with the children. They need some boundaries. But otherwise, I believe in letting them take the lead. If we go to a museum, we do what the child wants to do. If we do an art project, we make a mess if that suits the child's disposition. If we go to the park and he wants to dig in the dirt rather than play on the swings, we do that. We'll sing songs at the top of our lungs and splash water in the bathtub. Kids need freedom and space."

Sarah was taken aback. She'd never managed to deliver a spiel on her former vocation so eloquently. If it was rehearsed, it didn't come off that way. Then there was her choice of words—freedom and space. Aiden would have to reach to turn down Lily.

He sat forward and rested his elbows on his knees. "What else can you tell me?"

Lily launched into more of her philosophy of child-rearing, walking him through her typical weekly schedule for a toddler. She talked of long walks and afternoons in the park, of play dates and visits to the library.

Sarah had to step away as visions of Lily's plans appeared in her head. Oliver would have a wonderful, idyllic life and he'd be well cared for. It was everything she'd come looking for. If Aiden hired Lily, it would mean that Sarah had succeeded—she'd honored Gail's wishes and found Oliver his forever home. So why did she feel so empty? Why did it have to feel as if she were looking out the rear window of a car as it sped away?

"Sarah, can I speak to you for a moment?" Aiden's

voice worked its way into her psyche, her weakness for him harder to ignore with his presence.

She sucked in a deep breath and shoved aside her feelings. "Yes, of course. What's up?"

"Am I crazy or did I just find a nanny? Lily is perfect."

She smiled and nodded, fighting her irrational tears. "I agree. She's fantastic. You and Oliver will be very happy with her. I think you should offer her the job." It was best to keep pushing him away, or else her heart would be a pile of rubble by the end of the weekend.

"Okay, then. It's decided." Not wasting a second, he strode into the library while Sarah followed. "Lily, I'd like to offer you the job. Can you start first thing Monday morning?"

Lily smiled awkwardly. "Oh. The agency should've told you I have another offer on the table right now. A family that's moving to France. I haven't decided yet if I'm going to take it or not. I promised them I'd decide before the end of the weekend."

"Whatever they're paying you, I'll double it," Aiden said.

Aiden was clearly committed to moving forward. Sarah reminded herself this was supposed to make her happy.

Lily got up from the floor. "I appreciate that, but it's not the money. Honestly, it's the chance to travel."

"I love to travel. I'd love to take Oliver on adventures all over the world and you can come with us."

Sarah could imagine the three of them globetrotting together. Talk about feeling left out…

Lily cast her sights down at the baby. "He's so sweet and you make a compelling case. If it's okay with you, I'd still like to have the weekend to think about it. I know you need someone on Monday, but the other family wouldn't need me to start for another month, so I could at least take over from…" Lily glanced at Sarah and pressed her hand to her chest. "I'm so sorry. I've completely forgotten your name."

Sarah blanched. *I'm so out of the picture I'm a ghost.* "Oh, no worries. It's Sarah."

"I could take over from Sarah until you find a permanent replacement."

"I guess I can't ask for much more than that," Aiden said. "But please, think about the things I said. I'm sure you and Oliver are a great match."

Lily bid her farewells, which included several sloppy kisses from Oliver. Even the baby was practically ready to send Sarah on her way.

Aiden let out an exaggerated exhale as the elevator doors closed. "I'm so relieved that's worked out, at least for the next month. I didn't want you to think I was trying to hold you hostage. I just needed someone I felt good about."

Sarah nodded. "I'm relieved, too." *And feel so much worse.*

"Now you can go to Boston on Sunday." He strolled into the kitchen and poured himself a glass of water. "Actually, you could go home earlier if you wanted to. The paternity results are in tomorrow and they're sending over the legal team to take care of the paperwork. You could go home Saturday. I mean, if you're eager to go."

Seriously? Sarah felt as though her heart should just throw up its hands and stomp out of the room. It hadn't even been twenty-four hours since they'd slept together and he was shooing her out the door? Her instincts that morning had been 100 percent correct. She needed to get out, not get wrapped up in the guy who hated the idea of being tied down. "Okay. I'll leave as soon as it makes sense. Speaking of which, I have that conference call with Katie in a few minutes. I'll take it in my room."

Tears threatened again, but she had to keep it together. She turned to the stairs, but Aiden stopped her with a hand on her forearm.

"Sarah, wait."

She froze, the warmth of Aiden's fingers searing her skin. *What? Did you change your mind? Do you actually want me to stay through Sunday?*

"Use my office for your call."

Aiden wasn't sure what had gotten into him when he'd told Sarah she should leave before Sunday if she wanted to. It had seemed like the generous thing to do, but now he was kicking himself, even though he had to let her go sometime. Her actions suggested she hadn't wanted more than one night with him, and from the very beginning, she'd been laser-focused on the deadline. She'd delivered everything she'd promised. He'd done the same. Once the paperwork was done, their relationship could come to its logical conclusion. Except that Aiden had that uneasy feeling in the center of his chest again, the one that said something was wrong. He couldn't shake it, no matter how hard he tried.

Aiden played with Oliver in the library, unable to ignore how badly Sarah's call was going. She hadn't closed the doors to his office, so he couldn't avoid hearing her say things like, "I don't know. I'll have to get that together for you." Sylvia Hodge and her cohorts would likely only sink money into someone who was flawlessly prepared. He had to force himself to not walk in and offer his help. He'd done his part. He'd put her in the room with Sylvia Hodge. It was up to Sarah to make this happen.

Aiden's worst suspicions were confirmed when Sarah drifted out of the office. All traces of the excitement she'd had yesterday were gone.

"Well?" he asked.

"I feel like I just got hit by a train." Her voice was weary, as if she couldn't take another step.

"Those calls can be like that. It's not always a bad thing." He didn't want to give her false hope, but he couldn't stand to see her like this. Her upbeat air was gone and he missed it.

She pursed her lips and shook her head. "No. This was bad. There were so many questions I couldn't answer."

"I thought your financials were in order."

"They are, but they asked me things like what percentage of the market I can corner and how quickly I can do it. I can't answer that. That's what I need them for."

Aiden's stomach sank. Should he have prepared her more? Had he dropped the ball? "It's okay to not know the answer to everything."

"Judging by what Katie said, it's not. She said they don't work with companies that aren't as up-to-speed on the business end as they are on the design end. That's me, Aiden. I know the design end. I stumble through the rest of it."

"But you've accomplished a lot. They'll see that. And there's the value of your concept and product. I'm sure that it's Katie's job to be a bulldog, so Sylvia can step in and be your savior."

"I don't know why I tried to do any of this. Sylvia probably only agreed to have her people talk to me because I had her cornered and she didn't want to make a scene."

"Don't be so defeatist. You haven't had a definitive answer yet. And if this doesn't work out, you'll move on to the next thing. I've done it many times."

Sarah's jaw tensed in a way Aiden had never seen, not even that first day in his office when she'd been so frustrated. "There is no next thing, Aiden. I'm not you. I don't have a million amazing possibilities to juggle at one time. This is it for me. My career, my life, my paycheck. There's nothing else for me but this. This is the one thing I'm good at."

"Besides nannying."

"I don't know how many times I have to tell you that I'm done with that. Forever."

Yes, Sarah had said these things to him before, but he still didn't understand it. "Did something bad happen? Is that why you're so adamant about not going back to nannying?"

"Yes, something bad happened. Why else does a person decide they can't do something anymore?"

"Why didn't you tell me?"

"I don't talk about it with anyone, especially not someone I've known for a week."

Her dismissiveness felt like someone choking his heart. A week. In some ways it felt as if he'd known Sarah his whole life. "I'm just trying to help."

"I can't tell you. I'm too ashamed."

Now he *had* to find out what had happened. Sarah, ashamed? He couldn't imagine her doing a single dishonorable thing. "I'm not going to judge you. But I'd like to know what's going on. I think I've earned an explanation."

She stared at the ceiling, blinking back tears. "I got fired from my last job. I've never been let go in my entire life, and this family meant the world to me. It destroyed me. I took one more nannying job after that, but I only lasted a day. I had to do something else. I couldn't go back."

"So you were really attached to the children?"

"Child. Singular. A little girl named Chloe. She was a few months older than Oliver." She cast her sights down at the baby and pressed her lips together solidly. "I can't talk about this, Aiden. I really can't."

He pulled her into his arms, breathing in her sweet scent, overcome with the memory of how good this had felt last night. They fit together well. "It's okay to tell me. Maybe you'll feel better if you get it out. That's what you told me the night we sat up on the terrace and I was still upset about my mom."

She settled her head against his chest, trembling. "I became romantically involved with my boss. I fell in love with him."

"Go on." He choked back his discomfort at the thought of her with another man.

"I knew it was wrong, but I was so drawn to him and I adored his daughter and it just happened. His wife had passed away before I was hired and he seemed to need me and care about me, but I read the whole thing wrong."

He caressed her arm, closing his eyes and drawing in a deep breath. Her anguish poured into him. He longed to take it away. He also needed to know more. What kind of monster was this man who'd captured her heart and thrown it away? "What happened?"

Sarah looked up at him, but he didn't let go. He wanted her to know that he was there for her. "I told him the truth. I told him that I loved him. He actually laughed at me. He thought I was kidding. He thought we were having a fling. He'd assumed that I'd done it before, but I hadn't. And when I told him that it wasn't a joke, he fired me. He didn't want me around his daughter. He said he couldn't trust me anymore. Do you have any idea how awful that felt?"

"He couldn't trust you because you loved him?"

"Yes."

"That's horrible."

"It's the worst thing that's ever happened to me. Unrequited love is one thing, but it's quite another to have your bond with a child stripped away. I've always cared deeply for the children in my charge. I never knew another way. Leaving was always the hardest part, but at least it'd always been on good terms. This was just solid rejection. I was hollowed out. That's why I don't nanny anymore."

Oliver crawled over to them and pulled himself to standing with the help of Aiden's pant leg.

Sarah picked him up, tears streaming down her face. She smoothed his hair back and kissed his cheek. "I'm sorry. I know this is way more than you ever wanted to know about me. But now at least you know why Kama means so much. I can't go back to my old life."

Aiden had started over many times. He knew the appeal of a new beginning. "I understand. Completely."

She sighed and managed a smile before she handed over Oliver. "Thank you. I appreciate that. Now I need to go upstairs and regroup and try to figure out how I salvage this Sylvia Hodge thing. Are you okay to do bedtime on your own?"

"Yes, of course. I'm sure you want some alone time anyway." He really hoped the answer was that she didn't want to be by herself, that she wanted to stay up and talk after Oliver went to bed.

"I do. I need some time to think. Plus, a few more nights and you won't have me around to help. You might as well start acting like I'm not even here."

Fourteen

Sarah was working feverishly on an email to Katie and Sylvia Hodge Friday morning, when Aiden strolled into his home office, phone in hand. He grinned like a man without a single worry.

"Probability of paternity is 99.9 percent. Oliver is mine."

Sarah jumped out of the chair and raced from behind the desk, throwing her arms around him. "I knew it. I just knew it."

Unfortunately, the instant she was pressed against him, her body wanted to stay, especially when he returned the embrace with a firm squeeze, rocking her back and forth. With the clock ticking, should she take these happy moments? Even when they'd haunt her later?

"I knew in my heart that he was my son, but I don't think I realized how much it would mean to have the confirmation. Considering my own history, this gives me peace. Oliver and I are a family. No one can take that away from us." Aiden released her from their hug. It was impossible to ignore how enticing he was when he was so relaxed. Good news suited him well. "The lawyers will be by in an hour to do the final paperwork. They'll have it before the judge this afternoon. Then we'll be done."

Done. She was so close to being done, it wasn't even funny. She'd worried about awkward conversations after sleeping together, but Aiden hadn't said a thing. She respected a man who followed her lead, but part of her really wished he'd fought her on it beyond his minor protestation in Miami. His ready acceptance was another reminder that in the end, she was just another woman. Nothing more. "All sewn up. No more loose ends." *It's for the best. And you know it.*

He cleared his throat and walked over to the bookcase, straightening a book. "Have you thought at all about when you'll want to go?"

If only he knew how much that question hurt. "I'd like a little more time with Oliver." *And you, if I'm being honest.*

"I'm asking because I was thinking about having my family over tonight. For a celebration. Officially welcome Oliver into the Langford family. I definitely want you here for that."

Sarah could breathe a little easier. Maybe she was at least a notch above the other women he'd been with. "I'd love to be there. I think it's great you're involving your family. It's important to mend fences with your mom."

"This gives me another perfect opportunity to push her on it, but tonight's probably not the night, huh? Not when everyone is here."

"Agreed. Tonight should be happy. Leave the tough conversation for another day."

He turned to her while a soft smile crossed his face. "It means a lot to have someone to talk to about this."

Sarah grinned, even when she was dying a little more on the inside. Their ability to discuss painful things was one of the best parts of their friendship. He'd been so sweet with her when she'd opened up about Jason. He hadn't judged her. Not at all. "Good. I'm glad."

He knocked the bookcase with his knuckle. "I'll leave you to whatever you were working on. I'm going to get a workout in before the lawyers come by."

The afternoon was a flurry of activity. Documents were signed. Calls were made to the market to have food and drinks delivered. Oliver got an early bath before his first Langford family gathering. Sarah relished the hustle and bustle. It kept her mind off the clock, a constant reminder that it would soon be time to not only say goodbye to two people she cared about deeply, but after that came do-or-die time with Kama. What if everything with Sylvia Hodge blew up? Because that's where it seemed to be headed. The email she'd sent that afternoon had been answered with yet more questions. More doubts. More reasons they might say no. Then where would she be? Back in Boston, alone, her future a big fat question mark.

Aiden's brother Adam and his wife, Melanie, were the first to arrive. Adam was incredibly charming—just as magnetic as Aiden, with a smile that was nearly identical. That gave Sarah pause. Maybe Evelyn Langford wasn't keeping a secret. Sarah didn't have much time to think about it though, quickly hitting it off with Melanie, who was both down-to-earth and talkative.

"I have to say, Aiden. Fatherhood really agrees with you," Adam said as Oliver sat happily in Aiden's arms.

"Thank you. I really appreciate that." Aiden's response was more than polite conversation. His brother's kind words had resonated.

"I'll have to get some pointers from you when the time comes. Mel and I are trying to get pregnant," Adam said.

Melanie's eyes flashed. She swatted Adam on the arm. "I thought we weren't telling anyone."

Adam put his arm around her and pulled her closer, kissing her on the cheek. "We're with family. There are no secrets."

If only that were true with the Langfords.

Jacob and Anna arrived, both ecstatic to see Oliver. The baby had apparently fallen in love with his uncle Jacob during the Miami trip, since he readily went to him. Everyone chatted in the kitchen, wine and cocktails flowing, music in the background. No problems. No controversy. But despite Aiden's pledge to keep things light, Sarah had a sinking feeling that might change with the arrival of the final guest.

Aiden grabbed a carrot stick from a platter of veggies and dip. "Leave it to my mother to be late for her grandson's first party."

"Maybe she's stuck in traffic." Sarah arranged crackers on a plate.

"You know she likes making an entrance," Adam said. "It's annoying, but true."

The apartment buzzer rang. Aiden took in a deep breath and adopted the most forced smile Sarah had ever seen. "Mom's here." He soon returned with Evelyn.

She greeted everyone sweetly, saving Oliver for last. "There's my handsome grandson."

Oliver was content to stay with Jacob, but he humored his grandmother, laughing when she made a silly face and holding her finger with his pudgy hand.

Aiden smiled, but Sarah could see once again that he was having to try. What it must be like to live with something so big hanging over your head—Sarah could only imagine. It burdened him, greatly, and how could it not? It had made him the person he was today. Nothing was safe from the influence of the secret he was convinced his mother was keeping.

For nearly two hours, Sarah dedicated herself to being a comfort to Aiden, bringing him a fresh drink when needed, offering a reassuring smile or moment of eye contact, especially when he sat on the living room sofa with his mom. Every time he acknowledged Sarah with a smile or a nod, it shored up their solidarity. The friendship they'd forged would be one of her greatest takeaways from their ten days together. It could comfort her when she found herself wondering what would have happened if she hadn't put up a stone wall after Miami.

"How are you holding up?" She crouched next to him at the end of the couch when his mother had gone to use the bathroom. Things were winding down, which was good since Aiden seemed to have reached his limit. His eyes were tired, his jaw tense, brows drawn tightly together.

"She's making me crazy. She's spent the whole night planning things for Oliver's birthday next month and talking about how she wants to spend Christmas morning with him. It rubs me the wrong way. I can't help it."

Probably because she never did those things for you. Sarah bit down on her lip to keep from saying what Aiden already knew. "Maybe she's trying to make up for the past."

A slight smile crossed his face and he clasped his hand over hers. "You're so sweet. I love your optimism. But I'm pretty sure this is just her way of sweeping the past under the rug."

He was probably right. She didn't know why she had the need to put a positive spin on his mother's insensitivity, she only knew that she did. "So let's just get everyone to clear out."

"Yes. Oliver needs to get to bed anyway."

* * *

By the time Aiden's mom returned from the bathroom, he'd had enough for one day. Sarah was right. Everyone needed to go home. He got up from the couch. "I don't want to spoil the party, but I need to get Oliver to bed."

His mother smiled and nodded. "Such a good dad." She popped up onto her tiptoes and kissed Aiden on the cheek. "It's been a wonderful night. I only wish your father could've lived to meet his grandson."

That image left Aiden frozen with the words he wanted to say. It would be easier on everyone if he let it go, but after years on the periphery of his family, doubt festering in his head and heart, he not only wanted the truth, it was the only thing he could speak. "I'm not sure he would've accepted Oliver." *He sure as hell didn't accept me.*

"Of course he would have."

Again, the need—the thirst—for the truth was desperate. The fire inside him, the pain he lived with every day, blazed. "But he didn't accept me."

His mother's eyes were horror stricken. "Your father loved you."

Aiden calmly confronted her by looking her square in the eye. "Just tell me. I'm tired of wondering. I don't want to have to think about it anymore."

"But…"

He clasped his hand firmly over hers. "Mom. I love you, but there is no *but*. If you want to be a part of Oliver's life, you'll tell me the truth about who my father is."

Adam approached. "Everything okay?"

Aiden refused to let his mother off the hook. "Mom was going to finally tell me the truth about who my dad is. Weren't you?"

"You'd keep my grandson from me?"

Aiden nodded. "If you love me, you'll tell me."

His mother's eyes misted. Her lower lip trembled. "I don't want to hurt you. I never did."

"Mom, it's too late. This is your chance to start making it better." Aiden braced for what was to come.

His mother perched on the edge of a chair. "We tried to make it work, but your father…" She cast her eyes up at Adam, then Aiden. Anna joined them and took Aiden's hand, squeezing it tightly. "Your father couldn't deal with it. He looked at Aiden and all he saw was what he perceived as betrayal. That's why you were sent off to school. And I agreed, because I couldn't watch him be cruel to you and loving with Adam and Anna. Your father had such a temper. I was worried about what might happen if he got truly angry at you. That's why you were sent away."

Aiden swallowed, dogged by lonely memories from his childhood—birthdays in boarding school, phone calls from his mother where she acted as if this was all normal and summers at home as the odd man out. He was an expert at filing those things away, but he had to face them now. *This is it. The moment I've waited for.* "Then who's my father?"

Jacob, holding Oliver, had joined Anna. Melanie had crept closer, too, standing with Adam. They all had each other. Who did Aiden have? He turned and his vision landed on her—Sarah, standing there with concern painted on her face. She was his one true ally in this room.

"Your uncle Charlie is your biological father. I dated him before Roger. It was short, but that's when you were conceived. I lied to Roger when we first started going out. I didn't want him to know that I'd been with his brother. Roger and I fell in love and when we learned I was pregnant, we got married." She peered up at Aiden. The corners of her mouth were drawn down, deep creases between her eyes. She might be hurt, but she'd left him with the same scars. "It didn't take long after you were born for Roger to put two and two together. You have the same birthmark on your leg that Charlie had."

"The same one Oliver has." Aiden was amazed he'd said anything calmly considering the speed at which his mind and heart were racing.

"Yes." She gathered her composure. "Things were okay for a while, but everything changed when Adam was born. He always compared you two. He and Charlie had such a contentious relationship, it was no big surprise. And then Charlie died in the motorcycle accident and Roger couldn't handle it. It was such a tangle of emotion and you were the one it all got directed at, Aiden. I had to get you somewhere safe, where I knew you'd be okay. That's why I agreed to send you off to school."

Aiden stood there, thinking. With everything that had been launched at him, his mind was remarkably clear. The truth had washed away the dirt on the windows. He could see. The anger hadn't left, but it made sense now. He turned again to Sarah, who was standing back from the group. Of all the people in that room, she was the one he wanted to talk to. She was the one he wanted to confide in. He wanted to be alone with her. He wanted to feel good again. As to whether she wanted the same from him, he had no idea. Her face showed only sweet empathy as he walked Oliver over to her.

"I'm going to send everybody packing," he said softly.

"Good," Sarah said.

Aiden turned to his family. "Thanks everybody for coming today. It's been good for Oliver. And for me."

"Say something," his mother pleaded. "Please tell me you forgive me."

He could've been so cruel, but it wasn't in his heart. However misguided she might've been, she'd thought she was doing the right thing. "I forgive you, Mom. That doesn't mean I'm over it. We're talking about a lifetime of lies. It will take time. Someday I want you to tell me more about my real dad. For tonight, I think it's best if everyone goes."

Adam reached out to shake Aiden's hand. It might've been the first time that Aiden felt zero ill will toward his brother. They'd both been caught in the same dysfunctional dynamic. Adam might've reaped some of the good things, but he'd had his own burdens.

"You're my brother, Aiden," Adam said. "And I love you. I'm around if you need to talk about this."

"I'd like that," Aiden replied.

"I'm not sure what to say," his mother said. "Other than goodbye."

"Why don't we plan on you coming over next week for some time with your grandson?" Aiden answered. It was time for the healing to begin.

"I would love it." With that, Adam walked his mom and Melanie to the door.

Anna grasped Aiden's arm, tears in her eyes. "You were right," she muttered. "I didn't want to believe it. I'm so sorry."

He hugged his sister. "Don't apologize. You've never been anything but loving and supportive. You know, you're going to make such an amazing mom. I can't wait for Oliver to have a cousin."

Anna smiled through her tears and pecked him on the cheek. "I love you."

"I love you, too."

He walked Anna and Jacob to the entryway and watched as they stepped onto the elevator with Adam, Melanie and Evelyn, the door sliding closed. There were footsteps behind him. He knew it was Sarah, and not because she was the only other adult in the house. In only a week, he'd learned the tempo of her gait.

"If you want, I can do bedtime tonight," she said. "I'm sure you're exhausted."

Her voice was salve to his soul. He turned and it felt as if the universe was presenting him with the cure to all that ailed him. Whatever the problem, she made things better.

"Let's both put him to bed. Together."

"Oh. Sure. I'd like that."

The party had taken it out of Oliver. Aiden put him in his pajamas and Sarah read him a story, sitting with him in the rocking chair. Aiden leaned against the door frame, studying them together. If only he could capture that moment in a bottle, save it for later, after she was gone. Sarah's absence would leave a void in his and Oliver's life that would be impossible to fill. But it was what she wanted. She'd made that clear.

After only a few minutes, Oliver sacked out in Sarah's arms. She gently set him in the crib, and she and Aiden tiptoed into the hall.

"I'm sorry about tonight." Aiden reached for her arm. "I know we said that I should wait for another time, but I had to say something. It was killing me."

"I'm proud of you for doing it. Even though it hurts right now, be patient with yourself. Give yourself some time to process it. And in the end, Oliver's love will heal you. I truly believe that."

He would have smiled if it weren't so hard to breathe. She was so determined to make everything better, and that made her even more beautiful, that much more impossible to resist.

"I think I'll head to bed," she said. "I'm sure you want time to think about everything."

Could he risk his pride for a second time tonight? He had to. Even if she might say she didn't want him the way he wanted her. He might not get another chance. "Don't go, Sarah. Stay with me."

Fifteen

Stay with me. Sarah wasn't sure she'd heard his words correctly. They were surprising. They were scary—driving her to a place where she surrendered to her deep longing for him. Did he want her? She wasn't about to make presumptions about what Aiden had said. Not now. Not when she'd be opening herself up to more hurt. "Did you want to talk?"

He granted the smallest fragment of a smile, looking at her with his heartbreaking blue eyes, his gaze saying he didn't need to talk. He tenderly tucked her hair behind her ear, drawing his finger along her jaw to her chin. "I don't know what force in the universe brought you to me, Sarah. I only know that right now, I need you. I want you. And I'd like to think that you want me, too."

The air stood still, but Sarah swayed, lightheaded from Aiden's words. Their one night together had been electric, filling her head with memories she'd never surrender, but judging by the deep timbre of Aiden's voice, they might shatter what happened in Miami. "I don't want to ruin our friendship." *And no-strings-attached only breaks my heart.*

"Is that why you shut things down after Miami?"

"Yes." It wasn't the whole truth, but it was enough. As much as sleeping with Aiden might be a mistake, she didn't want to deprive herself of him. Would one more time really hurt? "And I've spent every minute since then regretting it."

"Then I say we have no more regrets."

Before she knew what was happening, he scooped her up into his arms. She'd never had a man carry her anywhere. Her small stature had always made her wonder why—apparently she'd had to wait for Aiden. She wrapped her hands around his neck and leaned into him. He took the few steps necessary to cross the threshold into his room. He set her gently on the bed and stretched out next to her.

She cupped the side of his face, the stubble of his beard scratching her palm. Her heart beat a frantic rhythm as she waited. Then his lips were on hers, soft and sensuous, and that made her pulse race faster. She closed her eyes to immerse herself in the world of Aiden—the silky soft sheets and his masculine smell, his solid, muscular body. He palmed her thigh, his hand inching along under her skirt, sending ribbons of electricity through her.

He rolled to his back, taking her with him until she was straddling his hips. Her dress was now hitched up around her and Aiden explored beneath her skirt again, slipping his fingers into the back of her lace panties and cupping her bottom. She rested her arms on the bed above his shoulders and dug her fingers into his thick hair, rocking her pelvis against his, his rock-hard erection rubbing against her apex. The need for Aiden had been building for two days, and everything he did made it more pronounced—his tongue exploring her mouth, his white-hot touch.

She sat back and scrambled her way through the buttons of his shirt. He untucked it, then shifted and rolled his magnificent shoulders out of his sleeves. She sat there in awe, reaching out and skimming her fingers along the contours of his shoulders. He was so incredible, inside and out. He clutched her neck, and brought her mouth back down onto his as she again rolled her hips, grinding against his crotch, making everything between her legs blaze with licks of fire—each pass was a tiny measure of gratification, and a bigger dose of torment. She needed him now.

"Touch me, Aiden."

She reached behind her and unzipped her dress, then Aiden threaded his hands beneath the skirt again and pushed the garment up over her head. She planted her hands on the bed next to his shoulders, and he traced the edge of her bra cups with his finger, dipping below the fabric edge and rubbing her nipple. The skin contracted hard beneath his touch, and goose bumps followed. A deep moan left her lips, just to let off a bit of the pressure. He was torturing her, his gaze never leaving her, the need in his eyes fierce and undeniable. He slid his finger under the strap and nudged it off her shoulder, then did the same on the other side. She was about to beg him to take off her bra when he snapped the clasp and the garment fell away. He cupped her breasts in his strong hands—such blissful relief that you'd think she'd waited a lifetime for his touch. She arched her back and her eyes drifted shut as he raised his head and flicked his tongue against one nipple, need shuddering through her. His lips closed on the tight bud, while his hand trailed down her stomach and slipped down the front of her panties, finding her apex.

His fingers teased, touching lightly, drawing gasps

from her lungs as he took full control. She settled her forehead on his shoulder as he masterfully brought her closer to climax with firm circles and a steady pace. The pleasure rose inside her, cresting. The tension would build, then ebb, then surge back until she was again at the very edge. When it finally became too much and she gave way, she smashed her mouth into his shoulder to quiet her cries of ecstasy.

But now she only needed him more. She climbed off him and watched as a sexy grin crossed his face when she unbuckled his belt and unzipped the zipper. Not having the fortitude to tease him, she slipped his pants and boxers down at the same time. He was so primed it nearly stopped her dead in her tracks. She appreciated the dark, lusty expression on his face as she wrapped her fingers around him and stroked firmly. He watched for only a moment before his eyes drifted closed and his shoulders let go of all tension. She leaned in and pressed her lips against his, loving the way the depth of his kiss told her how much he appreciated each pass of her hands. His skin was so warm and smooth, but the pressure beneath the surface was intense. Pleasing him like this was so gratifying, but she needed him fully. She needed him to make love to her. She wanted them joined that way again.

"Aiden, make love to me."

He rolled to his side and ran his fingers through her hair, covering her face with kisses. "I want to. Now." He sat up and opened a drawer in the bedside table, handing her the condom packet. She tore it open as he stretched out again. He drew in a sharp breath when she rolled it onto his waiting erection. Then he watched as she slipped off her panties and kicked them to the floor when they were to her ankles.

He positioned himself between her legs when she lay

back on the bed. "This is virtually the only thing I've thought about since we got back from Miami."

"Really?"

"Really."

He guided himself inside as she pulled his hips down and he sank into her, her body molding perfectly around him. He lowered his head and they settled into a long and tangled kiss. They moved together in their perfect rhythm, rocking back and forth as the kisses became more frantic, less refined. His breaths were ragged and shallow and it was clear he was close to climax. He reached down between them and placed his thumb against her center until she came and he quickly followed.

He collapsed next to her, catching his breath.

She was floating back down to earth, her mind a whirl of wonderful things. "That was incredible." *But I want more.*

He smiled, his eyes half-open. "I hope you aren't too tired. I want to make the most of our time together."

Make the most of it. Her thoughts, exactly.

In the new light of morning, Sarah again watched Aiden sleep. She lay on her side, one arm tucked under her pillow, studying his face, notably calm after last night. Aiden had let his guard down. He'd let her in and it had all been his idea. She hadn't had to push for a thing. She felt like a new person, emerging from her dark cocoon in the nick of time. One more day and she'd have been gone. Now, leaving was unimaginable. She'd be crumpling her own heart into a tiny ball. Certainly Aiden wouldn't let her. Their connection was too strong.

The events of the last week had turned everything upside down, but that meant she was out from under the menacing cloud, the one that had followed her for more than a year. Even more remarkable, the saddest thing she could imagine, Oliver losing his mother and Sarah losing her friend, had brought happiness. She could see a life with Aiden. She could imagine becoming Oliver's mom if that was where she and Aiden chose to take things. They could be a family.

There were still obstacles to overcome and the most pressing was no small thing—saying those three little words. But after last night with Aiden, riding out the aftereffects of a secret he'd feared his entire life, they'd cemented their bond. So as frightening as it was, she would take the leap of telling him her true feelings. When she'd sworn to never say it first again, she'd had no way of knowing that a man as extraordinary as Aiden would come into her life. He was different. They had a foundation. Synergy. There would be no sad ending after *I love you*.

Aiden shifted in the bed, scrunching up his face and groaning quietly. He snaked his arm around Sarah's waist and pulled her against him. "You're so far away."

She smiled as her eyes drifted shut and she inhaled his heady smell. "I'm right here."

He smoothed his hand over her bare bottom, gently squeezing. "So you are. My mistake." He nuzzled his way into her neck and she granted him access, even though it usually brought a fit of squealing. He peppered her skin with kisses that started soft and tentative but were now deeper and longer as their bodies pressed together.

"I usually don't like it if someone kisses my neck. After last night, you can kiss me wherever you want."

"It wasn't just last night. Earlier this morning was noteworthy, too."

She laughed quietly, but arched her back and hitched her leg up over his hip. Just thinking about it made her want him again. "It was wonderful."

He clasped her face and planted a kiss on her lips. "Thank you for everything last night."

"It's a little weird to say thank you for sex."

He shook his head and nudged at her nose with his own—such a sweet and tender gesture, it left her breathless. "No. I mean everything before we ended up in bed. You're just…"

She didn't want to be holding her breath, but she couldn't help it. Was he about to confess his feelings? Would he take her worry away and impart those three little words first?

He scanned her face, his eyes searching for something. "You're a miracle. I don't know how I got so lucky to have you and Oliver walk into my life, but I'm thankful. You've been there for me and I'm so appreciative."

She smiled wide, even though he hadn't relieved her of her greatest fear. "I like being there for you."

"I mean it, Sarah. I don't even want to think about the dark places my mind could have gone last night after everything with my mom. I've wasted so much time dreading that moment, worrying about what the truth would mean, but your presence made it all okay. You're like a magician."

A magician. A miracle. Both wonderful things to be called, but not quite what she was hoping for. It was hard to blame him. He'd been through so much with his family. It was no wonder that he was closed off, that he'd shored up his defenses so solidly that no woman had managed to make her way inside. She had to appreciate that he'd come so far since she'd met him. Maybe he needed a nudge. Maybe he needed to know that she wouldn't hurt him, that she would give her heart to him just as freely as she'd given her body.

Just do it. Just say it and let it come out. Open your heart. "I love you, Aiden." A warm wave hit her—contentment, satisfaction, accomplishment all rolled into one. This time she'd finally gotten it. She smiled and gazed into his eyes, but it became clear—within a few heartbeats—that something was wrong. His eyes weren't indifferent or angry…they were hurt. It wasn't at all what she'd expected. Of the many things she could've seen, that was not on the list of possible reactions to *I love you*.

Sixteen

I love you? No. This isn't happening.

Aiden had never before wanted so badly to be able to rattle off a string of words, but he couldn't. *I love you* was forever, and he wasn't ready for that. He was ready to ask if he could see her after their ten days were up, but the words she'd just said had ruined that possibility. There was only one good response, and he couldn't go there. "I don't take love lightly." In truth, he didn't take—or give—romantic love at all. He'd never told a woman he loved her. He'd never felt it. His relationship with Sarah was different, but they'd been caught in extraordinary circumstances and his feelings for Oliver were intertwined with his perception of her. Could it be love? His gut wasn't answering.

"I don't take it lightly either," Sarah pleaded. "But I love you. I know we haven't known each other for long, but this is what's in my heart. I had to say it."

Frustration nipped at him like an angry dog. Why was

she pushing this? Why did she have to take such a huge leap? He was racing to keep up, out of control, with no idea where or how this would end. "I have feelings for you, Sarah. And they're good feelings. I'm just not ready to go there yet. It's too soon." Did people fall in love in ten days? If they did, what happened to those people? Were they still in love a year later? What if everything between them faded and fizzled?

"It's not too soon for me. Some people fall in love in a minute. There is no timetable."

"But there is for us. You just spent the last ten days reminding me of a deadline. I don't like the idea of being forced into something." He hated his biting tone, but he saw her as his safe place, and she'd turned that inside out. She was sabotaging what was between them, just as she had in Miami. This time, she wasn't making a unilateral decision. She'd pulled him into this one and forced him to participate. Did she not see that he'd already taken big steps with her? He'd never spent more than three days with a woman.

"Forced? You made the first move last night." She sat up in bed and yanked the covers over her. "And you knew I was leaving tomorrow, but you took me to bed anyway, knowing that you didn't have an inkling of serious feelings for me?"

"Of course I knew you were leaving. You've spent every waking minute of our time together reminding me of it."

"And that made it easy to sleep with me. No pesky Sarah to worry about after tomorrow."

"That's not fair. I wanted you. I still want you." At least he could say that much without reservation.

Oliver yelped over the baby monitor. Aiden tossed back the comforter and pulled on his boxer shorts. "I'll get him. We'll have to finish talking about this later. I don't want to argue in front of the baby."

Sarah rolled away from him. "Honestly? I don't want to talk about it at all."

"Why not?"

"Because there's no coming back from what I just said to you."

She wasn't wrong about that.

Aiden stalked down the hall, his mind reeling. He'd been thinking he might invite Sarah to spend next weekend with them, and see how that went. He certainly hadn't been thinking about labels. Love hadn't crossed his mind. It wasn't even on the map.

He opened the door to Oliver's room. The little guy was standing, holding on to the top rail of his crib, unsteady on the mattress. He bounced up and down when he saw Aiden, squealing and grinning. He picked up Oliver and kissed him on the forehead, holding him close. Two labels he didn't have to question were that of father and son. What they shared was love. But he wasn't able to put a label on what he felt for Sarah. And if he told her what she wanted to hear, just to make her happy for now, and it later ended up hurting her, he'd never forgive himself. He might not be able to say *I love you, too*, but that was better than taking it back later.

He changed Oliver and brought him down to the kitchen, warming up a bottle and sitting with him on the sofa in the living room. He tried to read the rhythm of Sarah's footsteps upstairs—there was no telling what she was doing, but she was busy. Was she pacing the floor, angry with him because he'd let her down? Was she rethinking what she'd said? Was she doing the inevitable—packing up to leave? He wouldn't blame her if she were, no matter how much it might hurt. She was a vibrant and beautiful young woman. Any man in the world would be a fool to say no to her, making Aiden a class A idiot. Still, he couldn't lie to her. He couldn't say he loved her when he wasn't sure what it meant.

His loose plan of asking if she wanted to date, although tantamount to picking out china for him, would clearly not be enough for her. Not now.

I love you.

Yeah, I'm not sure. Can we just go out to dinner?

Starting on dramatically different pages wasn't a recipe for romantic success. It was a setup for disaster. She'd already been hurt by the guy she worked for. He wouldn't hurt her like that—he was different. So maybe he was back to where he'd thought he'd needed to be a few days ago—preserve the friendship and set aside romance.

Sarah was about to wear a rut in the hardwood floor of Aiden's guest room. *How could I have been so stupid?*

When it came right down to it, Aiden was a case of unrequited love. And although it stung like crazy, at least Sarah knew what it was. The heartache ahead had a name. A *label.* She could say with confidence, *I left because it was unrequited love. He wouldn't say it back to me and I'd already said it to him, so I had to leave. How does a girl come back from that?* Her friends would answer, *You don't come back from that. You leave. With your head held high and your dignity in place.* And Sarah could smile and nod, knowing she'd done the right thing. Even when the moments came when she was crumbling to dust on the inside, she would know she'd had no choice.

Oliver was another matter. She'd already been destroyed by the notion of leaving him, precisely her fear. His place in her heart would always be there. Their relationship was quite the opposite of unrequited. It was the purest love she'd ever known. Aside from her family's, Oliver's love was the only love she'd never doubted. She saw it on Oliver's face when she walked into his room in the morning or when he'd woken up from a nap. She felt it when he was upset and she held him close, the two of them clinging to each other. She lived and breathed their love when he laughed. Oliver's love had filled her heart for a month and its absence would leave an unimaginable void, and there wasn't anything to do about it. Oliver belonged with his father, and his father didn't love her.

She slumped down on the bench at the foot of the bed. "Now what?" she asked aloud. She couldn't go downstairs and talk about this more. It would only hurt. And she wasn't going to try to convince Aiden that he loved her. She wanted him to just love her. She didn't much like the idea of hiding out in her room until tomorrow. That left only one option, the one Aiden had so generously provided her with yesterday after deciding on the nanny—leave today.

She wasn't ready to say goodbye to Oliver, but the truth was that she'd never be ready. She could spend a lifetime preparing and it would never make it any easier.

Her phone beeped with a notification. She walked over to the bedside table and looked at the screen—it was an email, from Katie.

Sarah,
Despite the gaps in your financial forecast, Sylvia would still like to continue talks about acquiring Kama. Sylvia and I would like to come to Boston first thing Monday morning to tour your facility, look over designs for next year and discuss our options. Does 9 a.m. suit you? I know today's Saturday, but I need to know ASAP.
Best,
Katie

How many signs could Sarah get from the universe before she stopped fighting? Aiden hadn't returned *I love you*. Sylvia Hodge wanted her back in Boston, ready to talk business. And she'd set Oliver up for the life she wanted him to have. That meant Sarah needed to say goodbye, get on the next train and not look back.

She typed her reply.

Katie,
Thanks so much. Tell Sylvia I will see you both Monday morning. Looking forward to it.
Sarah

With no more time wasted on overthinking, she got out her suitcase and started packing. The sooner she got out, the better. Luckily, she didn't have much, so it only took a few minutes. She then hopped in the shower, cleaned up and dressed in the same old sundress she'd worn the day she met Aiden. That seemed like a lifetime ago.

As she took each step down the stairs, the tears threatened to take over. She imagined it was like trying to get out of the ocean when a storm has come up out of nowhere. The waves roll you back as you swim, the tide pulling just as hard, ocean spray in your face, but you keep going because you have to get to shore. You have to save yourself. For what, you aren't sure. You only know that it's your instinct to survive. You'll do anything to make it.

She and her suitcase reached the landing. She raised the handle, and rolled it toward the foyer.

Aiden's voice from the kitchen stopped her dead in her tracks. "You're leaving?"

Oliver was playing on the floor with some plastic bowls and wooden spoons.

She bit into her lower lip. *You can do this.* "Yes. I have to. I got an email from Sylvia Hodge's office. They need me in Boston ready to talk Monday morning. I need time to prepare. And you don't need me anymore, so I might as well get out of your hair and let you and Oliver enjoy your weekend."

"Sarah. We didn't even finish talking about everything." He came out from behind the kitchen island, but thankfully didn't touch her. He instead crossed his arms. "We're just going to leave it all unsaid?"

She forced a smile and an enthusiastic nod. She'd never felt less happy or eager to do anything. "I don't think we need to talk about it anymore. I get it, Aiden. I do. I'm not going to try to get you to say things that aren't in your heart. You didn't do anything wrong."

"I just wish you'd give me some time to wrap my head around it."

The thing was—she didn't need more time. She knew exactly how much she loved him. She felt it in the depths of her belly right now, a terrible burning. She knew exactly how bad it was going to hurt to step onto that elevator. She couldn't wait. She couldn't give him another chance. Aiden might never get to the place she needed him to get to. It wasn't his fault. He'd been deeply hurt by his past. And he'd always been very up-front—he needed space.

"It's okay. I shouldn't have said anything this morning. Just forget it." She rushed over to Oliver and crouched down, raising his face with the tip of her finger. "Goodbye, sweet…" her voice cracked into a million pieces. Her lip shook. Her chest convulsed. She couldn't say it. Her heart wouldn't let her. She leaned down and placed a single kiss on the top of his head, committing to memory his smell and the feel of his soft curls against her lips. She would miss that so much. Forever.

She straightened and turned away from Aiden. The tears were streaming down her face in a deluge and she couldn't let him know that he'd gotten to her like this. "I have to go. I'll miss my train."

"Are you sure about this?" he asked, doing the thing she'd dreaded—grasping her arm.

She didn't look back. She hid. "I'm sure."

"At least let me call down to John and have him take you to the station. Let me do that much. Just to say thank you for everything."

Don't fight him. Just go. Just walk out. Save yourself. She nodded. "Okay. Great. Thanks."

With that, she rushed to the elevator, jabbed the button and walked on board. She dropped her head as the door closed, her tears dotting the floor. She couldn't look up. She couldn't watch everything she'd ever wanted disappear.

Sarah went immediately into autopilot, putting on her sunglasses to hide her eyes and marching through the lobby outside. Luckily, John was always waiting for Aiden—this time it paid off for her.

"Ms. Daltrey. Penn Station?"

"Yes. John. Thanks." She climbed into the backseat, sucking in a trembling breath. *Just get me to the train. Then I'll be okay.*

Her phone beeped with a text from Aiden.

This is stupid. Come back. We should talk.

Words weren't enough this morning. Not sure what's different now.

I need time. I'm sorry.

It's okay.

She stopped herself from typing the words she wanted to. *I still love you even though you don't love me.*

"Ms. Daltrey?" John asked from the front seat. "I have

a message from Mr. Langford. He's asking me to bring you back to the house."

She blew out a breath. It was just like Aiden to snap his fingers and expect the world to conform to his wishes. "No. Please don't do that. Just pull over and drop me off and I'll get in a cab."

"Ma'am? I don't want to leave you, either."

Every sad feeling she'd had a few minutes ago was turning to frustration. "I'll text Mr. Langford. Please just keep driving."

She tapped out a message to Aiden.

Please don't put John in the middle of this. Let me go.

Waiting for Aiden's response was agony. She didn't want to argue. But she wasn't ready for the end, again.

Ok.

She tucked her phone into her bag. "All straightened out, John. It was just a misunderstanding."

"Oh, good. Okay. I'll have you at the station in no time."

"Great. The sooner, the better."

Seventeen

Day ten arrived with sunshine streaming through the windows and a giddy Oliver, full of energy and ready to take on the day. Right after breakfast, they'd started doing laps in the house. From the kitchen to the library to his office and back, Oliver walked while Daddy followed, holding his little hands to steady him. Oliver had discovered this new routine while they'd been playing last night before bed. Judging by the way he took to it and the enthusiasm with which he cruised along furniture, he'd be walking and running in a matter of days.

Aiden, however happy he was to share this milestone with Oliver, was dragging—no sleep and a gaping hole in your heart will do that to a guy.

Sarah was gone. And her absence was much more noticeable than Aiden had expected. The house felt strange and incomplete. Had it felt like this before she came along? He couldn't recall, exactly. It was quite different with Oliver there, but still, it wasn't the same without Sarah.

He missed everything about her—the way she hummed when she puttered around in the kitchen and her sweet smell when she walked past him. The way her face lit up when she laughed and the way she wouldn't let him get away with anything when she was mad. Memories shuffled through his mind—the day she managed to talk her way into one of the most secure office buildings in the world. She'd made his entire life turn on a dime that day, and done it in unflappable fashion. That night in the bathtub, when he'd first bonded with Oliver and Sarah had made it happen. That was also the night he'd caught her staring at him, the night he'd foolishly thought that seducing her would be like taking any other woman to bed. He'd relied on their ten-day deadline then. It made it easier for him to get what he wanted, no strings attached. Little did he know that Sarah was capable of tying up his heart and his head with those strings…and tugging them all the way back to Boston.

But what was he supposed to do? They were operating at different speeds. She was comfortable with bold strides. He needed to ease into it. He knew no other way.

His phone rang from the kitchen counter. His pulse picked up. Was it Sarah? He steered Oliver over and consulted the screen. Anna. Not the call he wanted, but maybe she could tell him to stop being such a wimp.

"Hey," Aiden said. "This is a surprise. It's a little early isn't it?"

"I figured you were already up with Oliver and I wanted to check in on you after the other night with Mom. How are you holding up?"

Aiden dragged a barstool around the kitchen island so he had a good view of Oliver, and sat down. "I'm doing fine. I've had years to stew over it. It's more of a relief than anything. And at least we can all get together now without it being hopelessly uncomfortable."

Anna blew out a breath. "Good. I'm glad you feel that way because I have something else I need to talk to you about. Jacob told me I should probably just butt out, and we kind of had a big argument about it, but I don't want to butt out. I can't not say something."

"What in the world are you talking about?"

"Sarah, Aiden. Don't you dare let her go back to Boston today without you two making a plan to keep seeing each other. I know how you are and I'm telling you right now that she's not like other women. She's a keeper, Aiden. I don't want you to blow it just because you've convinced yourself it's easier to play the field."

Aiden could only imagine what his face looked like right now—pure shock. Astonishment. "First off, why don't you tell me how you really feel? And second, how do you know there was anything going on between us?"

Anna huffed at what she apparently saw as Aiden's absurdity. "I saw the way you two were looking at each other the other night. And the minute that all of that stuff went down with Mom, she was the one you turned to. Right away. You didn't even hesitate. It's so obvious to me that you two are in love."

"How can you tell that from a look?"

"Am I wrong? There are feelings between you two, aren't there?"

"Well, yes, there are feelings between us. But that doesn't mean it's love. And besides, it's too late. She's already gone."

"What?" Anna shouted so loudly, she nearly blew out Aiden's eardrum.

"Careful or you'll go into labor."

"You let her leave? Why did you do that? Why would you be so stupid?"

Because she said she loved me and I couldn't say it back. The realization hit him, and the repercussions came at him just as hard. "It was moving too fast for me."

"The man who jumps out of airplanes thought it was moving too fast? Sounds to me like you're confused."

"Yeah. I guess I am. I just don't want to make a mistake. She means a lot to me. But I can't tell her I love her if I'm not sure. I don't even know how I'm supposed to know if it's really love. People always say that you'll know when it happens. Well, I don't know."

"Let me ask you this. How do you feel now that she's gone?"

"Horrible. Like somebody ripped my heart out of my chest."

"And what's the house like without her there?"

"Terrible. I'm thinking Oliver and I might need to move."

"And if you could do anything at all right now, what would you do?"

"Go see her. Apologize." *Oh God. I love her.* Aiden cast his sights down at Oliver, who was hitting the floor with a wooden spoon. *I really am an idiot. I'm a complete jerk.* He'd said to himself many times over the past ten days that he would never let Oliver go without. But in letting Sarah leave, he was not only depriving Oliver of the perfect mother, he was keeping himself from the one person who understood him and loved him despite his faults. Oliver had shown him unconditional love. But so had Sarah.

"Do you enjoy feeling like this?" Anna asked. "Because you know you can fix it."

"I can't fix it. I ruined it. She told me she loved me and I didn't say it back."

Anna gasped on the other end of the line.

"That's pretty much the end, isn't it?" His conscience

was impossibly heavy. He'd trampled all over the heart of the woman he loved. "I mean, how do I come back from that?"

"Groveling."

"Groveling?"

"It's the only thing that works. Flowers help. Jewelry. Chocolate. A gift certificate for a massage. But mostly groveling. You need to get your butt up to Boston and beg for her forgiveness. You need to tell her how you feel."

"You think it will work?"

"Not sure, but I think you'll regret it forever if you don't try. Jacob and I can be over in a half hour to watch the baby."

None of this will be right without Oliver. "No. It's okay. I'm taking him with me."

Sarah went into the Kama office Sunday morning. Although it was their headquarters, that word was generous—it was really just an old warehouse she'd been renting for the last year. Sleep last night had been pointless—too many painful things wreaking havoc in her head. Too many things running through her heart, like water through a sieve. She'd been so scared of what would happen if she got too close and now she knew how right she'd been to fear it. Losing Oliver and Aiden was the worst thing that had ever happened to her. No doubt about that.

She didn't bother flipping on the lights as she wound through the sewing room with its massive cutting tables, stacked high with boxes of inventory ready to ship. She went straight back to her office and got to work—the act of a woman invested in her own success, but it felt like an empty gesture. A show. More faking it. Her heart wasn't in it, as much as she might very well be standing on the precipice of great success. On the inside, she was

as empty as she'd ever been, which was a devastating realization. Her hard work was finally paying off, and she
felt horrible. She'd seen low moments, but not like this.

Not like last night, when she couldn't get a single minute of relief because her eyes were like a faucet. Her heart
had stubbornly chosen to ache and throb in her chest and
remind her with every pointless beat that the difference
between the love a person gives freely and the love they
receive in return is what ends up breaking us. This was
the second time she'd had to learn the lesson of how it
empties a person—giving and giving, never refilling the
tank. And she was as done as done could be. The fate of
her business felt as inconsequential as a speck of dust
floating in air. It was nothing worth holding on to if she
couldn't have what she'd truly invested in—Aiden and
Oliver.

But Aiden hadn't been able to go there. He just couldn't
say *I love you*. If only he knew—or cared—three little
words and she would've figured out a way to stay. She
would've told him that she'd meant it. She would've done
everything she could to make them all whole again, to
knit them into the family they could have been. But apparently, for a man wealthy beyond anything she ever
imagined, three words was too high a price to pay.

She tidied her office—going through the mail she'd
missed over the last week, filing away things, neaten-
ing stacks of paper. She made sure her computer screen
was free of smudges, and watered the pink orchid on her
desk. She did every mindless task she could come up
with, all in the interest of staying busy. If she couldn't
move forward, she could at least tread water. She could
keep her head above the rising tide. She had to fight back
her thoughts of her last night with Aiden, of the connection they'd shared. There was no doubt in her mind that
it had been more than sex that night. And she knew, deep

down, that Aiden knew it, too. He just couldn't admit it to himself. He was too wounded.

Tessa popped into view. "Morning," she said, stepping foot into the office.

Sarah jumped. "You scared me." She pressed her hand to her chest. Her heart was pounding. "What are you doing here? You didn't need to come in today. You should be at home relaxing. Tomorrow's a big day. I need you on top of your game."

A mischievous smile spread across her face. "I came by to let somebody in. He was pretty sure you weren't going to let him in on your own."

"What? Who?"

Just then, Aiden appeared in her doorway, Oliver in his arms. "I had to talk my way in. I needed to bring Oliver to you. He misses you. I miss you."

The grin on Tessa's face had only grown. "I'll leave you three alone. See you tomorrow."

Sarah walked out from behind her desk, in shock. Was this a dream? Were Aiden and Oliver a mirage? Surely a figment of her imagination couldn't have the pull on her that Aiden did right now. All she wanted to do was fling her arms around him and kiss him. Oliver reached for her. The minute she had him, Aiden's arms were around them both.

"Sarah, I'm here because I had to tell you in person that I love you."

"But…" Tears rolled down her face. How could she possibly cry more? "You don't have to do this. Don't feel like you have to say that to me. And you really shouldn't feel like you have to travel hours with a baby to say that to me in person."

"But I do have to do those things. I have to make it up to you. And I have to tell you the truth." He loosened his grip, to see her better. "I've been falling in love with you since the first night, when you put me in the bathtub with this little guy. It's grown so fast that I didn't know what it was. I couldn't see it. I don't know if I was afraid or confused or what, but the minute you left, I knew it wasn't right."

She nodded eagerly, feeling as though a weight had been lifted. Her hunch had been right. And it hadn't taken long for Aiden to see it, too. "I know it happened fast. I thought I was crazy to say that to you yesterday, but I had to. Especially after everything with your family." She studied his face, his blue eyes nearly taking her breath away. "I couldn't not tell you that I love you. You deserved to know."

He sighed and looped her hair behind her ear, caressing her cheek. "I've spent my whole life homesick for a home I never even knew. And you showed up out of nowhere, and made that home for me in ten days."

"Technically, it was nine."

A breathy laugh left his lips. "You showed me what love is. You opened up my closed-up heart. And that heart is going to shrivel up and die without you. The home you built isn't going to work without you."

"What are you saying, Aiden?"

"I'm saying that I love you and we have to find a way to make this work."

"But you're in New York. I'm here. How are we going to manage that? You don't even have a permanent nanny."

"I called Lily from the plane and convinced her to take the job. She's flying up here tomorrow morning to take care of Oliver while I go into the LangTel regional office downtown for a few hours."

Sarah wasn't sure she was hearing him correctly. "You're going to hang out in Boston? For how long?"

He shrugged. "Depends on what Sylvia Hodge tells you tomorrow. Then we'll figure it out. Anna said that if

Sylvia acquires Kama, she'll probably ask you to work out of New York so you're available for meetings and are more plugged in to the industry."

Sarah hadn't considered that. It was all still so new. "So we wait and see what happens tomorrow?"

"I was hoping Oliver and I can move in with you for a few days. I figure we'll put Lily in a hotel."

"I don't know. I need my space."

Aiden laughed and kissed the top of her head. "Darling, as long as you come back to me, you can have all the space you need."

Eighteen

For the third weekend in a row, Sarah was back in New York with Aiden and Oliver. She looked forward to these days more than anything, even when the back and forth was tiresome. Only one more week and the Kama office would move to Sylvia Hodge's Manhattan headquarters. She'd be in the city full-time. She, Aiden and Oliver would be together. Even though she and Aiden hadn't discussed their future, Sarah was more than content. It hadn't seemed necessary and her forcing of *I love you* had flopped—at least at first. Plus, Aiden was a complicated guy. Commitment wasn't easy for him. Just knowing that he loved her and wanted to be with her was enough for now.

Everything else workwise was already in place—when Sylvia decided to acquire Kama, it came together very fast. Last week, they'd moved everything into a new manufacturing space outside Boston. It was ten times bigger than the original facility and the air-conditioning worked—no small matter now that it was the middle of June. They'd hired ten new assembly people, three more employees to manage the warehouse. Tessa was overseeing the production facility, and she'd received a big fat raise for taking on her new responsibilities. Sarah couldn't have been any happier about being able to reward her for a job well done. The change also left much more time for Sarah to spend on designing, selecting fabrics and planning out the next several seasons. It was hard to believe, but everything on the work front was really coming together.

Saturdays at Aiden's were pretty low-key. Today had been no different, although they were anxiously awaiting a call from Jacob since Anna had gone into labor that morning. To pass the time, Sarah and Aiden had taken Oliver for a long walk, then grabbed some lunch. The baby had his nap after that, and they turned their dinner into a picnic up on the rooftop terrace. Now that it was nearly eight, Sarah was getting a bit of work done in Aiden's home office. Oliver was already in bed and Aiden had camped out with a book in the library.

Aiden's phone, which he'd left on the desk, rang. She glanced at the screen and grabbed it. "Oh my God. Aiden!" she yelled out. "It's Jacob. Get in here!" She answered the call. "Jacob? Aiden's in the other room. I figured I should answer. Is there news?"

"It's a girl," he said triumphantly. "Eight pounds, seven ounces. Twenty-one inches long. Big head of thick, black hair. She's beautiful."

Sarah loved hearing the good news, but Aiden was missing it. She got up from the desk to search for him. "Congratulations. I'm so happy. How's Anna?" She reached the library. No Aiden. *Weird.*

"She's tired, but she's doing great. We're both relieved

the baby's finally here and she's healthy. It's been such a rocky road."

"Oh, I know. She's your miracle baby. It's wonderful." Into the kitchen she traveled. Still no Aiden. "Do you have a name yet?"

"Grace. It's Anna's middle name."

Sarah glanced into the living room, which was also empty. "That's so beautiful. You must be so thrilled."

"I am, but I also have a million more phone calls to make. If you could tell Aiden, that'd be great. I'm sure Anna will want to speak to you both at some point."

Up the stairs Sarah went. "I don't know if you guys will be up for it, but we have Oliver's birthday party next Saturday."

"Oh, right. We'll have to see how it goes, I guess. We might need to call you for some baby advice."

"Absolutely no problem. Whatever you need. Love to all three of you. Can't wait to see her." She ended the call, but didn't dare yell now that she was in the hall. She'd wake Oliver. Where in the world was Aiden?

The door to his bedroom was closed. Now that they'd been cohabitating for nearly a month, she didn't hesitate to open it. But the knob wouldn't turn. It was locked.

She leaned against the door, but heard nothing. She rapped quietly and waited. She couldn't text him—she had his phone. She knocked again. Finally, he answered.

"Hey," he said, seeming flustered. He raked his hand through his hair, poking his head through the narrow opening he'd left.

"Your sister had a baby girl. Her name is Grace. That's what's up. Where have you been?"

His shoulders dropped. "Damn. I can't believe I missed that call. That's a bummer. Is everything okay?"

"Everything's great. I told them you send your best." She tried to peek into his room, but could see nothing.

"What are you doing in there? Can I come in?" He was behaving so strangely.

"I'm working on something. A surprise. But it's not ready."

She laughed quietly, curious what he was up to. Her birthday wasn't until October. "Like that's not cryptic. Do you want me to go away?"

"No. No. It's okay. I was going to call you up in a minute anyway. Just close your eyes and I'll lead you to the bed."

"If that's where we're going, it's not a surprise. Not that I won't enjoy it immensely." She elbowed him in the stomach, but he didn't take the joke. He was dead serious, so she decided to follow orders.

"Just a minute," he said when she was seated on the bed. "Be right back."

With her eyes closed, she listened for clues. He started singing. She'd never heard Aiden sing. Not once.

"How's it going in there?" she asked.

"You're so impatient." His voice was close—as if he were right next to her. He took her hand and she opened her eyes. "Ready?" He had a huge grin on his face.

"Yes." She trailed behind him into the bathroom. The lights were off. The marble countertops were covered in an array of lit candles. "Ooh. Bath night. So romantic."

"I had to make it romantic. For you."

She wrapped her arms around his waist, and he planted a soft and sensuous kiss on her lips. "That's adorable. I love that you made an extra effort for our Saturday night together."

He kissed her again, on her cheek, beneath her ear, on that extrasensitive spot on her neck. "It's more special than that."

Again, with the clues and mysterious phrasings. His kisses, however amazing, weren't helping. They made it difficult to think straight. "What kind of special?"

He cupped the side of her face and caressed her cheek with his thumb. "You're the best thing that's ever happened to me. I don't want to let you go."

Let me go? Oh my God. She clapped her hand over her mouth. "Aiden. Are you?"

"Shh. Just let me ask." He plucked a washcloth from the counter. A blue Tiffany box was beneath it. He popped it open, smiling wide and presenting her with the most gorgeous diamond ring she'd ever seen. "I love you so much. I want you to be my wife and Oliver's mother. Will you marry me?"

She blinked away tears, her heart about to burst from pure joy. "Yes. Of course." He placed the ring on her finger, and she popped up onto her toes, kissing him hard before stealing the chance to admire the diamond. "It's so gorgeous. Did you tell the people at Tiffany you were going to ask me in the bathroom?"

He laughed. "No. Do you know why I chose this room?"

She shrugged. "Because you like taking a shower with me?"

"That's part of it, but not the real reason." He took her left hand, straightening the ring. "That first night we gave Oliver a bath was the beginning of our life together. As a family. I wanted to acknowledge the start before we step into our future."

Tears welled again. "That is the sweetest thing ever."

"That was also the first time I caught you staring at me. That was sort of a big deal."

She swatted his arm. "I can't help it. You're just way too hot." Whatever she'd done to be lucky enough to have Aiden, she was glad she'd done it.

He cranked the faucet on the tub and turned his attention to her top, lifting it over her head. His heavenly lips skimmed her shoulder. "I can't wait to get in this bathtub with you and make love to you all night and talk about our future together."

Their future together. "Now I don't have to worry about the perfect guy walking into my life. I found him."

"Actually, I'm pretty sure you walked into his."

* * * * *

If you liked this story of a wealthy CEO
tamed by the love of the right woman,
pick up these other novels from
Karen Booth.

THAT NIGHT WITH THE CEO
PREGNANT BY THE RIVAL CEO
THE CEO DADDY NEXT DOOR
THE BEST MAN'S BABY

Available now from Mills & Boon Desire!

***

And don't miss the next
BILLIONAIRES AND BABIES *story*
FALLING FOR HIS WIFE
by USA TODAY bestselling author Kat Cantrell
Available May 2017!

***

He stepped in closer and whispered in her ear, "Outside."

For a second, neither of them moved. She could feel the heat of his body and she had an almost overwhelming urge to kiss the finger resting against her lips.

What was it about this man that turned her into a schoolgirl with a crush? She still had no idea what he did in his spare time or whether or not it broke any state or federal laws. And there was the unavoidable fact that acting on any lust would be a conflict of interest.

They were actively on a case, for crying out loud.

So instead of leaning into his touch or wrapping her arms around his waist and pulling him in tight, she nodded and pulled away.

It was harder than she thought it would be.

PRIDE AND PREGNANCY

BY
SARAH M. ANDERSON

First Published in Great Britain 2017
By Mills & Boon, an imprint of HarperCollins*Publishers*
1 London Bridge Street, London, SE1 9GF

© 2017 Sarah M. Anderson

ISBN: 978-0-263-92814-3

51-0417

Printed and bound in Spain
by CPI, Barcelona

Sarah M. Anderson may live east of the Mississippi River, but her heart lies out west. *A Man of Privilege* won an *RT Book Reviews* 2012 Reviewers' Choice Best Book Award. *The Nanny Plan* was a 2016 RITA® Award winner for Contemporary Romance: Short.

Sarah spends her days talking with imaginary cowboys and billionaires. Find out more about Sarah's heroes at www.sarahmanderson.com and sign up for the new-release newsletter at www.eepurl.com/nv39b.

To Dorliss Jones and Lynn Orr,
who were wonderful next-door neighbors
to my grandmother and have read every book.
You've been asking for Yellow Bird
for years—so here he is!

One

"Judge Jennings?"

Caroline looked up, but instead of seeing her clerk, Andrea, she saw a huge bouquet of flowers.

"Good Lord," Caroline said, standing to take in the magnitude of the bouquet. Andrea was completely invisible behind the mass of roses and lilies and carnations and Caroline couldn't even tell what else. It was, hands-down, the biggest bunch of flowers she'd ever seen. Andrea needed two hands to carry it. "Where did those come from?"

Because Caroline couldn't imagine anyone sending her flowers. She'd only been at her position as a judge in the Eighth Circuit Court in Pierre, South Dakota, for two months. She had made friends with her staff—Leland, the gruff bailiff; Andrea, her perky clerk; Cheryl, the court reporter who rarely smiled. Caroline had met her neighbors—nice folks who kept to themselves. But at no time had she come into contact with anyone who would send her *this*.

In fact, now that she thought about it, she couldn't imagine anyone sending her flowers, period. She hadn't left behind a boyfriend in Minneapolis who missed her. She hadn't had a serious relationship in…okay, she wasn't going to go into that right now.

For a frivolous moment, she wished the flowers were from a lover. But a lover would be a distraction from the job and she was still establishing herself here.

"It took two men to deliver," Andrea said, her voice muffled by the sheer number of blooms. "Can I set it down?"

"Oh! Of course," Caroline said, clearing off a spot on her desk. The vase was massive—the size of a dinner plate in circumference. Caroline hadn't gotten a lot of flowers over the course of her life. So she could say with reasonable confidence that the arrangement Andrea was carefully lowering onto her desk was more flowers than she had ever seen in one place—excepting her parents' funerals, of course.

She knew her mouth had flopped open, but she seemed powerless to get it closed. "Tell me there was a card."

Andrea disappeared back into the antechamber before returning with a card. "It's addressed to you," the clerk said, clearly not believing Caroline would receive these flowers, either.

Caroline was too stunned to be insulted. "Are you sure? There has to have been a mistake." What other explanation could there be?

She took the card from Andrea and opened the envelope. The flowers had been ordered from an internet company and the message was typed. "Judge Jennings—I look forward to working with you. An admirer," was all it said.

Caroline stared at the message, a sinking feeling of dread creeping over her. An unsolicited gift from a secret admirer was creepy enough. But that's not what this was, and she knew it.

Caroline took her job as a judge seriously. She did not make mistakes. Or, at the very least, she rarely made mistakes. Perfectionism might be a character flaw, but it also had made her a fine lawyer and now made her a good judge.

Once she'd found her footing as a prosecutor, she'd had an impeccable record. When she'd been promoted to judge, she prided herself on being fair in her dealings on the bench, and she was pleased that others seemed to agree with her. The promotion that had brought her to Pierre was a vote of confidence she did not take lightly.

Whoever would spend this much money to send her flowers without even putting his or her name on the card wasn't simply an admirer. Sure, there was always the possibility that someone unhinged had developed an obsession. Every time she read about a judge being stalked back to his or her house—or when a judge and her family in Chicago had been murdered—Caroline resolved to do better with her personal safety. She double-checked the locks on doors and windows, carried pepper spray, and had taken a few self-defense classes. She made smart choices and worked to eliminate stupid mistakes.

But Caroline didn't think this bouquet was from a stalker. When she'd accepted this position, a lawyer from the Justice Department named James Carlson had contacted her. She knew who he was—the special prosecutor who had been chasing down judicial corruption throughout the Great Plains. He'd put three judges in prison and forcibly retired several others from the bench after his investigations.

Carlson hadn't given her all of the details, but he had warned her that she might be approached to take bribes to throw cases—and he'd warned her what would happen if she accepted those bribes.

"I take these matters of judicial corruption seriously," he had told her in an email. "My wife was directly harmed by a corrupt judge when she was younger, and I will not tolerate anyone who shifts the balance on the scales of justice for personal gain."

Those words came back to her now as Caroline continued to stare at the flowers and then at the unsigned note. Those flowers were trying to tip the scale, all right.

Damn it. Of course she knew that people in South Dakota would not be less corrupt than they were in Minnesota. People were people the world over. But despite Carlson's warning, she'd held out hope that he was wrong. He had stressed in his email that he didn't know who was buying off judges. The men he'd prosecuted had refused to turn on their benefactors—which, he had concluded, meant they either didn't know who was paying the bills or they were afraid.

Part of Caroline didn't want to deal with this. Unknown individuals compromising the integrity of the judicial system—that was nothing but a headache at best. She wanted to keep believing in an independent court and the impartiality of the law. Short of that, she didn't want to get involved in a messy, protracted investigation. There was too much room for error, too much of a chance that her mistakes might come back to haunt her.

But another part of her was excited. What this was, she thought as she stepped around her desk to look at the flowers from a different angle, was a case without a resolution. There were perpetrators, there were victims—there was a motive. A crime needed to be solved and justice needed to be served. Wasn't that why she was here?

"How long do we have before the next session starts?"

she asked, returning to her chair and calling up her email. She had no proof that this overabundance of flowers had anything to do with Carlson's corruption case—but she had a hunch, and sometimes a hunch was all a woman needed.

"Twenty minutes. Twenty-five before the litigants get restless," Andrea answered. Caroline glanced up at the older woman. Andrea was staring at the bouquet with an intense longing that Caroline understood.

"There's no way I can keep all of these," she said, searching for Carlson's name and pulling up his last email. "Feel free to take some of them home, decorate the office—strew rose petals from here to your car?"

She and Andrea laughed together. "I think I will," the clerk said, marching out of the office in what Caroline could only assume was a quest to find appropriate containers.

Caroline reviewed the emails she and James Carlson had exchanged before she opened a reply and began to type. Because one thing was clear—if this were some nefarious organization reaching out to her, she was going to need backup.

Lots of backup.

Sometimes, Tom Yellow Bird thought, the universe had a sense of humor.

What other explanation could there be when, the very morning he was scheduled to testify in the court of the Honorable Caroline Jennings, he had received an email from his friend James Carlson, informing him that the new judge, one Honorable Caroline Jennings, had received a suspicious bouquet of flowers and was concerned it might be connected to their ongoing investigation into judicial corruption in and around Pierre, South Dakota?

It would be funny if the situation weren't so serious, he

thought as he took a seat near the back of the courtroom. This trial was for bank robbery, and Tom, operating in his capacity as an FBI agent, had tracked down the perpetrator and arrested him. The robber had had the bank bags in his trunk and marked bills in his wallet. A cut-and-dried case.

"All rise," the bailiff intoned as the door at the back of the courtroom opened. "The court of the Eighth Judicial Circuit, criminal division, is now in session, the Honorable Caroline Jennings presiding."

Tom had heard it all before, hundreds of times. He rose, keeping his attention focused on the figure clad in black that emerged. Another day, another judge. Hopefully she wasn't easily bought.

"Be seated," Judge Jennings said. The courtroom was full so it wasn't until other people took their seats as she mounted the bench that Tom got his first good look at her.

Whoa.

He blinked and then blinked again. He had expected a woman—the name Caroline was a giveaway—but he hadn't expected *her*. He couldn't stop staring.

She took her seat and made eye contact across the room with him, and time stopped. Everything stopped. His breath, his pulse—everything came to a screeching halt as he stared at the Honorable Caroline Jennings.

He'd never seen her before—he knew that for certain because he'd remember her. He'd remember this *pull*. Even at this distance, he thought he saw her cheeks color, a delicate blush. Did she feel it, too?

Then she arched an eyebrow in what was a clear challenge. Crap. He was still standing, gawking like an idiot, while the rest of the court waited. Leland cracked a huge smile, and the court reporter looked annoyed. The rest of the courtroom was starting to crane their necks so they could see the delay.

So he took his seat and tried to get his brain to work again. Caroline Jennings was the judge on this case and she was his assignment from Carlson—nothing more. Any attraction he might feel for her was irrelevant. He had testimony to give and a corruption case to solve, and the job always came first.

Carlson's email had come late this morning, so Tom hadn't had time to do his research. That was the only reason Judge Jennings had caught him off guard.

Because Judge Jennings was at least twenty years younger than he had anticipated. Everyone else who had sat on that bench had tended to be white, male and well north of fifty years old.

Maybe that was why she seemed so young, although she was no teenager. She was probably in her thirties, Tom guessed. She had light brown hair that was pulled back into a low ponytail—but it wasn't severely scraped away from her face. Instead, her hair looked like it had a natural wave and she let it frame her features, softening the lines of her sharp cheekbones. She wore a simple pair of stud earrings—diamonds or reasonable fakes, he noticed when she turned her head and they caught the light. Her makeup was understated and professional, and she wore a lace collar on top of her black robe.

She was, he realized, *beautiful*. Which was an interesting observation on his part.

He had no problems noting the physical beauty of men or women. For Tom, the last ten years had been one long observation of the human condition. Looking at an attractive person was like studying fine art. Even if a woman's physical attributes didn't move him, he could still appreciate her beauty.

But his visceral reaction to a woman in shapeless judge's robes was not some cerebral observation of conventional beauty. It was a punch to the gut. When was the last time he'd felt that unmistakable spark?

Well, he knew the answer to that. But he wouldn't let thoughts of Stephanie break free of the box in which he kept them locked up tight. He wouldn't think about it now. Maybe not ever.

He sat back and did what he did best—he watched and waited. Judge Caroline Jennings ran an efficient courtroom. When Lasky, the defense lawyer, started to grandstand, she cut him off. She wasn't confrontational, but she wasn't cowed by anyone.

As he waited for his name to be called, Tom mentally ran back through the email Carlson had sent him. Caroline Jennings was an outsider, appointed to fill the seat on the bench left vacant after Tom had arrested the last judge.

She was from Minneapolis—which was a hell of a long way from South Dakota. In theory, she had no connection with local politics—or lobbyists. That didn't mean she was clean. Whoever was pulling the strings in the state would be interested in making friends with the new judge.

Once, Tom would've been encouraged by the fact that she had already contacted Carlson about an unusual flower delivery. Surely, the reasoning went, if she was already willing to identify such gifts as suspicious, she was an honest person.

Tom wasn't that naive anymore. He didn't know who was buying off judges, although he had a few guesses. He couldn't prove his suspicions one way or the other. But he did know that whatever group—or groups—was rigging the courts in his home state, they played deep. He wouldn't put it past anyone in this scenario to offer up a beautiful, fresh-faced young judge as a mole—or a distraction.

"The prosecution calls FBI Special Agent Thomas Yellow Bird to the stand."

Tom snapped to attention, standing and straightening his tie. He should've been paying more attention to the trial at hand than musing about the new judge. The prosecutor had warned him that this particular defense lawyer liked to put members of law enforcement on the spot.

As he moved to the front of the room, he could feel Judge Jennings's gaze upon him. He didn't allow himself to look back. He kept his meanest gaze trained on the accused, enjoying the way the moron shrank back behind his lawyer. It didn't matter how intriguing—yes, that was the right word. It didn't matter how *intriguing* Judge Caroline Jennings was—Tom had to see justice served on the man who'd pulled a gun on a bank teller and made off with seven thousand dollars and change.

All the same, Tom wanted to look at her. Would she still have that challenge on her face? Or would he see suspicion? He was used to that. He'd been called inscrutable on more than one occasion—and that was by people who knew him. Tom had a hell of a poker face, which was an asset in his line of work. People couldn't figure him out, and they chose to interpret their confusion as distrust.

Or would he see something else in her eyes—the same pull he'd felt when she'd walked into this courtroom? Would she still have that delicate blush?

Smith, the prosecutor, caught Tom's eye and gave him a look. Right. Tom had a job to do before he dug into the mystery that was Caroline Jennings.

Leland swore Tom in, and he took his seat on the witness stand. Roses, he thought, not allowing himself to look in her direction. She smelled like roses, lush and in full bloom.

Smith, in a forgettable brown suit that matched his equally

forgettable name, asked Tom all the usual questions—how he had been brought in on the case, where the leads had taken the investigation, how he had determined that the accused was guilty of the crime, how the arrest had gone down, what the accused had said during questioning.

It was cut-and-dried, really. He had to keep from yawning.

Satisfied, Smith said, "Your witness," and returned to his seat.

The defense lawyer didn't do anything for a moment. He continued to sit at his table, reviewing his notes. This was a tactic Tom had seen countless times, and he wasn't about to let the man unnerve him. He waited. Patiently.

"Counsel, your witness," Judge Jennings said, an edge in her voice. Tom almost smiled at that. She was not as patient as she'd seemed.

Then the defense lawyer stood. He took his time organizing his space, taking a drink—every piddling little thing a lawyer could do to stall.

"Today, Counselor," Judge Jennings snapped.

She got a lawyer's smile for that one before Lasky said, "Of course, Your Honor. Agent Yellow Bird, where were you on the evening of April twenty-seventh, the day you were supposedly tracing the bills stolen from the American State Bank of Pierre?"

The way he said it—drawing out the *Yellow Bird* part and hitting the *supposedly* with extra punch—did nothing to improve Tom's opinion of the man. If this guy was trying to make Tom's Lakota heritage an issue, he was in for a rude awakening.

Still, Tom was under oath and he responded, "I was off duty," in a level voice. This wasn't his first time on the stand. He knew how this gotcha game was played, and he wasn't going to give this jerk anything to build off.

"Doing what?" That smile again.

Tom let the question linger in the air just long enough. Smith roused out of his stunned stupor and shouted, "Objection, Your Honor! What Agent Yellow Bird does in his free time is of no importance to this court."

The defense attorney turned his attention to the judge, that oily smile at full power. "Your Honor, I intend to show that what Agent Yellow Bird does on his own time directly compromises his ability to do his job."

What a load of bull. That perp was guilty of robbing a bank, and his defense team was throwing everything and the kitchen sink at the prosecutor's witnesses in an effort to throw the trial. Tom knew it, the prosecutor knew it and the defense attorney definitely knew it.

But none of that mattered. All that mattered was the opinion of Judge Caroline Jennings. She cleared her throat, which made Tom look at her. Then she leaned forward, elbows on her desk. "How so, Counselor?"

"Your Honor?"

"You're obviously building toward something. My time is valuable—as is yours, I assume. Someone's paying the bills, right?"

It took everything Tom had not to burst out laughing at that—but he kept all facial muscles on complete lockdown.

The defense lawyer tried to smile, but Tom could tell the man was losing his grip. Clearly, he'd expected Judge Jennings to be an easy mark. "If I could ask the question, I'd be able to demonstrate—"

"Because it sounds like you're fishing," Judge Jennings interrupted. "What illegal activity are you going to accuse Agent Yellow Bird of?" She turned her attention to Tom and there it was again—that *pull*. "Any crimes you'd like to admit to, just to save us all the time?"

Tom notched an eyebrow at her, unable to keep his lips

from twitching. "Your Honor, the only crime I'm guilty of is occasionally driving too fast."

Something changed in her eyes—deepened. He hoped like hell it was appreciation. All he knew was that he appreciated that look. "Yes," she murmured, her soft voice pouring oil on the fire that was racing through his body. "South Dakota seems made for speeding."

Oh, hell, yeah—he'd like to gun his engine and let it run right about now.

She turned her attention back to the attorney. "Are you going to make the argument that violating speed limits compromises an FBI agent's ability to investigate a crime?"

"Prostitutes!" the flustered lawyer yelled, waving a manila envelope around in the air. "He patronizes *prostitutes*!"

An absolute hush fell over the courtroom—which was saying something, as it hadn't been loud to begin with.

Shit. How had this slimeball found out about *that*?

"Your Honor!" Smith shot out of his chair, moving with more animation than Tom would have given him credit for. "That has nothing to do with a bank robbery!"

This was ridiculous, but Tom knew how this game was played. If he displayed irritation or looked nervous, it'd make him look shifty—which was exactly what the defense wanted. So he did—and said—nothing. Not a damn thing.

But his jaw flexed. He was not ashamed of his after-hours activities, but if Judge Jennings let this line of questioning go on, it could compromise some of his girls—and those girls had been compromised enough.

"That's a serious accusation," Judge Jennings said in a voice that was so cold it dropped the temperature in the courtroom a whole ten degrees. "I assume you have proof?"

"Proof?" the lawyer repeated and waved the manila envelope in the air. "Of course I have proof. I wouldn't waste the court's valuable time if I couldn't back it up."

"Let me see."

The defense lawyer paused—which proved to be his undoing.

Judge Jennings narrowed her gaze and said, "Counselor Lasky, if you have evidence that Agent Yellow Bird patronizes prostitutes—*and* that somehow compromises his ability to trace stolen bills—I'd suggest you produce it within the next five seconds or I will hold you in contempt of this court. Care to start a tab at five hundred dollars?"

Not that Tom would admit this in a court of law, but Caroline Jennings had just taken that spark of attraction and fanned it into a full-fledged flame of desire, because the woman was amazing. Simply *amazing*.

Lasky only hesitated for a second before he strode forward and handed the manila envelope over to Judge Jennings. She pulled out what looked to be some grainy photos. Tom guessed they'd been pulled from a security camera, but at this angle he couldn't see who was in the pictures or where they might have been taken.

He knew what they weren't pictures of—him in flagrante delicto with hookers. Having dinner with hookers, maybe. He did that all the time. But last he checked, buying a girl dinner wasn't illegal.

Even so, that the defense lawyer had the pictures was not good. Tom had a responsibility to those girls and his tribe. But more than that, he had an obligation to the FBI to make sure that what he did when he was off the clock didn't compromise the pursuit of justice. And if Judge Jennings let this line of questioning go on, Tom's time at the truck stops would be fair game for every single defense attorney in the state. Hell, even if this criminal wasn't found guilty, another defense lawyer would try the same line of attack, hoping to be more successful.

"Your Honor," Smith finally piped up into the silence, "this entire line of questioning is irrelevant to the case at hand. For all the court knows, he was meeting with informants!"

Not helping, Tom thought darkly, although again, he didn't react. If people suspected those girls were turning informant, they'd be in even more danger.

Judge Jennings ignored Smith. "Mr. Lasky, as far as I can tell, this is proof that Agent Yellow Bird eats meals with other people."

"Who are known prostitutes!" Lasky crowed, aiming for conviction but nailing desperation instead.

Smith started to object again, but Judge Jennings raised a hand to cut him off. "That's it? That's all you've got? He ate—" She turned to face Tom and held out a photo. "Is this dinner or lunch?"

Tom recognized the Crossroads Truck Stop immediately—that was Jeannie. "Dinner."

"He ate dinner with a woman? Did she launder the stolen money? Drive the getaway car? Was she the inside woman?"

"Well—no," Lasky sputtered. "She doesn't have anything to do with this case!" The second the words left his mouth, he realized what he'd said, and his entire face crumpled in defeat.

"You've got that right." Amazingly, Judge Jennings sounded more disappointed than anything else, as if she'd expected Lasky to put up a better fight. "Anything else you have to add?"

Lasky slumped and shook his head.

"Your Honor," Smith said, relief all over his face, "move to strike the defense's comments from the record."

"Granted." She fixed a steely gaze on Lasky.

Tom realized he'd never seen such a woman as Judge Jennings—especially not one for whom he'd felt that spark. He wanted nothing more than to chase that fire, keep fanning those flames. Stephanie would have wanted him to move on—he knew that. But no one else had ever caught his attention like this, and he wasn't going to settle for anything less than everything. So he'd stayed faithful to his late wife and focused on his job.

Except for now. Except for Caroline Jennings.

There was one problem with this unreasonable attraction.

She was his next assignment. Damn it.

"Agent Yellow Bird, you may step down," she said to him.

Tom made damn sure to keep his movements calm and even. He didn't gloat and he didn't strut. Looking like he'd gotten away with something would undermine his position of authority, so he stood straight and tall and, without sparing a glance for the defense attorney or his client, Tom walked out of the courtroom.

There. His work on the bank robbery case was done. Which meant one thing and one thing only.

Caroline Jennings was now his sole focus.

He was looking forward to this.

Two

As Caroline headed out into the oppressive South Dakota heat at the end of the day, she knew she should be thinking about who had sent the flowers. Or about James Carlson's brief reply to her email saying he had contacted an associate, who would be in touch. She should be thinking about the day's cases. Or tomorrow's cases.

At the very least, she should be thinking about what she was going to eat for dinner. She had been relying heavily on carryout for the last couple of months, because she hadn't finished unpacking yet. She should be formulating her plan of attack to get the remaining boxes emptied so she could have a fully functional kitchen again by this weekend at the latest and make better food choices.

She wasn't thinking about any of those things. Instead, all she could think about was a certain FBI agent with incredible eyes.

Thomas Yellow Bird. She shivered just thinking of the

way his gaze had connected with hers across the courtroom. Even at that distance, she'd felt the heat behind his gaze. Oh, he was intense. The way he'd kept his cool under fire when that defense attorney had gone after him? The way he'd glared at the accused? Hell, the way he'd let the corner of his mouth twitch into a smile that had threatened to melt her faster than ice cream on a summer day when he'd said he was guilty of speeding?

So dangerous. Because if he could have this sort of effect on her with just a look, what would he be capable of with his hands—or without an audience?

She hadn't had the time or inclination to investigate the dating scene in the greater Pierre area. She assumed the pool of eligible men would be considerably smaller than it was in Minneapolis—not that she'd dated a lot back home. It'd been low on her priority list, both there and here. Messy relationships were just that—messy. Dating—and sex—left too much room for mistakes, the kind she'd dodged once already.

No, thank you. She did not need to slip up and get tied to a man she wasn't even sure she wanted to marry. Her career was far more important than that.

Besides, she spent most of her time with lawyers and alleged criminals. Her bailiff was married. It wasn't like an attractive, intelligent man she could date without a conflict of professional interest just showed up in her courtroom every day.

Except for today. Maybe.

Because there was that small matter of whether or not he patronized prostitutes. That was a deal breaker.

Lost in thought, she rounded the corner of the courthouse and pulled up short. Because an attractive, intelligent man—FBI Special Agent Thomas Yellow Bird—was leaning on a sleek muscle car parked two slots down from her Volvo. Her nipples tightened immediately, and only one thing could soothe them.

Him.

She shook that thought right out of her head. Good Lord, a man shouldn't look this sinful—and in those sunglasses? He was every bad-boy fantasy come to life. But she'd watched him on the stand and seen flashes of humor underneath his intense looks and stoic expressions—and that? *That* was what made him truly sexy.

Was secretly lusting after an FBI agent in a great suit a conflict of interest? God, she hoped not. Because that suit was amazing on him.

"Agent Yellow Bird," she said when he straightened. "This is a surprise."

One corner of his mouth kicked up as he pulled his sunglasses off. "Not a bad one, I hope."

It wasn't like they'd had a personal conversation in court today. There'd been several feet of plywood between them. She'd been wearing her robes. Everything had been mediated through Lasky and Smith. Cheryl had recorded every word.

Here? None of those barriers existed.

"That depends," she answered honestly. Because if he were going to ask her out, it could be a very good thing. But if this was about something else…then maybe not so much.

His gaze drifted over her, a leisurely appraisal that did nothing for Caroline's peace of mind right now. She'd thought she'd been imagining that appraisal in the courtroom when she'd met his gaze across the crowded courtroom and everything about her—her clothes, her skin—had suddenly felt too tight and too loose at the same time.

No, no—not lusting after him. Lust was a weakness

and weakness was a risk. The heat flooding her body had more to do with the July sun than this man.

As his gaze made its way back up to her face, a look of appreciation plain to see, she knew she wasn't imagining *this*. When he spoke, it was almost a relief. "I wanted to thank you for having my back today."

She waved away this statement, glad to have something to focus on other than his piercing eyes. "Just doing my job. Last time I checked, eating dinner wasn't a conflict of interest." Unlike this conversation. Maybe. "I have no desire in being perceived as weak on the bench. I run a tight ship."

"So I noticed."

This would be a wonderful time for him to assure her that he didn't patronize prostitutes—in fact, it'd be great if he didn't eat dinner with them at all. She tried to keep in mind what Smith had said in his objections—perhaps Agent Yellow Bird had been meeting with informants or some other reasonable explanation that could be tied directly to his job.

Strangely, she wasn't feeling reasonable about Agent Yellow Bird right now. She steeled her resolve. She couldn't be swayed by a gorgeous man in a great suit any more than she could be influenced by cut flowers. Not even loyalty could corrupt her. Not anymore.

Everything about him—his gaze, his manner—was intense. And, at least right now, they were on the same side. She'd hate to be a criminal in his sights.

"Well," she said, feeling awkward about this whole encounter.

"Well," he agreed. He shoved off his car—an aggressive-looking black thing with a silver stripe on the hood that screamed *power*—and extended his hand. His suit jacket shifted, and she caught a glimpse of his gun. "We haven't been formally introduced. I'm Tom Yellow Bird."

"Tom." She hesitated before slipping her palm into his. This didn't count as a conflict of interest, right? Of course not. This was merely a...professional courtesy. Yes, that was it. "Caroline Jennings."

That got her a real smile—one that took him from intensely handsome to devastatingly so. Her knees weakened—weakened, for God's sake! It only got worse when he said, "Caroline," in a voice that was closer to reverence than respectability as his fingers closed around hers.

A rush of what felt like electricity passed from where her skin met his, so powerful that Caroline jolted. Images flashed through her mind of him pulling her in closer, his mouth covering hers, his hands covering...

"Sorry," she said, pulling her hand back. She knew she was blushing fiercely, but she was going to blame that on the heat. "I generate a lot of static electricity." Which was true. In the winter, when the air was dry and she was walking on carpeting.

It was at least ninety-four out today, with humidity she could swim in. She was so hot that sweat was beginning to trickle down her back.

He notched an eyebrow at her, and she got the feeling he was laughing. But definitely on the inside, because his mouth didn't move from that cocky half grin.

Her breasts ached, and she didn't think she could blame that on the sun. She was flushed and desperately needed to get the hell out of her skirt suit to cool down. What she wouldn't give for a swim in a cool pool right now.

Alone. Definitely alone. Not with Agent Tom Yellow Bird. Nope.

"About the flowers," Tom said, looking almost regretful about bringing up the subject as he leaned back against his spotless car.

Caroline recoiled. "What?" It wasn't as if the fact that she'd received the bouquet wasn't common knowledge—it was. Everyone in the courthouse knew, thanks to Andrea passing out roses to anyone who'd take some. Leland had taken a huge bunch home for his wife. Even Cheryl had taken a few, favoring Caroline with a rare smile. Caroline had left the remaining few blooms in her office. She didn't want them in her house.

Had Agent Yellow Bird sent them? Was this whole conversation—the intense looks, the cocky grins—because he was trying to butter her up?

Crap, what if Lasky had been right? What if Agent Tom Yellow Bird was crooked and prostitutes were just the tip of the iceberg?

Suddenly her blood was running cold. She moved to step past him. "The flowers were lovely. But I'm not interested."

Damn, she was tough.

"Whoa," Tom said, holding his hands up in the universal sign of surrender. "I didn't send them."

"I'm sure," Caroline murmured, stepping around him and heading for her car as if he suddenly smelled.

"Caroline," he said again, and damn if it didn't come out with a note of tenderness. Which was ridiculous. He had no reason to feel tender toward her at all. She was his assignment, whether she liked it or not. It'd be easier if she cooperated, of course, but he'd get to the bottom of things one way or the other.

He was nothing if not patient.

She began to walk faster. "I appreciate the gesture, but

I'm not interested. I hold myself to a higher standard of ethics and integrity."

What the hell? Clearly, she thought he'd sent the flowers. The idea was so comical he almost laughed. "Wait." He fell in step beside her. "Carlson sent me."

"Did he?" She didn't stop.

He dug his phone out of his pocket. If she wouldn't believe him, maybe she'd believe Carlson. "Here." Just as she made it to her car, he shoved his phone in front of her face. She had to stop to keep from slamming her nose into the screen. "See?"

She shot him an irritated look—which made him smile. She was tough—but he was tougher.

Begrudgingly, she read Carlson's email out loud. "'Tom—the new judge, Caroline Jennings, contacted me. An anonymous person sent her flowers and apparently that's out of the ordinary for her. See what you can find out. If we're lucky, this will open the case back up. Maggie sends her love. Carlson.'"

She frowned as she read it. This was as close as Tom had been to her and again, he was surrounded by the perfume of roses. He wanted to lean in close and press his lips against the base of her neck to see if she tasted as sweet as she smelled—but if he'd gauged Caroline Jennings right, she probably had Mace on her keys. Given the way she was holding her body, he'd bet she'd taken some self-defense classes at some point.

Good for her. He liked a woman who wasn't afraid to defend herself.

The moment that thought popped up, Tom slammed the door on it. He didn't like Judge Jennings, no matter how sweet she smelled or how strongly he felt that pull. This was about the case. The job was all he had.

She angled her body toward his, and a primal part of

his brain crowed in satisfaction when she didn't step back. If anything, it felt like she was challenging his space with her body. "And I'm supposed to believe that's on the level, huh?"

God, he'd like to be challenged. She was simply magnificent—even better out of her robes. "I don't play games, Caroline," he said. No matter how much he might want to. "Not about something like this."

She studied him for a moment. "That implies you play games in other situations, though."

His lips twisted to one side and he crossed his arms, because if he didn't, he might start smiling and that was bad for his image as a no-holds-barred lawman. "That all depends on the game, doesn't it?"

"I put more stock in the players."

So much for his image, because he burst out laughing at that. Caroline took a step back, her hands clenched at her sides and her back ramrod straight—which was completely at odds with the unexpectedly intense look of... longing? She looked less like a woman about to punch him and more like...

Like she was holding herself back. Like she wanted to laugh with him. Maybe do even more with him.

If he slid an arm around her waist and pulled her into his chest, would she break his nose or would she go all soft and womanly against him? How long had it been since he'd had a woman in his arms?

It absolutely did not matter—nor did it matter that he knew exactly how long it'd been. What mattered was cracking this case.

"I don't sleep with them."

"What?" She physically recoiled, pushing herself closer to the door.

"The prostitutes," he explained. "I don't sleep with

them. That's what you're worried about, isn't it? What I do in my free time?"

"It's none of my business what you do when you're off duty," she said in a stiff voice, shrinking even farther away from him. "It's a free country."

That made him grin again. "This country is bought and paid for, and you and I both know it," he said, surprised at the bitterness that sneaked in there. "I buy them dinner," he went on, wondering if someone like Caroline Jennings would ever really be able to understand. "They're mostly young, mostly girls—mostly being forced to work against their will. I treat them like people, not criminals—show them there's another way. When they're ready, I help them get away and get clean. And until they are, I make sure they're eating, give them enough money they don't have to work that night."

"That's…" She blinked. *"Really?"*

"Really. I don't sleep with them." For some ridiculous reason, he almost let the truth slip free—he didn't sleep with anyone. It was none of her business—but he wanted to make sure she knew he operated with all the ethical integrity she valued. "Carlson can back me up on that."

"Who's Maggie?"

Interesting. There was no good reason for her to be concerned about Maggie sending Tom her love, unless…

Unless Caroline was trying to figure out if he was attached. "Carlson's wife. We grew up on the same reservation together." He left out the part where he'd gone off to Washington, DC, and joined the FBI, leaving Maggie vulnerable to exploitation and abuse.

There was a reason he didn't sleep with prostitutes. But that wasn't his story to tell—it was Maggie's. He stuck to the facts.

The breeze gusted, surrounding him with her scent. He

couldn't help leaning forward and inhaling. "Roses," he murmured, his voice unexpectedly tender again. He really needed to stop with the tenderness.

She flushed again, and although he shouldn't, he hoped it wasn't from the heat. "I beg your pardon?"

"You smell of roses." Somehow, he managed to put another step between them. "Is that your normal perfume, or was that from the delivery?" There. That was a perfectly reasonable question to ask, from a law-enforcement perspective.

"From the flowers. The bouquet was huge. At least a hundred stems."

"All roses?"

She thought about that. "Mixed. Lilies and carnations—a little bit of everything, really. But mostly roses."

In other words, it hadn't been cheap. He tried to visualize how big a vase with a hundred stems would be. "But you're not taking any home with you?"

She shook her head. "I didn't want them. My clerk got rid of most of them. Leland took home a huge bunch for his wife."

"Leland's a good guy," Tom replied, as if this were normal small talk when it was anything but.

"How do I know I can trust you?" she blurted out.

"My record speaks for itself." He pulled a business card out of his pocket and held it out to her. "You don't know what you're up against here. This kind of corruption is insidious and nearly impossible to track, Caroline. But if there's anything else out of the ordinary—and I mean *anything*—don't hesitate to call me. Or Carlson," he added, almost as an afterthought. He didn't want her to call Carlson, though. He wanted her to call him. For any reason. "No detail is too small. Names, car makes—anything you remember can be helpful."

After a long moment—so long, in fact, that he began to wonder if she was going to take the card at all—she asked, "So we're to work together?"

He heard the question she didn't ask. "On this case, yes."

But if it weren't for this case…

She took the card from him and slid it into her shirt pocket. He did his best not to stare at the motion. *Damn.*

She gave him that look again, the one that made him think she was holding herself back. "Fine."

He straightened and gave her a little salute. "After this case…" He turned and headed to his car. "Have a good evening, Caroline," he called over his shoulder.

She gasped and he almost, *almost* spun back on his heel and captured that little noise with a kiss.

But he didn't. Instead, he climbed into the driver's seat of his Camaro, gunned the engine and peeled out of the parking lot as fast as he could.

He needed to put a lot of distance between him and Caroline Jennings. Because, no matter how much he might be attracted to her, he wasn't about to compromise this case for her.

And that was final.

Three

For a while, nothing happened. There were no more mysterious flower deliveries—or, for that matter, any kind of deliveries. The remaining half dozen roses on Caroline's desk withered and died. Andrea threw them away. People in the courthouse seemed friendlier—apparently, handing out scads of flowers made Caroline quite popular. Other than that, though, things continued on as they had before.

Before Agent Tom Yellow Bird had shown up in her courtroom.

She got up, went for a jog before the heat got oppressive, went to the courthouse and then came home. No mysterious gifts, no handsome men—mysterious or otherwise. No surprises. Everything went exactly as it was supposed to. Which was good. Great, even.

If she didn't have Tom's card in her pocket—and that electric memory of shaking his hand—she would have been tempted to convince herself she had imagined the

whole thing. A fantasy she'd invented to alleviate bore-
dom instead of a flesh-and-blood man. Fantasies were always safer, anyway.

But…there were times when she could almost feel his
presence. She'd come out of the courthouse and pull up
short, looking for his black muscle car with the silver stripe
on the hood, but he was never there. And the fact that disappointed her was irritating.

She had not developed a crush on the man. No crushes.
That was that.

Just because he was an officer of the law with a gun
concealed under his jacket, with eyes that might be his biggest weapon—that was no reason to lust after the man. She
didn't need to see him again. It was better that way—at
least, she finally had to admit to herself, it was better that
way while his corruption investigation was still ongoing.
The more distance between them, the less she would become infatuated.

Tom Yellow Bird was a mistake she wasn't going to
make.

It was a good theory, anyway. But he showed up in
her dreams, a shadowy lover who drove her wild with
his hands, his mouth, his body. She woke up tense and
frustrated, and no electronic assistance could relieve the
pressure. Her vibrator barely took the edge off, but it was
enough.

Besides, she had other things to focus on. She finally
finished unpacking her kitchen, although she still ate too
much takeout. It was hard to work up the energy to cook
when the temperature outside kept pushing a hundred.

Still, she tried. She came home one Friday after work
three weeks after the floral delivery, juggling a couple of
bags of groceries. Eggs were on sale and there was a recipe for summery quiche on Pinterest that she wanted to

try. She had air-conditioning and a weekend to kick back. She was going to cook—or else. At the very least, she was going to eat ice cream.

She knew the moment she unlocked the front door that something was wrong. She couldn't have said what it was because, when she looked around the living room, nothing seemed out of place. But there was an overwhelming sense that someone had been in her home that she didn't dare ignore.

Heart pounding, she backed out of the house, pulling the door shut behind her. She carried the groceries right back out to the trunk of her car and then, hands shaking, she pulled her cell phone and Tom's card out of her pocket and dialed.

He answered on the second ring. "Yes?"

"Is this Agent Yellow Bird?" He sounded gruffer on the phone—so gruff, in fact, that she couldn't be sure it was the same man who had laughed with her in the parking lot.

"Caroline? Are you all right?"

Suddenly, she felt silly. She was sitting outside in the car. It wasn't like the door had been jimmied open. It hadn't even looked like anything had been moved—at least, not in the living room. "It's probably nothing."

"I'll be the judge of that. What's going on?"

She exhaled in relief. She was not a damsel in distress and she did not need a white knight to come riding to her rescue. But there was something comforting about the thought that a federal agent was ready and willing to take over if things weren't on the up and up. "I just got home and it feels like there was someone in my house." She winced. It didn't sound any less silly when she said it out loud.

There was a moment of silence on the other end of the phone, and she got a sinking feeling that he was going to tell her not to be such a ninny. "Where are you?"

"In my car. In the driveway," she added. Cars could be anywhere.

"If you're comfortable, stay there. I'm about fifteen minutes away. If you aren't, I want you to leave and drive someplace safe. Understand?"

"Okay." His words should have been reassuring. He was on his way over and she had a plan. But, perversely, the fact that he was taking this feeling so seriously scared her even more.

What if someone really had been in her house? It hadn't looked like a robbery. What had they been after?

"Call me back if you need to. I'm on my way." Before she could even respond, he hung up.

Wait, she thought, staring at the screen of her phone—how did he know where she lived?

She turned on her car—all the better to make a quick getaway—and cranked the AC. She knew she shouldn't have bought ice cream at the store, but too late now.

She waited and watched her house. Nothing happened. No one slunk out. Not so much as a curtain twitched. It looked perfectly normal, and by the time Tom came roaring down the street, she had convinced herself she was being ridiculous. She got out of the car again and went to meet him.

"I'm sorry to bother you," she began. "I'm sure it's nothing."

Then she pulled up short. Gone was the slick custom-made suit. Instead, a pair of well-worn jeans hung low off his hips and a soft white T-shirt clung to his chest. He had his shoulder holster on, which only highlighted his pecs all the more. Her mouth went dry as his long legs powerfully closed the distance between them.

If she had been daydreaming about Agent Yellow Bird

in a suit, the man in a pair of blue jeans was going to haunt her dreams in the very best way possible.

He walked right up to her and put his hands on her shoulders. "Are you all right?" he asked, his voice low.

That spark of electricity moved over her skin again, and she shivered. "Fine," she said, but her voice wavered. "I'm not sure I can say the same for the ice cream, but life will go on."

He almost smiled. She could tell, because his eyes crinkled ever so slightly. "Why do you think someone was in your house?" As he spoke, his hands drifted down her shoulders until he was holding her upper arms. A good two feet of space still separated them, but it was almost an embrace.

At least, that's how it felt to her. But what did she know? She couldn't even tell if someone had been in her house or not.

"It was just a feeling. The door wasn't busted, and nothing seemed out of place in the living room." She tried to laugh it off, but she didn't even manage to convince herself.

He squeezed her arms before dropping his hands. She felt oddly lost without his touch. "Is the door still unlocked?" She nodded. "Stay behind me." He pulled his gun and moved forward. Caroline stayed close. "Quietly," he added as he opened the door.

Silently, they entered the house. Her skin crawled and she unconsciously hooked her hand into the waistband of his jeans. Tom checked each room, but there was no one there. Caroline looked at everything, but nothing seemed out of place. By the time they peeked into the unused guest room, with the remaining boxes from the move still haphazardly stacked, she felt more than silly. She felt stupid.

When Tom holstered his gun and turned to face her, she knew her cheeks were flaming red. "I'm sorry, I—"

They were standing very close together in the hall, and Tom reached out and touched a finger to her lips. Then he stepped in closer and whispered in her ear, "Outside."

For a second, neither of them moved. She could feel the heat of his body, and she had an almost overwhelming urge to kiss the finger resting against her lips. Which was ridiculous.

What was it about this man that turned her into a blubbering schoolgirl with a crush? Maybe she was just trying to bury her embarrassment at having called him out here for nothing beneath a more manageable emotion—lust. Not that lust was a bad thing. Except for the fact that she still had no idea what he did in his spare time or whether or not it broke any laws. And there was the unavoidable fact that acting on any lust would be a conflict of interest.

They were actively on an investigation, for crying out loud. It was one of the reasons she couldn't read romantic suspense novels—it drove her nuts when people in the middle of a dangerous situation dropped everything to get naked.

She was not that kind of girl, damn it. So instead of leaning into his touch or wrapping her arms around his waist and pulling him in tight, she did the right thing. She nodded and pulled away.

It was harder than she'd thought it would be.

When they were outside, she tried apologizing again. "I'm so sorry that I called you out here for nothing." She didn't enjoy making a fool of herself, but when it happened, she tried to own up to the mistake as quickly as possible.

He leaned against her car, studying her. She had met a lot of hard-nosed investigators and steely-eyed lawyers in her time, but nothing quite compared to Tom Yellow Bird. "Are you sure it was nothing? Tell me again how you felt there was something wrong."

She shrugged helplessly. "It was just a feeling. Everything looked fine, and you saw yourself that there was no one in the house." She decided that worse than feeling stupid was the fact that she had made herself look weak.

For some ridiculous reason, this situation reminded her of her brother. Trent Jennings had been a master of creating a crisis where none existed—and he was even better at making it seem like it was her fault. Because she'd been the mistake, the squalling brat who'd taken his parents away from him. Or so he was fond of reminding her.

That wasn't what she was doing here, was it? Creating a crisis in order to focus the attention on herself? No, she didn't think so. The house had *felt* wrong. Then something occurred to her. "Why are we outside again? It's hot out here."

"The place is probably bugged."

He said it so casually that it took a few moments before his words actually sank in. *"What?"*

"I've seen this before."

"I don't understand," she said, wondering if he was ever going to answer a straight question. "You've seen *what* before?"

For a moment, he looked miserable—the face of a man who was about to deliver bad news. "You have a feeling that someone was in your house—although nothing appears to have been moved or taken, correct?"

She nodded. "So my sixth sense is having a bad day. How does that mean there are bugs in my house?"

One corner of his mouth crept up. "They're trying to find something they can use against you. Maybe you have some sort of peccadillo or kink, maybe something from your past." He smiled, but it wasn't reassuring. "Something worse than speeding tickets?"

The blood drained from her face. She didn't have any

kinks, definitely nothing that would be incriminating. She didn't want people to watch when she used her vibrator—the thought was horrifying. But...

It would be embarrassing if people found out about her lapse of judgment in college. Although, since her parents were dead, she wouldn't have to face their disappointment, and the odds of Trent finding out about it were slim, since they didn't talk anymore.

But more than that...what if people connected her back to Vincent Verango? That wouldn't just be embarrassing. That had the potential of being career ending. Would she never be able to escape the legacy of the Verango case?

No, this was fine. Panicking would be a mistake right now. She needed to keep her calm. "I stay within five miles of the speed limit," she said, trying to arrange her face into something that wasn't incriminating.

Tom shrugged. At least he was interpreting her reaction as shock and not guilt. "They want something on you so that when they approach you again and you say you're not interested, they'll have a threat with teeth. If you don't want them to inform the Justice Department about this embarrassing or illegal thing, you'll do what they say. Simple."

"Simple?" She gaped at him, wondering when the world had stopped making sense. "Nothing about that is simple!"

"I don't have a bug detector," he went on, as if she hadn't spoken. "And seeing as it's Friday night, I don't think I can get one before Monday."

"Why not?" Because she couldn't imagine this oh-so-simple situation didn't justify a damned bug detector.

A muscle in his jaw twitched. "I'm off duty for the next four days. I'd have to make a special case to get one, and Carlson and I like to keep our investigations off the record as much as possible."

She couldn't help it—she laughed. She sounded horrible, even to her own ears, but it was either that or cry. This entire situation was so far beyond the realm of normal that she briefly considered she might've fallen asleep in her office this afternoon.

"The way I see it," he went on, again ignoring her outburst, "you have two choices. You can go about your business as normal and I'll come back on Monday and sweep the house."

It was, hands-down, the most reasonable suggestion she was probably going to hear. So why did it make her stomach turn with an anxious sort of dread? "Okay. What's my other choice?"

That muscle in his jaw ticked again, and she realized that he looked hard—like a stone, no emotions at all. The playful grin was nowhere to be seen. "You come with me."

"Like, to your home?" That was it. She was definitely dreaming. It wasn't like her to nod off in her chambers, but what other reasonable explanation was there?

"In a professional capacity," he said in what was probably supposed to be a reassuring tone.

Caroline was not reassured. "If they bugged my house and I'm new here, why would your home be any less susceptible to surveillance?"

And just like that, his stony expression was gone. He cracked a grin and again, she thought of a wolf—dangerous but playful. And she had no idea if she was the prey or not.

"Trust me," he said, pushing off the car and coming to stand directly in front of her. "Nothing gets past me."

Four

They had been in the car for an hour and fifteen minutes. Seventy-five *silent* minutes. Any attempt at conversation was met with—at best—a grunt. Mostly, Tom just ignored her, so she stopped trying.

Pierre was a distant memory and Tom was, true to his word, breaking every speed limit known to mankind and the state of South Dakota. She'd be willing to bet they were topping out well past one hundred, so she chose not to look at the speedometer, lest she start thinking of fiery crashes along the side of the road.

There was no avoiding Tom Yellow Bird. This muscle car was aggressive—just like him. He filled the driver's seat effortlessly, seemingly becoming one with his machine. She didn't know much about cars, but she could tell this was a nice one. The seats were a supple leather and the dashboard had all sorts of connected gadgets that were a mystery to her.

Just like the man next to her.

The landscape outside the car hadn't changed since they'd hit the open plains, so she turned her attention to Tom. They were driving west and he still had his sunglasses on. She couldn't read him. The only thing that gave her a clue to his mental state was how he kept tapping his fingers on the steering wheel. At least, she thought it was a clue. He might just be bored out of his mind.

It wasn't fair. She hadn't thought of the Verango case in, what—ten years? Twelve? But that was exactly the sort of thing a bad guy would be looking for, because she didn't have anything kinky hiding in her closet. And a vibrator didn't count. At least she hoped it didn't.

She liked sex. She'd like to have more of it, preferably with someone like Tom—but only if it were the kind that couldn't come back to bite her. No messy relationships, no birth control slipups, no strings attached.

Not that she wanted to have sex with *him*. But the man had inspired weeks of wet dreams, all because he had an intense look and an air of invulnerability about him. And that body. Who could forget that body?

She wished like hell she didn't have this primal reaction to him. Even riding next to him was torture. She was aware of him in a way she couldn't ignore, no matter how hard she tried. She felt it when he shifted in his seat, as if there were invisible threads binding them together. And that wasn't even the worst of it. Although he had the AC blasting on high, she was the kind of hot that had nothing to do with the temperature outside. Her bra was too tight and she wanted out of this top.

She'd love to go for a swim. She needed to do something to cool down before she did something ridiculous, like parading around his home in nothing but her panties.

And the fact that her brain was even suggesting that as a

viable way to kill a weekend was a freaking *huge* problem. Because getting naked anywhere near Tom Yellow Bird would be a mistake. Yes, it might very well be a mistake she enjoyed making—but that wouldn't change the fact that it would still be a gross error in judgment, one that might compromise a case or—worse—get her blackmailed. A mistake like that could derail her entire career—and for what? For a man who wasn't even talking to her? No. She couldn't make another mistake like that.

Rationally, she knew her perfectionism wasn't healthy. Her parents had never treated her like a mistake, and besides, they were dead. And she couldn't take responsibility for the fact that Trent had been a whiny, entitled kid who'd grown into a bitter, hateful man. She didn't have to do everything just right in a doomed effort to keep the peace in the family.

Yes, rationally, she knew all of that. But her objective knowledge didn't do anything to put her at ease as Tom drove like the devil himself was gaining on them.

Finally, Caroline couldn't take it anymore. She had expected a fifteen-minute car trip to a different side of town. Not this mad dash across the Great Plains. It was beginning to feel little bit like a kidnapping—one that she had been complicit in. "Where, exactly, do you live?"

"Not too much farther," he said, answering the wrong question.

But he'd actually responded, and she couldn't pass up this chance to get more out of him. "If you're spiriting me away to the middle of nowhere just to do me in, it's not going to go well for you." She didn't harbor any illusions that she could make an impact on him. He was armed and dangerous, and for all she knew, he was a black belt or something. She was good at jogging. She had taken a few self-defense classes. She wasn't going to think about how long ago, though.

That got a laugh out of him, which only made her madder. "I have no intention of killing you. Or harming you," he added as an afterthought.

"You'll forgive me if I don't find that terribly reassuring."

"Then why did you get in the car with me?"

She shook her head, not caring if he could see it or not. "I just realized that when I said something felt off at my house, you trusted me. Anyone else would've told me I was imagining things. I'm returning the favor." She leaned her head back and closed her eyes. "Don't let it go to your head."

"I doubt you'll let that happen."

The car slowed as he took an exit. But he was going so fast that she didn't get her eyes open to see the name or number of the exit. They were literally in the middle of nowhere. She hadn't seen so much as a cow for the last— what, ten or twenty miles? It was hard to tell at the speeds they'd been traveling.

"Dare I ask how you define 'not too much farther'?"

"Are you hungry?"

She was starving, but that didn't stop her from glancing at the clock in the dashboard. The sun was low over the horizon.

"Do you always do that?" He tilted his head in her direction without making eye contact. At least, she assumed. She was beginning to hate those sunglasses. "Answer a question with an unrelated statement?"

She saw his lips twitch. "Dinner will be waiting for us. I hope pizza is all right?"

See, that was the sort of statement that made her wonder about him. He'd clearly said he was taking her to his house. Was he the kind of guy who had a personal chef? That didn't fit with the salary of an FBI agent.

But she couldn't figure out how to phrase that particular question without it sounding like an accusation. Instead, she said, "So that's a yes. And," she added before he could start laughing, "pizza is fine. Better if it has sausage and peppers on it. Mushrooms are also acceptable. Do you have any ice cream? Wine?"

"I can take care of you."

Perhaps it was supposed to be an innocent statement— a reflection of his preparedness for emergency guests. But that's not how Caroline took it.

Maybe her defenses were lower because she was tired and worried. But the moment his words filled the small space between them, her body reacted—hard. Her nipples tightened almost to the point of pain as heat flooded her stomach and pooled lower. Her toes curled, and she had to grip the handle on the passenger door to keep from moaning with raw need.

Heavens, what was with her? It had been a long day. That was all. There was no other explanation as to why a simple phrase, spoken in a particularly deep tone of voice, would have such an impact on her.

She locked the whole system down. No moaning, no shivering, and absolutely no heated glances at Tom. Besides, how would she know if his glances were heated or not? He still had on those damn sunglasses.

Instead, in a perfectly level voice, she said, "That remains to be seen, doesn't it?" She took it as a personal victory when he gripped the steering wheel with both hands.

Silence descended in the car again. If she'd had no idea where she was before, she had less now. They'd left the highway behind. The good news was that Tom was probably only doing sixty instead of breaking the sound barrier. With each turn, the roads bore less and less resemblance to an actual paved surface. But she didn't start to panic until he turned where there didn't seem to be any road at all, just a row of ragged shrubs. He opened the glove box and fished out a...remote?

"What are you doing?" she demanded.

He didn't answer. Of course he didn't. Instead, he aimed the remote at the shrubs and clicked the button.

The whole thing rolled smoothly to the side. She blinked and then blinked again. Really, her head was a mess. She was going to need a whole bottle of wine after this. "Be honest—are you Batman?"

He cracked a grin that did terrible, wonderful things to her body. Her mouth went dry and the heat that she had refused to feel before came rushing back, a hot summer wind that carried the promise of a storm. Because there was something electric in the air when he turned to face her. She wanted to lick his neck to taste the salt of his skin.

Maybe she would strip down. Her clothing was becoming unbearable. "Would you believe me if I said I was?"

She thought about that. Well, at least she tried to. Thinking was becoming hard. She was so hot. "Only if you've got an elderly British butler waiting for you."

His grin deepened and, curse her body, it responded, leaning toward him of its own volition. "I don't. Turns out elderly British butlers don't like to work off the grid in the middle of nowhere."

That got her attention. "I thought you said you had a home?" She looked around, feeling the weight of the phrase *wide-open spaces* for the first time. There was nothing around here except the highly mobile fake shrubbery. "I don't see..."

Then she saw it—in the direction where the ruts disappeared down the drive, there were trees off in the distance. "This is a real house, right? If you live in a van down by the river, I'm going to be pissed. A real house with pizza," she added. "And a real bed. I will walk back to Pierre before I crash in a sleeping bag."

It wasn't fair, that grin. His muscles weren't fair, his jaw wasn't fair and the way he had of looking at her—that, most of all, wasn't fair. Especially right now, when it was pretty obvious to everyone—all two of them—that her filters were failing her.

"I do have a housekeeper of sorts," he added, glancing at the clock in the dash. "She should have dinner underway. And in the meantime, if you'd like to swim…"

He had her at a complete disadvantage, and the hell of it was, she wasn't sure it was a bad thing. There was a part of her that desperately wanted to believe it was a good thing. At least, the part about being here with him was a good thing. There was no way to put a positive spin on someone breaking into her house and planting bugs.

"You have a pool out here?" She stared at the trees again.

"Not exactly," he said, sounding almost regretful about it. "But I have a pond—spring fed, nice and cool. If you need to cool off."

Somehow, she'd gotten close enough to him that he could cup her cheek with the palm of his hand. Her eyelashes fluttered and she couldn't help leaning into his touch. Even though this had been one of the stranger afternoons in her life, she still felt safe with him. Maybe she shouldn't. They were a million miles from nowhere. But she did.

"Let me take you home."

A pond? She didn't love mud squishing between her toes, but at this point she wasn't sure she cared. "Promise me we'll get there soon. I don't know how much longer I can wait."

She meant for the food and wine. For the cool pond. But

she felt his body tense and realized that she hadn't been talking about dinner at all.

She didn't know how much longer she could wait for this man. This confusing, confounding man who cared what happened to her.

"Ten minutes. You won't regret this."

"I better not."

Neither of them moved for a second. Then, so slowly that she could feel the electricity between them crackle, he stroked his thumbs over her cheekbones. His hands were rough, but his touch was gentle and she was too tired to fight the shiver of attraction anymore.

Damn his sunglasses. Damn her exhaustion. Damn the fact that they were parked in the middle of nowhere instead of at some romantic restaurant or, even better, a bedroom. Any bedroom. Damn this corruption case she was unwillingly a part of because, better than a glass of wine and a pint of ice cream, falling into Tom Yellow Bird's arms would definitely relieve some of her stress.

He held her there, stroking her cheeks, and she thought he was going to kiss her. She wanted him to. She also didn't—what she really wanted was for the world to go back to making sense—but that wasn't going to happen. So she'd settle for a kiss.

"We need to get going," he said, pulling away from her with what she chose to believe was reluctance. Because that way, it didn't sting as much.

"Of course," she said, staring at the trees in the distance. "Let's just go."

It almost didn't even matter where anymore.

Five

In his life, Tom had made mistakes. Beyond being unable to rescue Maggie and overlooking the fact that he should have been behind the wheel instead of Stephanie in the car accident—he had screwed up.

He'd lost the notoriously violent pimp Leonard Low Dog not once but twice and, as a result, the man had nearly killed Maggie. He'd lost the trail on Tanner Donnelly's killer until Tanner's sister, Rosebud, and her now-husband, Dan Armstrong, had cracked the case open. And Tom hadn't yet been able to uncover who was paying off judges in South Dakota.

All of those were epic errors in judgment, ones that he'd tried hard to rectify. Leonard Low Dog was serving twenty without parole. Shane Thrasher was doing forty for killing Tanner. Tom had put three judges in prison and had a hand in forcing others to retire from the bench.

But none of those mistakes were in the same category as bringing Caroline Jennings home with him.

She gasped when he finally rounded the last bend and his cabin came into view.

Aside from the Armstrongs and the Carlsons, Lilly and Joe White Thunder—people he trusted beyond the pale—he'd never brought anyone else back here. This was his sanctuary. This was where he could be close to the memories of Stephanie.

"Good God," Caroline exhaled. "Where the hell did this come from?"

"I built it." It was the summer home he and Stephanie had planned, once their careers had been established. Once they would've been able to take a month off in the summer.

And now Caroline was here. It was a mistake, but if there was one thing life had taught him, it was that there was no going back. Own up to what you did and keep moving forward. She was here, and he was sworn to protect her.

"You built it? Like, by yourself?"

"I had a few contractors, but only ones I could trust." He didn't see Lilly's pickup truck anywhere—good.

The low-slung building practically glowed in the fading sunset, the solar panels on the roofs of the house and garage glinting in the light. The panels had been a compromise. Someone could easily see his house from the air, but he was off the grid.

He hadn't exactly sworn to protect Caroline. He'd promised to take care of her. And when he'd made that promise, he'd felt the shiver pass through her body.

This was fine. Yes, he had to be in DC Monday evening, but she wouldn't be with him that long. He'd keep an eye on her this weekend until he could sweep her house. Early Monday morning, Tom would take her to work, and she'd go home Monday evening as if nothing had happened.

"This is amazing." Her voice was breathy—and that was

before she turned those beautiful eyes toward him. "You live here full-time? In the middle of nowhere?"

He shrugged. "I needed a place to think. I have an apartment in Pierre, but it's not as secure."

Right. That was why he'd brought her here. Security. He would do anything to keep her safe. Even break the rules—his own rules.

Bringing her to his house? That broke every rule he'd ever set for himself. That was him putting his selfish wants ahead of his job, and that was a risk not just for him, not just for her, but for all the years he and Carlson had spent on this case. That was an unacceptable level of risk.

But what was he supposed to do? He couldn't leave her. The pull he felt to take care of her wouldn't let him. But it was more than that.

Caroline hadn't cut him a single bit of slack. Except when he'd touched her, her soft skin warm in his hands.

He pulled into the garage. It wasn't until she gasped again that he looked at her. "Who the hell are you?" she asked, staring at his vehicles.

There were a couple of nondescript cars that he used for surveillance, his motorcycle, the old pickup truck he used when he went to the reservation and the new one he used when he was hauling supplies—not to mention his fire engine–red Corvette Stingray, which he only took out when he needed to give off an aura of wealth. "I know you may not believe this, but I don't make a habit of lying."

Based on her expression, if he thought that was going to fly, he had another thing coming. "You must not be including lying by omission in the definition."

He snorted as he got out of the car, pleased that she followed. He snagged her bags out of the trunk. "This way."

He led her to the wide porch that wrapped around three of the four sides of his house. "I have a few things I need to see to, so if you'd like to take a dip in the pond, now would be a great time." That would give him a chance to contact Carlson and see about getting her house swept for bugs.

But it'd also give him a chance to get his head back in the game. Lilly White Thunder should have gotten dinner started, and hopefully she'd had enough time to put fresh sheets on the beds.

But the thought of Caroline curled up in his bed, her hair mussed and the sheet slung low around her waist—

"Come on," he said, dropping her duffel just inside the door. The scent of pizza baking in the oven filled the cabin, but the windows were open and the house smelled fresh and clean.

As much as he loved Lilly, he was glad the older woman wasn't here. He didn't want to introduce Caroline to her, didn't want to risk the chance that Caroline's presence would slip out and make the rounds on the res.

Because that kept Caroline safer. Not because he didn't want Lilly looking at him with her warm eyes and getting any funny ideas.

Unable to help himself, he took Caroline by the hand. She was too hot and tired to meet new people, anyway. The sooner she got out of those clothes and cooled down, the better she'd be.

And her being nude had nothing to do with him. Not a damn thing.

He was rock hard as he led her through the patio doors and down a small flagstone path to where he had dammed the natural spring to create a small pool.

Caroline stumbled to a stop when she saw it. "It's…red. The water's red?"

"It is. Higher iron content. It flows into the Red Creek River," he said, stepping in close to her and pointing down the riverbanks. "That's where the name comes from. Don't worry, it won't dye your skin."

The next thing Tom knew, she whacked him on the arm. "Why didn't you tell me about this?" she demanded, her voice sounding unnaturally high. "If you had just told me you had a luxury log cabin complete with stone fireplaces and leather furniture and…" Her voice cracked. "And a little pond that isn't even a pond." She sniffed. "You lined the bottom with stones, didn't you?"

It was the most accusatory statement he'd heard—and it wasn't about a crime or a case. It was about his little pool. "If I want to feel mud squishing in between my toes, I'll swim in the river."

She slapped him on the arm again and he let her. "You could've told me. I didn't even bring a swimsuit."

"I didn't know you needed to cool down until we were in the car." He turned his gaze out to the trees, where his spring flowed into the river. He specifically did not look at her. "If you want to soak, it's about three feet deep," he added. "Not enough to do laps."

She sighed and he glanced back at her. She was staring at that water like it was a long-lost lover that she'd never thought she'd see again. And Tom knew he was crazy, because he was suddenly jealous of the pool. "If you look, I'll gut you in your sleep," she said, sounding so tired that Tom felt like a cad.

He knew he was not an easy man to get along with. Never had been—that's why Stephanie had been so good for him. She had never let him get away with anything. She'd challenged him and pushed him and held him to a higher standard. She had met him on the playing field as an equal, and Tom had loved her for it, completely and wholly.

But even Stephanie had never threatened to gut him like a fish.

Grinning, he said, "Then I best not look."

Caroline turned away from him and grabbed the hem of her shirt, slowly lifting and revealing the pale skin of her lower back. She had the shirt halfway off and she looked at him over her shoulder and if he hadn't been lost before then, he sure as hell was now. "Shouldn't you be hiding the knives?"

"You know I'm used to sleeping with one eye open, right?" She started to lower the shirt, so he quickly took a step back. "I'm going. I won't look. I'll let you know when dinner's ready."

"At the rate we're going, it's going to be breakfast," she said with a sigh.

He turned on his heel before he did something stupid, like give in to the urge to pull her into his arms. He'd been battling that urge since he'd pulled up in front of her house that afternoon, stomach churning with dread. She'd sounded so scared on the phone—she'd been trying to laugh it off, but Tom had heard the truth in her voice. All he'd wanted to do was hold her then and make sure she knew she was safe with him.

Instead, he'd gone into her house, ready to shoot any intruder who'd stolen her peace of mind. He'd told her to pack for a weekend away and driven her way out here. She was well within her right to gut him.

And now he had to make it through the next forty-eight hours alone with her. The only things to do out here were hike and hunt, soak in the pool, and sleep. There was no television, no internet, and the only cell service was his satellite phone.

She was safe now, and he was pretty sure she knew it. After all, wasn't she actively stripping out of her clothes? Wasn't she, at this very moment, stepping into the shallow pool he'd built, seemingly just for her? Wasn't she lowering her nude body into the water, feeling it lap at her inner thighs, her stomach, her breasts?

Jesus, how was he going to make it until Monday morning?

The water was deliciously, blissfully cold. It shocked Caroline awake and kept right on shocking her. Which was good. It was so much easier to sit and think about goose bumps than to let her mind wander over the events of the last four hours. Had it really only been four danged hours? Sheesh, what a day.

Her stomach grumbled. She would kill for a glass of wine but, bathed in the last light of dusk and letting this not-pool wash the day's sweat and anxiety away, she was content.

However, no matter how cold the water was, it couldn't erase all the heat from her body. Safely submerged beneath the waterline, her nipples were so puckered they were painful, and the heat between her legs? This water would have to be a whole lot colder before it knocked *that* down. Even though her skin was chilled, she was warm from the inside out.

She was lying naked in a pond that Tom Yellow Bird had built. She could almost pretend he'd built it for her, but she knew that was ridiculous.

Still, it was a nice fantasy. Why hadn't that man told her about this place? She could see leaving out detailed directions. He was more than a little paranoid, but maybe in his line of work, he had to be.

She floated sideways so she could get a better look at the house. She hadn't seen any sign of a maid or a house-keeper—or a British butler, for that matter. The only sign that anyone else knew where this house was had been the scent of pizza in the oven.

The house had also been spotless, as if this supposed housekeeper came in regularly to dust and air it out. Tom had hurried her through the house pretty quickly, but she'd gotten glimpses of the rough-hewn logs, a massive fire-place done in stone with a chimney that rose up to the ceiling. It was rough and overwhelming—much like Tom himself.

The whole house was a long structure, but not tall. It probably didn't even have a second story. It rode low to the ground like it didn't want to be noticed—except for the solar panels that covered the entire roof. There were trees close enough to the building to throw some shade on the porch, but otherwise, all they did was block the view from the road, however distant that was.

The logs were great behemoths of wood, and she let her imagination play over the image of Tom cutting and fitting them together like life-size Lincoln logs. Undoubtedly, he would've worked shirtless, sweat running down his neck and over his chest. Of course he would know how to use tools. And then he would lift each log into place, his muscles straining and—

"I'm coming down." His voice rang out over the plains, breaking up her reverie. "Are you decent?"

"I'm still in the water," she called back. "I...I don't have a towel or anything." And she had stripped a good six feet away from the pool because she had been so anxious to get out of her clothes. And her shoes—they weren't waterproof flip-flops. She couldn't just shove her feet back in them without ruining the leather ballerina flats, and she wasn't sure she could make it up the flagstone walk without slipping. "I may be trapped in here forever."

His laughter, deep and rich, was another pleasant surprise. She hadn't heard him laugh like that yet. "I would be a terrible host if I left you in there to turn into one giant prune. I brought you a towel."

"I haven't yet decided if you're terrible host or not. It better be a fluffy towel."

"The fluffiest. I'm not looking."

"You better not be," she said, standing slowly to let the water sheet off her body. But when she turned for the towel, she saw that he was standing by the pool, holding out the unfolded towel, his head ducked and his eyes closed. "What are you doing?" she demanded, sinking back into the water.

"The rocks are slick. I'm making sure you don't slip." He said it as if this were just an everyday occurrence instead of a giant leap of faith on her behalf.

Oh, hell—what was she talking about? How was the risk of him catching a glimpse of her nude somehow a bigger leap of faith than getting into a car with him and letting him whisk her away to the middle of nowhere?

She had already leaped. Now she just had to trust that he would catch her before she fell.

So she stood again, her skin tingling as the water rushed off it.

Moving carefully so she didn't do something embarrassing like face-plant, she stepped into the towel. His arms came around her, but he didn't step back. And he didn't open his eyes. She was so glad those damn sunglasses were gone. "You never lie?"

He shook his head. "I didn't look."

She shifted so that the towel was secured under her arms. It was a *very* fluffy towel. Then she took a deep breath and rested her hand against his cheek. His eyelashes fluttered, but they stayed closed. "Why did you bring me out here? And I don't want to hear that line about how you were keeping me safe."

"That line is the truth."

"There were a hundred ways to keep me safe inside city limits, Tom. Stop lying by omission. Why did you bring me out here?"

His hands settled around her waist, holding the towel to her body. She shivered, but it had nothing to do with the temperature of the water or the air. "I can take you back. If you want, we can leave after we eat."

She wanted to throttle him and kiss him and slap him and drop the towel. She wanted to drag him into that pool of water with her and spend time exploring. She wanted to go home and she never wanted to leave. "What if I don't want to go?"

His fingers dug into her waist, pulling her close. They were chest to chest now, her sensitive nipples scraping against the towel. Against his chest. Unconsciously, her back arched, pushing her even closer to him. "What if I want to stay?" she asked him, pushing up on her tiptoes.

"You feel it, too, don't you?" His voice was so soft she had to tilt her head to catch the words. "I never thought I'd feel this again."

Again? What the hell did that mean, *again*? He'd brought her here on the pretense of protecting her!

She pulled away from him—but she didn't get far. Her feet slid out from under her and she started to fall—but the impact never came. Instead, she found herself swept into Tom's arms as if she were something precious.

"Whoa," she said, impressed despite herself. It was ridiculous because this entire situation was ridiculous. Tom Yellow Bird was literally sweeping her off her feet. "You can put me down now."

"I didn't bring you all the way out here for you to crack your head on the stone pavers," he said, his voice the very picture of cool, calm and collected. And he did not put her down.

She had no choice but to lock her arms around his neck. "Why did you bring me out here?"

It took a lot to rattle Tom. He'd stared down cold-blooded killers and talked his way out of more than a few bad situations.

But catching a damp Caroline in his arms? Cradling her to his chest? Carrying her all the way inside and then setting her down and turning his back instead of heading straight into the bedroom and spending the rest of the night feasting on her body instead of dinner?

His hands shook—*shook*, damn it—as he stoked the fire in the pit. Then, when he judged that she'd had enough time to get dressed, he opened the wine and carried it down to where he'd arranged the patio chairs around the little table close enough to the fire that the worst of the bugs would stay away. It was better to focus on these tiny details than what was happening inside his bedroom.

Or what he wanted to happen in his bedroom.

Finally, he couldn't take it anymore. He took a healthy pull of his wine. Normally he didn't drink much. He didn't like having his senses dulled.

Right now? Yeah, he needed to be significantly less aware. Less aware of Caroline's scent combined with the fresh smell of the spring. Or of her weight in his arms or the bare skin at the back of her knees where he'd held her. He wanted to lick her there and see if she was ticklish—but he didn't dare.

Damn it all. He was failing at thinking about Caroline with any sense of rationality. So he did the only thing he could—he thought of the one person who could always hold his attention, who got him through the worst of the stakeouts and helped him sleep after the bad days.

Stephanie. His wife.

God, she had been too perfect for this world. The first time he'd seen her in that formfitting white dress, her jet-black hair and vivid blue eyes turning every head in the room...

Oh, he could still see the way her whole face lit up when they made eye contract. He could still feel that spark that had lit in his chest as he'd cut through the crowd to get to her—the spark that had told him she was *it*. That woman, whoever she was, was his forever and ever, until death did them part.

But for the first time in a long time—years, even—that memory of Stephanie didn't hold his attention. Instead of lingering in the past, he couldn't escape the present.

He heard the patio door swish open, then closed. He heard the sound of tentative footsteps crossing the porch and moving down the two stairs. He heard the evening breeze sigh through the grasses and the gentle burbling of his spring as it flowed out of his pool and made its way down to the river.

And when Caroline took her seat, he turned, and damn it, there was that spark again, threatening to jump the barriers he'd tried to erect around it, threatening to catch in the prairie grass, burning everything in its path. Including him.

Caroline wasn't Stephanie. Stephanie wouldn't have been caught dead in a pair of old cutoff shorts and a faded gray T-shirt. Flip-flops would have never crossed Stephanie's toes. Stephanie wouldn't have been seen with her hair curling damply around her shoulders. And Stephanie never would have picked up the empty glass and said, "There better be some of that left for me."

"I told you," he replied, filling her glass, "I'm not a terrible host. I'll be right back with the pizza."

He plated up the pizza and snagged some napkins. God bless Lilly for pulling something together on such short notice.

Caroline hadn't moved from her spot, except to draw up her feet. She wasn't perfect. But by God, the woman looked like she fit out here. "Sausage," he said, handing over her plate.

She took the pizza, and for a while, neither of them spoke. Tom was used to ignoring hunger when he was on a stakeout and delivery would have blown his cover, but Lilly had, once again, made just what he wanted, almost by magic.

He knew it was coming, though. Caroline was not going to sit quietly over there for long. Finally, she set her plate aside and turned to face him. "So?"

"So?" he agreed, refilling both their glasses. "You have questions?"

"You're damn right I do." It could have come out snappish—but it didn't. Her voice took on a languid tone, one that matched the hazy quality of the fire. "Explain this house to me."

"Like I said—I built it."

"By yourself."

"That's correct." He waited, but he knew he wouldn't have to wait long.

He didn't. She was sharp, his Caroline. "With what money? Because that was one of the nicest bathrooms I've ever been in—and it's not like Minneapolis has a lack of decent bathrooms. And the kitchen—it's a chef's wet dream."

He laughed and she laughed with him, but he knew he wasn't off the hook. "Quality is often worth the price."

There was something sharp about her eyes, and he wished he could see her in action in the courtroom as a lawyer. Not from behind the bench, but in front of it. "But that's just it. Who's paying for it? An FBI agent doesn't make this kind of money—no matter how special you are. You have a top-of-the-line cabin on what I can only assume is a pretty big spread of land."

"Eighty acres from the road to the edge of the Red Creek Reservation. I grew up about thirty miles from here." He met her gaze. "I enjoy my privacy."

He could see her thinking over that information. "You maintain an apartment in Pierre."

"And one in Rapid City." Her eyes got wide. "I have a lot of territory to cover. Plus, I have a safe house in Pierre where I can hide people for a while." Only after he said it did he realize what he'd just admitted.

He could have put her in the safe house. Sure, it might have been uncomfortable for a judge to suddenly find herself bunking with former prostitutes and recovering drug addicts, but she would have been perfectly secure.

Instead, he'd brought her out here.

"In the interest of full disclosure," he added with a wave of his hand.

"About damn time," she murmured. But again, she didn't sound angry about it. She was looking at him with those beautiful eyes and suddenly he couldn't figure out why he hadn't told her all this up front. "You own all these various and sundry properties?"

"Yup." He stretched his legs out toward the fire and, amazingly, felt some of the tension of the afternoon begin to drift away, like embers in the wind.

He was not a man who relaxed. There were too many criminals to track and arrest. He'd made so many enemies just doing his job that he rarely let his guard down.

But here? Sitting by a fire with a pretty woman on a clear summer night, a bottle of wine to share?

"Who paid for it?" she asked, her voice curious without being accusatory.

"My wife."

Six

She hadn't just heard that, had she?

"Your *wife*?" Well, that certainly made sense with the "again" comment from earlier. He was married. Of course he was. So what had happened down by the pool? "Where is she?"

He dropped his gaze to his wineglass. "Buried next to her grandparents in Washington, DC."

The air whooshed out of Caroline's lungs. "I'm sorry." Could she be any bigger of an idiot? She might as well have accused him of adultery.

He shrugged, but his face was carefully blank—just like it'd been on the stand when that defense lawyer had tried to trick him. "She died nine years ago in a car accident—hit by a drunk driver. I should have been behind the wheel—but I'd stayed at the party. I had some business to deal with."

The way he said *business* sent a shiver down Caroline's

back. She had the distinctive feeling that he hadn't been getting stock tips.

"In DC?"

He nodded and leaned back, his eyes on the stars. Caroline followed his gaze, and what she saw took her breath away. The night sky was unbelievably gorgeous, not a single star dimmed by city lights.

"The FBI was my way off the res," he began. "But I wasn't alone. Rosebud, the little sister of my best friend, Tanner, got a scholarship to Georgetown and we stuck together—two Lakota fish way out of water."

Caroline had some questions but decided that, since Tom was actually talking, she'd best not interrupt him.

"She and Carlson were in class together and started dating—she's the lawyer for the Red Creek tribe now. James and I got along, and he made sure I went with them to all the fancy parties that his parents made him attend. It always struck me as an odd way to rebel, but…" He shrugged. "That's how I met Stephanie."

He spoke with such tenderness that, once again, Caroline felt like an idiot. He'd loved his wife. Was it wrong to be jealous of a dead woman? Because she couldn't help but be envious of the woman who could hold Tom Yellow Bird's heart.

"She and Carlson were childhood friends—I think their mothers wanted them to marry, but they both settled on two dirt-poor Indians with no money and no family names." He laughed, as if that were funny. "Carlson came west because Rosebud and I needed his help with this case, and he met Maggie—it's quite a story. Ask Maggie about it sometime." A melancholy silence settled over him. "He treats her well, which is good."

The way he said it made it clear that if Tom didn't think Carlson was treating his wife well, there'd be bloodshed. "So you've been working with Carlson for...how long?"

Belatedly, she realized what else he'd said. He'd just assumed that she would meet one of his oldest friends. Maggie probably knew all his embarrassing childhood stories, every dumb and brilliant thing he'd ever done. Carlson was Tom's most trusted friend.

And Tom had just made the assumption that Caroline would meet them. More than that, that she'd meet his friends in a social setting instead of in a law office or a courtroom.

Almost as if Tom expected to be doing a lot more of this—sitting out under the stars, having wine and pizza, and talking—with Caroline.

"We've known each other for over fourteen years now."

Nine years since Stephanie died—Caroline did the quick math.

Tom looked at her. "I was married for almost four years. Since I know you're trying to figure it out."

"That's not the only thing I'm trying to figure out," she murmured. "She was well-off?"

"Her mother was an heiress and her father was a senator." He exhaled heavily. "We tried not to talk politics. They did their best to accept me, which is more than a lot of people in their place might have done. But I was from a different world." He was quiet for a moment, and Caroline couldn't figure out if he was done or if he was just thinking. "I still am."

"I'll give you that—this place is different." She looked back at the stars, galaxies spread out before her, their depths undimmed by something as innocuous as fluorescent lighting.

A little like the man next to her. She topped off her glass and his when he held it out. "I'm sorry about your wife," she said again, because it seemed like the thing to say—even though it wasn't enough. He'd lost someone he cared for, and that was painful no matter what. She reached over and gave his hand a squeeze. He squeezed back, lacing his fingers with hers.

Neither of them pulled away.

"So this was all because of her money?"

"I invested wisely. She ran a charity. Her mother still runs it." He opened his mouth, as if he were going to expand upon that statement, but then he shook his head and changed the subject. "How about you?" He lolled his head to the side, and for a moment, he looked younger. The faint lines of strain were gone from around his eyes and his mouth was relaxed. He looked ten years younger. "Any dead husbands—or other bodies—in your closet?"

She kept her face even. As much as she didn't want to turn the spotlight back onto her occasionally questionable choices, she was relieved that they weren't going to keep talking about his late wife. "Nope. I always figured that once my career was established, I'd settle down, start a family. I've got time."

A look of pure sadness swept over his features before he went back to staring at the sky. "I used to think the same thing."

She didn't like that sadness. "I was almost engaged once, in college," she heard herself say, which surprised her. She never told anyone about Robby. "We were young and stupid and thought we could make it work, us against the world. But we couldn't even make it through senior year." That was glossing over things quite a bit.

The truth of the matter was that she and Robby couldn't make it past a pregnancy scare. She hated making mistakes, and that particular one had nearly altered the entire course of her life.

She and Robby had talked about getting married in that wishful-thinking way all kids did when they were crazy in lust, but when her period had been three days late…

She shuddered at the memory and once again gave thanks that it had been stress, not pregnancy, that had thrown her cycle off.

"Things didn't go as planned," she admitted, which was a nice way of saying that when she'd told Robby she was late, he'd all but turned tail and bolted for the door. The fantasy of living happily ever after with him had crumbled before her eyes, and she'd known then that she'd made the biggest mistake of her life—up to that point, anyway.

Which was ironic, considering that Trent's nickname for her when she'd been growing up had been "the mistake." Not that her parents had ever treated her like that, but Trent had. He would have loved it if Caroline had made the exact same mistake in her own life. "I thought it was going to be perfect, but all it turned out to be was heartbreak."

"You didn't marry him, though?"

"Nope."

Tom shrugged. "No one's perfect—especially not in relationships."

Oh, if only it were that simple. "Regardless, I don't tell people about that. It reflects poorly on my judgment, you understand."

"Of course. I imagine he couldn't keep up with you."

She chuckled at that. "If I agree with you, it'll make me sound egotistical."

His laughter was warm and deep, and it made her want to curl into him. "Perish the thought."

Long moments passed. She sipped her wine, feeling the stress of the day float away on a pleasant buzz. He didn't think less of her because she'd almost tied herself to the wrong man.

Maybe he wouldn't think less of her because she'd made a mistake trusting the wrong man.

"Tom?"

"Yeah?"

"You still haven't answered my question."

Why was she here? What was going on between them? Because she couldn't imagine that he brought other potential witnesses out here and let them skinny-dip in the pond and hold his hand under the stars.

She wanted to think this was different, that he was different with her. Not like he was with his socialite wife in the rarefied air of DC politics and power—but not like he was when he was stalking bad guys and saving the world.

It wasn't egotistical—it was *selfish* to want a little bit of Tom Yellow Bird all to herself. But she did. In this time, this place—hidden away from the rest of the world—she wanted him. Not as a protector and not as a law-enforcement colleague—but as something else. Something *more*.

It was worse than selfish. It was stupid, a risk she shouldn't even contemplate taking.

So why was she contemplating it so damn hard? God, it'd been such a long time since she'd risked letting off a little steam with some good sex. And out here, so far removed from neighbors and courtrooms…

It felt like they'd left reality behind and she and Tom were in a bubble, insulated from the real world and any real consequences.

Would it be so bad to let herself relax for a little bit? Tom would be amazing, she knew. And now that she'd seen where he lived—how he lived—she trusted that no one would ever know what happened between them. No nefarious stalkers planting bugs here. Tom simply wouldn't allow it.

Surely, she thought, staring at his profile, she could

enjoy a little consensual pleasure with him without ruining everything, couldn't she? Take the necessary precautions, not let her heart get involved—not compromise the case?

He didn't answer for a long time. Then, suddenly he stood. "It's late," he said, his voice gruff as he pulled her to her feet. "Let me show you your room."

Yes, she wanted more—but it was clear that, at least right now, she wasn't going to get it.

Tom had always liked this bed. This was a top-of-the-line memory-foam mattress—king size, with fifteen-hundred-thread-count sheets. The ceiling fan spun lazily overhead, making the temperature bearable. Dinner had been delicious and the wine excellent. This was as close to peace and quiet as he got.

So why couldn't he sleep?

Because. Caroline was at the other end of the hall.

He forced himself to be still and let his mind drift. Even if he couldn't sleep, he could rest, and that was all he needed. He didn't need to be on full alert. He had a lazy weekend ahead of him. He just needed enough to keep himself—and his dick—under control.

He let his mind go over his plans for Monday. A morning flight to Washington—it was the only flight, so he hadn't had much of a choice there. Then he'd have dinner with Senator and Mrs. Rutherford—his in-laws. From there, they'd go to the gala fund-raiser for the Rutherford Foundation, the charity Stephanie had founded with her trust fund money. Celine Rutherford, Stephanie's mother, ran the foundation in her daughter's name, but Tom liked to help out whenever he could. It was his way of honoring his late wife.

He didn't love gala fund-raisers, because he'd never quite gotten over the feeling that he was an interloper. He didn't love going back to DC for the same reason, although if he went for work, he was usually fine. And while he greatly respected the Rutherfords, seeing them was still painful. Celine strongly resembled her daughter, and it hurt Tom to look at her and know that was what Stephanie would have looked like if they'd gotten the chance to grow old together.

Usually, he didn't go back for these sorts of things. He had cases to solve, bad guys to catch—and the Rutherfords understood that. They never questioned Tom's work ethic. Instead, they all seemed content with chatty emails from Celine every month or so, plus cards at the holidays.

But once a year, he made the trip out East. He sat down with the Rutherfords and celebrated his wife's life and legacy. The Rutherford Foundation was dedicated to furthering education for girls and women around the world, and thanks to Tom's involvement, he'd gotten some of those funds allocated to Native American reservations around the US.

The timing *sucked*. When he'd made the executive decision to bring Caroline out here, he'd reasoned that he'd have plenty of time to get her back, get the equipment he needed and sweep her house. But in talking with Carlson while she'd soaked in his pool, Tom had realized he wouldn't be able to make his flight if he swept the house himself. As it was, they were going to have to get up before the crack of dawn on Monday so he'd have enough time to get back to his place in Pierre and grab his tuxedo.

At least Carlson could do the sweep on Monday. Tom would feel better if he checked every inch of Caroline's house himself, but he trusted Carlson implicitly. After this, Tom was getting his own sweeper. To hell with using the department's. The things he could buy on the internet were almost as good. Good enough to have checked Caroline's house, anyway.

All these plans buzzed through his head as he lay there, which was fine. It was much better to think of airport security lines and tuxedos than it was to dwell on the mental image of Caroline lying nude in his pool.

He'd left her out there for almost twenty minutes while he'd called Carlson and gotten the pizzas Lilly had made out of the oven. And the whole time, he hadn't been thinking about his late wife or about gala fund-raisers. In all actuality, he'd barely been thinking about corrupt judges or bugged houses.

All he'd been able to think about was Caroline. Lying nude in his pool.

Even now, he could see her out there, the hazy golden light of sunset glimmering around her hair, the reddish spring water dancing over her skin. God, she must have been gorgeous. But he hadn't looked. He'd promised.

At some point in the still of the night, he became aware of movement. Wild animals sometimes prowled around at night—the smell of pizza could've drawn them. Without moving, he woke up and listened.

The sound he heard—the regular if light sound of footsteps, the faint squeaking of the floorboards, the sound of a knob turning—weren't coming from outside. He didn't react as Caroline stepped into the room. Instead, all he could think was that he hoped she didn't gut him like a fish.

He waited until, nearly noiselessly, she'd made her way over to him. "I told you I was a light sleeper."

She made a little noise of surprise. "You're awake?"

"So are you."

"I…" He heard her take a deep breath. "I couldn't sleep."

That got his eyes open. "Yeah?"

But the sight of her in a short cotton gown that fell to just above her knees, her hair rumpled with sleep—God, he didn't know if he could be this strong. "Do you really think someone is going to try and blackmail me?"

"No guarantees in life, but probably. Do you have something to hide?" He desperately wanted her to say no. Maybe it was because it was late or maybe it was because he hadn't been able to stop thinking about her since he'd seen her in her courtroom, ferocious and beautiful.

Or maybe it was just because she was standing in his bedroom in the dead of night, looking for reassurance. And if there was one thing Tom could provide, it was reassurance. Hands-on, physical reassurances. A lot of them.

For years—*years*—he had put all his energy into doing the job, because what else did he have? Not his wife. Not the family they'd planned for.

All he had was the never-ending quest for truth, justice and the American way. He gave the FBI nearly everything he had, and what he held back, he gave to rescuing girls from prostitution.

No matter what, he wanted Caroline to be honest and true. And he wanted her all for himself, selfish bastard that he was. He wanted Caroline for himself, not because she was a new lead or a key component of this damnable case.

He wanted her. God, it felt so good to want again. Even better to be wanted.

There was a pause that made him wonder if maybe he'd read the situation wrong. Then she said, "I don't have any kinks." He heard her swallow. "At least, I don't think I do..."

Tom's body was instantly awake. "You're not sure?"

"Who can say if it's something that's going to be used against me?"

Moving slowly, he sat up, ignoring the way his body jumped to attention. "I could," he offered, not even bothering to convince himself that it was knowledge necessary to keep her safe. This had nothing to do with protecting her, and they both knew it. "You could tell me what you like and I'll let you know if it's a hazard to your reputation or not."

He heard her swallow again, the soft click of her throat muscles working. Would she turn and go back to her bedroom, shut the door and lock it? Or would she…

"I like men," she began, her voice so soft he almost couldn't hear the waver in it.

So far, so good. "Just men?"

He could see her head bob—thank God for the full moon tonight.

"Nothing illegal about that. I think it makes you normal. Unless…" He breathed deeply. He would not lose control. Simple as that. "Do you do anything with your partner that might be dangerous?"

He saw her chest rise and fall as she exhaled. "I…I like to be on top. I have been told that I have extremely sensitive breasts. I like it when my lover strokes them and sucks them. But not biting—they're too sensitive for that."

Adrenaline slammed through his system, his heart pounding and his dick throbbing. He could see it in his mind's eye, her riding him, his face buried in her breasts. "That doesn't seem unusual." His voice cracked.

He needed to have her over him. He needed to feel the warm wetness of her body surrounding him, holding him. He needed to pull one of her nipples into his mouth and suck on it until she screamed with pleasure.

God, he wasn't sure he had ever needed anything so much in his entire life.

He didn't dare move. He didn't want to break the spell that had her sharing her deepest desires. "Is there anything else that could be considered unusual?"

"I…" She took a step toward him. It wasn't a big movement, but he felt it down to his toes. That spark that had always existed between them—it was no longer an isolated flash of light in the darkness. It was burning hotter and brighter than anything he'd ever felt before. It lit him up. *She* lit him up. "I like it when a man bends me over and takes me from behind."

For all of his years keeping his emotions blank and unreadable, Tom could not fight back the groan that started low in his chest and burned its way out of his throat. "Yeah?" he choked out.

"That's not dangerous, is it?" Her voice shook again, but it didn't sound like nerves. It sounded like *want*. "I sometimes fantasize about a man coming into my chambers and bending me over my desk because he wants me so much that we can't wait. He—he might hold me by my hair or dig his fingers into my skin. He can't even wait to get undressed." She took a shuddering breath. "Is it wrong, do you think? It's so risky…"

"Wrong?" He laughed, a dry sound. "I've never heard anything so right in my entire life." Her face practically glowed with what looked a hell of a lot like relief. "I wouldn't try it until your office has been swept for bugs, though. And only with a man you trust completely."

She took another small step closer. His breath caught in his throat—he could see her legs now, long and bare. She had an unearthly glow where the moonlight kissed her skin. He'd never been jealous of the moon before. "That's the problem, you see? There aren't very many men I trust."

"There aren't?"

She shook her head. "Only you."

Tom was on his feet before he could think better of it. Then she was in his arms and he was kissing her.

No, *kissing* was too generic a word that covered too many things.

It didn't cover this—he was *consuming* her. He devoured her lips and sucked on her tongue while he ran his hands down her back and over her bottom, squeezing hard.

"Anything else," he whispered in her ear before he sucked her lobe in between his teeth and nipped, "that could be used against you?"

"I don't like prissy, cautious sex." Her body was vibrating in his arms, and he could feel her nipples, pointed and scraping against his chest. "I like it wild and rough. Loud and—"

He couldn't take another moment of this exquisite torture. He swept her legs out from under her for the second time in a few short hours and threw her onto the bed. "I wanted to do this earlier," he told her. "But I didn't know what you wanted."

"You." He grabbed at his T-shirt. Her hands went to the waistband of his shorts, shoving them and his briefs down. It wasn't gentle or patient. He grabbed the hem of her nightshirt and yanked it over her head, leaving her bare before him just as his erection sprang free. She gasped and then palmed him. Desire ran ragged through him.

When she looked up at him, her eyes luminous in the moonlight, she said, "I want you. Because I feel it, too."

Tom paused for just a second, a wild look of need in his eyes, and Caroline wondered if she'd said the wrong thing.

Please, she found herself praying as she clung to him, *please don't let this be a mistake.*

It wouldn't be, and that was final. She wasn't a naive college girl living in her own little world anymore. She and

Tom were consenting adults and it was perfectly reasonable to burn off a little excess energy doing consensual things. What happened in this room had nothing to do with corruption or cases or the errors of her ways.

But the next thing she knew, Tom had pulled free of her grasp and fallen to his knees. Her hands were empty and she felt oddly bereft.

He grabbed her by the hips and hauled her to the edge of the bed, his fingers digging into her skin. "Caroline," he groaned and then his teeth skimmed over her inner thigh. "Did you ever think of this?"

Then his mouth was upon her, licking and sucking her tender flesh. She sank her fingers into his hair and gave herself up to the sensation. Tom shifted, lifting her legs over his shoulders and spreading her wider for his attentions.

"Sometimes," she got out in a breathy voice. But not very often.

Oral sex was just…one of those things. Her previous lovers had either not been enthusiastic about it or hadn't been good—the worst was when it was both combined. They would go down on her for a few minutes and consider that an even exchange for fellatio.

But Tom? Not only was he enthusiastic—and that would've been more than enough—but he knew what he was doing. He found the bud of her sex and tormented it relentlessly with his tongue. One hand snaked up over her stomach until he was fondling her breast, rubbing his callused thumb over her nipple until it ached. His other hand? When he slipped a finger inside her, she almost came off the bed. She wanted to cry with satisfaction. She didn't. Instead, she just held on for the ride.

Jesus, her fantasies weren't this good. Tom found a rhythm and worked her body. He teased her nipple and licked her sex and thrust his fingers into her body. He gave her no quarter, no space for her mind to wander off and debate the wisdom of this. He kept her in the here and now, in this bedroom, with him. He pushed her body relentlessly as the orgasm built. He must've been able to tell she was close, because suddenly, he wasn't just flicking his thumb back and forth over her taut nipple—he pinched it between his thumb and finger and made a humming noise deep in the back of his throat.

Caroline came undone. Her thighs clenched around his fingers as she rode the waves of pleasure until they left her sated and limp. Slowly, Tom withdrew. He went from licking to pressing gentle kisses against her sex. Instead of pinching her nipple, he stroked his fingers all around her breast and then down over her stomach. Slowly, he pulled free of her body. She shivered at the loss.

She felt she needed to say something, show her appreciation somehow. She should be polite and reciprocate, at least.

But she found she couldn't do any of those things. She was boneless with satisfaction, able to do little more than smile at him. "Hopefully," she said, her voice sultry even to her own ears, "that wasn't a hazardous activity."

Tom got to his feet. The moonlight kissed his skin, giving him an otherworldly look. His erection jutted out from his body, and she lifted her foot to nudge at the tip. "No," he said, his voice deep and commanding, "I don't think there was anything damaging about that." He grabbed her foot when she nudged him again and lifted it, pressing a kiss to the sole.

It tickled and she laughed.

He leaned over her, holding his body above hers. The scent of sex hung between them as his erection brushed her hip. Unexpectedly, her eyes watered. This man—more

than his dammed spring, more than his wine and pizza—
she'd needed this from this man. "You decide."

She touched his face, letting her fingertips trace the
map of his skin. "On what?"

Even in this dim light, she could see his eyes darken.
"Do I flip you over or make you ride me?" She gasped at
his words, her body arching into his. He'd paid attention,
bless the man. He went on, "Should I suck your breasts
or slap your ass?"

She pulled him down onto the bed, rolling as he went.
"I'm on top."

"God," he muttered, shifting so they were in the middle
of the bed, "I love a woman who knows what she wants."

Seven

"Condoms? Something?"

It took a second for Caroline's words to sink in, because Tom was having trouble getting past the way she straddled him, her breasts ripe for the plucking. His erection ached with need—and it only got worse when she settled her weight on him. He could feel the warmth of her sex against his dick—so close, yet so far away. He flexed his hips, dragging against her sensitive skin.

She made a noise high in the back of her throat as she shifted, bringing him against her entrance. But before he could thrust home, she leaned up, breaking the contact. "*Tom*. Condom?"

"Um…" Right, right. Birth control was the responsible thing here. As much as he hated to lift Caroline off him, he couldn't risk her health just because he couldn't think of a single thing beyond how her body would take his in. "One second."

He kept a fully stocked emergency cabinet in the storeroom that could help him survive a few months out here—and along with the necessities in the kit were unlubricated condoms. He just had to find them—which he had to do naked, while not looking at the pictures on the wall.

As he searched, Tom could almost feel Stephanie's eyes on him. Which was ridiculous. But he couldn't bring himself to glance at their wedding photos. He couldn't display them out in the open, but he also couldn't put them in an album on the shelf. So they lived here, in his storage room.

She would've wanted him to do this, he told himself, rifling through the emergency supplies. Stephanie had loved him beyond the point of reason, and she wouldn't have wanted him to spend the rest of his life alone. Not that having sex with Caroline had anything to do with the rest of his life. Those two things weren't directly connected.

Except…for that spark.

Stephanie would have wanted him to be happy. Polished, quiet Stephanie, who liked slow seductions and quiet submissions and sex in a bed. Only a bed. Never in an office or on a desk.

Finally, he found the condoms and a tube of all-purpose lube. It felt like he'd been looking for hours, but it'd probably been no more than five minutes. By the time he made it back to the bedroom, he was afraid the magic of the moment had been broken.

He paused at the bedroom door, trying to play out all possible outcomes. Would she have fallen back asleep? Changed her mind? Would he have to go sit in his spring-fed pool to keep himself under control?

He could take care of himself—he'd been doing it for years. But he didn't want to. He wanted to get back to that place where he and Caroline were two consenting adults about to get what they needed.

He needed her.

He had from the very beginning, when she'd been magnificent in her courtroom.

"Tom?" Her voice was soft, sultry. Not the voice of a judge, but the voice of a woman. A woman who needed to be satisfied.

For a fleeting second, he wished he were bringing a little more experience to the table. He didn't want to think he'd forgotten how to do this, but it'd been a long, long time since he'd had sex with another person.

But then he licked his lips, the taste of her sex still on his mouth, and he figured, what the hell. Sex was like riding a bike, only a lot more fun. "I'm here."

She was splayed out on her side, moonlight kissing her in the most intimate of places. Places he'd kissed. Places he was going to kiss again.

He watched as she slid a hand over her breast, cupping it and stroking her own nipple. He went painfully hard at the sight as her head lolled back. "Did you find a condom?" she asked in a breathy voice.

Instantly, he was hard all over again. His mind might have some performance anxiety, but his body was raring to go. "I found several."

"Oh, thank God." She pushed herself up and patted the bed next to her. "Come to bed, Tom."

He dropped the supplies on the sheets and crawled over to her. "You look good in my bed," he murmured, rolling onto his back. "I like you there."

He reached for the condom—but before he could, her mouth was on him. "Caroline," he groaned, trying to pull her up.

"You didn't tell me what you liked," she said, her voice throaty as she licked up his length.

He sank his fingers into her hair, trying to pull her up

and trying to hold her where she was at the same time. His brain short-circuited as the unfamiliar sensations rocketed through him. Her mouth was warm and wet and she was just as fierce as he'd hoped.

"This…this is good," he ground out, his hips moving on their own. She gripped him tightly as she licked at his tip. "God, Caroline."

Then he looked down at her. She was staring up at him as she licked and sucked, a huge grin on her face as she pleasured him. "This isn't a hazardous activity, is it?"

He wasn't going to make it. He sat up and pulled her away. He needed the barrier of the condom between them, because it was too much—she was too much. "I can't wait," he told her, rolling on the condom and applying the lube. "I need you right now."

"Yes," she hissed, straddling him again. This time, when his erection found her opening, she didn't pull away. Instead, she lowered her weight onto him, slowly at first, and then, with a moan that made his gaze snap to hers, she sank down the rest of the way, taking him in fully. "Oh, *yes*, Tom."

His mind blanked in the white-hot pleasure of it all. It'd been so long—but his body hadn't forgotten. The smell of sex hung heavy around them, and Caroline's body pinned him to the bed. He blinked, bringing her into focus. He let go of her hips only long enough to shove the pillows under his shoulders.

Because he hadn't forgotten what she'd whispered to him. "These are amazing," he told her, doing his best to focus on her needs, her body—and not how he was already straining to keep his climax in check. He stroked his fingertips over her breasts. "Simply amazing."

Her back arched as her hips began to rock. "Do you like them?"

"I do. But," he added, reaching around her waist with one hand and pushing her down to his mouth, "I like them more here."

With that, he sucked her right breast into his mouth and teased her left nipple with his fingers. He didn't bite—but he didn't have to. Caroline went wild as he lavished attention on her breasts. She moaned as her flesh filled his mouth, his hands. He wasn't gentle, either. She wanted loud? She wanted to feel like he couldn't hold back?

It wasn't a stretch, that. He lost himself in her body, her sounds, her taste. She grabbed onto the headboard and rode him wildly. It was all he could do to hang on long enough.

But he did. When she threw her head back and screamed out his name, he dug his fingers into the smooth skin of her hips and, thrusting madly, let go. God, it felt so good to let go again.

She collapsed onto his chest, panting heavily as he wrapped his arms around her and held on tight. In that moment, he felt like he'd come home again.

Who knew that by losing himself in her, he'd find himself again? But he was alive from head to toe, truly *alive*.

"Tom," she whispered against the crook of his neck.

"Yeah." He exhaled heavily and wished he were a younger man, one who had it in him to roll her onto her back and take her again. He shifted, lifting her off enough that he could get rid of the condom before settling her back against his chest. "Wow."

After a long time—Tom had begun to drift—she propped herself up on her elbows. "So," she said, the happiest smile he'd seen yet on her face. "What are the plans for the rest of the weekend?"

And then, because he wasn't as old as he thought, he did roll her onto her back and cover her with his body. "This," he said, flexing his hips and grinding against her. "Pizza and wine and the pool and *this*, Caroline."

"Finally," she murmured against his lips as she wrapped her legs around his waist. "A straight answer."

He was already thrusting inside her when he realized that the sensation was more intense than it'd been last time. He withdrew long enough to get another condom before he buried his body in hers again.

He'd finally come home, and he damn well intended to stay here.

Eight

This was a mistake, Tom thought as he stood next to the bed, staring down at Caroline's sleeping form. A rare tactical error. A series of errors, each compounding the other until what he was left with was a huge mess of his own making.

He shouldn't have brought her out here, knowing damn well he had to fly out of South Dakota first thing Monday morning. And he shouldn't have fallen into bed with her, either.

But he'd done both of those things, anyway. For once, he hadn't put the case first. And now he had to deal with the consequences.

She wasn't going to like this.

"Caroline."

She startled, blinking sleepily at him in the soft light from the bedside lamp. "What? Time to get up?"

"Yes."

Tom handed over the cup of coffee. She sat up to take

it, which made the sheet fall down around her waist. He almost groaned at the sight of her breasts. Damn it, this was not how he'd wanted to wake her up, either. But the die was cast.

She smiled sleepily at him, an invitation and a promise all rolled into one. "How much time do we have?"

He gritted his teeth. He'd indulged himself all weekend long. That was a luxury neither of them had right now. "Get dressed."

She blinked at him. At least this time, her eyes were almost moving at the same speed. "Are we back to this? You're not going to answer any question directly? Come on, babe."

Crap. It wasn't even five fifteen in the morning, and all he wanted to do was climb back into this bed with her and forget about the rest of the world, just like he'd dared to do for the last two days.

The rest of the world, however, wasn't about to be forgotten. He sat down on the bed. Which was a mistake, because when he did that, he reached over and cupped her cheek. "There's been a change of plans."

She leaned into his touch, looking worried. He didn't like that look. "How bad is it?"

There was probably a diplomatic way to inform her of the change in their travel plans. But he didn't have time to figure out what it was. "You're coming to Washington, DC, with me."

Her mouth fell open, and she jolted so hard she almost spilled her coffee. "But I'm supposed to be at work today…"

Tom forced himself to stand and move away from her. "There's been an emergency. Your house will not be secure by the time you get off work today, and I'm not willing to risk you going back there without having it swept. So you're coming with me."

She blinked again and then, in one long swallow, finished the coffee. When the mug was empty, she smiled widely. "Funny. Real funny, Tom. It's a little early for practical jokes, but it's good to see that you have a sense of humor at any hour." Her voice trailed off when he didn't return her easy grin. "Wait—you aren't joking?"

He shook his head. "This trip has been planned for months. I thought I'd be able to secure your house before my flight left this morning, but when I realized I wouldn't have time, Carlson was going to do it for me. But he's had an emergency and I don't trust anyone else to do it."

The ticket desk at the Pierre Airport wasn't open yet, so he'd have to buy her ticket when he got there. He hadn't once been on a full flight from Pierre to Minneapolis to Dulles, so it shouldn't be a problem.

"I have to go to DC because you have to go to DC," she repeated, as if she were trying to learn a foreign language. He nodded. "Because the only other person you trust to sweep my house for bugs that may or may not exist is dealing with an emergency."

"That's correct."

She flung off the covers, and despite the early hour, despite the less-than-ideal circumstances, his pulse beat a little harder as she stomped around his bedroom wearing nothing.

"I have cases on the docket," she announced, her voice suddenly loud. The caffeine must have kicked in. "I can't just jet off with you. There has to be someone else—"

"No, there isn't. I told you—Carlson and I keep our activities quiet. That way no one can compromise our investigations. His wife is having pregnancy complications and I'm not about to mess with our operating procedures—procedures that have led to several successful convictions—just because—"

"You're being ridiculous," she snapped, throwing on her clothes.

Maybe he was. Maybe he shouldn't be taking her anywhere. After all, it hadn't taken more than a few hours out here, away from prying eyes and ears, before they'd wound up in bed together. It was one thing to indulge in a long, satisfying weekend with her at his isolated cabin—it was something completely different to take her to DC.

Then, before he could come up with any sort of witty retort to "ridiculous," she pulled up short. "Wait—Maggie's having complications?" She spun on him. "Is she okay?"

The fact that she was suddenly concerned for one of his oldest friends—whom she did not know—despite the fact that she was furious with him made something tighten in his chest. "She's got the very best watching over her. She's had some problems with high blood pressure, but they're controlling it." He hoped like hell Maggie would be okay. He couldn't bear the thought of losing another woman he cared for.

"That's good. I hope she's okay. But I can't fly to Washington, Tom."

"Take a sick day. Two," he corrected. "We'll fly back tomorrow."

She jammed her hands on her hips. She'd gotten her bra and shorts on, but she hadn't zipped them up. He knew what she was going to say before she said it, though. "No."

"*Yes*, Caroline." He began grabbing the rest of her things and shoving them into her bag. They could argue in the car. And, knowing Caroline, they would. "I don't know what kind of man you think I am, but after what's happened between us this weekend, you have to realize that I'm not about to do a damn thing that would put you at risk."

"Except drag me across time zones."

"I'm not leaving you behind, and that's final."

"I'll stay at a hotel," she announced, pulling her shirt over her head.

For a moment, he considered that. Hell, a hotel was where he should have put her in the first place. Anyone else, he would've done just that.

But could he trust that whoever had bugged her house hadn't also bugged her office? That they wouldn't be waiting to track her back to wherever she went—her home, a hotel, the safe house?

Bringing her out here hadn't been his tactical error. Not the big one, anyway.

No, where he'd really screwed up was thinking that he could separate this weekend with her from everything else—his work with the foundation, his job investigating the corruption case, his life. All of it.

He hadn't put the case first. He'd made an exception for Caroline because when he'd looked at her, he'd felt this spark—and the power of that pull had completely erased his professional distance.

She was his assignment. That was all that should be happening between them.

But now that he'd gotten in this deep with her, he couldn't walk away. Or fly away, as the case might be.

"No," he announced.

"Why the hell not?" It was easier to have this argument with her now that she was fully dressed. She grabbed the duffel from him and gave him the kind of look that most likely had wayward attorneys wetting their pants. She was ferocious, his Caroline. "Give me one good reason why, Tom. One really freakin' *good* reason."

He could run through the list of collateral damage this corruption case had left over the years. Lives destroyed, reputations ruined. Justice subverted.

Or he could argue about her personal safety. He could go into excruciating detail about how he'd seen other people's houses get bugged and that information had been used to wreck their lives. He could scare the hell out of her, because a scared witness was willing to do anything to stay safe.

He could also tell her what, up until sixty hours ago, had been the truth—that one person's inconvenience and discomfort meant nothing—not hers, not his. Breaking this case open was the only thing that mattered, and he would do whatever it took to finally get to the bottom of who was buying and blackmailing judges.

He did none of those things. Instead, he closed the distance between them, pulled her into his chest and kissed the holy hell out of her. She tasted of coffee and Caroline, a jolt to his system that he was already addicted to.

"Because," he said when he broke the kiss. Her eyes were closed and she was breathing hard, and if they weren't pushing deadlines, he'd lay her out on the bed and to hell with the rest of the world. "Come with me, Caroline. I…"

He almost said he needed her. Which was *not* true. He needed to know she was safe. He needed to know she was beyond the grasp of blackmailers and violent criminals.

It wasn't like she was someone he couldn't live without.

"Just come with me," he finished, which was not a good reason. It barely qualified as a bad reason, but damn it, it was early and he had to get her to the airport.

Her brow furrowed and her tongue traced the seam of her lips. It was physically painful, resisting the urge to lean down and replace her tongue with his own, but he managed to keep his distance. "Please," he added, way too late.

Her shoulders sagged. "I am *definitely* going to regret

this," she murmured as she shouldered her duffel. "What the hell. Let's go to DC. But," she added, jabbing him in the chest with her finger, "you better make it worth it."

"I will," he promised, trying not to grin and failing. "Trust me, I will."

Nine

"Celine. It's me. Listen, there's been a change of plans."

Caroline had no idea if she was supposed to be eavesdropping—but it was hard not to. Tom was pacing in a small circle about five feet away from her. That was all there was room for at the gate in Minneapolis, while they waited for their connecting flight.

But even that small space couldn't contain his energy. Caroline couldn't stop staring at him. Even though she was beyond irritated with the man, there was still something about him that called to her.

Tom's voice was pitched low, and she had to strain to hear him over the noise in the terminal.

She'd had no plans to be in Minneapolis today. Sure, it was always great to come home again, but being stuck at the airport for a ninety-minute layover wasn't exactly a homecoming.

"I'm bringing a guest," Tom went on.

Well. At least Caroline had been upgraded from security risk to guest. That had to count for something, right?

Tom's gaze cut over to her. "For a case… No. Don't worry—she'll be fine. But we might have to change dinner plans."

Caroline was tempted to point out that nothing about this situation was fine, but she didn't want to interrupt. Who was Celine? Not a girlfriend, she was pretty sure. But not a hundred percent sure, because she wasn't one hundred percent sure about any of this. Had she really been pulled onto a plane by the man of her dreams without luggage, toiletries, coffee…?

"We're traveling light, so if you could have something for her tonight?… Yeah. I'm sorry to be such a pain."

Wait. Had Tom Yellow Bird just apologized? Oh, she had to meet this Celine. Because Caroline was reasonably sure she'd never heard the man apologize for anything, and he'd quasi-kidnapped her twice now.

No, he hadn't kidnapped her. That wasn't fair to him. She had, after all, willingly gone along with him both times.

And why had she done that? There wasn't any rational reason for why she had thrown caution, common sense and her professional reputation to the wind. Sure, Tom would try to dress the last four days up as a matter of her safety. Yes, there'd been something off in her house.

But who were they kidding?

She'd come with him because she couldn't help herself. Tom Yellow Bird made her want to do things that she shouldn't—want things she shouldn't. And as ridiculous as this whole situation might be, she'd come with him because it'd meant another few days with him. It'd meant learning a little more about Tom Yellow Bird.

It'd meant another night in his arms and, apparently, that was worth the risk.

A sour feeling settled into her stomach. At this point, at ten fifteen on a Monday morning, when she was supposed to be in court, Caroline was completely out of rational reasons for any of the choices she'd made since calling Tom on Friday night.

It was hard to even remember how this had started—her house had felt wrong. Tom thought it was bugged. Someone was potentially planning to blackmail her.

So what had she done in response to a blackmail threat? Run away with the FBI agent assigned to the case and thrown herself at him. And now she was running away with him again, this time to Washington, DC.

For someone who prided herself on making the right choices ninety-nine out of a hundred times, Caroline was sure screwing things up.

"Hold on, I'll ask her." Tom turned to her. "What size do you wear?"

It wasn't like he hadn't seen her naked and didn't have a really good idea of her weight. So this was just another indignity. "Eight."

Tom repeated the number and then said, "What?... Oh. Yeah, okay." Then he handed the phone to her. "Be polite," he said in a low voice.

She scowled. When was she not polite? "Hello?"

"If you could just give me your dress size, shoe size, hair color, eye color, skin tone and body type, that would make this so much easier," a cultured woman's voice said with no other introduction.

Whoever this was, she certainly sounded like a Celine.

"Excuse me?" Maybe this was some sort of personal assistant? Frankly, at this point, nothing would surprise her.

"For tonight?" Celine said, as if she were speaking to

a child. "Thomas has indicated you will need something to wear."

Thomas? She looked up at him. He was frowning, but that could have just been his normal expression at this point. "What's happening tonight?"

Tom's frown deepened. If she hadn't spent the weekend wrapped around him, she might be intimidated.

"Why, the Rutherford Foundation's annual gala benefit," Celine announced, as if that were the most obvious thing in the world instead of a complete surprise. "Thomas is, as usual, the guest of honor. And if he thinks enough of you to bring you as his guest, we can't have you looking like you just walked off the plane, can we?"

The Rutherford Foundation? Later, she was going to strangle the man. Slowly. But she'd promised to be polite— and she had to admit, she desperately wanted to meet the woman Tom not only apologized to freely, but would let call him Thomas. "Oh. Yes. He mentioned something about that," she lied. "I'm a size eight and I wear a seven and a half in shoes."

"Hair color? Eye color? Bra size? Are you pear shaped or top-heavy?"

This was not awkward at all, she kept repeating to herself as she answered the questions. Her face felt like it was on fire with embarrassment, but she answered as honestly as she could.

"Thank you," Celine said, and oddly, she did sound genuinely grateful. "If I could speak with Thomas again? Oh—I didn't even get your name."

"Caroline. Caroline Jennings." Should she mention she was a judge? Or was that on a need-to-know basis? "Thank you for your help," she said, remembering her manners. "Will I have the chance to meet you tonight?"

Celine laughed, a delicate, tinkling sound. "Oh, I wouldn't miss it for the world."

With that vaguely ominous statement, Caroline handed the phone back over. What the hell had she gotten herself into?

This wasn't her world. Her world was predictable and safe. She lived her life to minimize the number of risks she took. Risks like running off with a man who was little more than a stranger, or falling into bed with said stranger.

Or jetting across the country to attend a gala benefit for a foundation with a dress code that required her body shape to be up for analysis, for God's sake.

She was skipping work. That was a hazard to her professional reputation. And Tom…

"We'll see you in a few hours," he told Celine, his gaze cutting over to Caroline.

Tom was definitely hazardous.

Tom ended the call and loomed over her. Unlike in Pierre, where they had been the only people in the airport besides a ticket clerk who'd also been the baggage handler, the Minneapolis Airport was crowded with people. Tom had only been able to snag one seat at their gate, and he had insisted Caroline sit in it.

It was sort of chivalrous. Thoughtful, even—which was quite a change of pace from him waking her up at the butt crack of dawn and informing her she was flying to the nation's capital with him, no discussion allowed. But that one small chivalrous act was barely a drop in an ocean of other things that were the complete opposite of thoughtful.

"We're going to a gala benefit for the Rutherford Foundation?" she asked, wondering if she should pinch herself—hard—to wake up from this strange dream. "You don't think you might have mentioned that before I had to give my body type to some woman named Celine?"

"I wanted to make sure you would be welcomed at the benefit," he said, choosing each word carefully.

She tried to be understanding. Really, she did. If she were to look at the situation objectively, Tom's behavior made perfect sense within a certain context. And that context was that he was a widowed officer of the law. He'd lived alone for years. He was used to giving orders and having them followed. He was used to being right, because who was going to contradict him? The criminals he arrested?

No, she had known from the very first moment Tom had walked into her courtroom that he did things his way, and honestly, that was part of his appeal. Or it had been, until this morning.

But damn it, she was not some common criminal he was shuffling from courthouse to jail. Hell, she wasn't even a witness that he was protecting at all costs. She didn't know what she was, except the woman who couldn't resist doing whatever he told her to.

She was definitely going to regret this.

"For the record," she began, standing so he wasn't staring down at her, "you should have told me first. Even better, you should've asked me to go as your date. It's a lot more effective than ordering me around and keeping me in the dark."

"I'm not—it wasn't—"

"You were and it was," she interrupted. "I like you, Tom. I hope you realize that. I wouldn't be here if I didn't."

He took a breath that looked shaky. "I am aware of that."

God save her from men who couldn't talk about their feelings. Caroline pressed on. "But if you keep treating me like…like a chess piece you can move around the board whenever the whim strikes you, this won't end well for either of us."

She wasn't ready for what happened next. His scowl slipped, and underneath, she saw... vulnerability. Worry. "You're not a chess piece, Caroline." He stepped in closer to her. She felt him all the way down to her toes. "Not to me."

Her whole body leaned toward him without her express permission. Something more—that's what he was to her. That's what she was to him, right?

No. Get a grip, she ordered herself. She'd rather be mad at him. There was nothing wrong with angry sex, after all. But tenderness was dangerous. For all she knew, affection could be deadly.

So she didn't allow herself to feel any of that. "Good," she said, making sure to keep her voice firm, "Now, why don't you tell me about this gala benefit I'm accompanying you to this evening?"

Celine had done as she'd promised. More than she'd promised, Tom realized when he and Caroline walked into the room at the Watergate Hotel. Celine and Mark always offered to put him up in their guest room, but he'd been staying at this hotel for years. It was better this way. The room was a small apartment, really, with an office, dining room, kitchen and a generous bedroom—with a generous bed.

There, right there in the middle of the room, were boxes from Bloomingdale's, stacked seven high on the coffee table. Hanging over the back of the bedroom door were two garment bags, one long and one shorter.

An unfamiliar twinge of nervousness took him by surprise. He couldn't be nervous. He did this every year. He'd attended enough formal events that he could push through feeling that he was an impostor. He belonged here now.

At first, coming back to DC, getting suited up in his

tuxedo and pressing the flesh with the political movers and shakers had almost been more than Tom could bear, but he'd done it to honor Stephanie's memory and pay his respects to her parents.

By now this trip was old hat to him. He was on a first-name basis with those movers and shakers. His custom-made tuxedo was cut to conceal his gun. He could chat with Mark and Celine without feeling like his heart was being ripped out of his chest. There was no reason to be nervous.

"Holy hell." Caroline's voice came from behind him. She sounded stunned. "Look at this place! And—whoa." She stepped around him and stared at the boxes. "How much clothing did she get for me?"

It was a fair question. In addition to the seven boxes on the coffee table, there were three more on the floor. "Knowing Celine, she probably got you a few options, just in case something didn't quite work." A huge clothes-horse, Celine would have enjoyed the opportunity to shop for someone else.

But he didn't say that. He felt out to sea here, because he hadn't had a date, as Caroline had started calling this evening, in...

Okay, he wasn't going to think about how long.

It wasn't a date, though. He was not dragging her around the country just so he could have sex with her whenever he wanted. This was a matter of safety. Of public interest. He couldn't compromise this case any more than he already had.

Yeah, he wasn't buying that, either.

Caroline reached over as if to pick up the top box and then pulled her hand back. "I don't think I can afford what she picked out."

"I'm paying for it." She turned and launched another

blistering glare at him. "I'm the one who dragged you out here," he reminded her. "The least I can do is foot the bill for the appropriate evening wear."

She chewed at her lip, and even though his head wasn't a mess and he wasn't nervous about tonight, he wanted to kiss her anxiety away. He wanted to do a lot more than kiss her. He wanted her back in his bed, where they should have been this morning.

"And her husband—that's Senator Rutherford, right?" She nervously twisted her hands together. "I can't believe that he was your father-in-law. And I really can't believe that I'm going to a party with them tonight." Her brow wrinkled as she stared at the boxes.

"You'll do fine," he said—not so much because it was what she needed to hear, although it might be. But it was because he needed to hear it, too.

He was just introducing the only woman he'd slept with since Stephanie to her parents. No big deal.

"We've got a few hours," he said, carrying his bag into the bedroom. He needed to hang his tux and make sure his shoes were shined. "I need to check in with the office."

The look on her face let him know loud and clear that he'd said the wrong thing. "Oh."

Damn it. He immediately saw his mistake. What kind of jerk was he to drag her to DC and then ignore her? "What I meant to say is, after I check in, if there's something you want to see, we could go do that."

She snorted in what he hoped was amusement, but her face softened and he got the distinctive sense that she knew he was trying. Mostly failing, but trying anyway. "Play tourist with you? Now you're getting the hang of this date thing. Sadly, I don't think we have time to wander the Mall. I need to see what I'm dealing with here—" she gestured to the boxes "—and I definitely need a shower." She looked again at all the boxes. "I hope there's some makeup in there or something."

The mention of a shower caught his attention. Shower sex was definitely one of his fantasies. Nothing in this day had gone according to plan. Yeah, he was rolling with the punches as best he could, but...

He wanted to relieve some of the tension that had started to build the moment she'd sat up in bed this morning, the sheet pooling at her waist.

He wanted to get her naked and wet, their bodies slick and then he wanted...

But he couldn't. He had ignored his responsibilities long enough. He had to do his job. Long after whatever this thing with Caroline was had ended, the job would still be there.

So instead of leading her to the shower and stripping her bare, he took a step back and said, "I'm sure there is. And if there isn't, I'll get you some." She notched an eyebrow at him. "I'll have someone who knows something about makeup get some for you," he corrected. "Deal?"

"Deal." She cracked her knuckles and made for the boxes. "Let's see what we've got."

Ten

What they had, Caroline concluded an hour later, was half a department store's worth of clothes. *Good* clothes. The kind of designer names that made her bank account weep with frustration.

Armani. Gucci. Halston, even. Celine Rutherford had exceptional taste and apparently an unlimited budget.

How on earth was she supposed to let anyone else pay for all of this? Four gowns—gowns!—plus two summery sundresses, a pair of Bermuda shorts, a pair of twill trousers, four different tops to pair with the pants, matching accessories and shoes for every outfit. For God's sake, there was even lingerie in here. Really nice lingerie. The kind a woman wore when she was intent upon seducing a man. Pale pink silk, delicate black lace—damn.

And of course there was makeup. Hell, the stuff in one of those bags wasn't even the brands she sometimes splurged on at the department stores. Tom Ford? Guerlain?

She was looking at a complete wardrobe that had probably set Tom back close to ten thousand dollars. More, if the stones in the necklaces and earrings were real diamonds and emeralds and not reasonable facsimiles. She hoped like hell they were fakes.

Her chest began to tighten as she surveyed the luxury goods. This wasn't right. This was like when she'd been a first-year prosecutor, drowning under the weight of her student loans, and had woken up one day to discover that, somehow, all of her debts had been mysteriously paid off.

It had been a mistake then not to undo that. It would be a mistake now to accept all of this finery.

What complicated things even more was that she was afraid she was falling for Tom. Some of him, anyway. She wasn't in love with the domineering parts of him that gave orders first and made requests second. But a part of her even found that appealing. He was just such a strong man, confident and capable, willing to run toward danger. But underneath that was a streak of vulnerability that tugged at her heartstrings.

Wrap that all up in his intense eyes and hard body and— well, was it any wonder she was in Washington, DC, willing to compromise her morals *again* just to be with him?

She glanced back at the doorway that led to a small office. Tom had disappeared in there when she'd started unpacking the boxes—he obviously wasn't the kind of guy who was heavily invested in women's fashion. Every so often, she could hear him talking—was he working or was he checking in on Maggie?

It almost didn't matter. Caroline strongly suspected that, when it came to his friends, his focus was just as intense as it was when he was working a case. He took his job seriously and she respected the hell out of him for it, even if she selfishly wanted him all to herself.

If this whole crazy weekend turned into something

more…what would they even look like as a couple? She couldn't ask him to stop working—it was clearly such a huge part of who he was, just like being a judge was fundamental to who she was. It wouldn't be selfish to ask him to pull him back from his duties to spend more time with her—it would be unconscionable.

A flare of guilt caught her by surprise. No, she couldn't compromise his ability to do his job—any more than she already had. And she couldn't compromise her reputation any more than she already had, either. Gifts as extravagant as this wardrobe looked bad, and when it came to conflicts of interest, appearance was everything.

Which meant she couldn't keep the clothes.

She'd have to wear one of the dresses and the shoes. But she wouldn't take the tags off anything else. The rest of it was all going back.

Now she just had to figure out how to tell Tom that. She didn't want to seem ungrateful, but she didn't want it to look like she could be bought for the price of designer formal wear.

She needed a shower to clear her head. "I'm going to start getting ready," she announced after she tapped on the office door. "Is it okay if I shower first?"

He shot her a look that kicked the temperature of the room up a solid five degrees, and Caroline found herself hoping that he'd offer to join her. Then he said, "Be my guest."

She was not disappointed by this. She needed to shave and exfoliate, and it was hard to do all those things with a man in the tub with her. So this was just fine. Really.

She was rinsing her hair when the door to the bathroom clicked open. She turned to find Tom leaning against the sink, watching her.

There was something about the way he was holding his

body that made her nipples tighten in anticipation. Maybe he had come to join her, after all. She shouldn't want him here. She shouldn't willfully keep making the same mistakes, over and over.

But here he was, and she was powerless to send him away.

"Are you waiting on the shower?" As she asked, she ran her fingers over her chest and down her stomach, rinsing the soap off.

Even at this distance—maybe six feet between them—she could see his eyes darken. He practically vibrated—but he didn't move.

"Or," she said, musing out loud, "you could join me. Plenty of room." She made a big show of scooting to one side.

He made a noise that echoed off the tiled walls. His clothes hit the floor, and the next thing she knew, he had her pinned against the wall, his erection nudging at her. "Did I mention that this is one of my fantasies?"

"Is it, now?" She dug her fingers into his hair, tilting his head back so the water sluiced over him. "I don't recall you mentioning your fantasies. Just mine." It felt dangerous to tease him like this, but God help her, it felt right, too. Somehow, she knew she was safe with him.

"Caroline," he groaned. He flipped her around—and none too gently, either. "I can't wait—I have to have you right now." He nudged her legs apart with his knee and tilted her bottom up. "Okay?"

"Yes," she hissed, arching her back to give him better access.

He was against her and then he thrust inside her in one smooth movement, filling her so effortlessly that she almost screamed from the pleasure of it. But she just managed to keep her noises restrained.

The he wound her hair around his fist and pulled her head back. "You have no idea," he whispered in her ear, his voice hoarse, "*no* idea how much I love hearing you scream." As he spoke, his other hand reached around and took possession of her breast, his fingers expertly finding her nipple and tormenting it mercilessly.

Caroline shimmered as she surrendered to the sensations. Her body adjusted to his and then he began to thrust, long, measured strokes timed with his fingers tugging on her nipple, his hand pulling gently but steadily on her hair and his mouth, his teeth on her neck and shoulders.

This weekend had been intense, a fantasy played out in real time. But this? She flattened her hands against the wall and gave herself up to him completely.

"Scream for me, Caroline," he whispered in her ear, his voice desperate, his hands on her body as he drove into her again and again.

It was all she could do, the only gift she could give him. And she gave it freely. "Tom—*Tom!*"

He growled and sank into her. Caroline's world exploded around her in a shimmering white light. Seconds later, Tom relinquished his hold on her hair and breast and dug his hands into her hips. He slammed into her with a ferocity that she knew she'd never find in another man. A second climax had her screaming his name again as he froze, her name a groan of pleasure on his lips.

They sagged against each other, the wall holding them up. Without warning, Caroline began to laugh. It came from deep inside—a release that she hadn't known she'd needed.

Tom spun her in his arms and tilted her head back. "Okay?" he asked, an amused smirk on his lips.

She was laughing so hard tears ran down her face. All these years and *this* was what she'd been chasing. She'd had a bunch of mediocre sex and occasionally some good sex, all because it was careful. Safe. But this?

She'd always known something was missing. And all it took was one cryptic FBI agent with an overprotective streak and the fantasies she'd nurtured quietly for years to show her how much she'd settled for.

And the hell of it was, she'd *known*. From the first moment she'd caught him staring at her across the courtroom, so caught up in her that he forgot to be seated—she'd known he was something special.

"I've never been better," she said when she finally had herself under control as she pulled him back into her arms. "Never."

"Good," he said against her lips. "Because I have a few more fantasies I want to try out."

She tried to look coy, which was something of a challenge, given that they were naked underneath a stream of water. "Don't we have to go to some gala?"

He cupped her face in his hands. "I'm not talking about just tonight, Caroline."

The full meaning of his words hit her. Dating. A relationship, even. *"Oh."*

His grin was wolfish. How could a man look so hungry when he'd just been sated so spectacularly?

"Let's get through tonight," he told her. "Then…"

"Right. Tonight." She had to put on a gown and what were probably real jewels and hobnob with heiresses and power brokers.

What else did he have in store for her?

She tried on the black dress, but, as expected, she couldn't wear either her serviceable beige bra or the silky strapless pink one Celine had provided. She decided to go with the plum gown. The color was deep and rich, not quite purple and not quite maroon. It wasn't bright enough that she'd stand out in a crowd, but it wasn't black, either.

Although the floor-length dress was sleeveless, it had two little straps that met at the center of the neckline, a V nestled between her breasts that provided just enough support that she wouldn't spend the evening tugging at the top. She paired it with a cuff bracelet that she hoped like hell was covered in rhinestones and not real diamonds. Along with that went sparkly chandelier earrings. She chose the kitten-heeled silver sandals.

She managed to get the dress zipped on her own and then turned to look at her reflection in the full-length mirror on the closet door. What she saw stunned her—was that really her?

Because the woman looking back at her was glamorous—gorgeous, even. That woman bore only a passing resemblance to Caroline.

Maybe she could do this—waltz into this world of power and wealth, and if not fit in, at least fake it for an evening.

"Caroline? We need to leave," Tom called out from the living room.

"Have you heard anything about Maggie?" she yelled back, touching up her lipstick. Not that her lipstick needed to be touched up. It was possible she was stalling.

None of this seemed real. The clothes, the jewelry, being in a DC hotel room with Tom—she was afraid to break the strange spell he'd cast over her.

"They managed to get the contractions stopped and everything is stabilized. They're still keeping her another night, but better safe than sorry at this point."

"Good. I'm glad to hear it." It was obvious Maggie was important to him, but more than that, Caroline didn't wish pregnancy complications on anyone.

Finally, she couldn't stall any longer. She wanted to make a good impression on his…were they still his in-laws? Former in-laws? She didn't know, but she did know it was bad form to keep them waiting.

She took a deep breath and opened the door. "How do I look?"

Tom looked up, and his mouth fell open. Then he dropped his phone and came to his feet.

Her pulse began to beat hard as he took in everything—and as she stared at him in return. Good Lord, he was wearing a tuxedo. Which shouldn't have been a surprise—she'd seen him unpack it, after all. And this was obviously the sort of event where tuxedos were de rigueur.

But the way the tuxedo fit him? Sweet merciful heavens. It was like a tall, dark, handsome James Bond had just walked off the screen and into her hotel room. Tom made a suit look amazing, a pair of jeans even better.

But Tom in a tux was something else entirely. Her nipples went rock hard at the sight, and suddenly, the dress seemed a half size too small.

As if she wasn't nervous enough, a creeping sense of doubt moved up her back. She'd pushed it aside earlier, in the shower. But now reality reared its head.

Tom was still staring, that unmistakable hunger in his eyes. There were so many things she didn't know about him. She knew he'd loved his wife, but had he moved on from her death?

This was not her world. It had been Stephanie's world, and Caroline knew that she could never compete.

He still hadn't said anything yet. She looked down at the dress and shot him a nervous smile. "Is this okay?" She did a little turn so he had full view of the dress in the back.

When she got turned around again, he was giving her

such a hard look she recoiled back a step. "Tom? Is it all right?"

"Good," he said, his voice tight.

She began to panic. She'd thought this gown was the best option, but maybe it didn't make her look as glamorous as she'd thought. "I've never been to a gala benefit for a foundation before. There were other dresses…"

"No," he cut her off. "That one's perfect. You look amazing."

She blinked at him. "Was that a compliment?"

The look of confusion on his face almost undid her right then and there. "Was it?"

This man. "No, the correct answer is, of course it was."

She gave him a long look and she'd swear the room brightened when the lightbulb went off over his head. "Of course it was. You look amazing, Caroline."

Even though she'd had to walk him up to the words, the sincerity in his voice made her cheeks warm. "Okay, good. Everything else can be returned—except for the makeup and…" She looked down at the dress. She didn't want to discuss the lingerie with him right now. That seemed like a bad idea because they had to be someplace very soon and she suspected that, if she brought panties into the discussion, she'd find herself removing them within seconds. "Everything I'm wearing right now. It's far too much money for me to casually accept the rest as a gift. I don't want to create the appearance of impropriety."

His eyes crinkled, and she got the feeling he was trying not to laugh at her, because there was nothing proper about any of this, appearances or otherwise, and they both knew it.

"Caroline," he said and suddenly he was looking at her with undisguised hunger, his voice the sound of sex on the wind, "try not to think like a lawyer tonight, all right? This is a date, not a court hearing. You look amazing."

She was many things—intelligent, competent, dedicated—but so very rarely was she *desirable*. Or glamorous. And right now, she was both.

She was keeping this dress.

He was the most dangerous man she had ever met. Not because he had the capacity to be deadly or because he filled out that tuxedo.

It was because of the way he made her feel. Glamorous and desirable—those were terrifying emotions. They made her do unpredictable things, like skip work and crash a gala. Worse, she was afraid of what would happen if they were combined with other emotions—tenderness, affection and who could forget sexual satisfaction? All those things swirled around inside her until they formed a superstorm of something that felt much stronger than infatuation, more potentially damaging than a hurricane.

She had once fancied herself in love. With Robby, of course. Looking back now, she couldn't remember what, exactly, she had loved about him. She didn't recall him being a particularly good student, nor was he exceptionally kind to small animals. He was just…there. He'd liked her, for whatever reason. She'd been young. Being liked was half the battle.

She liked to think she wasn't stupid anymore. And she definitely wasn't young.

So this wouldn't be the same thing she'd had with Robby. She was older and wiser. Tom had hinted that they'd have something more after this weekend—but there was no law that it had to be marriage. They could keep doing this—having a consensual, satisfying relationship that didn't involve messy emotions or the potential for heartache. She should keep some distance between them and cling to the safety it provided.

Yes, that's what she should do. But what she did instead was sashay toward him, her hips swaying seductively. "Tom…"

He looked at her with such longing that she wondered how late they could be. But then he said, "We should go."

She wasn't disappointed at that. Not even a little. "We should."

But after this little gala, they were coming back here. And in the morning, she wasn't leaving until she'd found out how far he was willing to take this.

Eleven

"Nervous?"

Caroline rolled her eyes at Tom. "No, why would I be nervous? I'm just wearing a gown and accessories worth thousands of dollars, after riding in a limo far nicer than the one I took to high school prom, next to an armed man wearing a tuxedo, on my way to meet your former in-laws, who happen to be insanely wealthy and also powerful, all while attending a gala benefit filled with the elite in honor of your late wife. Why would I be nervous?"

The corner of his mouth ticked up, but he didn't smile. He couldn't, not with her on his arm as they made their way into the crush of the annual Rutherford Foundation Gala Benefit and Ball. When she'd walked out of the bedroom in that dress, the fabric clinging to her every curve, he'd been stunned past the point of coherence, physically shaking with the effort it took to restrain himself from mussing up her hair and peeling that dress from her body.

He hadn't, because Mark and Celine Rutherford were waiting on them. He had to keep up appearances.

He freakin' hated appearances.

He didn't get nervous anymore—but at times like these, he couldn't help flashing back to the first time Carlson had dragged him along to one of these events. Or the second time. Hell, even the tenth time, he'd still been painfully aware that he didn't belong. It'd gotten better after he'd married Stephanie, but...

But Stephanie, God rest her soul, wasn't on his arm. He didn't have her social graces smoothing the way and making sure he fit in.

Instead, Caroline was with him.

And there was no turning back.

He remembered how, the first few times they'd attended a function together, Stephanie had kept up a steady stream of survival tips, designed to put him at ease. So he did the same for Caroline. "It's open bar. But I'd recommend going easy on champagne."

"If it's all the same to you, I'd like to avoid making a complete and total fool of myself in front of—how many members of Congress will be here?"

"Probably no more than thirty. Or did you want to include former senators and congressmen?"

She stumbled, but he steadied her. Once she had her balance back, she whispered, "I can't tell if you're being serious or if you're teasing."

He was definitely teasing her. "Don't panic. There probably won't be more than two Supreme Court justices in attendance."

She hit him with her clutch. Hard. "Later, I'm going to get even with you."

He damn near grabbed her and marched her right back out to the limo. They didn't even have to make it to the hotel—the limo was big and had an abundance of flat surfaces. He'd wrinkle her dress with wild abandon before he peeled it right off her luscious body.

But he didn't. Instead, he kissed her hand, his lips warm against her knuckles. "Caroline."

She took a deep breath that did some very interesting things to her cleavage, but then she turned her gaze up to his face. Her eyes were so full of hope and affection that suddenly his own breath caught in his chest. "Yes?"

Yeah, he'd been trying to convince himself he'd brought her here for noble reasons. But now? After he'd taken her in the shower? Moments before he introduced her to the Rutherfords?

He realized how damn wrong he'd been. The case wasn't the reason they were here. Her security wasn't why she was wearing that gown, nor why he was about to introduce her to the Rutherfords.

She was the reason. He hadn't been able to put her in a hotel and forget about her. He hadn't been able to leave her behind.

He wasn't sure he could.

"I'm glad you're here with me."

She gasped, a delicate blush on her cheeks, and he felt himself leaning toward her. The rest of the crowd fell away, and it was just him and her and this spark that had always existed between them.

Just then, he heard, "Thomas!" The sound of Celine Rutherford's voice snapped him out of his insanity.

Celine swanned toward him, glamorous as usual in a lacy evening gown that managed to make her look at least twenty years younger than she actually was.

"Celine," he said, bending over to kiss her cheek. "You look lovelier than ever."

She did. He braced himself for the pain of seeing her

again but it didn't come. Not in the almost overwhelming waves that usually left him dazed, anyway.

A dull ache radiated from his chest, but it wasn't as bad as it normally was. Manageable, even.

"You sweet talker, you." Celine beamed, playfully patting his arm.

Tom grinned good-naturedly. "My apologies for being late. I always forget there's traffic here."

She waved this away. "The important thing is that you're here now. You look wonderful, Thomas."

Beside him, Tom was pretty sure he heard Caroline snort in what he hoped was amusement. And he knew why, too. No one called him Thomas for very long.

Except for the Rutherfords. "Celine, may I present Judge Caroline Jennings? She's my guest this evening."

Caroline stepped forward, looking starstruck. "It's a pleasure to meet you, Mrs. Rutherford. I cannot thank you enough for going to all the trouble of pulling that wonderful selection of clothing for me. I hope this meets your specifications?" she asked in a rush, as if the dress Tom had not been able to stop staring at for the last forty minutes was a feed sack on her.

Celine laughed, a light sound. "I think you made the right choice. You look marvelous, dear. That color suits you perfectly."

For years, seeing Celine Rutherford had been the most painful thing Tom had to survive. Stakeouts and violent criminals and occasional shoot-outs—he'd take those any day of the week compared to the mental torture of his annual visit to the Rutherfords. It was easier now, because Stephanie was forever fixed in his mind at twenty-seven years old and Celine got a little older and a little grander every year.

But it still hurt. There was a small, selfish part of him

that wished the Rutherfords weren't so kind to him, that they could all let the relationship drift away and Tom wouldn't have to face these memories on a regular basis.

Normally, he would get through this evening by drinking more champagne than was healthy and finding a few other people from the FBI he could talk shop with.

This time? He didn't want to deal with questions about who Caroline was and why she was here. It was bad enough that he was introducing her to Celine.

What the hell was he doing here? There wasn't supposed to be anything between him and Caroline, beyond her role in an ongoing investigation.

But had that stopped him from bringing her to DC? Or introducing her to his in-laws? Or thinking about a relationship after this?

Nope. All those things he shouldn't be doing, he was doing them anyway. Just to keep her closer.

Celine went on, "And it was no trouble at all. I had so much fun putting the outfits together. I so miss shopping for Stephanie." Her voice trailed off and her eyes got suspiciously shiny. "But then, I suppose I always shall. I do try to keep her spirit alive. This was her foundation, you know. She started it with her trust fund money. Thomas and I keep it going to honor her memory."

"I've always admired what the Rutherford Foundation does," Caroline said, and oddly, she sounded serious about it. "I don't think Tom knows this, but I've actually donated a fair amount of money to the Rutherford Foundation over the years. I admire your objectives about educating girls and women around the world."

"You have?" Celine smiled broadly, any lingering remnants of grief vanished from her eyes. "Why, that's wonderful! It's always a pleasure to meet people who appreciate what we're doing—isn't it, Thomas?"

"It is," he said, staring at Caroline with curiosity. "Why didn't you tell me that?"

She lifted an eyebrow. "I prefer surprising you."

"Oh, I can see we're going to get along famously," Celine said, linking her arm with Caroline's and pulling her away from Tom. "Thomas needs someone who can keep him on his toes. Come, I must introduce you to everyone. Thomas?" she called over her shoulder. "Are you joining us?"

For a long second, he couldn't move. He couldn't talk, even. All he could do was look at Celine and Caroline fast becoming friends and trail along behind the two women, shadowing them like a bodyguard. He was fine. It was just the shock of seeing Celine give what looked a lot like a seal of approval to Caroline. That was throwing him for a loop. Every few feet they paused and greeted someone. Celine introduced Caroline as if they were the oldest of friends.

What would Stephanie think of this? Would she have laughed at him because, as usual, he was taking everything too seriously? Would she have been hurt that Tom was bringing another woman to Stephanie's event? It wasn't like Caroline was replacing anyone. She and Stephanie didn't look alike, didn't have the same sense of humor and definitely didn't have the same background.

All they had in common—besides the ability to fill out an evening gown—was that, for some inexplicable reason, they both cared for Tom.

And he cared for them.

Caroline laughed at something Celine said to Representative Jenkins, and Celine beamed at her. Celine liked Caroline.

Caroline kept him on his toes and didn't let him get away with anything. Even when he steamrolled her, she didn't simper or whine. She gave as good as she got, and he loved it when she did.

Stephanie would've loved Caroline. The realization made his chest tighten.

Mark Rutherford fell into step next to him. "Tom," he said, giving Tom a strong handshake. "Good to see you."

"Mark," Tom said. He nodded to where Celine was showing Caroline off. "I would introduce you, but Celine has already staked her territory."

Tom liked his in-laws—he always had. They had never made him feel like he was a dirt-poor Indian who didn't belong. Even if that's what he had been, once upon a time. Tom wondered if they'd approved of Stephanie marrying him, but he'd never know. They had always treated him with warmth and respect.

Mark had aged quite a bit since Stephanie's death. He and his daughter had always been close. His hair had gone almost white within the year, and he had not sought re-election after his term finished in the Senate. His appearance was just another reminder of how much time had actually passed.

"How have you been?" Tom asked.

"Getting by. I'll be glad when this fund-raiser is over. It consumes Celine for months on end. And you know how she is when she gets focused on something." They shared a laugh, but Tom couldn't help looking at Celine and Caroline, who were continuing to make new friends. He knew exactly how his mother-in-law was when she focused on something—and right now, Caroline was the beneficiary of that focus.

"I'm sorry this is awkward," he began, because it felt awkward to him. "But it was unavoidable."

Mark waved this away. "No need to explain. We're thrilled to meet her."

Tom was so focused on Celine and Caroline that he almost missed what Mark had said—and put it together with something Celine had said earlier—about how Tom needed her to keep him on his toes.

Oh, *no*. Yeah, he'd been thinking about keeping Caroline closer—but he didn't know what that meant right now. It didn't mean wedding bells and babies, that was for sure—and he couldn't have the Rutherfords jumping to that conclusion. He needed to nip this in the bud. "I'm not here *with* Caroline."

Mark gave him a look that Tom had seen many times over the years, one that always made Tom squirm. "Am I reading this wrong? You show up with a gorgeous woman you can't stop staring at and I'm supposed to believe you two aren't involved?"

"She's part of a case." To his own ears, Tom sounded defensive. "You know how important my work is," Tom went on. "The job's not done."

True, none of that had exactly stopped Tom from sleeping with Caroline. Nor had it prevented him from bringing her here. Or telling her he wanted to see her after this trip, too.

His stomach felt like a lead balloon. It'd been one thing when they'd been tucked away in his house or at the hotel, far from prying eyes. But he hadn't been able to leave their relationship there. He'd convinced himself that it was all right—no, vital—to bring Caroline to this party and introduce her to the Rutherfords. And it was a lie. A selfish, willful lie just because he couldn't bear to leave her at a damned hotel in South Dakota.

What had he done? Celine and now Mark were both taken with Caroline. They were welcoming her into their world with open arms. Tom realized he was setting the Rutherfords up for more heartbreak when this…*thing,* whatever it was with Caroline, ended. He couldn't bear to hurt his in-laws. They'd already lost their daughter.

But more than that, Tom had essentially announced to the whole world that she was important to him when he was supposed to be hiding her, keeping things quiet. He was supposed to be protecting her, and instead, he'd opened them both up to more scrutiny. If someone were looking for something to use against either of them, Tom had just handed it to them on a silver platter.

This was too much. He'd left himself exposed and that made Caroline vulnerable. Hell, it made Celine and Mark vulnerable, too.

What *had* he done?

Mark's eyes sparkled with humor. "I've known you a long time, Tom. I've watched you force yourself to attend these things year after year when it's obvious you'd rather be anywhere else. And I've watched women flirt shamelessly with you." He clapped Tom on the shoulder and chuckled. "You could've had your pick, but they've all been invisible to you. But her?" he said with a nod of his head to where Caroline was laughing at something the House minority whip was saying, "You *see* her. Tell me, is that more important than a job?" Sadness stole over his face again. "It's not. Trust me on this one."

Tom gaped at the man, fighting a rising tide of indignation. "I was married to your daughter, sir. I loved her."

Mark looked at him with a mixture of kindness and pity. "And she died. We'll never forget her—she's the reason we're all here. But we moved on." He leaned in close, kindness radiating from him. "Maybe you should, too."

Twelve

"I can't believe I met the Speaker of the House!" Caroline marveled as she collapsed back in the seat of the limo. The whole evening had an air of the unreal about it.

Celine Rutherford had—well, she'd worked miracles. Caroline had felt perfectly dressed—because Celine had gone shopping. Caroline had met seemingly every mover and shaker in Washington, DC—because Celine introduced her.

And then there was Tom—who was currently sitting silently on the other side of the limo, staring out the window as the lights of DC went zipping past. He seemed…lost.

If she'd thought she'd understood that he was the strong, silent alpha male—then this evening had blown that image out of the water. He'd made the rounds by her side, smiling broadly and making small talk like a pro.

Now that the high of hobnobbing with the rich and famous was wearing off, she was acutely aware that she'd been awake since before dawn, had taken two connecting flights and socialized in a high-stress situation.

Still, she reached over and laced her fingers with Tom's. This was not how she'd planned to spend her day, but she was glad she'd come. "I had a wonderful evening. Celine and Mark were a delight."

At one point, she'd seen Mark Rutherford put his arm around Tom's shoulder in a fatherly manner.

But more than that, he'd spoken warmly with his in-laws—it was obvious that he cared for the Rutherfords a great deal, and they obviously thought the world of him.

It was the sort of loving relationship she'd lost when her parents had passed.

Tom had lost so much. She was glad he had the Rutherfords. He needed more people who cared about him in his life. It bothered her to think of him feeling as alone as she sometimes had after her parents' death.

She was being maudlin—which was probably just due to the exhaustion. It had been a long day, after all.

Tom might suck at talking about his feelings, but his actions spoke for him. It was one more piece to the puzzle that made up Tom Yellow Bird.

Dangerous FBI agent. Reserved private citizen. Thoughtful former son-in-law.

Incredibly hot lover.

Somehow, it all came together into a man she couldn't help but be drawn to. Ever since she'd first seen him in her courtroom, she'd felt something between them, and that something was only getting stronger.

"I'm glad to hear this evening wasn't too hard for you."

There was something in his smile, in his tone that gave her pause. "Was it for you?"

He shrugged, as if his pain were no big deal. "No matter how many times I do this, I still don't belong."

She gaped at him in shock. He'd blended in seamlessly while she'd struggled not to be starstruck. How could he possibly think he hadn't belonged?

"But you do," she told him. "Celine and Mark—they adore you, and you obviously care for them, too. You fit in better than I did." If it hadn't been for Celine, Caroline would have been hiding in the corner with a glass of wine, too anxious to brave the crowd.

He pinned her with his gaze—one she'd seen before. It was the same look he'd given the defendant in the court case—the day she'd met him.

Her back automatically stiffened. Why was he glaring at her? But then, just underneath that stone-cold exterior, she glimpsed something else—something vulnerable.

Scared, she thought as he began to speak. "Do you know where I came from?" he demanded, his voice quiet. It still carried in the limo. "Do you have *any* idea?"

She blinked in confusion. "You said…I thought…the reservation that's less than thirty miles from your house?"

"Yes, but that doesn't tell you where I'm from. Because I *don't* belong here." His scowl deepened. If she didn't know him like she did, she might have been afraid.

But she wasn't. "The Red Creek tribe is pretty small— fewer than four thousand people. I grew up on the banks of the Red Creek curve in a little…" He looked out the window, but not before she caught a flash of pain on his face. "My town was about four hundred people. We didn't even have a gas station. We had electricity at my house, but we pulled our water from the river."

She could tell that admission had cost him something. He was such a proud man—but he'd grown up in what sounded like very poor circumstances.

How many people knew this about him? His late wife,

for sure—but did the Rutherfords know? Any of those people who had been so happy to shake his hand tonight?

She sure as hell wouldn't have guessed it—not from his slick suits and his muscle cars and that cabin that had the finest money could buy, because quality was always worth it.

Why was he telling her this? Was he trying to scare her off—or convince himself that he still didn't belong? "We were all scraping by on government surplus foods," he went on, as if being poor was somehow a character flaw. "The only way to change your fate was to get off the res—so that's what I did. I decided to be an FBI agent—don't ask why. I have no clue where I got the idea."

As he spoke, she could hear something different in his voice for the first time. There was an accent there, something new in the way he clipped his vowels. It was the prettiest thing she'd ever heard.

She smiled, trying to imagine Tom Yellow Bird as a kid. All she got was a shorter guy in a great suit. "But you actually did it," she said softly, hoping to draw him out.

"I did. I got a college scholarship, got my degree in criminal justice and headed for DC. It was this huge city," he added, sounding impossibly young. "I'd never been anywhere bigger than Rapid City, and suddenly there were cars everywhere and people and they were all wearing nice suits—it was *crazy*. If I hadn't had Rosebud and, through her, Carlson—I honestly don't know if I could've made it."

"It was that big of a culture shock?"

"Bigger. I was used to the way people on the reservation treated me—as someone to be proud of. I was an athlete and I was smart enough to get a scholarship. I was a big fish in a very small pond, but DC—that was the whole ocean and it was filled with sharks. And I…" He shook his head and she could feel some of his tension fading away.

"I was nothing to them. With this last name? Nothing but a curiosity."

She tried to picture it. After all, she was from Rochester, Minnesota, originally—and that was a lot smaller than Minneapolis. But she had been a girl moving from a mostly white town to an even larger mostly white town. People never looked at her as a curiosity, because she blended in.

No, she couldn't imagine what it would've been like to go from living on government surplus cheese to being invited to bigwigs' parties in DC because your friend thought it would be fun.

She thought about Tom's house, how it was off the grid but still in the lap of luxury. He squeezed her hand, which she took as a good sign.

Had something happened at the party to upset him? Or was it just seeing his in-laws? She didn't know.

"Is it still like that on the reservation?"

"A few years ago they built a hydroelectric dam. The tribe owns forty percent of it and they used a lot of local labor in the construction. The res still isn't a wealthy place, but it's better. Ask Rosebud about that when you meet her—it's her story to tell."

Caroline blushed from the tips of her toes to her hair, because he'd again, just casually, tossed off the fact that she *would* be meeting one of his oldest friends. That she'd be part of his life moving forward.

Which was what he'd said in the shower, too. But…

She wanted to spend time with him. But she couldn't keep doing what they'd been doing—running away together and ignoring the real world. The last three and a half days had been risky and dangerous and if she kept up this sort of behavior, it might well come back to haunt her.

Still, she wanted to meet his friends. She had the feeling it was another piece to the puzzle that was Tom Yellow

Bird. "I'll do that." She was trying to hear what he wasn't saying, because if she knew anything about Tom, it was that what he didn't say was almost as important as what he did. "Have *you* changed the reservation for the better?"

"I try," he went on. "I honor Stephanie by keeping most of her money in the Rutherford Foundation. I have the safe house I told you about. I also fund a bunch of college scholarships. If there's a kid who wants to work hard enough to get off the res, I'm going to help them do it. And no," he added before Caroline could ask the obvious question, "it's not all her money. I invested wisely. It's amazing how easy it is to make money when you already have it," he added in a faraway voice. "Simply *amazing*."

She knew how damned hard it was to start from nothing, to be buried under such debt that a person couldn't breathe, couldn't sleep. "I don't know many FBI agents who run charities. You could have retired, you know."

"The job wasn't done. It still isn't." Something about the way he said that sent a shiver down her spine. "Besides, I don't run the charities. I pay people to run them for me."

"Are any of those people members of the Red Creek tribe?"

His lips curved into a smile that was so very tempting. "Maybe."

And that, more than anything else, was why she was in this car with Tom Yellow Bird. He was just so damned honorable. Yes, he was gorgeous and financially independent—but there was more to him than that.

She had a momentary flash of guilt. He was protecting his people and fighting for what was right. Hell, he was protecting her. He was protecting her and sweeping her off her feet, and she wasn't worthy of him. Because she couldn't make the same claim to being honorable.

She had done her best to make up for her grand mistakes—

but a mistake was something you did accidentally. That was the definition of her pregnancy scare, sure. But more likely it was a mistake she'd made by being involved with Robby, by not taking the proper precautions. And after that scare, she'd buckled down. No more Robby; no more casual attitudes about birth control. From then on, she was careful, and it'd paid off. She hadn't experienced that kind of heart-stopping terror again.

But her pregnancy scare was a world of difference from what had happened with the Verango case. There had been nothing noble about her actions, and what she'd done was exactly the sort of thing someone might use against her.

She came *this* close to telling Tom about it. After all, he'd opened up to her. They were moving into uncharted territory here. How easy would it be to say, *I did a favor for a friend and my debts were paid off in full*? One sentence. Less than twenty words. It wasn't like she'd accepted a bribe intentionally—her law professor had manipulated her. But she hadn't returned the money because she hadn't known how.

Instead, she'd made donations—once she had a salary—to charitable causes, including the Rutherford Foundation. By her rough estimates, she'd given away slightly more than the original amount of the loans that had been paid off with dirty money.

"I don't talk about that. About any of that," Tom said, sounding more like himself. "It's…"

If he was trying to convince her that his hardscrabble life and his wife's death were things he should somehow be ashamed of, she was going to kick his butt. "It's brave and honest and true, Tom. To take something like losing your wife and turn it into something good? Not even good— amazing?" Tears pricked at her eyes, and she cupped his cheek. "You are the best man I've *ever* known."

He slid his arm around her shoulder and touched his forehead against hers and said, "It was different tonight. And that was because of you."

Her confession died on her lips. Whatever this was between them, it was good. She cared for him and he cared for her, and there was that something between them that neither of them could deny. This wasn't pretend. This was real.

If she told him about her one mistake, would he still look at her with that tenderness, with that hunger? Or would he see nothing but a criminal?

The most she could hope for was that no one would put her student loans and Vincent Verango's plea deal together. It was perfectly reasonable that a first-year prosecutor would offer a plea deal to a supposed first-time offender.

"Caroline..." His voice was barely a whisper. "I..."

Yes, she wanted to say. He'd taken her to his house, brought her to Washington. He'd taken her to a gala benefit and introduced her to his late wife's parents. He'd made crazy, passionate love to her. He'd said he wanted to see her after tonight. She'd cast aside common sense to follow him, because there was something between them that was real and true.

Whatever he wanted, the answer was *yes*.

Suddenly, he pulled back, all the way to the other side of the limo. It hurt worse than a slap to the face. "After we get back tomorrow, I'll sweep your house myself."

Maybe that was supposed to be a tender gesture from a man who had forgotten how to discuss emotions. *When you care enough to sweep the house yourself,* she mused.

But there was no missing the way Tom had pulled away—not just physically, but emotionally. Caroline swore she could feel a wall going up around him. "When will I see you again?"

The silence stretched until she was at her breaking point. "We have to be careful to avoid the appearance of impropriety," he finally said.

He wasn't so much throwing her words back at her as using them as laser-guided weapons, because they hit her with military precision. "Oh. Right."

Objectively, she knew this was true. She'd fallen into bed with him this weekend. She'd skipped work today—and tomorrow—by claiming she had the flu. She was wearing ungodly expensive clothing and jewelry that he'd paid for. She was taking stupid risks with her heart, her health and her career. She hadn't had this much sex in years.

If someone really were looking to blackmail her, this weekend would be a great place to start.

So, yes, she knew they needed to put some distance between them. It just made rational sense.

But there'd been that promise of something more in the shower today. She'd started to believe that this wasn't just a crazy weekend—that this was the start of a relationship.

That explained why Tom's mixed signals hurt so much.

"I have to put the job first," he went on, not making it any better. "My feelings for you…"

Hey, at least he had feelings he was admitting to. That had to count for something. "No, I understand. We both have jobs to do. I just…forgot about that for a little while."

Maybe it was just her, but she thought he visibly sagged in relief. "It's easy to forget everything when I'm with you. But when we're back in Pierre…"

Yeah. When she went back to being Judge Jennings and he went back to being Agent Yellow Bird, neither of them would forget.

Damn it all.

Thirteen

"Fourteen." Tom flung the small bag of recording devices onto James Carlson's desk. "Fourteen damn cameras in her home."

It took a lot to piss Tom off. He'd been doing this for a long time. He'd thought that his rage had burned out of him in the years after Stephanie's death.

Apparently, he'd been wrong.

Carlson looked up at him, eyebrows quirked. "That does seem a little excessive."

"A *little*? There were two cameras in her bathroom—one in the shower and one guaranteed to get an up-skirt shot on the toilet. And three in her bedroom! You and I both know the only reason you would need three separate angles of her bed was if someone was planning on mixing footage."

Several years ago, Rosebud Donnelly had been secretly filmed with her husband, Dan, and the tape had been used in an attempt to blackmail Rosebud into dropping a lawsuit against an energy company. She had come to Carlson and Tom for help.

One minute of Rosebud having her privacy violated and her dignity assaulted. It had been a trade-off then because Carlson and Tom had thought—after all these years—that they'd finally found the man behind the curtain, as Tom thought of him. Dan Armstrong's uncle Cecil was an evil man. For years he'd been blackmailing people and paying off judges—including the judge who had made a mockery of the judicial system by using Maggie so very wrongly.

That should have been the end of the case. If this were a movie, it would've been. But it wasn't. Fourteen cameras made it loud and clear—this wasn't over by a long shot.

Why wasn't it over?

Tom sat in the chair in front of James's desk, vibrating with anger. He was capable of violence, but he rarely resorted to it. However, right now? Yeah, right now he could shoot someone. Repeatedly.

What would've happened if he had let Caroline convince herself that she was imagining things? What would've happened if he had left her alone all weekend? If he'd dropped her off Monday morning and gone on his merry way to DC alone?

He'd been right to take her with him. Fourteen cameras proved that. But he'd also been so, so wrong to do so, because he'd still put her in a position of risk.

"You seem a little worked up about this," Carlson said casually, picking up the bag. "What did Judge Jennings say when you told her how many cameras you found?"

"I didn't. I mean, I haven't—yet." He wasn't sure he could bring himself to tell her, because he knew what it would do to her. It would destroy her sense of peace. She wouldn't be able to sleep, to shower—to do anything personal and intimate.

Like this weekend. When she'd stripped and floated in his spring-fed pool under the fading sunlight. Or when she had straddled him and ridden him hard, crying out his name. Or in DC, when he'd paid God only knew how much to outfit her in gowns and jewels so he could introduce her to his in-laws. Or when he'd taken her in the shower.

If he told her about the cameras, she wouldn't be able to be herself. He would take that freedom away from her.

He wasn't sure when he realized that Carlson wasn't talking. It could've been seconds later, it could've been minutes. He looked up to find one of his oldest friends staring at him. Anyone else and Tom might've been able to keep his cards close to his vest. But Carlson was no idiot, and they knew each other too well.

Tom dropped his head into his hands, struggling to find some equilibrium—or at least a little objectivity. But he didn't have any. He hadn't since he'd heard her voice on his phone on Friday, small and afraid.

Hell, who was he kidding? He hadn't had any objectivity when it came to Caroline Jennings since she had walked into that courtroom. And after the last four days, he couldn't even pretend there was distance between them. Because there wasn't. He had been inside her, for God's sake.

"Do you ever think about her?" he heard himself ask. "Stephanie?"

"I do. She was a good woman."

Silence.

Normally, silence would not work on Tom. Waiting was what he did best. In the grand scheme of things, what was a few minutes when someone was hoping to make him slip up?

What was almost ten years without his wife—without anyone?

"Do you think…" He swallowed, calling up the image

of Stephanie at that last party, her body wrapped in a silky blue cocktail dress and her mother's sapphires. Stephanie, telling him she was tired and ready to go. Stephanie, smiling indulgently when he said he had just a little more business to see to—he'd catch a cab. She should take the car. The car *her* money had paid for, not his.

Stephanie kissing him goodbye—not on the lips, but on the cheek. Stephanie, walking away from him for the very last time.

He had loved his wife with every bit of his heart and soul. But in the end, he'd only known her for four years. It hadn't been enough. It would never be enough.

In the end, he'd put the job ahead of her. He should have been with her and he hadn't been, because he'd been chasing a lead, hoping for someone to slip up under the influence of alcohol.

Had it been worth it? Tom couldn't even remember what that case had been. He hadn't finished it, he was sure. He'd been lost in burying his wife.

No. The job hadn't been worth it. Maybe it never would be. Wasn't that what Mark Rutherford had said?

"She would've wanted you to move on." Tom looked up and realized that Carlson was no longer sitting behind his desk. He was now leaning against the front of it, looking at Tom with undisguised worry in his eyes. "It's been almost ten years, Tom."

Mark's words, almost exactly. Tom let out a bitter laugh, because it was that or cry, and he didn't cry. Not ever. "It's not like I've been moping. I've been busy."

Carlson smiled indulgently. "That you have. But can you really do this forever?"

"I'll do it until it's finished." Yes, it was easier to think about the job—corruption, the people who were hurt by faceless men of evil.

"No one questions your commitment to this case."

Tom collapsed back into the chair, defeated. "I took her out to the cabin. And then I took her to DC with me. I introduced her to Celine and Mark. There. Happy now?"

It was difficult to shock Carlson, but in that moment, Tom was pretty sure he had succeeded. He knew for certain when Carlson said, "No shit."

"It might have been a mistake," he conceded—which was an understatement, to be sure. Because before Caroline had called him, fear in her voice, Tom had been content to watch her from a distance. But now?

No distance. None. Which was why he'd practically begged for distance that night in DC. It had hurt like hell to push her away, but it'd been the right thing to do. This proved it.

He glanced back at Carlson, and if he didn't know better, he would say his friend was trying not to laugh. And if Carlson laughed, Tom was going to punch him. It would feel good to punch someone right about now.

"I've got to meet this woman. Maggie will love her."

Tom groaned. This was only getting worse. "I might have compromised the case." Because he had definitely compromised Caroline Jennings. Repeatedly.

Carlson did burst out laughing. "Right, because I've never done anything—including sleeping with a witness—that might have compromised a case. Or do you not remember how I met my wife?" Carlson actually *hooted*, which was not a dignified noise. Tears streamed down his cheeks. "Damn, man—you've been an FBI agent for too long. There's more to life than arresting the next bad guy, Tom." He leaned over and picked up a picture of Maggie. He had several scattered around the office, but this one was newer—a soft-focus shot of her in the hazy afternoon sunlight, cradling her pregnant belly. "So much more."

Tom worked real hard not to be jealous of his friends' happiness, but he was having a moment of what could reasonably be described as weakness, and in that moment, he was green with envy. "Be that as it may, I'm not going to continually compromise this case. Someone sent her flowers. Someone bugged her house. I'm going to go sweep her office after this, but I'm not going to be shocked if it's bugged, too. Sooner or later, someone's going to reach out to her."

Carlson looked at him for a moment before silently agreeing to go along with the subject change. "Do they have anything on her?"

Tom shook his head. "She's so clean she squeaks. I think that's why they resorted to the cameras—there's nothing else to blackmail her with." Except for how he'd flown her across the country and showered her with gowns and jewels and...

"We need her," Carlson said, any friendliness gone from his voice. "If they reach out to her, I want her to play along and see how much information she can get before they become suspicious. This could be a game changer, Tom."

Carlson wasn't just stating an obvious fact—he was reminding Tom to keep his pants zipped from here on out.

He stood, knowing what he had to do and knowing how damned hard it was going to be.

He wanted her. But that need scared him—because it endangered her, of course. His wants and needs had nothing to do with this. Not a damn thing. The only thing that mattered was that he couldn't risk her. "I need to keep an eye on her, do regular sweeps of her house and office. But I'll do anything to keep her safe between now and then. Including not seeing her."

Carlson considered this. "Does she mean that much to you?"

If it were anyone else but Carlson, he'd lie. And Tom hated lying. But Carlson was one of his oldest friends, and he owed the man nothing less than the truth. "She does."

"Well, then," Carlson said, pushing off the desk and resting a hand on Tom's shoulder. "You do what you need to do."

Tom nodded and turned to go. But when his hand was on the doorknob, Carlson spoke again. "She would've wanted you to be happy, Tom. You know that, right?"

It was like a knife in the back. Tom opened the door and walked out without responding.

Fourteen

Caroline did her best to go back to normal, but it wasn't easy. The trip left her drained in ways she hadn't expected. Apparently getting up at crazy hours and jetting across the country was exhausting.

But that minor inconvenience wasn't the only problem.

Where the hell was Tom Yellow Bird? He was like a ghost in her life. She hadn't seen him in the weeks since they'd come back from DC, but she got regular text messages from him that included the date, time and location he'd swept for bugs. He apparently had checked her office and her house on alternating days—but never while she was there. And he didn't tell her if he'd found anything, just that her house was clean now.

Not that she needed a text to know he'd been in her home. Just like she'd felt it when someone had broken in several weeks ago, she could feel Tom's presence. It was unnerving how easily she could tell that he'd been in her home. Maybe it was the faint smell of him that lingered in the air. Whatever it was, it led to some of her wildest dreams yet.

But when she texted him back to thank him or ask how he was, she'd get one-word replies, if that. It was as if he were still barreling across the highway, inscrutable behind his sunglasses and avoiding any and all questions.

Where was the man who'd swept her away to DC? Who couldn't keep his hands off her? The one who helped her live out some of her favorite fantasies? The man who caught her in his arms when she slipped on wet rock rather than let her fall and couldn't bear to let her out of his sight? She missed *that* man.

Maybe she shouldn't be surprised that he hadn't come around. She didn't quite understand what had changed at the Rutherford Foundation gala, but clearly something had. The Rutherfords had been warm and welcoming—but there was no missing the fact that they were Tom's late wife's parents. Maybe it'd messed with his head to see them all together.

If she could talk to the man, she'd reassure him that she wasn't trying to replace his wife. How could she? She'd never be Stephanie—not in looks, not in family history and not in the way she loved Tom.

Because Stephanie had loved a different Tom than the one Caroline had entrusted with her safety—and quite possibly her heart. Stephanie had loved a younger, more insecure Tom, a man more desperate to prove he belonged in the rarefied DC air. Perhaps Stephanie's Tom hadn't been quite so dangerous, so inscrutable.

That wasn't Caroline's Tom. The man she missed more every single night was unreadable and playful, commanding and commandeering. He could blend seamlessly into a courtroom, a cabin on the high plains and a DC ballroom.

Caroline wanted more than a wild weekend with him and, despite the ghosting, she was sure he wanted more, too. She just had no idea when she might get it because, aside from the flowers she'd received almost two months ago—and the constant sweeps of her home and office— she had no other indication that there was any sort of nefarious activity happening. She got up, exercised and went to work. She came home and slept. Then she did it all again.

Which was fine. Being with Tom had been a whirlwind of impulse and attraction, one that had led her to take crazy risks. At least there hadn't been any lasting consequences from her time with Tom—except that she missed him.

All she could do was hope that he missed her, too.

Ironically enough, a few weeks after she called in sick to work, she started to get sick for real. She'd been feeling draggy, which she'd chalked up to the stress of, well, *everything*. She had no idea where she stood, both with the corruption case and with a certain FBI agent.

She slept more on the weekends, but she couldn't get caught up with her rest. Then she got sick to her stomach in court and barely called a recess in time to make it to the bathroom. Afterward, she felt fine. It must have been something she ate? She threw out the rest of the chicken salad she'd taken for lunch. It smelled funny.

Then the same thing happened the next day—she felt fine until right after lunch, when her stomach twisted. Again, it was a close call, but she made it to the bathroom in time. As she sat on the floor, waiting for her stomach to settle, she realized something.

It hadn't been the chicken salad.

She'd been tired. Now she was sick, but not with the flu or anything. Caroline did the math. It'd been three weeks since her whirlwind weekend with Tom. And her period...

Oh, *crap*.

She should have gotten her period last week.

Caroline was sick again. The whole time, she kept thinking, *No*.

No, no, no, *no*. This couldn't be happening, not again. She'd dodged this bullet once before. She'd missed a period due to stress and it'd made her see that she shouldn't marry Robby, that she couldn't prove her stupid brother right—she wasn't a mistake.

Oh, God. She'd lost her head and her heart to Tom Yellow Bird. For one amazing weekend, she'd thrown all caution to the wind and put her selfish wants and needs before rational thought and common sense.

Had she really been stupid enough to think she'd managed to avoid the consequences of her actions? *Idiot.* That's what she was. Hadn't she learned that anytime she stepped outside the safety of making the correct choices—*every* time—fate would smack her down?

Now she was most likely carrying Tom's child.

Oh, *God*.

She sat on the floor of the bathroom, the tile cool against her back, and tried to think. The first time her period had been late, all the way back in college, her life had flashed before her eyes. She'd been terrified of telling Robby, then her parents. They would have gotten married and she would've had to notify the law school that she'd have to defer a year—or withdraw completely. Her career prospects, all of her plans—all of it would have been wiped away by a positive test result. She'd been sick then, too—but with sheer dread as she waited on the pregnancy test results.

No. She'd known it then and she knew it even better now. Marrying Robby and having his baby would have been the biggest mistake of her life.

Now? Oh, she was still panicking. Unplanned potential pregnancies were an anxiety attack waiting to happen.

But instead of filling her with dread, this time when her life flashed before her eyes, she felt…hopeful. Which was ridiculous, but there it was.

She saw her body growing heavy with Tom's baby. Instead of ghosting through her life, she saw Tom coming home to her at the end of the day, cuddling a little baby with his dark hair and eyes. She saw nights in his arms and trips to visit both his friends on the reservation and the Rutherfords and…

Oh, no.

She wanted that life with Tom. She didn't want this to be a mistake.

She needed to talk to him immediately. Or, at the very least, as soon as she had peed on a stick.

Okay. She had a plan. After work, she'd go buy a pregnancy test. And then she was tracking down Tom Yellow Bird if it was the last thing she did.

"Judge Jennings."

The silky voice pulled her out of musing about baby names in the parking lot on her way home from work that day. She found herself standing a few feet away from a man in a good suit wearing mirrored sunglasses. But it wasn't Tom. This guy was white with light brown hair that he wore stylishly tousled. He was tall and lean—much taller than she was—but due to the cut of the suit, she could tell he had plenty of muscles.

He could've been attractive, but there was something in the way his mouth curved into a smirk that she didn't like. Actually, that wasn't strong enough. There was something about this guy that was physically repulsive.

"Yes?" she said, trying to gauge how far she was from

her car without actually looking at it. Too far. She'd have to go back into the courthouse. Which was fine. The security guards were still there and they were armed.

"I'm glad we've finally met," the stranger said, his smirk deepening. "I've been looking forward to getting acquainted with you for quite some time now."

Oh, crap. "If that was supposed to sound not creepy, I have to tell you, it didn't make it." She smiled sympathetically, as if he were socially awkward and doing the best he could instead of scaring her.

"Excellent," he said, the smirk widening into a true grin. "A sense of humor. It makes everything so much easier, don't you think?"

Oh, she didn't like that smile at all. She took a step back. If she kicked out of her heels, she could run a lot faster. And screaming was always a viable option.

The man straightened. "Relax, Judge Jennings. Did you enjoy the flowers?"

Double crap. She was starting to panic—but even in the middle of that, James Carlson's last email came back to her. *If they reach out to you, play along.* So she straightened and stood her ground, trying to look like she was the kind of woman who could be swayed by several hundred dollars' worth of cut flowers. "They were lovely, actually. Am I to thank you for that?"

He waved the suggestion away. "I must say you are a very difficult woman to get a handle on," he said, as if he had a right to get a handle on her at all. "I have been deeply impressed by your record on the bench."

How was she supposed to play along when he was making her skin crawl? She couldn't. "Still creepy," she said, backing up another step. "If you'd like to make an appointment to discuss something of merit, feel free to call my assistant and schedule a time. Other than that? I don't think we have anything to talk about here."

"Oh, but we do. We do, Judge Jennings," he repeated, because apparently annoying was just a way of life for this guy. "It would be such a shame to see a fine judicial career destroyed because of one naive mistake, don't you agree?"

The world stopped spinning. At least, that was how it felt to Caroline as she suddenly struggled to keep her balance. "What? I don't know what you're talking about." The protest sounded weak, even to her own ears. "I don't make mistakes."

He advanced on her, two quick steps. She tensed, but he didn't touch her. She couldn't run, though—she could barely hold herself upright.

"Excellent," he said again. He was overly fond of that word. "Then the Verango case was intentional, was it? Terrence Curtis was your mentor, after all. It's funny how these things work out, isn't it?" He said that last part so softly Caroline almost leaned forward to catch the last words.

She didn't dare. "I've had a lot of cases," she said, wondering if she sounded like she was on the verge of blacking out. "I can't say for certain which case you're talking about." It wasn't much of a lie, but it was all she had right now.

Tom had known this was coming. He had warned her, and she had willfully ignored his warning because...

Because she'd thought the shameful truth wouldn't get out. No one had ever drawn a connection between her and Verango, between Verango and Curtis. Because she had convinced herself that there was no connection beyond the mentor and mentee relationship.

"Yes," the man said in what might have been an understanding voice coming from anyone else. "I can see that you know exactly what I'm talking about. And won't our mutual friend, FBI Special Agent Tom Yellow Bird, be interested to know about this new development?" He snapped his fingers. "Better yet, I could call James Carlson up and inform him that, despite his hopes and prayers, he has yet another judge to prosecute, hmm?"

"What do you want?" she demanded, trying to sound mean and failing miserably.

"Not much," he said, his tone giving lie to his words. "Merely an exchange. I keep your unfortunate mistake between you and me—like friends do—and in exchange, when a case of interest to me comes before you, you'll give me a moment of your time to make my case." His mouth tightened, and Caroline was afraid that was the real guy, finally cracking through the too-perfect exterior. "Although I won't be scheduling an appointment with your assistant. I'm thinking more along the lines of…dinner?"

"You want me to throw a case?" On some level—the logical, rational level—she knew this was great. This was exactly the break that Tom and James Carlson had been waiting for. Whoever was buying off judges was actively trying to blackmail her!

But there was nothing great about this. Not a damned thing. "He can't watch you forever, no matter how hard he might try," the man said, leaning forward and finally letting the true menace in his voice bleed through. "Do you really want him to know how easily you can be bought?"

There was no need to ask who *he* was.

"No," she whispered, shame burning through her body. Because that was the truth. Tom would find out what she had done all those years ago and it would change things.

Even more than things had already changed. She might be carrying his child.

God, how she didn't want to regret what had happened between her and Tom. She didn't want to regret him. But he might damn well regret her.

Who would want to be saddled with a woman who'd lied by omission about her past, who'd gotten pregnant? She could ruin his career as well as her own. All because she'd lost her head for one weekend.

All because she couldn't say no to Tom Yellow Bird.

Her stomach lurched dangerously, and she fought the urge to cover her belly with her hand. "I don't."

"Excellent," he repeated yet again. "Judge Jennings, it has been a pleasure making your acquaintance." He pulled a business card out of his pocket and held it out to her. But when she went to reach for it, he held it just out of reach. "We understand each other, don't we? Because I would hate to see a promising career like yours destroyed over a little mistake like this."

Caroline swallowed down the bile in the back of her throat. "We understand each other," she agreed. Because she did. Her promising career had indeed been cut short.

She waited for this vile man to say "excellent" again, but he didn't. Instead, he reverted back to a smirk and handed the card over. "If you have any questions or need anything from me—anything at all—I can help you. But only if you help me."

She didn't even look at the card. She slid it into her purse and tried to smile. She didn't know how she would ever smile again. "Of course," she said, impressed that she managed to make it sound good.

With a nod of his head, he turned on his heel and walked off. He didn't get into a car. He merely walked away. When he rounded the corner of the courthouse, Caroline counted to five and then followed. If she could get a car, a license plate—something…

But by the time she could see around the corner, he was gone. Not a car in the street, not the back of his head—nothing.

Her stomach rolled. She was going to be sick.

And it was no one's fault but her own.

Fifteen

The only reason Tom didn't leave flowers for Caroline at her house after every time he swept it was because he didn't want to freak her out. After all, she didn't exactly have positive associations with random floral displays in South Dakota.

But he was tempted. After the initial sweep, he hadn't found any other bugs in her house or office. Which was good. He probably didn't need to be checking things on a regular basis. He should return her key to her. But he couldn't stop. He had to make sure she was safe.

But it was the only thing he could do while keeping his distance. In the meantime, he and Carlson waited for the other players to make their next moves. He knew from a career of waiting that counting each tick of the clock wouldn't make it move a damned bit faster.

He hated not having the ball in his court. Whoever had bugged her house knew that Tom had pulled the devices. They probably knew Tom was doing regular checks. And it was safe to assume that the bad guys had put two and two together and knew that Tom and Caroline had spent at least part of that weekend together. They were no doubt plotting their next move, and all Tom could do was wait to react defensively.

The wait was going to kill him. Slowly.

Because he *missed* Caroline. That, in and of itself, was new. He didn't miss people, not like this. The only other person he'd felt this consuming loneliness for was...

Well, Stephanie. But she'd been dead and he'd been grieving the loss. Caroline was pointedly not dead. In fact, she was within an easy drive. All he'd have to do was park in her driveway and knock on the door.

He couldn't. He was on a case—several cases.

As the days passed, he couldn't stop thinking about what Mark Rutherford and Carlson had both said—that maybe it was time to move on. Maybe Tom already had, but he hadn't realized it until the moment he'd seen Caroline across the crowded courtroom.

He'd spent an electric weekend with her. He'd kicked back and relaxed. He'd enjoyed the explosive sex. He'd taken her to meet the Rutherfords. All of those were things he didn't normally do. That was the only thing that was messing with him. He'd tried something new.

That was all it should have been.

But it wasn't. Because he missed her.

He'd wanted...he wasn't even sure what he'd wanted with Caroline. Sweeping her house and keeping his distance wasn't it, though.

If he were being honest, he'd wanted to see her more. A lot more. But doing that would jeopardize the case.

Spending more time with Caroline...

It had felt like a betrayal of Stephanie. But the thing that Tom couldn't get his head around was the fact that no one else seemed to think that. Not Stephanie's parents. Not Carlson—and they'd all known Stephanie for a much longer time than Tom had. Every single one of them had said the same thing—Stephanie would have wanted him to move on.

Was that what Caroline was? Was Tom finally moving on?

These were the thoughts that occupied Tom constantly as the days dragged on. Tom was tracking down a lead on a different case—sadly, crime waited for no man—when his phone buzzed and he answered it. "Yellow Bird."

"Tom." It was Carlson.

Tom felt a flare of hope. Had someone made a move on Caroline? He hoped like hell they had so this case could end—although he was irritated that she would have gone to Carlson instead of him.

Carlson went on, "There's been a development. You need to come in to the office."

"When?"

"Now."

The last of the lunch rush was thinning out, so it only took Tom twenty minutes to make it over to Carlson's office. He called Caroline to make sure she was all right, but she didn't answer.

He had a fleeting moment when he wished that he had called her at some point during the last few weeks or come up with some sort of excuse to stop by the courthouse and see her. Texting hadn't been enough. He knew there were solid reasons why he hadn't. He didn't want anyone to make a connection between them. He didn't want to compromise the case any more than he already had, so he'd kept his distance.

A growing sense of dread was building inside him and he wasn't sure why. A development should be exciting—

another step closer to finishing this case and finding out who was behind the corruption. This was what he lived for, right?

As he thought about what he lived for, though, it wasn't slapping cuffs on a dirty judge that came to mind. It was Caroline. The way she looked curled up next to the fire pit, wineglass in hand. The way she looked curled against his chest the next morning, a little smile on her face as she slept.

He could hear Mark Rutherford asking him if the job really was the most important thing. And suddenly he knew—it wasn't. He could give everything he'd ever had and ever would have to the job, but what could it give him in return? The promise of more criminals committing crimes. The certainty that the job would never be done.

The realization that he might have given up his dreams of living a long and happy life with Stephanie, but he hadn't given up those dreams of a home, a family.

A wife.

After this, he was going to take some time off, he decided as he walked into Carlson's office. He needed to start over with Caroline. She was probably furious with him—and she was well within her rights to be so, considering he hadn't seen her in much too long. But he knew now that he couldn't keep putting the job first, because it would never return the favor.

And then, as if he'd summoned her just by thinking about her, there she was, standing up from the chair in front of Carlson's desk. Carlson, sitting behind the desk, didn't move at all.

Tom blinked a couple of times, trying to make sense of what he was seeing. Caroline was here and his heart gave an excited little leap—but she wasn't happy. There was something wrong—her eyes were red and watery and her mouth was tight. Instinctively, he moved closer to her. "What's going on?"

Something bad had happened—he knew that much. It was physically painful when she turned her gaze to his. The way she was looking at him—it was like someone had killed her puppy. And she didn't have a puppy.

No one said anything. Tom went to her and put his arms around her shoulders. She sagged against him a little as she drew in a shuddering breath, and in that moment, Tom knew he would kill for this woman. Whoever had hurt her, they would pay.

Carlson's face was drawn and worried. He had arranged his features into a stern look, but Tom could tell he was concerned. "Is someone going to tell me what's going on or not?"

"I'm so sorry," Caroline whispered against his chest.

That didn't sound good. In fact, that sounded bad. He held her tighter and glared at Carlson. "Well?"

"As anticipated, someone reached out to Caroline. We have his name and contact number, as well as a description."

"Okay…" That was fine. They'd expected that. "I know they didn't have any bugs in your house and they didn't have anything on you. What were they trying to use for blackmail?"

Caroline shuddered again and then inexplicably pushed him away. She sank down into her chair, staring at the floor as if it held all the answers. "They do have something on me," she said in a voice so torn with anguish that Tom crouched down next to her to catch all of her words.

"What? I checked you out. You're completely clean."

She shook her head. "No. Not completely."

She wouldn't look at him. Why wouldn't she look at him? Anger flared. He'd really like to punch something.

"Caroline has explained the situation," Carlson began. Tom wanted to ignore him, but he was the only one talking and Tom still didn't know what was going on, so he had to pay attention. But he didn't look away from Caroline. Tears dripped down her cheeks, and each one was like a knife in his heart.

"When she was a first-year prosecutor in Minneapolis, her college mentor approached her. He had a friend of a friend who'd been arrested. It was the usual line—the charges were baseless, the friend was really innocent. He pressed Caroline to drop the charges. She wasn't able to do that, but she offered a plea agreement, which led to a suspended sentence and no time served. As a result, her student loans were paid off."

It all sounded so clinical coming of Carlson's mouth. There was a dinner, a conversation. A plea agreement. Loans were paid off.

"How much?"

Carlson didn't answer, and after a moment, Caroline replied, "Almost two hundred thousand dollars." She still wouldn't look at him.

He stood so suddenly that she recoiled in the chair. If he'd been a younger man, Tom would've put his fist through the wall. Maybe even the glass of the door. But he was older and wiser and he knew that breaking his hand wouldn't solve any of life's problems.

No matter how good it might feel.

"They're counting on her doing anything to keep that series of events quiet," Carlson went on. "The fact that she has come forward to voluntarily share this information before allowing it to compromise yet another case is to be commended. She also detailed how, over the years, she's donated a comparative amount to various charities—

including the Rutherford Foundation—in an attempt to make restitution."

Tom glared at his friend. Carlson was trying to make this sound good—but there was no way to put lipstick on this pig. Caroline had lied to him. He had asked her—repeatedly—if there was anything in her history that could be used against her. Okay, maybe most of that conversation had gotten distracted by sex—but he had asked. She had said no.

Not only had she lied to him, but…

She could be bought.

He didn't just want to punch something. He wanted to shoot something. Repeatedly.

Because they were supposed to be equals. One of the things that made them good together was the fact that they both took their jobs seriously and upheld the law. They didn't throw cases, they didn't accept bribes and they didn't subvert justice.

"Tom," Carlson said, his voice more severe this time, "it was a long time ago. And since that time, Judge Jennings has upheld the law with honor and dignity."

He knew what Carlson was trying to do. He knew what Carlson wanted—he wanted Caroline to play along. He wanted her to find out more information not just about the man who had approached her, but about who that man was working for. He wanted to use Caroline.

Tom's vision narrowed, growing into a murky red around the edges. "Is there anything else?" His voice sounded wrong even to his own ears.

Panic clawed at the edge of his awareness, because he knew this feeling. *Nothing.* He felt nothing.

It was the same horrifying numbness that had overtaken him as he'd stood next to his wife's bed in the hospital and watched life slip away from her broken body.

He couldn't afford to feel anything right now, because if he did, he would lose his mind, and there would be no coming back from that.

He'd thought he'd known Caroline. More than that, he'd taken her to his house. He'd introduced her to the Rutherfords. He'd…he'd trusted her. And he'd thought she'd trusted him. But had she, really?

"Actually, there is." Carlson came around the desk. Without further explanation, he walked out of the office and closed the door behind him.

Bad sign. Getting worse.

"Tom, sit. Please." Caroline's voice broke, but it didn't hurt him. It couldn't.

He sat and waited. How much worse could this get?

"You have to understand—I was so young. I was twenty-four, in my first job. I was drowning under the weight of my student loans. I was having trouble sleeping and was falling behind on my bills and…" She covered her mouth with her hand, but he wasn't going to be moved by it. "Terrence Curtis was my mentor. He always pushed me to be better, and I trusted him. He wrote me letters of recommendation and helped me get into law school…"

"Sure. You owed him."

"It wasn't like that," she snapped, sounding a little more like her old self. Good. He wanted her to fight him about this. He didn't want her to make a pitiful plea. "I should've known better. But he asked me out to dinner to talk about how things were going. I was struggling. We talked and then he mentioned the case that I had coming up—Vincent Verango. He said he knew Vincent personally and it was all a big misunderstanding and he would vouch for the man. And I had no reason not to trust him. I shouldn't have, but I did."

"There's a bit of a gap between trusting a mentor and taking that much cash."

"It wasn't like that," she protested. "He never said, 'If you let my friend off easy, I'll pay off your student loans.' He was too smart for that. I… I was too smart for that. He twisted everything around, and I didn't even know that the loans were going to be paid off until suddenly, they were gone. Vincent was gone, too. Out of state. He's since died, I heard. It was only then that I began to get suspicious. I dug a little deeper and discovered that Vincent had a long list of plea deals and dropped charges—racketeering, money laundering—he was in deep with so much and…and Curtis was in bed with him. Curtis protected him. He used me," she said, sounding angrier by the second. "He knew I trusted him and he used that, and for what?

"God, I was such an idiot but I couldn't see how to undo it without ruining my career. So…" Her anger faded as quickly as it had come on. "I didn't do anything."

"It's a great story, Caroline. I'm not sure any of it's the truth, but it's a great story. You make a very convincing innocent bystander." The color drained out of her face, but Tom didn't care. "Was there something else you needed to tell me? Because if not, I have things to do."

She looked terrible. Not that he cared anymore, because he didn't. But if he had, he would've been legitimately worried about her. She looked on the verge of passing out. Maybe he would ask Carlson to track down something for her to drink—he couldn't leave her like this.

She didn't answer, which unfortunately gave Tom time to think.

He'd spent years coping with the fact that there would be no happy endings for him, not after Stephanie. And then Caroline Jennings had shown up and given him a glimpse of a different life—of the different man he could be with her.

That was the cruelest thing of all, Tom decided. Just

a glimpse at what could've been, and now it was being snatched away.

If she'd never come here and he'd never laid eyes on her, he wouldn't know what he was missing. But now he would. From here on out, every time he went out to his cabin and lay in his bed, he'd think of her, probably for the rest of his life. His miserable, lonely life.

He could definitely shoot something. He'd start with her mentor, work his way through this Vincent guy and then finish off with whoever had confronted her today.

"I'm so sorry," she whispered again.

For some reason, that made him feel like he was the bad guy here when he most definitely wasn't. He had done nothing wrong. Was he yelling? Was he flipping the desk? Was he threatening bodily harm—at least, was he doing it out loud? No. He was doing none of those things. He was politely listening to her tale of woe.

Damn it, he wanted to reassure her that it would be all right. He wasn't going to, but he wanted to. "About the bribe you took, or is this particular apology in regards to something else?"

She moved then, reaching down and pulling her purse into her lap. Her hands were shaking so violently that it took her a few tries to get it unzipped. Tom watched her curiously.

Then she held something out to him. It was a white stick, maybe four inches. One end of it was purple and there was a small digital screen on it.

He blinked. Desperately, he wanted to believe that was a digital thermometer, but he knew better. Jesus, he knew better. Because sometimes, when a girl wanted to get off the streets, it wasn't for her—but for the baby she was carrying. He kept a supply of pregnancy tests in the safe house.

"I…" she said, holding the pregnancy test out to him. "We…"

This wasn't happening. He was hallucinating. Or having a nightmare. Did it matter at this point? No. What mattered was that he had left reality behind and was stuck in some alternative universe, one where his second chance at happiness betrayed his trust and got pregnant with his child at the same time.

He was tempted to laugh because this was crazy. Simply insane. The only reason he didn't was because Caroline was crying and it hurt him. Damn it all to hell.

"We used protection," he said out loud, more to himself than to her. He tried to think, but his brain wouldn't function. Nothing was functioning.

She nodded, wrapping her arms around her waist and curling into a ball. "That's what I thought, too. Then I was tired and then I got nauseous. And I thought…the shower? In DC?"

Jesus, she was pregnant. With his baby, no less. All those dreams of fatherhood that he had put away years ago—they tried to break free and run rampant around his head. He wouldn't let them. He couldn't afford to.

She was right. He'd been so swept up in living out his fantasy of shower sex that he hadn't taken the most basic of precautions. "That's…" He swallowed and then swallowed again. "That's my fault."

She nodded. "Mistakes happen."

He closed his eyes, but that was when all of those hopes broke free. Caroline, in his bed every night. Caroline, her belly rounded with his child. Caroline, nursing their baby while Tom made her dinner. A thousand visions from an everyday, ordinary life flashed before his eyes—a life that, until twenty minutes ago, he had wanted.

But now?

"Why didn't you tell me about the bribe?"

"I put it behind me. No one ever connected Curtis to Verango, much less to me and my student loans." She sighed, looking more like the judge he knew. "I knew it was wrong, but I couldn't go back and undo it. How was I going to unpay the loans? Who would I give the money to, even if I could come up with that much cash?" She shook her head. "It's not a good excuse, and I know it. But I figured that, since no one had made the connection, no one ever would. I didn't…" She sniffed and Tom got a glimpse of the younger woman she'd been, trying so hard to be an adult and not quite making it. "I didn't want to own up to my poor judgment. But more than that, I didn't want you to think less of me.

"But now that it's out in the open, I wanted to tell you, because I knew that if you could just see that I'd been young and stupid, you would do what you always do."

"And what do I always do, Caroline?" It came out more gently than he'd intended.

She looked up at him, her eyes wide and trusting. "You protect me, Tom. You keep me safe."

He stood and turned away, because he couldn't be sure what expression was on his face right now. Damn it all. He wasn't supposed to care about her at all. She was a part of an ongoing investigation. That should have been the extent of it.

Except now she was pregnant. With his child. Because he hadn't done his goddamn job and put the case first.

He'd put *her* first.

"I didn't…I mean…" She made a hiccuping noise that about broke his heart. "I understand if this is a deal breaker, of course. But it was never malicious. And I *never* meant to hurt you."

She was making this worse. "How long ago was this?"

"Almost thirteen years ago."

He dropped his head in his hands. Thirteen years ago, Stephanie had still been alive. He hadn't yet let her walk out of that party alone. He had desperately been trying to prove that he was good enough for her and wondering if he would ever feel like he belonged.

He turned to face Caroline. God, even now, meeting her gaze was a punch to the gut. "Anything else I should know?"

She nodded tearfully. "I had a pregnancy scare in college. With the guy I almost got engaged to. I was…I was terrified. I hadn't been careful enough. I'd made a serious mistake, and I realized when it happened that I didn't love the guy. And I was going to have to marry him and it was going to kill my career aspirations and my parents were going to be so disappointed in me. They'd finally see what my stupid brother had been saying for years, that I was a mistake."

He was going to shoot her brother if he ever got the chance.

But more than that, each word was like a knife to his chest. Yeah, he could see how an unplanned pregnancy would have changed the course of her life back then.

Just like it could do right now.

"What happened?" he asked in a strangled voice.

"I was just late. It was the stress of senior year." She tried to smile, as if she wanted to display how relieved she was. "I didn't want anyone to know, because it was a serious lapse in judgment and if I couldn't make the right choices to avoid something entirely preventable, like an unplanned pregnancy, then why should anyone take me seriously as a professional?"

"Right, right." He looked down at the little stick. "This isn't just stress, is it?"

She shook her head. "I'm so sorry."

Yeah, he was sorry, too. It would be easy to blame her for this, but hell—she didn't get pregnant by herself. "I'm almost afraid to ask—but anything else?"

"No. I made a serious error in judgment my first year as prosecutor and I'm pregnant. I think that's enough for one day." She paused and looked at him, still nervous. "Tom, this guy—he said you couldn't protect me forever."

Tom moved without being conscious of what he was doing. He hauled Caroline out of her seat and crushed her to his chest.

He was mad, yeah—but he couldn't walk away from her. "He doesn't know me very well, then, does he?"

She wept against his chest, and he held her tight. He couldn't help himself.

His trust in her had been misplaced. And maybe he wouldn't get that second chance. But he'd be damned to hell and back before he threw her to the wolves. He protected people.

He was going to protect her.

He stroked the tears away from her cheeks with his thumbs. "I've ruined everything, haven't I?"

She was going to have his baby. She was in real danger. He'd compromised the case. He'd compromised her.

She hadn't ruined anything. He, on the other hand, might have destroyed everything he'd dedicated his life to.

Oh, if only Stephanie could see him now. What would she say? Would she laugh and tell him to relax, like she used to when he got uptight about some fancy shindig in DC? Would she give him that gentle look and tell him he was being an ass?

Or would she tell him that there was more to life than work? That he, more than anyone else, should know not to let life slip through his fingers, because it could all go away tomorrow?

He and Stephanie had always wanted a family. Would she tell him he'd be insane to let this second chance with Caroline pass him by?

A light tap cut off his jumbled thoughts. The door swung open, revealing a very worried Carlson. "Is everything okay in here?"

Tom glared at the man, but he knew he couldn't get rid of him. Not only were they in Carlson's office, they were friends. "Now what?" It came out more of a growl than a question.

"You aren't going to like this," Carlson warned.

Tom tensed, because he knew how far Carlson would go to root out this corruption. Carlson would want Caroline to get closer to her contact and get as much information as she could without endangering herself. He'd want her to wear a wire, maybe flirt—anything to get the information the case needed.

He stared down into Caroline's eyes. How was he supposed protect her—and their child—if she did any of that?

"No," he said, turning his body so that he stood between Caroline and Carlson. "We do this my way or we don't do it at all."

Sixteen

Suddenly, after a career of waiting, Tom didn't have patience for a single damn thing.

This Todd Moffat scum had contacted Caroline and threatened to ruin her career if she didn't go along with what he wanted.

Caroline had withheld the truth from Tom.

She was also carrying his child.

How was he supposed to do anything but spirit Caroline as far away from the likes of Moffat as possible? Worse, how was he supposed to trust her?

The wheels of justice turned mighty slowly. Tracing Moffat took time, as did getting the appropriate warrants. Neither Tom nor Carlson wanted to get a case dismissed on a technicality—especially not about something as important as this. They couldn't rush this just because Tom couldn't sleep, couldn't eat—couldn't breathe.

He'd compromised the case. He'd compromised Caroline.

God, he hoped like hell he hadn't ruined everything.

Yes, it was important, what he was doing. This years-long investigation was connected not only to judicial corruption, but also to environmental rights and tribal sovereignty—all of it was very, *very* important. Damned important, even. Lives hung in the balance.

But he couldn't let what Caroline had said about her so-called mentor go. She'd lied to Tom about her past—but had she lied about what had actually happened? Had she glossed over her real role or had her mentor used her like she'd said he had?

Tom needed to know. He couldn't let it go. It took a few days because he moved through nonofficial channels, but eventually he tracked down the telephone number for one Terrence Curtis.

When Curtis said, "Hello?" in a voice that shook with age, he sounded ancient.

Tom announced himself. When Curtis spoke again, he sounded more confident. "Agent Yellow Bird, how can I help you today?" He did not sound like a suspect trying to hide his guilt.

"I need to ask you a few questions about one of your former students—Caroline Jennings? Do you remember her?" Tom kept his voice level, almost bored.

"Oh, yes—Caroline. One of my best students—and I say that as someone who taught for decades. We've fallen out of touch, but I've kept up with her career. She's done great things, and I know she'll go on to do even better things."

He sounded like a proud father, not a man who had hoodwinked his best student into abetting a criminal. But the fact that Curtis remembered her fondly made Tom feel a little more kindly toward him. "So you remember her."

"I just said that, Agent Yellow Bird," Curtis said, sounding exactly like a teacher scolding a student. "Is everything all right with Caroline?"

"What can you tell me about the Verango case?" Tom said, hoping to catch Curtis off guard.

"The…I'm sorry," he said quickly. "I'm not sure what you're talking about."

"You're not? That's a shame. Because Caroline, one of your best students, remembers the conversation very clearly. The one where you convinced her to settle for a plea agreement that would let your friend Vincent Verango go free?"

There was a stunned silence on the line, and for a second, Tom thought the old man had hung up on him. He didn't want that to happen. Curtis still lived in Minneapolis and it was a hell of a long drive.

"That's…" Curtis said flatly. "That's not how it happened. Verango and I were not friends. I never—"

"Oh, but you did, didn't you, Mr. Curtis?" Tom cut him off. "It's not a point of contention up for debate. I'm just trying to corroborate her story. Because Caroline, your best student, has done great things, and as you say, she could conceivably continue to do great things from the bench—if her entire career isn't derailed by a corruption scandal. One that traces directly back to *you*."

Curtis made a strangled noise, somewhere between a choke and a gasp. "What—who?"

"All very good questions. Here's what I think, Mr. Curtis. You were her mentor. She looked up to you. She trusted you—maybe she was a little naive about that, but you were both working for the good guys, right?" Silence. "She says that, when she was struggling during her first year as a prosecutor, you took her out to dinner to offer her some moral support. A pep talk. And while you were there, you mentioned you had a friend, Vincent, who had been unfairly arrested. You vouched for him, and as a result of your conversation, Caroline did not throw the book at him. She pulled her punches and Vincent walked." More silence. Man, he really hoped Curtis hadn't hung up on him. "Shortly thereafter, all her student loans were paid off in full. Am I leaving anything out?"

"I..." Curtis sounded older—and definitely more scared.

"And that's why you fell out of touch, isn't it? Because when she figured out that you had abused her trust—it was gone, wasn't it? She kept her distance because it was the only way to protect herself."

"I needed the money," he said, his voice shaking. "I made sure she got a good cut—"

"I don't give a shit what your reasons were. I just need to know whether or not Caroline Jennings was your dupe or if she was an active participant in the miscarriage of justice."

"Of course she didn't know!" Curtis erupted. "I didn't think she'd mind—I was trying to help her out. I should've known better. She always was one of the smartest students I've ever had."

Tom had what he needed—proof that Caroline had not intentionally broken the law. She'd just put her faith in the wrong man.

That pregnancy scare in college, this thing with the Verango case—each time Caroline had slipped up, it was because she'd trusted the wrong man.

And now she was pregnant with Tom's child because she'd believed him. When he'd told her he needed to take her out to his cabin to keep her safe, she'd gone. Same for the trip to Washington. She'd questioned him, sure, but in the end, she'd put her faith in him.

They'd both trusted that what happened at the cabin and then in DC was somehow separate from their jobs.

Well, it wasn't separate anymore.

Tom looked up to where Carlson was listening on another receiver. "Anything else?" He was asking both Curtis and Carlson. Carlson shook his head.

"If you talk to her," Curtis said, sounding tired, "tell her I'm sorry. She was one of my best students, you know."

"I'm sure she was." Tom hung up, feeling almost lightheaded. Caroline wasn't a dirty judge. Yeah, she still should have told him about this, way back when he'd asked if there was anything that could be used against her.

But damn it all, he understood that impulse to bury a past mistake. Hadn't he been doing the exact same thing? Ten years of his life focusing on the job so he could justify living while Stephanie had died.

"Well?"

"I think I have everything I need," Carlson said, making some notes. "I wasn't going to charge her—you know that, right?"

"She wouldn't expect any special favors. Neither would I." Tom knew that about her. Justice was blind.

Technically speaking, the job wasn't done. The department was closing in on Moffat, but no arrests had been made yet. There was a part of Tom that wanted to be the one to slap the cuffs on his wrists, to look him in the eye and make sure he knew that Tom Yellow Bird had been the one to serve justice. Finally, after all this time.

That was still important to him. But it wasn't the most important thing. Not anymore.

Caroline was his second chance.

He wasn't going to let the job ruin that for him.

Tom stood. "Do you need me for anything else?"

Carlson smiled knowingly. "No. In fact, if I see you in the office in the next five days, I'll have you arrested. Show your face within the next two days, you'll be shot on sight."

Tom was already heading out the door. He paused only long enough to look back over his shoulder. "Go home to your family. Trust me on this, James—you don't want to miss a single moment."

Because everything could change in a moment.

No one knew that better than he did.

Seventeen

Really, not that much had changed over the last several weeks—at least, not on the surface, Caroline thought as she packed up at the end of yet another ordinary day.

She got up, she walked—instead of jogging, which was her only concession to being pregnant and even then, it had more to do with the crippling summer heat than her physical state. She went to work, she came home and she did it all over again.

She did not run away with Tom. In fact, after their confrontation in Carlson's office, he had all but disappeared off the face of the planet. She couldn't blame him. After all, she'd screwed up. She'd made a series of unfortunate mistakes that had compounded upon each other. She'd done serious damage to both of their careers, and if she knew one thing about Tom, it was that his career was everything to him.

She hadn't talked to her brother, Trent, in years. They'd

managed a semi-civil nod across the aisle at Mom's funeral several years ago, but Caroline chalked that up more to the influence of his wife than any sentimentality on Trent's part.

Even though she'd cut him out of her life—and vice versa—his hateful words from when she was just a little girl had never left Caroline. She was a mistake and she ruined everything.

She'd heard it so often, in so many ways, that she'd completely internalized Trent's hatred.

Okay, so—yes. She had screwed up. She'd made mistakes. But that didn't make *her* a mistake any more than her parents having her late in life made her a mistake. She might not have been a planned child, but she knew in her heart that she'd made her parents happy.

Yes, Caroline was now pregnant and it could reasonably be described as a mistake.

But that's not what this child was. No, this child was a gift.

Her brother was a hateful man who had blinded her to the truth—far from being a mistake, Caroline had been a gift to her parents. They'd loved her, even if Trent couldn't.

She hadn't planned for this—not for any of it. She hadn't planned to make love with FBI Special Agent Thomas Yellow Bird. She hadn't planned to have her errors in judgment thrown back in her face when she'd least expected it. She had absolutely not planned to get pregnant.

But, yes—unplanned or not, this child was a gift. That didn't mean she and Tom were going to raise this baby together. Even though she was wishing for exactly that.

Because just like it took two to make a baby, it took two to raise one. Oh, sure, Caroline could do the single-mom thing. Women had been successfully raising babies on their own for millennia. But she didn't want to.

She wanted long drives into the sunset and long week-ends at a cabin in the middle of nowhere. She wanted to meet the people Tom had grown up with, and she wanted her child to know his roots. She wanted to spend time with Celine and Mark Rutherford and do what she could for the Rutherford Foundation.

She wanted Tom. All of him, not just the parts that looked good in a suit. She wanted the insecure young man carving out a place for himself where none had previously existed and she wanted the overconfident agent who did what he thought was best, come hell or high water. She wanted the fantastic lover and the man who made sure she had the right clothes for events so she wouldn't be nervous.

And if she couldn't have him—all of him—then...

Then he couldn't have her. She wasn't going to settle for anything less than everything. They'd have to share custody or something.

Frankly, the very idea pissed her off. As did the fact that he still hadn't called. Was that just it, then? She'd lied by omission and he was done with her? If that wasn't the pot calling the kettle black, she didn't know what was. Getting a straight answer out of that man about anything was only accomplished by magic, apparently. He hadn't told her he was taking her to his luxury cabin. He hadn't told her she was going to the Rutherford Foundation gala. He hadn't told her anything until the information became vital.

Was that because she wasn't important enough to trust with the information? Or was it just that the job would always come first?

Deep down, she was afraid she was on her own, because in all honesty, she wasn't sure if Tom would ever be able to put her and the baby before his job. She couldn't replace his late wife, and he lived and breathed being an agent. She might be up against forces beyond her control.

When she finally did see him again, she didn't know if she'd kiss him or strangle him, frankly. It depended heavily upon the hormones.

Caroline was staring at her refrigerator, battling yet another wave of not-morning sickness and trying to decide if there was anything that was going to settle her stomach when someone pounded on her front door.

"Caroline!"

Adrenaline dumped into her system as the fight-or-flight response tried to take hold, because who on earth could be banging on her door at six thirty in the evening? Was it a good guy or a bad guy? She couldn't handle any more bad news.

"Caroline! Are you in there?"

Wait, she knew that voice. She sagged—actually sagged—in relief. *Tom.* He was here. Oh, please, let it be good news. Please let it be that they had arrested all the bad guys in the entire state of South Dakota and—and—

Please let him have come for her.

She peeked through the peephole, just to be sure—but it was him. Alone. She threw open the door and said, "Tom! What are you—" but that was as far as she got because then she was in his arms. He was kissing her and kicking the door shut and walking her into the living room and she knew she needed to push back, find out why he was here. But she couldn't. She had missed him *so* much.

But that wasn't her fault. A flash of anger gave her the strength she needed to shove him back. "What are you doing here?" she demanded, gaping at him. He had a wild light in his eyes she could only pray was a good thing. "The case—"

"Screw the case," he said, pulling her back into his arms. "It doesn't matter."

"How can you say that? Of course it matters. What if someone followed you here? What if someone puts us together?"

He was grinning at her. Grinning! He was in the middle of her living room, cupping her face in his hands and looking down at her like she was telling a joke instead of having a panic attack about what the future held. "They better put us together," he said, touching his forehead to hers. "Babe, I am so sorry."

"For what?" She pulled completely out of his grasp, because she couldn't think while he was touching her, couldn't formulate words when he was holding her so tenderly. She stomped to the other side of the living room and crossed her arms over her chest. "I'm the one who screwed up, remember? I'm the one who compromised the case because I lied about my past. I'm the one who threw a case all those years ago. I'm the one who lied to you, Tom. Why are *you* apologizing to *me*?"

She was yelling, but she didn't care. He was here. She was happy and furious and saddened all at once. Stupid hormones.

And he was still smiling at her, the jerk! "Why are you smiling at me?" she shouted.

"Have I ever told you that you're beautiful when you're furious?"

That did it. She threw a pillow at him—which, of course, he caught easily. "You're not making any sense!" Her voice cracked and her throat tightened and she was afraid she would start crying, which would be terrible. She might have ruined her career and she might be unexpectedly pregnant, but that didn't mean she wanted to break down in front of him.

"I'm just so glad to see you. But," he added, before she could launch another throw pillow at him, "I actually came to tell you something." He held up his hands in the sign of surrender. "Okay, you screwed up. But you're acting as if no one else has ever made a mistake in the history of the world, and you're wrong. I've screwed up more times than I can count, Caroline. Including with you. I got it into my head if I just kept my distance from you, that would keep you safe. That would also keep me safe. And all it did was make us both miserable. I miss you. I need you."

He fished something out of his pocket and held out his palm to her. "I want to be with you. Not just now, not just for the weekend—for the rest of my life. Because I feel it. I've felt it since the very first second I saw you."

"What—what are you doing?" Was that a ring?

"I'd given up on a happy ending, Caroline. I'd fallen in love once before and had it ripped away from me, and I figured that was it. No happy endings. No family. Just my job. And then you showed up." His eyes looked suspiciously bright as he took a few steps across the room. "I saw you and I felt it again—hope. Desire. *Love.* I hadn't been with a woman since the night before my wife died and then you came along, and suddenly, I couldn't keep my hands off you. And that led to *my* mistake. I had no intention of getting you pregnant, and I had no intention of leaving you alone to deal with it by yourself. I'm sorry that I haven't been here. But if you'll have me, if you'll forgive me, I will always be here for you."

Okay, so she was crying. It didn't mean anything. She wiped the tears out of her eyes and looked down at his hand, which was now before her. It *was* a ring. Of course it was. A perfect ring with a really big round diamond and a bunch of smaller diamonds on the band. It was the kind people wore when they got engaged. When they meant to spend the rest of their lives together.

She looked back up at him, trying to keep it together and failing miserably. "But the case—the job—"

Tom shook his head. "For so long, it was personal. I had to prove I belonged by being better than everyone else, and then, when Stephanie died, I…I didn't have anything left. Everyone in my family had passed. I was a long way from home. All I had was the job, and I gave it everything because it was the only way to make things right."

She didn't like the image of him all alone. "Is that why you've been radio silent for so long? You're making things right?"

Tom pulled her into his arms. He looked tired. Was that because of the job or because of her? "I'm not going to let anyone intimidate or threaten you, Caroline. That's a promise. But I don't have to give everything to the job. Not if it keeps me from you." He rested his free hand on her belly. "Not if it keeps me from *this*. I've missed you so much, Caroline. You mean everything to me and I've let you down. If you give me another chance, I won't let you down again."

She swiped madly at the tears rolling down her cheeks, but they were replaced too quickly. "I missed you, too," she sobbed. "I've missed you so much."

Unexpectedly, he fell to his knees. "Caroline Jennings, will you marry me? Because you will always be more to me than a case or a job. I love you. I have from the very first. And I want to spend the rest of my life proving it to you."

She tried to look stern, but it wasn't happening. "I don't want this to happen again," she told him, starting to hiccup. "I don't want you to disappear for days and weeks on end. I don't want you to leave me alone, wondering…"

"I won't. It was a mistake to do so. But," he went on, climbing to his feet and holding her hands in his, "I have one thing I need to tell you."

She groaned. "What now?"

"I spoke with Terrence Curtis." She gasped, but he just kept going. "He admitted that he convinced you to amend the charges and that you had no idea he had an ulterior motive. He also told me to tell you that he's proud of everything you've accomplished since then. You were one of his best students."

"You tracked down Mr. Curtis for me?"

Tom had said he would protect her. She'd always assumed he meant physically—safe from bad guys and evildoers.

But this? This was her reputation. Her career. And he'd protected it.

"I wanted it on the record that you hadn't intentionally or maliciously broken the law. Carlson won't be pressing charges, either."

"What about…"

"Moffat? We're building the case. We know who he is and who he's working for. We've got him—thanks to you."

She stared at him, because that was all she could do. There weren't any words.

He was back to grinning wildly at her. "Say yes, Caroline. Be my wife, my family. Our family," he added, stroking her stomach. Instantly, the air between them heated, and she felt that spark catching fire again as his hand drifted lower and then higher. She burned for his touch—but with fewer clothes. A lot fewer clothes.

"I took a couple of days off," he murmured. "Let me show you how much I love you."

"Yes." Yes to it all—to his touches, to his proposal,

to his love. "I love you, too. But I'm going to hold you to your promises, okay?"

"I'm counting on it."

She couldn't stop the tears, but she smiled anyway as she pulled him into her. "Good. Because I feel it, too. And I'm never letting you go."

Epilogue

Once upon a time, Tom had considered tracking down criminals and arresting them to be difficult but rewarding work. It involved a lot of sleepless nights and hours of patiently waiting for a few moments of intense activity—the arrest—and then, much later, the payoff, a guilty verdict.

All in all, it had been remarkably good training for being a parent.

"Never thought I'd see the day," James Carlson said. Carlson was speaking to Tom, but his gaze was fastened on his wife.

Maggie sat next to the fire pit with Rosebud Armstrong, Celine Rutherford and Caroline. The women were laughing and chatting, all while Maggie rubbed her pregnant belly. Everyone was hoping to make it through this Memorial Day barbecue without the untimely arrival of the second Carlson child.

"See what?" Tom kept an eye on Margaret as she picked up leaves and handed them to Caroline. Tom knew his thirteen-month-old daughter could sit in one place for a while sometimes—but not when Carlson's two-year-old, Adam, was chasing the Armstrong boys around. The twins, Tanner and Lewis, were almost seven and didn't have time for a two-year-old. Instead, Rosebud and Dan's kids were splashing in the spring-fed pool. Poor Adam kept getting soaked, but instead of fussing, he was giving as good as he got, giggling the whole time. Dan Armstrong was nearby, keeping the kids safe in the shallow water.

Margaret watched the whole scene with fascination, and Tom knew it wouldn't be much longer before she tried to follow the older boys into the water. It didn't matter that she could barely walk, much less run. She'd be after them in moments, shrieking with joy. She was such a happy baby. Just looking at her made Tom's heart swell with joy.

"You," Carlson laughed, taking a long pull on his beer as he flipped a buffalo burger.

Tom gave his old friend a dull look. "You see me all the time." Margaret pushed herself to her feet, almost falling into Caroline's legs. Although Caroline kept her attention focused on Rosebud—who appeared to be telling a story about the twins' most recent exploits—she easily caught her daughter and cuddled the baby to her chest.

For years, Tom had waited. He and Stephanie had wanted to make sure they had their careers set before they took time off to have a family, and then…it'd been too late. He'd figured that he missed his window and fatherhood wasn't in the cards for him.

He had never been more thrilled to be wrong as he was right now.

"No," Mark Rutherford said, watching all the children, "I know what he means. We never thought we'd see you this *happy* again."

Caroline looked up and caught him watching her. And,

just like he always had, Tom felt that spark between them jump to life. Every time he saw her, he fell in love with her all over again.

"Yes," Carlson laughed, flipping another burger. "Just like that."

Tom didn't know how to respond to that. He was in uncharted territory here. In addition to being a Memorial Day party, this barbecue at his cabin also marked the end of the corruption investigation that he and Carlson had pursued for years. It also potentially marked the end of Tom's full-time commitment with the FBI. The job was finally done, hopefully permanently.

Todd Moffat had been arrested, tried and convicted. His employer had been revealed to be Black Hills Mines, a mining company that had been locked in several protracted legal battles with the various tribes over uranium rights. Uranium mining was a dirty business, but there were huge deposits underneath the land that made up many of the reservations in South Dakota. Black Hills Mines wanted the right to strip the uranium out of the ground. Understandably, the tribes preferred not to have their reservations destroyed and contaminated. Moffat had turned in favor of a lighter sentence and everything had fallen into place.

The job was over—for Tom, anyway. He was taking a leave of absence from the agency. He'd continue to be available as a consultant—he was still the best agent to deal with cases that involved tribal issues. But he was turning his attention to the Rutherford Foundation.

They were building a new school on the Red Creek Reservation. Tom was going to make sure it was everything his tribe needed.

So this wasn't a farewell party. The agency had gotten him a cake for that at the office. This?

This was a welcome home party. Margaret was at a really amazing age, and he couldn't bring himself to spend his nights sitting in a surveillance vehicle in the hopes that the bad guy did something when he could be at home with his wife and his daughter.

However, no matter how perfect this moment or any of the moments in the previous twenty-three months had been, he knew he didn't have all the time in the world. Maybe he was jaded, but he knew better than anyone else that it could all end tomorrow and he wouldn't waste another moment on something as impersonal as a career. His career would never love him back. It would never give him a family or those thousands of small moments every day that made up a good life.

Margaret was going to start running and talking soon. And Tom was going to be there to see it with his own eyes. He was going to show his little girl the world—powwows and parties and everything that made him who he was, everything that would make her who she was, too.

For years, he'd made his own family—finding members of his tribe and others who were lost and needed a way home. And he hadn't given that up. He might have stepped aside from his job, but he would never turn his back on those who needed him. He had a charity to run, scholarships to fund and people to help. But he didn't need a badge to do that. Not anymore.

He just needed to know that, at the end of a long day, Caroline was coming home to him. She'd returned to her seat on the bench once her maternity leave had ended, and Tom was proud of what she'd accomplished.

Margaret looked up at him and smiled, her fingers in her mouth. She'd probably be up late tonight, fussing at her sore teeth. But right now, she grinned at him and all Tom could think was, there she was—the most perfect little girl in the world.

It was different, the love he felt when he looked at his daughter. It was full of hope and protection and sweetness, whereas when he looked at his wife, it was full of longing and heat and want. But it was love all the same.

"She would have been happy for you," Carlson said, shaking Tom out of his thoughts. "This was what she'd have wanted for you. You know that, right?"

Tom looked at his wife and daughter and fell in love again, just like he did a hundred times a day. Some days—like right now—he thought his heart might burst from it.

When he'd first fallen for Caroline, he'd struggled to give his heart to her completely. But he knew now—loving Caroline and Margaret didn't take away from the love he'd felt for Stephanie. It didn't make him less. It only made him more. So much more.

"Yeah," he said, staring at the loves of his life. "Yeah, I do."

"We should get a picture," Rosebud called out. "Something to mark the retirement of one of the best special agents the FBI has ever seen."

Everyone agreed, even though it felt like overkill to Tom. He was still adjusting to this new reality, where he wanted people to take pictures of him and his family—wedding pictures and baby pictures he didn't hide in a storage closet, but displayed on the walls of his cabin. He'd paved the road down to the cabin and done away with the shrubbery hiding the turnoff. He didn't have to hide who he was anymore. He belonged, just as he was.

It took time to wrangle all of the kids. Dan had a new tripod for his phone, so he was able to set it up to take a photo of all of them.

Tom's throat tightened as he watched his family and friends arrange themselves around him. Caroline leaned into him, her touch a reassurance. "Okay?" she asked in a quiet voice meant just for his ears.

He stared down at his wife and knew that later, after everyone had left and Margaret had fallen asleep—at least for a few hours—he'd take the spark that had always existed between them and fan it into a white-hot flame. Because he had known from the very beginning—there she was, the woman he was going to spend the rest of his life with.

He kissed her, a promise of things to come, because he would never be done falling in love with her. "I've never been better."

* * * * *

*If you loved PRIDE AND PREGNANCY,
pick up these other connected novels from
RITA Award–winning author Sarah M. Anderson.*

*A MAN OF HIS WORD
Dan and Rosebud's story.*

*A MAN OF PRIVILEGE
James and Maggie's story. Available
now from Mills & Boon Desire!*

*And check out these other books
from Sarah M. Anderson.*
*A REAL COWBOY
NOT THE BOSS'S BABY
THE NANNY PLAN*

* * *

MILLS & BOON®

Desire™

PASSIONATE AND DRAMATIC LOVE STORIES

Join Britain's BIGGEST Romance Book Club

50% OFF your first parcel

- **EXCLUSIVE** offers every month

- **FREE** delivery direct to your door

- **NEVER MISS** a title

- **EARN** Bonus Book points

Call Customer Services
0844 844 1358 *

or visit
ıillsandboon.co.uk/subscriptions